Cousins to the Kudzu

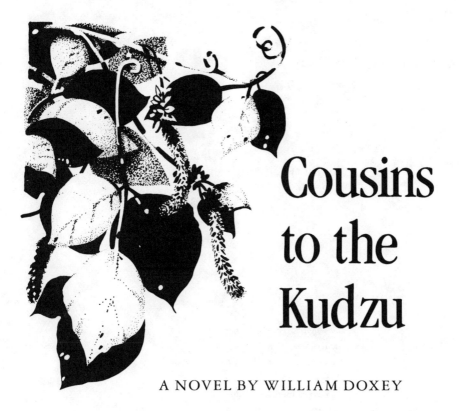

Cousins
to the
Kudzu

A NOVEL BY WILLIAM DOXEY

LOUISIANA STATE UNIVERSITY PRESS
BATON ROUGE AND LONDON 1985

For Betty Jobson

Copyright © 1985 *by William Doxey*
All rights reserved
Manufactured in the United States of America
Designer: Joanna Hill
Typeface: Linotron Garamond
Typesetter: G & S Typesetters
Printer and binder: Edwards Brothers

LIBRARY OF CONGRESS CATALOGING IN PUBLICATION DATA

Doxey, William.
  Cousins to the Kudzu.

  I. Title.
PS3554.0974C6   1985   813'.54   84-21317
ISBN 0-8071-1225-9

So God created man in his own image, in the image of God created he him; male and female created he them. . . . And God saw every thing that he had made, and, behold, it was very good.

Cousins to the Kudzu

Chapter One

In early summer of 1933, Eugene Spaulding left Baltimore with a battered suitcase, a secondhand black bag, and a degree in medicine. His shiny wool suit bore eloquent testimony to years spent in the teaching wards of hospitals. The scattered spots of blood and other evidence of the human condition he had sponged away from the fabric with various compounds of his own concocting, and the traces that remained, both of bodily material and cleansers, while not visible to the unpracticed eye, were apprehensible to every nose. When he took his seat in the day coach for the long, hot trip south to Atlanta, he was greeted by as many twitches as a new rabbit in an overcrowded hutch.

The young doctor's only living relative was his great aunt Consuelo who lived across the street from Grant Park in a two-story frame house that had been only partly burned during the Battle of Atlanta. One of her most vivid memories was of having lived through that conflagration and of having seen the awesome eagle called Abe, which was the mascot of one of the encircling Union armies, soaring through the smoke above the fated city. She had prayed that this feathered symbol of yankee might be fried like a chicken by a sudden updraft of flame. But God was listening elsewhere that day, and the eagle flew on and on and on, disappearing finally into the night skies of her mind, where it still cocked its head and took wing whenever she saw black folks strolling near the park as though they were good as anyone else.

Dr. Spaulding was in the debt of this venerable lady, for she had supplied barely enough money to see him through medical school. He came to the Grant Park house to call on her and to reveal the plan of his future. She was sitting on the swing in the shade on the side porch, cooling herself with a church fan showing three wide-eyed lads in a fiery furnace, and an occasional glass of lemonade slopped from a cut-glass pitcher specked with lazy flies.

He did not know if she recognized him, and later supposed that she both did and did not. She called him, variously, "Young man," "Ernest," "Uncle Thad," "Sweetheart," and "Gene." He sat with her for a while, then went inside and spoke with the white lady who took care of her and the house. She was a good woman in that she saw her duty and did it, from dusting the crystal chandelier over the unused dining room table once a week, to seeing that the aunt's undergarments were clean. She was also a practical woman, and had taken the job because the pay was twice what she made in a carpet mill. There was also a place in the household for her son, a somewhat afflicted young man of twenty-five who loved popcorn and Coca-Cola as much as life itself, and who learned at last how to cut the lawn with a push mower without endangering his toes, but still could not figure out why people let grass grow in their yards if they had to cut it down every week.

The doctor spoke to the housekeeper and told her his plans. He had been so touched by the suffering caused by the Depression that he would establish his practice in a small town in Georgia where he could be of most use. She was washing dinner dishes when he revealed this. She stopped scrubbing and looked at him as though she hadn't heard, and for a moment he thought she was hard of hearing. He was about to repeat himself when she said, "Well."

And that was all she said, nor did she say more of substance during the several weeks Eugene stayed in the old house while his license to practice in the state was being granted. He passed the time walking the park and riding the streetcar through the sprawling city, and he spent many a blistering afternoon in the damp, cool darkness of theaters watching movies and especially newsreels showing the depressed state of the union in the flickering, listless faces of nameless

2

persons standing in endless lines looking for work. On Sunday mornings he did not go to church, but sat on the porch outside his upstairs room listening to the ringing bells sounding across the treetops of the city, and finding comfort in the joyous noise that communicated the unspeakable more directly than words, and made him momentarily forget those faces.

The license was duly issued and he took leave. The housekeeper nodded when he told her he would be in touch from time to time, and that her salary would still be promptly paid, along with expenses for the upkeep of his aunt and the house, by the family lawyer. He said good-bye to his aunt, kissing her rouge-spotted cheek while her bright blue eyes stared mindlessly at the equally bright blue sky, then, bags in hand, strolled through the park. On the other side he was approached by a man no older than himself who asked could he spare a dime. Eugene observed him professionally as he fished in his trouser pocket, and judged his slumped shoulders and pinched face as being indicative of advanced TB. He gave him a year to live, at most, as well as a quarter. Then he caught a streetcar that took him to the train station.

He headed south first, toward Macon. Cotton was still being made then in the wide fields spreading away from both sides of the tracks. Black and white women wearing loose faded dresses overlain by faded aprons, their heads protected from the heat by bonnets, moved up and down the rows under the sweltering sun, chopping weeds with flashing hoes on handles made slick by the friction of their own skin against the coarse-grained wood.

This was the South he knew, and he smiled at the sight of a half-dozen or more buzzards slowly wheeling against a backdrop of distant clouds as fluffy white as the cotton showing here and there from bursting bolls. It was a land of rickets and pellagra, of worms and weak lungs, of knifings and incest, a land of fierce believers who handled snakes and drank poison to test their faith, of primitive atheists who tested theirs with snuff, white likker, and toothless despair. It was a country in which to be born was sufficient grounds to doubt the existence of Purpose, and to be born ugly was to be in perverse harmony with things, while to be born pretty was to be as a creature formed without natural defenses to protect it from the

3

onslaught of mighty germs that would in short order cripple and kill.

The train stopped at one town, and while cars were being switched, the young doctor swung down into the July heat, coat over his shoulder, panama hat cocked back on his head, sweat oozing from around the edges of his suspenders and down his legs into his black elastic socks. He went into the depot and talked to the ticket agent, that one person in every trackside town who knew the comings and goings of everyone and the whys and wherefores.

Long before the conductor cried ALL ABOARD for the remade train, Eugene was back in his seat. The agent told him all he needed to know: the health of the community was in the hands of three doctors, two of whom were father and son. In station after station down the track through fields of cotton and, finally, across the noisy trestles spanning the Ocmulgee River, running red and shallow into the sweeping rail yards of Macon, the news was always the same. There were physicians aplenty, yet still Eugene could not help wondering— though he knew the answer—if this were true, why were so few of the faces raised to the passing train aglow with good health?

He headed west, then, toward Alabama, then north again, not thinking that word but rather that he was "going up" the state. Though a man of the world, educated by fine professors who themselves had practiced their art on the best cadavers of Paris and Heidelberg, he was still a man who knew his roots, a man whose family, according to Great Aunt Consuelo, hadn't had occasion to look north since in the seventeenth century their ancestors embarked from a city near London and sailed to Charleston.

So up the state he went, traveling a day, then detraining in one town and taking a room at a hotel on the square where he washed his body first, then his shirt and socks, and touched up his suit with a few pungent drops from a bottle in his medical bag. This was an interesting town, named La Grange after General Lafayette's home in France. It was a prosperous community, marked by mills which spun on as though there had been no Crash. But his worst suspicions were confirmed: the medical profession was well represented, and there was even a surgeon in residence, as evidence of the town's wealth.

He left this city at 8:42 the morning after he had arrived and at 10:17 found himself on the platform of another station. The sky was

4

blue and already it was hot; from green trees beyond the tracks jays were scolding. Children stood on the right-of-way admiring the shining six-foot wheels. Eugene glanced at the name board nailed to the depot wall and discovered he was breathing the air of Oughton, elevation 916.

In his mind's eye he conjured a map of the state and saw that Oughton was fifty miles, more or less, west of Atlanta on the road to Anniston, Alabama. He noted that bales of cotton and crates of goods were being loaded into freight cars on the siding and also that the men doing the work were laughing good naturedly. He entered the depot and found that as well as a ticket agent there was a telegrapher, and that messages were coming into and going out of Oughton as fast, or faster than, he could handle them.

The ticket agent was a six-foot, big-shouldered young man. His cheeks were full and firm, and when he nodded and smiled, Eugene saw that his teeth were healthy. In reply to his questions, the agent said that the only medical man in town was a Doctor Whatley; he was very old and wished to retire to a piece of beach-front property near Panacea, Florida, but could not and would not until he found another doctor to take his place. There were also two veterinarians, one of whom occasionally pulled teeth for those not wanting to make a trip down to La Grange to a real dentist. "My name," said the ticket agent, extending a huge hand, "is Robert Mosely, and I know about doctors because my mother is a nurse and has worked with Doc Whatley ever since I can remember."

Eugene introduced himself. Mosely grinned and said that perhaps he should call upon the physician, adding that the West Point Railroad had been known to bring the answer to more than one prayer to Oughton. He allowed Eugene to leave his bags behind the counter near the telegrapher, whose hand had not left his clicking key while the two young men were speaking, but whose ears had heard all. As Eugene went outside he flashed him a friendly smile and wished him luck, lazily calling him "Doc," as though he had never been sick a day in his life.

Eugene walked two blocks up a gentle hill to the square where the ubiquitous statue of a confederate soldier marked the geographical and cultural heart of the community. A few tattered pigeons eyed him from the stone walk, and two old men were sitting on benches, canes clutched between their knees, staring into space.

The doctor's office was on the square in three rooms above Wilson's Bakery. Whatley was a small, energetic man who, after Eugene had introduced himself, wasted no time. He examined Eugene's diploma and announced that he, too, was a product of Hopkins. This called for a libation. They saluted Baltimore and Asclepius, as well as Cos and Hippocrates, with moonshine sipped from specimen jars. Then they got down to business. Eugene's license was in order; he was young and healthy; Oughton was a town like all others: people let themselves become ill and had to be guided back to health, while others shot or knifed or beat each other to the point of death; women bore children here, too; and folks grew old and died. Whatley had been in practice for twenty-eight years, coming from Columbus shortly after the turn of the century; had married a local girl who had passed away a year ago May. His only child, a daughter, was married and lived in Minnesota where her husband, a doctor, too, was helping to open a new hospital.

They had another drink, which was followed by first aid for a grocer named Roberts who hobbled in, one shoe in hand, his right sock dripping blood. He had dropped a tub of lard on his big toe. The nail was hanging by a thread. Whatley gave him a shot of the whiskey and removed the nail, then applied collodion to stop the bleeding. After two drinks Roberts departed staggering rather than hobbling.

Three days later Whatley's practice was Eugene's. He bought the doctor's professional place in the community for eleven hundred dollars. He paid two hundred in cash, taking the bills from a roll stashed in a large pill box in his medical bag which was marked boldly DEADLY POISON—DO NOT TOUCH, illustrated with a skull and crossbones. He signed a note drafted by Whatley for the balance, payable at twenty-seven dollars per month to be sent via money order the 25th day of each month for three years to a Florida address. The extra two dollars per payment was interest.

Eugene also secured the departing physician's office space from Mrs. Wilson, who ran the bakery downstairs and owned the building as well. His first patient was her eldest daughter, Doreen, a sturdy girl of nineteen or twenty who smelled of yeast and cinnamon. Her complaint was an irritating scalp mole two inches above her left ear. It turned out to be a well-fed tick. Eugene removed the creature but, knowing how delicate the sensibilities of some young women were, told her that to avoid such moles in the future she must brush her hair vigorously twice a day. He wondered, though, how she had picked up the vermin, then ceased when, several days later, he saw her go off hand in hand with a red-haired farm boy named Emmett who delivered fresh eggs, milk, and butter to the back door of the bakery.

A year passed, then another and another. As the people of Oughton discovered that under his care fevers cooled and babies were born with the usual number of fingers and toes, they showed their acceptance by shortening his name to the honorific Doc, as they had his predecessor's. He made his home in two rooms at the McIntosh House hotel one block off the square. It was owned and operated by Tom Leeds and his wife Martha, a fine cook who set a bountiful table three times a day for the traveling men who made the hotel their headquarters while in town on business and for the regular boarders who lived there.

Eugene entered into the life and times of the town. He met old Kermit Westmoreland, whose fate it had been to be the manager of a Cuban sugar plantation during the Spanish American War. He had left the tropics then, had crossed paths with Miss Cora Middleton, daughter of William Middleton, prosperous cotton grower and mill owner of Oughton, had married her and lived here ever since. He still considered himself an outsider, and liked nothing more than to take his ease on the porch of the McIntosh and share his observations of Oughton life with all who would listen. Eugene enjoyed the tales as well as the teller, and although there was thirty years between them, they became good friends.

The young doctor was invited into the homes of citizens with daughters of marrying age. They fed him well, and he responded to one and all with that charm that comes from knowing you are sought after because you are special. But he asked no young lady to be his bride, nor did he sit alone with any on a porch in the moonlight. Beyond the city limits were other places such as Mt. Nebo where a young man might go when moonlight was on his mind.

On Sundays he sometimes went to church but more often did not. Since he was a certified and licensed man of science, it was assumed that his mind, like Whatley's had been, was more open and by necessity independent. When he did feel the urge to pass an hour under stained glass, Eugene visited the churches in turn, going Baptist, then Presbyterian, then Methodist and finally Episcopalian. There were no Catholics. The two Jews, lacking the requisite minyan, went once a month by train to Atlanta to worship. Johnny Demos, who with his two sons ran a store just off the square that sold everything from the latest newspapers and magazines to ten-year-old fireworks, took his family to La Grange twice a year for Greek Orthodox services. Beyond the city, in the world of cotton fields and pine woods bisected by dusty roads, there were bold streams to wash away sins and fierce snakes to be held up to heaven in display of abiding faith.

Eugene gained weight and bought a new wool suit, as well as one of lighter weight for summer wear. By 1938 he had saved enough money to catch the eye of his banker, Steven Floyd, who invited him fishing at his cow pond and, between slapping gnats and damning the heat and Mr. Roosevelt, told him it was time he put down real roots in Oughton. The best way to do this, he counseled, was to drop his savings, like a ripe seed, into the fertile soil of a nice piece of property his bank happened to own.

"Ten acres, more or less, of high ground on the Atlanta Highway just beyond the city limits. Four acres in woods, rest in improved pasture. Barn and outbuildings in good repair, house, too." He stuck out his lower lip and blew his breath up his face to stir the gnats from his eyes. "Few years and the city'll be out there. Run a couple of roads through and you've got good development property. Man could do worse, a lot worse."

Eugene asked him why if the land were so fine the bank was willing to part with it. He got the answer he half expected: "Why son, banks are in the money business, not real estate!"

That evening, as he sat on the porch of the McIntosh House and watched the lightning bugs, he told Kermit Westmoreland about Floyd's offer. Kermit laughed and said, "Steve's in the money business, all right—other people's money!" He went on to explain that the banker had been investing heavily in a Florida land scheme and that the bubble had burst with a bang that shook windows on Wall Street, at least those that still had glass in them after the big crash.

Eugene bought the parcel for fifteen hundred dollars, paying half in cash and giving a five-year note at 5 percent for the balance. He had never had land of his own before and he really didn't know what to do with it besides walking out to look at it every day or so, as though to make sure it was still there. He had no desire to leave the hotel and the fussy care of Mrs. Leeds, much less her good cooking. He hired a man named Dunway to keep the place up and took his real pleasure in considering how someday he would retire to those acres and, straw hat on head, bring forth from the rich earth bountiful crops of corn, tobacco, cotton—or whatever one raised on his own land.

And so it was that in September of the next year, 1939, Eugene was at thirty-one a respected and rather prosperous member of the community. His lightly freckled skin was beginning to wrinkle around the corners of his green eyes and his sandy hair had begun its slow yet steady journey away from his brow. Among his friends he was known as a man with perhaps a bit more than his share of wit and with a tongue that was fastened to it on one end, like a whip to its handle, that could flick the flies of pretense from the rump of a politician at twenty paces and leave the fellow smiling.

He had his own rocker on the porch of the McIntosh, and men three, four, even five years older or younger would gather round him and Kermit Westmoreland in the evenings and solve the many problems of the world. The German invasion of Poland did not so much concern them, however, as did the falling price of cotton and the fate of that year's Georgia Bulldogs on the gridiron.

Eugene was sitting there, in his chair, one foot propped against the rail when the southbound express which passed through Oughton every evening at exactly 8:05 made its first whistle blast at the north end of the yards. Reflexively, all the men pulled out their watches and checked the time, then snapped them shut and slipped them back into their pockets and smiled at one another without speaking. It was reassuring to know that while cotton was either up or down, and while some fellow named Adolf Hitler was stirring up trouble across the seas, the West Point Railroad rolled on as steady as the stars across the night.

Then there was the screech of brakes, the hiss of steam, the groan of huge bands of steel squeezing together to stop the train.

The night fell silent. Eugene looked at Kermit, who looked at

9

Eugene while the others looked at both of them. A dog howled. Another answered. Then the whistle blew and the wheels of the express churned up the tracks, gathering momentum. A whistle blast at the south end of the yards and the train was gone.

"Most peculiar," said the young lawyer Ben Lewis.

Kermit grinned. "Oh, maybe old Rudolph forgot to kiss his wife good-bye and stopped to telegraph a peck or two!"

They all laughed at this, because Rudolph the engineer was a bachelor whose only love was the gleaming locomotive he urged on through sun and rain, snow, sleet, hail, and wandering cattle, up and down the tracks, as sure and certain as death and the final judgment.

They got to talking about Rudolph's exploits, telling tales each had heard a dozen times and loved to hear again as much for the telling as the tale. Then they heard the steady clop-clop-clop of hooves on pavement and looked toward the square. Frank Bailey, who was principal of the high school, said, "That's Old Red's wagon."

"Not Old Red driving, though," someone said from the shadows. "That's his boy Sam. Looks like he's got a passenger."

By now the wagon had crossed the square and was nearing the hotel. Eugene got up and leaned against the porch railing. Old Red was an elderly black man who made a living hauling freight to and from the station. His boy Sam was about nineteen. As the wagon come into the circle of light cast by the porch lamps, Eugene saw a woman sitting on the seat beside the driver. She was dressed in black and wore a hat and veil. She swayed and clutched a pale hand to Sam's muscular arm to steady herself. This action made the young black so nervous that without being spoken to, he said, "This lady don't feel good. She stop mister Rudolph's train and got off cause she don't feel good!"

Eugene took his jacket from the back of his rocker and slipped it on as he came down the steps. Young Pete Corday was steadying the mule while Ed Roberts was reaching toward the lady in distress. Eugene and he helped her down. Her voice was hardly more than a whisper and her body trembled as she said, "Thank you, I don't feel . . . I need to . . . rest . . ."

Now Mrs. Leeds came through the front door. Aided by Eugene, she put the mysterious woman in a downstairs room beside her own, the same one that she reserved for family. Sam followed with the lady's luggage. Eugene paid him generously for his trouble and sent him on his way, then told her he was a doctor and took charge with his best bedside manner.

She removed her hat and Eugene paused as he reached to touch her brow. Her skin was pale yet youthful and her moist eyes seemed as green as fresh mint. He liked the shape of her small chin and the arch of her pink lips.

Her brow was feverish. He took her pulse and found it elevated. "Have you traveled far?" he asked.

"From Nashville," she whispered. "That was yesterday. From Rome today."

"You poor thing," said Mrs. Leeds from the foot of the bed. "You'll stay here till you're yourself again."

"But . . . but you know nothing about me," she said, looking first at Mrs. Leeds, then at Eugene.

Gene said, "We know you aren't feeling well. That's enough for now." He told her his name and went to his room for his bag.

The next day her fever was gone and she was able to sit up in bed when Eugene called after lunch to see how she was. She told him her name was Ellen Wilkerson and that she was traveling south to visit relatives. As he took her pulse, she confided that she had recently been under the care of a Dr. Chambers in Nashville and that she had not felt well for some time. Eugene's professional eye had already seen as much. His male vision, however, saw a lovely woman in her middle twenties, alone and defenseless in a strange town. Long after he had counted the heart beats in her wrist, he held her hand in his and peered into her green eyes. At last she had said all she knew to say, or all she wished, and gently withdrew her hand and said, "I am a widow, doctor. My husband passed away five months ago." She closed her eyes, then, and did not open them even when, finally, Eugene took his leave, telling her that he would look in after supper.

That afternoon he could think of nothing but her, and he wondered exactly what her medical problem was. He went to the train station and sent a telegram to her doctor in Tennessee. Less than two hours later, Old Red's son Sam brought him a reply:

MRS WILKERSON IN DELICATE CONDITION STOP EMOTIONAL
DEPRESSION CAUSED BY RECENT TRAGIC LOSS OF HUSBAND
AND TWO SMALL CHILDREN STOP NO IMMEDIATE FAMILY STOP
SUGGEST TREATMENT FOR NERVOUS DISORDER STOP

Eugene read the message three times, then put it away in his desk. Nervous disorder? Did this Nashville doctor think he was Freud and Oughton was Vienna? What Ellen Wilkerson needed most was friends, and one thing he knew was that Oughton was a friendly town.

And so Eugene's curative treatment of Ellen Wilkerson began. Within two weeks she was sitting in his rocker on the porch of the McIntosh House smiling at Kermit's stories. Two weeks later she had changed from her widow's black to dark blue, and when the time of harvest home came in October, when the moon grew fuller and fuller and there was a snappy crispness to the air, she went to Corday's on the square and bought a lavender skirt and matching sweater outfit that brought the taste of wine to Eugene's lips.

He took her for a ride then in the '34 Ford coupe he used for making country calls. The top was down and she wore a white scarf against the wind. There was the bittersweet smell of woodsmoke in the evening air. They went out the Atlanta Highway and took the dirt road up the hill to his property. Corn stalks stood dry and rustling in the fields. The house was milk white under the rising moon. He stopped beyond the well and asked her how she liked it.

"It's very nice," she said. "It has a homey feeling. How long have you owned it?"

"What makes you think it's mine?" he replied, smiling.

She laughed softly. "I don't suppose a man would show someone another man's property."

They were married in December, a week before Christmas, in the lobby of the McIntosh House. Kermit Westmoreland was Eugene's best man, while Mrs. Leeds was Ellen's matron of honor. After the vows were said, there was rum punch and a tiered cake from Wilson's Bakery. There was dancing, too, in the lobby and out on the porch, even though a few of the guests were so Baptist that they shook their heads in disapproval as they ate the refreshments. After several glasses of punch, however, they were shaking them in time to the victrola's music.

December was mild, a false spring, some said, hinting at terrible weather to come. Eugene and Ellen had no honeymoon to speak of. They drove to Atlanta and spent two days and three nights in a hotel near Stone Mountain. Then they came back to the house and the acres outside of town. He painted rooms and hauled furniture as she directed, and never had so much pleasure in his life. By New Year's they felt as settled and happy in their married ways as a couple that had been together through twenty years and half as many children. Oh, it was true that sometimes Ellen went to a window and looked out at the sky and seemed to forget that Eugene was in the room. And there were times when he came home for lunch and found her eyes moist as though she had been crying. She had told him about her husband and son and daughter before he asked her to marry him. There had been a fire while they were visiting his people in Murfreesboro. Her husband had perished trying to save the children who were sleeping upstairs.

Eugene commiserated with her, and treated her tenderly at all times, especially when he saw that she had been sorrowing. He wanted to have children of his own, but he knew it was too soon to broach that subject, so he left it alone and concentrated on making her happy.

The first of February the mild weather changed and winter came during one night's darkness in a howling wind as though it had been lingering elsewhere and suddenly remembered it had missed an appointment in Oughton. The little house on the hill shook and groaned. Cold drafts sprang from unseen cracks like leaks in an otherwise sound ship. When the well froze, they moved into two rooms at the McIntosh and Ellen wired a storage company in Nashville to send her steamer trunk in which she had packed away her winter clothing.

It was snowing the morning, a week later, when Old Red and Sam brought the trunk from the station. Mrs. Leeds made them wait on the porch while she took a broom and swept it clean of flakes. They carried it up to Eugene and Ellen's rooms. Ellen gaily told Mrs. Leeds to let her have just fifteen minutes and she'd give her a fashion show the envy of New York.

13

Mrs. Leeds went back to the kitchen to see about the roast she was cooking for lunch. A half hour passed before she wondered what was keeping Ellen. The mashed potatoes needed attention, and then the green beans, so another twenty minutes went by before she wiped her hands clean on her apron and went upstairs. She called Ellen's name, and when there was no answer, she knocked on the door and found it ajar.

The opened steamer trunk stood between the door and the bed. Again she called Ellen's name. Again there was no reply. It wasn't until she peered over the top of the trunk that Mrs. Leeds saw the young wife. She was sitting on the floor, hugging her knees and rocking back and forth, her green eyes fixed and staring at something in the trunk. She spoke sharply to her, touched her, shook her. Her body was as hard as iron, her skin dry and hot.

Mrs. Leeds looked into the trunk. There, on one hanger after another, were the skirts and blouses, the dresses, the trousers, jackets, and shirts, and, on racks in the bottom, the shoes—some scuffed brown and white, some shiny patent leather—of her children.

The storage company in Nashville had sent the wrong trunk.

Yes, a mistake was made, a simple one that anyone might make; and when informed, the firm offered to send the other trunk at no cost. But it was too late then for winter clothes.

Eugene cared for his wife himself at first. Old Red's daughter Emmaline stayed with her while he was at the office, and he came home several times a day to check on her. Ellen was not violent. But they had to feed her, to bathe her, to take care of her every need. Eugene took her to a psychiatrist in Atlanta, a man who had studied with Jung in Switzerland. The prognosis was not favorable. He suggested shock treatments. Eugene had seen that sort of thing once in medical school, the electrodes connected, the mouthpiece affixed to protect the subject's tongue, the terrible bowing upward of spine and muscle as the charge surged through the body, the lingering smell of singed hair and flesh, the inconclusive results. He loved Ellen too much to submit her to that.

In August of that year he found a sanatorium near Asheville, North Carolina, which specialized in severe depression cases. Mrs. Leeds and Emmaline accompanied him on the journey. He was a medical doctor who was professionally trained to deal with terrible illness and agonizing death. But he was not equipped, either as a physician or as a man, to cope with the living death of the beautiful young woman he loved. As they parted, he broke down and the attending psychiatrist, another Johns Hopkins graduate, had to give him a strong sedative.

What saved his own sanity was an epidemic of influenza that winter. As he worked round the clock day after day, he came to realize that his life was not his own, and that by purchasing Whatley's practice he had really sold himself to the community. He was their priest of life, their intercessor against the evil of disease. They owned him body and soul and he could not long indulge his personal sorrow while babies were suffocating on their own mucus.

Chapter Two

Dex Roberts put aside the evening newspaper and went into the kitchen. His wife Dawn followed. He stood in the darkness, his hands on either side of the sink, looking out the window at the autumn light.

"Dex, you hungry?" Dawn asked.

"What?" He spun, blinking as though he had been startled from a dream.

She switched on the overhead light. "I asked if you were hungry. There's cold chicken in the refrigerator, and some brownies in the cookie jar, if the kids didn't get them."

"I don't want anything."

"Beer?"

He said no and went into the living room. Dawn turned off the light and trailed him. As Dex settled in his chair, she said, "Honey, what's wrong? You've been acting this way for a week. Have I done something?"

Dex shook his head and opened the paper to the sports section.

"Talk to me!" Dawn demanded. "I won't be put off like this. Are you bothered about something? Is business bad?"

"No, I don't know," Dex replied.

"Is that all you can say?" She took the paper from him, threw it on the floor, and made him look her in the eye, "Who is she, Dex?"

16

"She?"

"You know. Why don't you tell me and then we can make plans."

Dex stood up. "Listen, I haven't felt well lately, that's all. I've been married to you nine years and not once have I even looked at another woman!" Now he was pacing the floor, throwing his arms in the air. "If I knew what's wrong I'd tell you." He wheeled and thrust a finger at her. "Don't you trust me?"

"Yes, of course I do. It's just that—well—you worry me. I love you, Dex, I always have and I guess I always will. I know I'm not very pretty and a lot of nice looking girls come into the store. It's—"

"Don't talk this way," said Dex. "Don't nag." He rubbed his eyes, then the back of his head. "I don't mean you nag. Look, just believe me. There's nothing wrong."

"All right, if you say so."

"I say so. Now let's go to bed. It's almost eleven and I'm dog tired. Tomorrow's Friday."

But tired as he was he could not rest. He changed into his pajamas, brushed his teeth, gave Dawn a hug and a kiss, closed his eyes, and out of habit said a few silent words to God. For a while he thought sleep might come quickly. Dawn made rustling noises as she settled beneath the covers, and it seemed in seconds she was fast asleep, emitting the little purring sound which turned into snores when she rolled over a certain way.

From the room across the hall came the incoherent mumbling of his son Ted, who was seven and who often had nightmares and walked in his sleep. His four-year-old Bonny slept peacefully like her mother. The house creaked as though it too were relaxing, and he heard the dreamy sounds of the wind in the trees clustered in the back yard. Now and then a dog barked. In the lulls Dex recognized the beating of his heart. Or was it only his imagination?

What's the difference? he asked himself. It was the same, and as long as his heart made those sounds he was all right. Of course, the time would come when it would go silent. What was man born for except to die? And get into trouble first. Life was funny. No one got out of it alive.

So why am I wasting my time in bed? he wondered. You spent one-third of your life unconscious. He rolled over. Everyone else did, at least! Rest was necessary, though. Men weren't machines. Flesh and blood. They slept and they ate, too. Did they ever! The food that passed through his grocery store in just one day! Sold a lot of toilet paper too. He rolled on to his back and listened to the autumn wind.

They came into the store and filled their baskets and went out and next week came again. Over and over. Worse on Friday, lots of SPE-CIALS. And for what? The wind moaned. Yes, it all added up to that. What caused wind anyhow? Beans! No, temperature differences. Hot went to cold or was it the other way? Food was one thing everybody needed. And shelter. He pulled the blanket up to the tip of his nose. Something in your belly and a dry place out of the weather. The basics.

Give a man those and he might survive, for a while. There were other things, though. Man didn't live by bread alone. Sex. Dawn was all right. Of course, her breasts weren't for *Playboy*. But kids did that to a woman and you couldn't have everything, preachers said. Those women who came in the store were something else. Sometimes they shopped early in the morning wearing tight pants and their hair in curlers and no bras. See them bending over the display cases fingering meats. The best set belonged to Lauree Lewis, daughter of the solici-tor, Ben Lewis. She was in her second year at Athens.

Dex rolled on his side and considered touching Dawn. She'd be willing, always was, even before they married. Lauree's were just right. Large stargazers, very firm, and the nipples were big and very red, like cherries. She was probably doing it at the university. And if she didn't get knocked up or out she'd come home to Oughton, marry one of the locals who went to law or med school, build a fine home in Sunrise Hills, and live happily ever after. Coming into the store in tights with curlers and no bra.

That was life? He rolled away from his wife and looked across the bedroom to the window. A full moon was rising through the trees. He watched the wind dance the bare branches in the pale light and he felt the same urge which had been torturing him for the past weeks. An indefinable force compelled him to rise and move around, to go some place—where, he wasn't sure.

He slid from beneath the covers and, moving quietly not to wake Dawn, went to the window. The light of the moon split his body into regions of white and black. The neighboring houses were dark. Leaves blew like ashes across the lawns. The moon was huge and as perfectly

18

round as a bullet hole. It was strange to know a man had walked upon it. There were people who worshiped it. Human sacrifices even. He shuddered and touched his hand to his stomach.

Even in Oughton. He learned about them when he was a child. Not the blacks either. They feared the night. White folks. When the moon was right they did things. No one could prove it, but they happened. Murders. Rapes. Animals butchered in the fields. It was enough to make preachers in their pulpits say—well—nothing specific. But the Bible passages they harped on dealt with evil spirits and shadows of death.

Dex shut his eyes and tried to force his mind off that subject. He conjured up Lauree's breasts and imagined one in each hand. It was nice manipulating those cherries between his thumbs and forefingers. Once she wore a loose, billowing dress, and when she bent low he saw all the way down to her panties. He felt his fingers crawling down her flat tummy to that realm of white.

A dog howled, then another.

His eyes opened. The moon was higher now, and the limbs held it like a net. His wristwatch read twelve. How long have I been here? he wondered. His legs tensed and he felt in his chest a sensation which called to mind the crazy turnings of an uncased compass needle. He recognized the old urge—he had to go.

"I won't!" he told himself. He searched for a reference point, for some solid contact with reality to stop the mad whirling behind his eyes. The window sill steadied him momentarily. But he knew it wasn't enough. Nothing was.

As he put on his clothes over his pajamas what happened at work the day before flashed through his mind like a movie rerun. He saw himself restocking soup. One minute it was can after blasted can— tomato, split pea, noodle—the next he was almost a mile away walking down Maple Street, still wearing his long white apron and holding the price marker set at two for fifty-eight. What brought him back to his senses—if that's what they were—was a horn. Tom Davis passed in his truck and asked did he want a ride? As they drove back to the store Tom laughed and asked was he opening a branch cross town?

Very funny. But he laughed right back and, winking, said he was tending to some—ah, hum—*business*. Tom ran a service station and a lot of women trusted him with their cars. He winked back.

19

Dex tied his shoelace, gave his hair a quick brush, and stole from the house. One wink was worth ten thousand words. Tom would spread it round and pretty soon at Jaycees or Rotary some wise guy would joke about his banana or peaches or meat department. He paused in the shadows on the porch. That sort of thing was fun and it never hurt to have a reputation even if it wasn't exactly true. But what was happening to him?

He half expected a ghost to rise from the shrubbery and moan "Follow me." The houses up and down the street were dark, lifeless shapes. He sat on the top step. What were they up to? Were they really asleep? Suppose they pulled blackout curtains over the windows and were wide awake doing things?

He looked at the Corday house on its huge lot down the street. Pete Corday was dead a year and now his widow Alice was alone. Dex squinted at the spot on the second floor wall where he reckoned the bedroom window was. Alice Corday was in her middle thirties but she still looked good. He had never seen her breasts though. She shopped Jack Brown's A&P. Too good for an independent grocer. Once she came in for a jar of vaseline and a package of BC's. Still, she was a nice lady, friendly, and her calves were like springs. He closed his eyes and saw her bouncing from his store.

He opened them two blocks away. His head was spinning. And his body followed, first to this side of the street, then the other. He struggled to regain control. What if I'm seen? They'll say I'm bombed! A dog snarled at his heels. The Bailey's doberman. A plenty mean bitch. He snarled back and the dog was quiet.

But he could not quiet himself. His legs kept moving. He could neither stop nor direct them. It was out of his hands, or feet. Am I asleep? Is this a dream? he asked himself.

He heard his voice whisper he *must* be asleep. He tried to be rational. Sleepwalking was caused in most cases by bladder pressure. Doc Spaulding said when Ted did it get him to the bathroom pronto. Dex tore at his fly. The pajamas got in the way. And it wasn't easy doing it while walking down the middle of the street. He had to concentrate for all he was worth. Now it was working. Yes, but a car was coming!

He wanted to run but his feet would not leave the centerstripe. The

20

headlights exposed him, and now the driver switched on his brights. Dex turned his face away and tried to fasten his trousers. Damn, caught in the zipper! The car slowed. Tomorrow's headlines flashed in the darkness: local grocer, father of two, booked on drunk and indecent charges, after struck down by hit-and-run.

The car swerved and passed. In the backwash of light Dex saw a white, scowling face and a clenched fist. The license tag was out of town. Did the guy think pissing in the street was a hallowed Oughton custom?

Dex started to yell at him, but his voice died in his throat. No need waking the neighborhood. Wake? He freed the zipper. I'm not sleepwalking, he realized. No, his bladder was untensed and still his legs led on.

As he walked through the sleeping town, turning down one street, up another, cutting through backyards, following alleys, snarling at dogs, doubling and redoubling his path, Dex surrendered unconditionally to the blind force that urged him through the night like a shifting wind hurling a rudderless ship. Above, the full moon shone like an anti-sun, recalling legends of werewolves and vampires. Had he become a creature of darkness? He ran his fingers over his head and face. He needed a shave and could stand a trim at Gus White's barber shop, but he wasn't animal shaggy. His teeth hadn't grown into fangs, yet. He wasn't drooling and he felt no hunger for blood. He passed Bird's Funeral Home without noticing it.

A little piece of tail maybe, he joked to himself as his legs sped him on to the high school football field. At the fifty he broke into a jog, and as he circled one goal and headed for the other, he remembered all the cute tricks that cheered, legs Y-ed, ponytails flying, when he played ball. There was plenty of good stuff on the cheering squad those years. Jenny Meyers came across for a touchdown and would let you tickle her for a recovery and would tickle you for an interception. They were conference champs his senior year. He turned left at the ten and angled off the field.

Beyond the campus the town gave way to the country. Dex found himself running through the woods. It was so dark he felt blind. But he did not so much as stub his toe or brush a low-hanging branch. It was lonely in the woods. He did not like it. He wished he would collide with something. Maybe the shock would turn off whatever forced him on. He tried to veer from the path set by his feet, but they held fast and for all his trouble he got nothing but worse proof he was powerless.

He climbed a kudzu-covered barbed wire fence and moved through a cornfield. Pumpkins growing between the rows shone in the moonlight like scattered heads. The dry stalks rubbed him with a noise of snakes and struck at him time and again. His legs were leaden; his breath burned like fire. His heartbeat was a painful throb. "I can't—I can't go on!" he moaned. The sound of his voice stopped his feet.

He stood stone-still at the edge of the field facing the forest. He tried to move but he could not even close his eyes. I'm crazy, he told himself, crazy! But that was impossible. There was no insanity in his family, not even a wild-eyed aunt who prayed for the Last Days. His ancestors were pioneers who fled the debtor's prisons of England to make a new life in a new world. They killed the Indians, were killed by them in turn, and slowly won the land for themselves. A little strange maybe, thought Dex, but crazy? Never!

People went crazy, though. Every family had its first. Papers and TV were full of it. Dex tried to move. The wind and moonlight held him tight. People flipped, bugged out, came loose. Some killed others and/or themselves. What was it all about anyhow? Nobody was immune. Preachers stole church funds and ran away with deacons' wives. And other people piss in the middle of the street!

He saw the moon from the corner of his eye. The son-of-a-bitch! Like a big white face watching, always watching. Maybe he was under a spell? Yes, people lived in Oughton who could do it. He saw a doll with his face. It was pinched in a vise. They were getting the pins ready.

But that was crazy! Who would do that to him? I never hurt a soul, not one! he told the moon. He was a good husband and father. Ted respected him. Okay, so he didn't play with him like he should. He worked hard and at night he was tired. He was faithful to his wife. He wasn't any nutty puritan, but still, if he did mess around a little he was a man, and it wasn't because he was looking for another woman to take her place. The checkout girls understood. Give them a little squeeze

22

when business was slow just to pass the time. Could go looney in a grocery store with all those vegetables and cans and boxes sitting there. They didn't mind. They did a little squeezing themselves. It was nothing that didn't go on at the A&P. They were nice girls and attractive, but slow upstairs. Sometimes it was repulsive, like with animals. Not that he ever did that, but Marlow Redmann the butcher made jokes. Besides, Dawn was no cherry when I got her, he reminded himself. She never would say who. But she went with Craig Pike in junior high and Steve Floyd later.

But all this wasn't grounds for a sharp needle through the heart! The moon ducked under a cloud. Dex shivered. There was something moving in the kudzu between the field and the forest. He tried to run but he could not move a muscle. They were coming to get him. He did not know who they were but he knew what they would do. Take down his pants. Cut it off. Yes, then the cruel bastards would give him first aid so he couldn't bleed to death. They'd tell everybody. The nutless wonder of Oughton County! Crowds would flock to the store just to see him. How could he explain to Dawn! She was still a young woman.

The moon reappeared, brighter now than before, it seemed. Dex searched the field. A face, pale and spotted with shadows, looked at him. And now a second face, thinner and darker than the first, appeared. He heard a voice, faint and mumbled, then another, loud, rough.

"Dammit, Julius, speak up! There ain't nobody within five miles!"

Two men stepped from the shadows and stood at the edge of the field. Dex knew them. The loud man was Reg Dunway. His short companion was Julius, his brother. They worked sometimes at the wire factory doing common labor.

"Don't like it," Julius said. "No use temptin' fate. Never tell when you're seen. The night's got eyes."

"Bullshit!" said Reg. "Only thing looks like a man round here is that damn scarecrow yonder." He pointed at Dex.

Julius jumped back and crouched, his hand in his pocket.

Reg laughed and grabbed his sleeve and pulled him up straight. "You don't wanna go cuttin' no bag of straw. Come on, we ain't got all night."

The two men went back into the forest. Again Dex tried to run

23

away. But he was frozen to the earth. Thank god they don't recognize me, he thought. What were they doing here anyhow? Dex felt himself shaking. At least he was still alive. Still? The Dunways were bad actors. If they suspected—now he strained not to move.

They were coming back! He heard them trampling through the brush. They were dragging something. A long, thick bundle. He heard them grunt. Then Reg stumbled and yelled, "Dammit, Julius, pick up your end!"

"You ain't carryin' the pick and shovel, too," Julius said.

They moved to the edge of the field, dropped the bundle, and started digging. They worked fast, cursing under their breath but not talking, and when it was knee deep they climbed out, rolled the bundle in, and covered it up. When they finished, Julius sprinkled dead leaves over the raw earth and swept away their footprints with a broken pine branch.

"That'll do her fine," Reg said.

Julius found the pick and shovel, looked straight at Dex, and said, "We been here too long. Let's go."

Reg laughed and clapped him on the back. "What's the matter, boy, you scared of the dark? You fraid some old ghost gonna get you? Boo!"

A cloud nibbled the edges of the moon, then swallowed it whole.

"It ain't the dark," Julius said.

"She'll wish it was dark forever and ever," Reg said.

Dex heard them going through the brush. Her? What had they done? The moon broke free of the clouds and its blinding glare lit the field with a whiteness that reminded him of a photo negative. He trembled. They had tried to hide the grave, but he knew where it was. His eyes were trained on the spot. Far away a dog was howling. His flesh crawled. He smelled fresh-turned earth. The cold wind tore at his shirt and spilled down the back of his neck. If only he could fasten his collar button. But he was paralyzed. He strained his arm. It responded by lunging at his throat, knocking him backward. He was free! Whatever force held him let go.

"And go I will!" he cried.

Reg and Julius had gone into the forest. He turned and started across the field in the direction he had come. The pumpkins rolled under his feet and dashed him into the corn. A terrible noise wrapped about him like a cloak. He tried to shake it off, to go quietly. If those two heard! Back there in the earth was a body and one was enough. Yes, they killed her and—

Dex stopped in the middle of the cornfield. How do I know? he asked himself. He shook his head trying to dislodge the dangerous ideas forming there. If the Dunways had killed someone he was a witness. He knew where the body was. It was his duty—

"Screw duty!" he cried out. Then, tilting his face to the moon, he shook his fists and screamed, "Screw you too!"

As he turned and went back through the field he forced Lauree Lewis into his mind. Those tits! The straw in the field was soft. Lay her in the moonlight. The checkout girls were okay and they asked no questions. Alice Corday bought vaseline and headache powders the only time she came in the store. Was that before or after Pete died? It must've been before because he was one hell of a big man and caused her enough trouble—folks said—for head pains no nostrums could cure.

He reached the edge of the field. Yes, this was the place. There were leaves and the ripe odor of raw earth. He dropped to his knees and clawed at the dirt with his bare hands, throwing it behind like a dog digging a bone. As the hole opened darkly before him he told himself he was really crazy. What would the others do? Tom Davis? Wouldn't catch him uncovering somebody else's victim. He wanted to stop but he couldn't. On his knees, bent over, rocking back and forth steadily, he saw in the dancing shadows the dark places of checkout girls and smelled their cheap perfume.

He sniffed the air. He *did* smell perfume. His fingers touched cloth. He jumped to his feet and shook his hand madly like it had been burned. The odor tickled his nose and throat. Visions of powdered breasts spun in the moonlight. There was a woman buried in the earth!

He leaped into the hole. The dirt caved in beneath his weight. Yes, and now something moved under him. He flung the dirt wildly, crying, "I'm coming, I'm coming!"

A moan rose from his fingertips. He thrust his hands deep, felt the angular roundness of a shoulder, and, bracing his feet against the sides

25

of the hole, pulled the body to the surface. He heard coughing, felt a stirring. The rough cloth shroud was tied with cord at the top. He broke it open.

The face of a young woman stared at him. Her lips were black with blood. Her crazed eyes strained as though they would squirt from the sockets. She snorted and whinnied like a wild animal.

"I've saved you!" Dex cried. "You'll be all right now!"

The girl bared her teeth and snarled. The silver disk of the moon swam in her unblinking eyes. She groaned, and Dex tried to reassure her, but she lunged at him with her jaws, and when he pulled away she vomited.

Dex scrambled from the grave and brushed himself off. She was out of her mind. What could he do? "I saved your damn life," he told her. "Now it's up to you, hear?"

She gnashed her teeth and rocked back and forth like a child humming its babydoll to sleep. The moonlight changed the vomit into a silver gown. Dex studied her face. It was hard to tell, but he could not recall her. Of course, she ran with Reg and Julius. She wasn't ugly, though. Her kind never were. She was all right. Her body felt good when he was digging her up. He heard himself laugh. She was out of her head. He could give her a good poke and who'd be the wiser?

"Hey!" He kicked a clod of dirt to get her attention. "Hey, you wanna do it, hey, you wanna fuck?"

For the first time she blinked her eyes. She frowned and then she threw her hands to her ears and screamed. She was still screaming when Dex crossed the barbed wire fence. Minutes later he fancied he heard her as he ran across the football field.

If she wants to scream let her, he told himself. But it was one hell of a way for a girl to act toward a guy who saved her life. You could be damn sure the Dunways were getting in her pants, if she wore any. He kept to the sidewalks and moved from shadows to shadows. The moon was in the west now. The courthouse clock said four-thirty. But what did that mean? In France it was mid-morning. The chinks were having lunch. He sold a lot of chow mein. Women liked it because it was simple to fix. Eighty-nine a can. Noodles extra. He passed Holliday's Rooming House. A light burned upstairs.

She was off her noodle all right. Damn, what a terrible thing!

26

Julius and Reg were two bad ones and they should be locked up. "But I'm not the one to do it," he told himself. He knew what they were capable of. Maybe an anonymous phone call to set the wheels turning?

Dex looked over his shoulder. The streets were empty and the houses dark. Reg called him a scarecrow. He'd scare those two birds. Maybe the girl would come for a job some day. If her mind straightened out. She wouldn't remember him, and if she did he'd deny it. Girl like that, slip her some groceries and bingo!

Dex locked the front door behind him, crept into the bathroom, and shed his clothes. They were filthy with clay and briars. Dawn would ask questions. He rolled them in a tight bundle and tucked it behind the toilet. There was a laundromat across from the store.

He tiptoed to the bed and carefully crawled beneath the covers. Dawn was snoring like a buzz-saw, her small face upturned, her thin lips parted, her graceful white throat exposed. Had the girl left the grave yet? The whirlings in his head were gone and he felt only tiredness. It was damn strange what had happened to him. Maybe he *was* sleepwalking. Or? Doc Spaulding would know. But I can't tell him, thought Dex. It would mean revealing Julius and Reg. He knew he could never tell a soul.

He relaxed then and listened to his heartbeat. Steady as a clock. It felt good to be tired this way, like after doing a difficult job. He wanted to enjoy the sensation. But before he could savor it, he fell asleep.

Chapter Three

The morning after the housewarming at Davey Rutledge's, Polly Green had an inspiration which she formed into palatable shape while fixing breakfast and served to her husband, the judge, along with his grits, ham, and eggs.

Waiting till he got a mouthful, she said, "Sidney, we're going to find Davey Rutledge a wife."

During the long moment he tried to swallow, the judge was silent, but his eyes, wide and wild, spoke volumes, all beginning and ending with NO! He shook his head, grunted, and, after a gulp of tomato juice, said, "*We* ain't gonna do no such thing and neither are you!"

Polly smiled sweetly. "Watch your grammar, dear. You're not at Gus White's barber shop. Why aren't we? Weren't his parents our friends? Isn't Davey a promising state senator with a bright political future? Don't—?"

"Order in the dining room!" the judge bellowed, striking the table with the flat of his meaty hand. "Davey's doin' well enough as is, so let him be. I mean it, Polly, you poke your nose in that boy's business and I'll—I'll—"

"Give me twenty years, dear?"

"Worse than that!"

He finished his breakfast in silence. As he went out the front door,

Polly helped him with his overcoat, kissed his leathery cheek and told him to be nice in court.

"Any sentence over a year and a day's on your head," he replied, putting on his hat. "I'll be home for lunch, and you leave Davey alone, hear?"

Polly was a dutiful wife, but it was quite out of her hands by now. As the judge's car disappeared beyond the seventh tee on the country club course, she closed the door and made plans. Davey Rutledge was indeed a good boy. They had known him all his thirty-one years and were best friends with his parents before they were killed two years ago in a terrible car accident. He was born the same year as her son, Frank, who died in an Air Force jet crash eight years ago. It was a staggering blow, from which she and the judge would never fully recover. Frank's picture stood on the walnut table in the living room bay window. Polly paused on the way to the kitchen and looked at her son. He was a smiling, clean-cut boy, but he wasn't as handsome as Davey Rutledge. No, and like his father he was built low to the ground like a badger. In the photo his face was still slender. Were he alive today he'd probably have a double chin and a bald spot, like Sidney at thirty.

She glanced out the window across the broad, leaf-strewn lawn to the street. It was a brisk November morning and the country club lake and clubhouse were visible through the bare trees. A nice estate in Sunrise Hills was a far cry from their first apartment. In those days a young lawyer had it tough. And what did it count if his wife graduated from Agnes Scott? Nothing, less she came from money, had connections, or, at least, could do something to help keep the wolf at bay.

Polly frowned. Their door hadn't been exactly clawmarked. Sidney's people owned land. He had intelligence, strength, and ambition. Played guard for Georgia in '42. Same team with Sinkwich and Trippi that won the Rose Bowl. It was a great honor and the plaques and photographs looked good on his office wall. After the war they helped build a lucrative practice and secure a judgeship.

A figure came into view on the road. A man running. Polly recognized him by his yellow sweatsuit. Steve Floyd, another of Frank's friends. Poor Steve, his sweet young wife Louise had almost died in childbirth the month before. The baby was in the Masonic hospital in Atlanta. Deformed. Sometimes it made you wonder.

Polly went into the kitchen and put the butter in the refrigerator. Leave the rest for Clusta, the colored girl who came every day. That was part of being a judge's wife, though God knew how many dishes she washed in her lifetime. When Frank was a boy he helped her, and sometimes now when she felt sad and alone she told Clusta never mind and closed the kitchen door and did them herself, by hand.

If only Frank had married. Grandchildren were a link between the living and the dead. He had a sweetheart, Molly West, but she married an engineer from New York named Rojack who worked here in town. They lived nearby. Her children, two boys, were handsome. Sometimes Polly fancied they looked like Frank. It was absurd. But they had hair the same brownish color as his.

There was a knock at the back door. Clusta came in and said mornin'. Polly told her clean the kitchen and then do the wash in the baskets by the machine. Afterwards she could make the beds and run the vacuum. And, oh yes, be sure and set out those chops in the freezer. "I want to have a nice lunch for the judge," she said.

As Clusta scraped the dishes, Polly went upstairs, slipped off her robe and gown, and showered. The warm soapy water felt good coursing down her body. For a woman over fifty I'm in good shape, she decided. Her flesh was the type that, rather than spreading, in middle age seems to contract. Her breasts were smaller and more shapely now than when she married, even though they were wrinkled. Her slender waist and flat tummy turned the girls at the club green, especially summers when she went swimming every day and wore a bikini with no more qualms than those svelte coeds home for vacation. She ate whatever and how much she wanted and it never showed. If it weren't for the wrinkles, she told herself, shutting off the water, I might live forever and forever be fair.

She dried in the bedroom in front of the dresser mirror. The party at Davey Rutledge's new house was fun. Senator Rutledge. She said the word aloud, "Senator." It was a grand title for so young and unassuming a man. Of course, he was only a state senator, and historically many men were elected younger, but to gain broad public confidence at thirty-one spoke well. She envisioned him standing by the window. He was very tall—at least six three—and slender, but not skinny. His

30

shoulders were broad and in a swimming suit he looked quite muscular. He and Frank were teammates in high school, and Davey went on to play varsity baseball at Georgia while Frank fought for a place on the football squad. Poor dear Frank. He tried so hard but he never played first team. But Sid was proud nonetheless. They liked each other. Why did men want to fly? Those damn Wright brothers! Now she would no more consider setting foot in an airplane than—than—

"Than becoming a streetwalker!" she declared.

"Ma'am?" said a voice at the door.

It was Clusta, come to make the beds and run the vacuum. Polly draped the towel round herself. Clusta had seen her before. She was a maid, and sometimes helped her dress for those grand Atlanta parties they attended two, three times a year.

"Do the guest rooms first," Polly said. "Change the sheets and pillowcases and put fresh towels and new soap in the baths."

"We gonna have company?"

"We might, if you get the rooms ready."

Clusta laughed and went down the hall singing a happy song whose words were, to Polly's ears, only three: Yeah, baby, yeah!

Yeah, that was it! She tossed the wet towel in the bathtub and got dressed in a comfortable pants suit. Then she phoned Atlanta, dialing direct.

The judge was finishing his second chop when the doorbell rang and Clusta appeared in the dining room to say, "Company calling!"

"What company?" asked the judge. "Polly, have you—?"

"I?" said Polly, rising, "There's no reason we shouldn't have callers. We don't live in a hut on the Gobi Desert."

"Maybe," said her husband, "but I gotta sentence a first offender this afternoon, and don't you forget it."

How many men are hanged because judges argue with their wives? Polly wondered as she followed Clusta to the foyer. Of course, it was still justice. Think how many crimes occur cause criminals fight with theirs.

The guests were neither criminal nor judicial. It was Polly's oldest and dearest friend, Margery Hampton, and a really attractive young woman whom Margery introduced after hugging Polly's neck.

"This precious jewel is my niece, Abby Dorsch. You remember my

31

younger sister Grace? The one who married Leon, the Louisville banker? Abby is her child. Isn't she lovely?"

Polly saw she was more; she was positively striking. A tall, slender girl with long dark hair, she wore a tailored black wool coat with a red silk lining. Her gray dress was tastefully plain and accented with a single strand of pearls. Her face was exquisite: high cheekbones, well-defined lips, expressive green eyes. She smiled warmly and her teeth were perfectly even and very white.

"Who is it, Polly?" called the judge.

"Sidney, it's I!" Margery replied. She hurried into the dining room without pausing to give her mink to Clusta.

"Lord God!" cried the judge. "Not you!"

Polly laughed and, having taken Abby's coat, escorted her through the foyer. "My husband, the judge," she explained, "dated Margery before me. She and I were classmates at Agnes Scott and she introduced us. It was after the Bama game and Sidney had played so well they gave him the ball. He was some sight! A beautiful blackeye and scratches all over his face."

As they entered the dining room, Clusta came out with Margery's mink over her arm. She stroked the fur as though it were a purring kitten, and Polly told her to bring some coffee for the guests. At her voice, the judge looked up, then came to his feet as he saw the handsome young woman on his wife's arm. He sped around the table as though he were leading an end sweep, extended his hand, smiled, and said, "I'm Sid Green, owner of this here property."

Margery cackled. "Don't mind him, Abby. He graduated *cum laude* and he still talks like the Grand Ol' Opry!"

"Abby? Your name is Abby?"

"Abby Dorsch, dear," Polly said. "She's Margery's sister Grace's daughter."

The judge's eyes narrowed ever so slightly. "Oh? How come we ain't seen you in Oughton before now? Margery been exposin' you to Atlanta society?"

"Aunt Marge has shown me a good time," said Abby. "But the last two years I've been in Peru."

"That so?" said the judge. "We been considerin' a South American cruise ourselves."

"I was in the Peace Corps." She smiled. "It's a little different."

32

"A terrible sacrifice," Margery declared. "Such a waste." She gave her niece a hug. "Two wonderful years when she could have done so much. But that's water under the bridge, isn't it? We must look on the good side."

"Oh, why?" said the judge.

The girl laughed openly, loudly.

"Isn't it time for the afternoon session, dear?" asked Polly. "You have an important sentencing."

"Be merciful!" said Margery. "After all, someday you'll be called to account for your horrible sins, Sid Green, and it wouldn't hurt to be able to say something good in defense."

The judge wiped his lips and dropped the linen napkin on his empty plate. "My goodness is self-evident, like sunshine and rain. How's your soul, Margery!"

His voice was so affectedly ominous that even Clusta, who was bringing his hat and coat, laughed defensively. He said good-bye and started for his car, but in the driveway he called back to Polly and motioned for her to join him.

It was cold in the wind without a coat but she stood by the Buick and listened. "This is no chance visit, is it?" he asked. "You cooked it up for Davey Rutledge. Well, I warned you don't mess with his life. That's a nice lookin' girl, but let Davey find his own, hear?"

Again Polly heard, but what was she to do? They were here and hospitality required they be entertained. Clusta put their overnight bags in the guest rooms and hung their clothes in the closets. It wasn't like she'd really down and out *planned* to ambush Davey. No, she would permit nature to take its course, no matter what.

As they sat round the dining room table having coffee the thought struck Polly that it was all predestined, and she was Episcopalian not Presbyterian. Of course it was! At this moment in eternity the reason for her existence was to bring together these young people, else why on earth was she set down in a country town like Oughton? And please tell me why I didn't live a hundred years ago instead of right now?

"What's so amusing, dear?" asked Margery.

"Oh? Nothing. Why?"

"You were grinning like the proverbial cat."

33

Polly shook her head. "Sorry, but there's not one canary in town."

"That's not surprising," Margery replied with a sour intonation. "There's hardly anything in this wasteland." She turned to Abby. "Don't you find this area much like the back country of Peru? I mean the natives are so simple."

"Plumbing isn't simple," said Abby. "Neither are electric lights."

"She's become a regular technocrat," Margery said. "You'd think she went to MIT rather than Sweetbriar."

"I wish I had."

Polly said, "I'd like to hear about your adventures."

"You'll hear soon enough," said Margery. "Right now we've got serious talking to do. Abby, why don't you explore the judge's *property*. There's a million things to do. Too chilly for a swim, though. Polly, you still have that mare?"

"I don't care to ride," said Abby. "I did enough of that at Sweetbriar to last a lifetime. Aunt Marge mentioned the judge is some kind of shot."

"Oh, he is indeed," said Polly. "Do you shoot?"

"Only like Sergeant York," said Margery. "Her daddy Leon taught her from the time she could say 'pull.'"

"You're most welcome to use one of Sid's guns, and there's plenty of shells, but who'll handle the targets?"

"Let her use that maid, Polly. She looks strong enough."

"Clusta? Well, I don't think she knows what skeet is."

Abby stood. "I'll teach her, if it's all right."

Margery nodded, so Polly said fine. She'd find Clusta in the kitchen. The guns, shells, and targets were in the judge's study. Clusta knew where. As Abby went upstairs to change clothes, Margery poured another cup of coffee and pulled her chair closer to Polly.

"Your phone call was a god-send," she said.

"Oh? I thought Abby was the belle of Atlanta."

"She is. Still, there's such a thing as over exposure." Margery added cream and sugar and stirred slowly.

Polly tried to fathom her expression. Was something wrong? She had the feeling that Margery was a little too—too, well, too much Margery. The girl Abby was lovely and seemed very bright. However . . .

34

She hid her doubts and said, "She's such a pretty girl and so intelligent."

Margery nodded and sipped her coffee. "I know what she is. What I don't know is this young man of yours."

"To begin with he's a senator."

"Oh, aren't Nunn and Talmadge still serving me in Washington?"

"A state senator. But he's just thirty-one and everybody—even Sidney—says he has a bright future."

Margery removed a gold cigarette case and matching lighter from her handbag. She lit a cigarette and exhaled a small cloud of blue smoke over the table. "Background? Family? Money?"

"The Rutledges have been in west Georgia since the Indian Wars," Polly began.

Margery raised an eyebrow. "That was only in the 1820s."

Polly ignored her. "They've given statesmen to government, college presidents to education, and captains to industry."

"Did the Chamber of Commerce write that?"

"Davey's parents were killed two years ago September in an automobile accident. His father owned Rutledge Farms and had many other interests. Davey runs the farm and controls two local insurance agencies. He just built himself a new house. It's down the street, cross from the sixth hole. You passed it coming in."

"That colonial thing?"

Polly nodded. "You should see the furnishings, and like our place there's pasture behind."

"Net worth?"

"What?"

Margery flashed a scornful smile. "How much dough does he have?"

"I—," Polly began, then stopped. She heard Abby coming downstairs. She wore faded blue jeans, a washed-out sweat shirt, heavy shoes, and her hair was pulled back and secured with a green rubber band.

"Hi!" she said, smiling, "Clusta and I are going. If you need us you know where we are, okay?"

"Have fun, dear," said Margery.

"Be careful," Polly said.

"We will. Bye!"

Dressed like that she looked sixteen rather than—how old was she?

"Twenty-four last July," said Margery when Polly asked.

"Davey's thirty-one."

Margery flicked a cigarette ash in her saucer. "I see. He and your Frank were friends?"

"Yes, they were close. But I don't think of him as my son, if that's what you 'see.'"

"Temper, temper," said Margery. "My, this coffee makes me nervous. Give a gal a real drink?"

"You know it's in the sideboard."

As Margery filled a water glass with bourbon, Polly asked her pointblank why she was entrusted with exposing Abby to polite society.

Margery frowned, sipped her drink, and sat down again. "Think you smell a rat? Don't deny it, Polly Green. I know you better than you know yourself. Truth is, Abby's a complicated case. She's young and pretty and smart as a whip, and her family has money, but she's a stubborn little fool! Damn the Peace Corps! Commie, that's what it is! One of the Coca-Colas was most interested in her, but she told him 'Go to hell!' cause big business is shirking its 'global responsibilities.'"

The hollow "thump" of a shotgun report made Margery flinch.

Now it was Polly's turn to smile, but she did not. Rather, she said, "Abby has a mind of her own?"

"Bull-headed is what she is! And I'll tell you something else. I have good reason to suspect she, well, *associated* on the personal level with Peruvians, and I don't mean those with fine Spanish backgrounds. She was stationed in the interior where there's only *Indians*!"

Another shotgun report broke into Margery's declaration. She sipped her bourbon, then said, "You know about her mother, my sister Grace?"

Polly knew only that she was younger and lived in Louisville. She shook her head.

"You're the only woman in Georgia who doesn't. It's not very pretty but it's a fact. Grace had—*problems* with young men, if you know what I mean. If you don't, then guess. She was rather too—*democratic*, and I don't mean politically. One weekend she entertained half the SAE house."

36

"Margery, I can't believe that!"

"Wish I didn't have to. Daddy arranged her marriage with Leon to clear the air and her reputation. Why else would a refugee name like 'Dorsch' be acceptable to our family? Louisville's far enough away and distance breeds respectability."

Margery drained her glass and lit another cigarette. "Nowadays, of course, Grace's behavior isn't untypical. And as far as I know Abby's pure as the driven snow. I'm telling you all this, Polly, because—first—I thought you knew about Grace, and—second—because I don't want you hurt."

"Me? Why, what could hurt me?"

There was a knock at the front door, then the sound of a male voice and of a girl's laughter. When Polly reached the foyer she found Abby, Clusta, and a policeman. It was Deputy Wills. He carried the judge's shotgun crooked over his arm. Abby had her hands in the air and was trying not to laugh. Clusta stood behind her giggling.

"I caught these two down in the judge's pasture, Mrs. Green," Wills said. "They say you'll vouch for them."

"I want my lawyer," said Abby.

"Put your hands down, ma'am. This's no joke."

"He'll shoot us, Clusta. He really will!"

"I know them," Polly said. "The young lady is my houseguest. Clusta's my maid. They have my permission to shoot in the pasture."

"Yes ma'am. It's not that I didn't believe them, not exactly. But I never seen a—a colored girl shoot skeet before." He offered Abby the gun, and when she refused to lower her hands, he gave it to Polly, saluted, and left.

Polly watched him march down the drive to the patrol car. The heavy gun strained her arms. A shotgun. She glanced at Abby and Clusta. The father of the bride wore a twelve-gauge Browning?

Abby took the gun from her, saying, "I'd better clean it before the judge gets home. Come on, Clusta-baby, you can help."

As the two girls went into the study, Margery said, "See what I mean? I realize it's the Age of Aquarius, but goddamn!"

The judge was just as moved by the incident, but instead of cursing, he roared—with laughter.

Upstairs in the privacy of their room while both changed for supper, he said, "Polly, I wish you could've heard Wills reporting to me. 'There was a nigra gal shootin' skeet in your pasture, judge, and a white gal was pullin' targets. Strange thing is she was pretty durn good. Broke six for seven till I moved in.' Six for seven! By God, that *is durn* good!"

Polly said, "I never dreamed Abby wouldn't do the shooting."

"Hell, don't make no difference to me."

"It doesn't?"

"No. What time's Davey comin'?"

"What makes you think I invited him?"

"More than thirty years of being married to you. I may be a judge, but I ain't no fool."

"No one suggested you are," Polly replied.

"There's a chill in the air colder than November," the judge declared. "I got me a sneakin' suspicion you got second thoughts. Don't shake your head. It's a dead giveaway. Yes sir, ol' Polly Matchmaker's got the I-wish-I-hadn't-blues."

"Oh, and you're happy I did?"

"I'm not unhappy. That girl Abby's all right in my book. You see how she cleaned the gun? Couldn't do better myself without trying. And she's got real style, as well as good looks. Only thing bothers me is tossin' her away on Davey Rutledge. What a waste of good material!"

"Maybe you'd like a divorce so you can have her?"

"Oh-oh, think I struck a nerve. Better get while the gettin's good!" The judge pulled on his suit coat and left the bedroom.

Polly sat at the dresser and looked at her face in the mirror. Old men are all the same—fools! I should know; I'm married to one! She remembered with no little pain how Sidney looked at Alice Corday, and he even admired that bitch Jennifer Myers! That movie star who used to live in Oughton—Susannah Wheatly—made him break out in a sweat.

She felt like pulling a Bette Davis and hurling a jar of Merle Norman into the mirror, and she actually grabbed the greasy jar. But what would that prove? Sid would know he'd struck a nerve indeed. Davey was coming, any minute. She called him in the morning right after speaking with Margery. He was such a nice boy. "Supper tonight? Why, yes ma'am, I'd like that." He sounded like he really meant it.

Polly put on her lipstick. But what did Sid mean about wasting good material? Would be the other way around. I'm not one to judge, she told herself, but Abby's probably worse than her mother. Oh, that was a terrible thing to say! She was sorry she thought it. But now it was out in the open.

She rose and went to the closet. Not that she couldn't sympathize—or was it empathize? On a basic level all women dreamed of doing the SAE house. She looked at herself in bra, panties, hose, and heels. That's what the female creature was for. But if we all acted like Grace what would this world come to? The family would become extinct. That would be a terrible loss, because—well—because—

She found the blue dress she searched for. It would be a great loss because without the family where would society be? Hmmm, a moot question, as Sid would say. That bastard! We'd all be bastards then. "It's good for people to marry and live respectable lives," she told the dress before stepping into it. Why should Davey or Abby, or even Clusta, be exempt? "If Frank were alive he'd be married."

To a girl like Abby Dorsch? Polly did the zipper and checked the hem. God forbid! Still, it was a sad but true fact that men are stupid. Even Frank. He didn't have to join the Air Force, and, once in, no one made him become a pilot. Now he was gone. She felt like crying. What's the use, anyhow? But if she cried her makeup would run and she'd be an ungodly mess.

Polly found a simple string of pearls in her jewelry box and did them round her neck. Sidney bought them in Paris their last vacation. Men were stupid, yes, but.

There was a soft knock on the door. "Come in," said Polly. Abby materialized in the mirror. For a moment Polly didn't know what to say. She wore the same smart outfit she arrived in, only now, in the evening, she seemed more beautiful.

"Hi," said Abby. "I'm sorry barging in like this, but I thought we should talk."

"Really?" said Polly. "About what?"

She watched the girl's lovely face in the mirror and was taken aback by the sound of her own voice. It was Margery she heard, not herself!

39

"I know what you and Aunt Marge are trying to do."

"Oh? And what is that?"

There it was again, the razor-edge dipped in acid!

"Let's not play games, Mrs. Green. I've been through too much. You want to marry me off to your 'fine young man.' It's that simple. Well, I don't give a damn about marriage and when I do I'll find my own man. That's what I want you to know."

Polly turned slowly to face her. She seemed smaller than she appeared in the mirror. But she was even lovelier. For a very long moment Polly had no idea what she should say. The gall of the girl enraged her, and, yet, she could not help admiring her. It was mad—absolutely insane—but she heard her own voice—not Margery's—saying the first thought that came into her head:

"Was it fun sleeping with Indians?"

The girl's sudden smile was as unexpected as a hug. "Don't you mean 'fucking'?"

"Well?" said Polly.

"Indians are all right, when there's nothing better. But just between me and you, mom, blacks are best. Ummmm, yeah! Ask Clusta, she'll give expert testimony."

"I'm glad we understand each other," said Polly, not understanding her at all. What I mean, she told herself, is that—

"What do you mean 'understand'?"

Polly tossed the question back like a hot potato. "What do you mean?"

Abby shrugged her nice shoulders. "You know."

Later, as she lay in bed listening to the November wind thrash the dying trees, Polly realized sometimes she knew and sometimes she didn't. Sidney was asleep. She heard him grunt and turn over. Are all judges restless sleepers? she wondered. At least he slept. There were pills in the medicine cabinet. Doc Spaulding prescribed them long ago when Frank died. But how could she think while sleeping?

Supper went off without a hitch. Davey Rutledge was his usual attentive, well-mannered self. Very handsome in a double-breasted navy suit. And Abby was charming as well as beautiful. By dessert they seemed as though they'd been engaged for months. At his questioning, she told several harmless stories about Peru—teaching children to read, planting a garden for herself. He reciprocated by describing his new house, and after brandy he drove her over to see it. They were back in thirty minutes. Polly examined her closely—not a hair out of place, clothes in order, lipstick unsmeared. He remained for a drink, and as they sat round the fireplace, Sidney told the tale of Abby's skeet shooting. Davey laughed as though he found it cute rather than merely amusing, and Abby beamed as though she were sincerely pleased he was happy.

All in all it was a perfect evening. Everyone seemed to have a good time. Margery got friendly drunk. Clusta didn't drop a dish. And Sidney treated the two young people as though they were his own.

Perfectly wrong!

Polly went to the bathroom and took a capsule. The face in the neon-lit mirror was gaunt, and its hair was pulled back so tightly the scalp shone in pale lines. Sidney grunted from the darkness. He had come to bed in heat and after a terribly long time they managed to bring it off. But she got the feeling he was pretending she was Abby and so she faked her part. What did it matter anyhow? They were dead inside. Oh, the instant was still pleasurable, but afterwards it was just another mess to clean up.

Polly got back into bed and pulled the covers to her nose. The winter wind rattled the windows. Earlier she suspected her actions were part of a plan, that she was predestined to do what she did. The house creaked on its foundation. Now she no longer suspected.

When Margery called her three weeks later and screamed the "good" news that Abby and Davey were engaged, Polly was shocked but she wasn't surprised. As her trembling hand returned the phone to its place, she saw the pieces falling in their pattern. Beyond the window, Steve Floyd jogged through a misting rain. Frank's death was as logical and necessary as that misshapen child. And there was no reason in the world why Clusta should not break ninety-nine out of one hundred.

Chapter Four

S am Roberts eased into the flow of traffic, turned left at the light, and drove for the expressway.

An hour was plenty early. Marian called at noon to remind him. A reception for the new priest. About time they found one. Episcopalians! It was his wife's church. He was raised a Baptist. Lot of freedom there, not all robes and hocus-pocus. Impressive though, like an art show every Sunday. And they stuck to the book. Fifteenth-Sunday-after-Something. Page seventy. Gave a sense of belonging to know all over the world they were reading the same passages.

He worked his way into the exit lane. It was universal, like life and death.

At the top of the ramp he checked the oncoming traffic, then raced down the merge strip and found an opening. He glanced at the dash clock. Another fifty minutes and home.

To meet the new minister and his wife. He frowned. Those gatherings could be deadly. Should stop for a drink. But where? The city was giving way to the country and there was no place. Booze at the house, anyhow.

Home booze. That's what got Joe York, the last priest. Sam drummed his fingertips on the steering wheel and conjured up Joe's florid complexion. Quite a man! Tiger in the pulpit. When he could find his way to it. How long did he last, six, seven years? Pretty good, for that church. And they didn't fire him because of the drinking. It was a little, human thing. Told one of the good ladies of the congregation to kiss his royal arse. Ben Lewis' wife Susie.

Sam snorted. "Royal arse!" The "royal" angered folks. Smacked of pride. Did him in. A pity. He was a damn fine chap, for an episco. Not too much older than me, thought Sam. Maybe forty. Also played poker and shot a good game of golf. His tennis was weak, but you can't have everything. He didn't. Louise his wife was—well—

Of course, they had problems. Who wanted that job, anyhow? He recalled the Baptist preachers he'd known before he met Marian and her "upper-class" notions. With those fellows it was root hog or die and a lot died. Booted by their flocks. The image of sheep kicking skinny gentlemen in their butts popped into his mind like a cartoon.

Sam chuckled. A car behind beeped. He focused on the highway and speeded up.

The new priest had been a chaplain in Vietnam. Lost an eye in combat. Of course, Ben Lewis and the vestrymen didn't ask his opinion about him. Well, it was to be expected since he wasn't one of them. He went and gave his money, but he never submitted to Marian's pleas to take instructions. He was what he was. As the branch is bent so grows the tree. After several years she gave up.

Still, might have been interesting to have a say in the proceedings. Hell, it was his money too! Would a guy with a patch be a milktoast who'd never say "kiss my arse" royal or otherwise? Who were they trying to kid with all their bowing and scraping and chanting like a tribe of Anglo-Indians?

Sam glanced at the countryside. The first churches were the forests. Some writer said so and he was right. Look at those trees. Deep shadows cleaved them like—yes—the valley between a woman's breasts. He gripped the wheel tighter and whistled an aimless tune. Kids today were going back to nature. They had the right idea.

A stream sliced the forest like a silver knife. In a twinkling it was gone and there was the road before and behind him and deep woods on either side. Cars and trucks boxed him in. The exhaust fumes were thick. Thank God for air-conditioning.

But what about time? Did He provide any? Sam checked the clock beside the speedometer. Forty minutes to home. Just follow the four-

43

lane and take the Oughton exit to Sunrise Hills. What kind of name was that? A poet-developer. Modern living for the family that wants to rhyme? And has the cash to. Well, it was better than slums.

But not as good as a tree house. Sam studied the forest blurring past. He rolled down the window and tried to draw a deep breath. God! Where was the good smell of pine straw and sun? He shut the window. Couldn't stink up the whole world. Or could they?

Highways could. Always pushed them through the woodlands where they'd do the least commercial harm. Suddenly Sam wanted to leave the four-lane, to take another way home. He was ahead of schedule. Try a long-cut. Commune with nature.

He watched for exit signs. The next was Post Ferry Road. He knew it. The ferry was long gone, but the road was two-lane, one each direction, and ran through some beautiful country that hadn't yet been spoiled. Even a farm or two. He tripped the turn blinker, angled for the right lane, slowed, and came down the ramp.

The entrance to Post Ferry Road stood like the mouth of a tunnel cunningly hollowed from a dense stand of ancient trees. Sunlight came now in muted patches making him blink. He slowed, opened the window and turned off the air-conditioner. A moist odor of earth, sun, and leaves charmed the sterile coolness surrounding him.

The road was deserted. All the other drivers took the expressway in their haste. Sam lazed along, one arm dangling from the window, a cupped hand swooshing air into his smiling face. He loosened his tie and hummed a happy, wordless tune. Life, basic and uncomplicated, surged in his veins. He realized with a pleasant astonishment that he felt good.

Yes, it was this way in the old days when he was growing up in Oughton. He looked at the dash clock and was half surprised its hands weren't running backwards. He felt younger and gentler, yet, at the same time, fiercer. He was tempted to rip off his clothes and run through the woods.

"Put that in a sermon and they'll make *me* head bishop!" he exclaimed.

The road curved down a hill, ran through a field golden in the sun, climbed a steep grade, and dipped into a tangle of trees which shut out the sky and dangled a net of green shadows.

Another car was parked on the roadside.

Red. A sports car. Out-of-state tag. Hood up. Not the best place in the world to have car trouble.

A woman stepped out and waved. Sam slowed. The spell was broken. It was just the world after all and he was an old man of thirty-nine and cars broke down in God-awful places. Being a gentleman, he of course would render aid. And get dirty in the process. He pulled off beyond the sports car, and as he fumbled for the door handle, looked at the woman in the rearview mirror.

Very nice. In her twenties. Middle at most, maybe early. Wore a short skirt. Fine legs. Face wasn't exactly beautiful. But she had a trim waist and healthy breasts. Her long dark hair was tied back with a green ribbon.

"I'm having trouble," she said with a sad smile.

"Yes, see what I can do."

He leaned inside the open hood and peered at the greasy engine. The fools who crammed so much into so small a space should be sent to Milledgeville. All the sparkplug wires were connected. The carburetor linkage was okay. He touched the radiator. No overheating.

"Tell me, when did this——," he began. Now the young woman stood beside him. The musky odor of her perfume—or was it bath soap?—roused his senses. Her thigh touched his.

"——happen?"

"Oh, a few minutes ago."

"You didn't run out of gas?"

"No, I filled the tank this morning."

"Yes, I'm not——" he almost said "a mechanic," but quickly substituted, "——certain, but I think I know the trouble. Why don't you try starting it and I'll listen?"

"Sure." She walked around to the driver's side. She moved very nice, getting the most out of her legs with a poise that showed she knew what she had.

As the starter turned, Sam spotted the trouble. Loose distributor cap. A simple push and twist. Might not even get greasy. He reached for it. And stopped short. Out of the corner of his eye he saw her face framed in the slit between hood and windshield. Her eyes were very expressive, and her mouth was a bit large and pouty, like that actress—what was her name, in *Zhivago*—Lauree something. Yes, and she gripped the wheel with both hands. Not a ring in sight.

Sam shook his head like a boxer tossing off a stunning punch.

Jesus, what am I thinking? he wondered. A sudden warmth rushed through his chest down into his stomach. The cap sat cocked out of place a half-inch below his fingers. Birds were singing. The wind strummed the leaves. It smelled like fresh-cut grass. Wouldn't be a soul along. Not a soul. Whoa, stop, he cautioned himself. The shadows of the forest beckoned him as strongly as the awareness of the girl.

"Well, can you help me?"

He pulled his head from under the hood. She sat behind the wheel, the door thrown open, one leg extended toward him. He saw an expanse of incredibly golden skin and a triangle of white.

Sam closed his eyes and wished she would vanish. When he looked again she was still there. Well, she had her chance.

He nodded. "Yes, I can help you. If you'll help me."

"Help you?" She frowned. "What does that mean?"

Sam cleared his throat. "You know."

She climbed out, shut the door, and leaned against it. "You won't fix my car if I don't?"

Why didn't she say yes or no and get it over with? He was tempted to laugh it off, and any other time or place he might. But here, now. He looked straight into her green eyes and said, "That's about the size of it."

She glanced at the shadowy road. "I can wait for someone else."

"You may have a long wait."

"What kind of man are you?"

Sam was asking himself the same question. At first she frightened him. Now, the more she spoke the less he feared her. He was beginning to enjoy himself.

"Well?"

"Just an ordinary guy, sweetheart. So if you're not interested, I'll—," he waved and started for his car.

As he passed she caught his sleeve. "I guess I have no choice, do I?"

Sam liked the feel of her hand, but she wasn't getting off that easy. "You always have a choice."

She shrugged her shoulders. "Like hell."

Sam led her into the forest. They broke through the underbrush by the road, then found their way between the dark trees to a small

46

clearing roofed with swaying branches. Hazy light sprinkled the cool grass with patterns like stained glass. In the deep shadows beyond, a brook danced over water-green stones.

The young woman faced him. "You want me to take off everything?"

"Yes."

She unzipped her dress and dropped it about her ankles, stepped out of her panties, and undid her bra.

"All right," she said, defiantly, "this is me. What about you?"

The revelation of her full, tanned body excited and embarrassed him.

He was flabby around the middle, and his skin hadn't seen the sun in months. When Marian saw him it didn't matter. The lights were dim and she was the same. But this creature. She was time rolled back like a heavy burden to his college days.

He slipped off his jacket and tie and undid his shoes.

Her youthful strength caught him with a grim vengeance, as though she would fight him with the only weapon she had. Sam waited for her to bite or scratch or smash the back of his head with a rock. But she did nothing, save what she had promised.

When it was done, Sam rose, fixed his trousers, and shoes, brushed bits of grass from his knees, and said he would go ahead and fix her car while she dressed.

She grabbed his foot. "You aren't trying to trick me?"

"Of course not. I'm a man of my word."

My word, I am? thought Sam, walking through the woods to the road. Jesus, what a time! He couldn't believe it happened. He felt worn-out. And rejuvenated. Joined for a moment with her was like being plugged into a time machine.

He came through the underbrush and headed for her car. Out in the open he sensed a change in his feelings. He stopped, looked, listened. Had he been seen? Was it a set-up? Impossible. How could anyone know he'd leave the expressway and take this back road when he didn't himself?

Still, it didn't seem right. What the hell had come over him?

He heard the wind in the leaves. His courage returned. Was there some law against helping young women in distress? He laughed. Hell no! The knight of the back road. Lancing dragons and et cetera. Her

47

odor clung to his face and hands like a silken trophy a lady might give her champion to wear.

Nice thoughts, yeah, but more practical matters were at hand. As he leaned on the fender and glanced under the hood his eyes fell upon his wristwatch. Had to hurry for the reception. He reached for the distributor cap. Was there no end to a man's responsibilities? Couldn't even drive down a country road and commune with nature without being pressed for time.

His finger touched the cap.

Trouble with the world was people always did the expected. Be prompt, pay the bills, go here, there, smile when sad, control self when happy. Play the game. Give and ye shall receive. Let's make a deal.

His fingers fumbled with the distributor.

The cap slipped off. He paused and looked as though seeing it for the first time. Why the hell was he doing this?

Suddenly he knew, and the awareness raised him up and caused him to bang his head against the hood.

His skull throbbed like a war drum. But rather than pain, it was a pleasant sensation. Overhead the branches moved like dancers swaying.

He smiled, then laughed. He wasn't under contract to fix her car. Who was she anyhow? He'd never see her again. Teach her a lesson. And himself, too. Yes, by God, that was it!

As he got into his car he felt a happy agitation in the pit of his stomach which signaled the rise of new lust. For an instant he was tempted to rush back into the forest. But he started the engine, rolled up the window, turned on the air-conditioner, and raced off down the road.

He stopped once at a service station to wash his face and hands, comb his thinning hair, and vigorously brush his clothes. He almost told the attendant there was a car broken down on Post Ferry Road. But he laughed instead, and the attendant grinned and said yes it was a nice day.

Marian was dressed and waiting when he opened the front door. As he changed his shirt he explained.

"I ran into some car trouble."

48

"Oh?"

He knotted his tie. "Yes. A loose distributor cap. Banged my head on the hood."

"That's too bad. We're already late."

The reception was at the country club. As he drove into the parking lot, Sam scanned the area for red sports cars. But the only sports model was bright blue with a yellow racing stripe, and he recognized it as belonging to Davey Rutledge, the whiz-kid politician. The new priest was nice enough, though Sam kept wondering if there was anything at all underneath his black patch. His wife was a tall, pleasant young woman who seemed mainly interested in asking questions about the local schools.

Sam took Post Ferry Road every afternoon the next week. But he never saw the young woman again. He did not forget her, though. When the pusy discharges began he went for treatment to Doc Spaulding, who, of course, would not report him to the health department.

Dr. Spaulding took one look at Sam's anguished member and bellowed, "Jesus, Mary, and Joseph! What the hell have you been up to?"

Sam told him as little as possible. The old doctor made him look through a thick medical book filled with horrible photos showing the effects of VD. Many were in color. Then he cured him with one shot and chewed him out for not acting his age and urged him to seek professional help, if not from a psychologist at least from his minister.

Sam swore on his sacred honor he would. But when his symptoms disappeared he decided he didn't need any help, especially not from a guy with one eye. So he compromised. Every day he could manage, he left work early, drove the back roads home, and had a meaningful communion with nature.

Chapter Five

B eing buried alive's no fun. I wish them two peckerwoods done it to me would try it out for size. Then they'd know I'm saying the truth!"

She pushed her silky blond hair away from her pretty face and waited for the fellow in the bathroom to finish so she could wash all trace of him away. The crisp five-dollar bill was tucked in the toe of her shoe. He had plenty; he'd never miss it. Could've taken more.

She lay back on the tumbled bed, lifted her feet and sighted down her nice legs to her hose rolled up like tan doughnuts on her slim ankles. She smiled about the cash. For Christmas and won't Lucy Diamond have fun with all her toys!

Jim Bird was in the bathroom running the water loud so she couldn't hear him pee. Jim Bird. She squinted at the gold timex on her left wrist: after ten. He said his name was Jim Bird. When he stopped his big new car as she walked past the Burger King, he said, "Hi, sweetheart! Ride?" And as she huffed down the walk, but giving a nice swing to her cute swinger, he followed and said, cross the front seat and out the rolled-down window, "My name's Jim Bird and I'm a gentleman."

Her feet hurt so she got in. No, it wasn't just her feet. Was that a vision she had right then, like wasn't it Peter or somebody on the road somewhere in the Bible who saw a big light and heard a bigger voice? Only she saw the mill and all those Singers.

She checked the time again. Getting later by the minute and she had to be on the corner when the bus picked them up at six A.M., and here she sat in some motel room waiting for some Jim Bird to finish peeing so she can wipe him out with a wet towel and not come up pregnant again. And all the time the mill where she sewed men's suits gawked over her shoulder.

He was all right, though. At least he was clean and didn't have those pusy heat bumps on his behind like—*they* did. Not too spunky though. Said he worked in an office. She'd take a man works outside for a good fuck every time. Something about sitting all day long drains a man quick.

Cepting Charlie, foreman of the shift. First time he laid eyes on her he gave her boobs a pull and didn't even say 'scuse me. "I do that to all my girls," he said, "and if you plan working here you'll take it as a compliment." He also screwed them regularly on the rolls of fabric in the warehouse behind the mill. Wasn't much to him, though. He was getting on in years and couldn't get it up too good, even though he made the girls try all sorts of things to do it. Told four of them to strip at once. Got it in gear then, but Henny was first and she knocked it out of him so all the rest could get back to work. Pays by the piece, so when you lay Charlie you lose time and money, but if you don't you lose your job and what else can a girl with a baby daughter and no husband do?

"Hey, you coming out of there in the next ten days?" she yelled at the bathroom door.

He turned the water on louder. She looked closely at herself. Wasn't much to him, so. She climbed from the bed, pulled up her hose and hooked them to her black garter belt, slipped on her panties—real nylon and as blue as summer sky—got into her bra, and pulled her yellow dress over her head. She pulled on her shoes. The pleasant lump made by the five-dollar bill caused her to smile. That Jim Bird should be taught not to keep a lady waiting! She slipped the billfold from his trousers, found another five-dollar bill, and put it in the toe of her other shoe. She got her purse and coat and went out.

They had already drained the motel pool for the winter. It stood black and bottomless between her and the street. Made her head dizzy.

She pulled on her coat against the chilling wind, slung the purse over her shoulder, and cut across the motel lawn to the walk. Her shoes made rustling sounds through the fallen leaves. She turned and looked back at his car. Had a local tag. Behind the motel the wire factory furnaces blazed in the black sky. She saw showers of sparks, heard the bang-bang-bang of presses and the voices of workmen.

She moved down the walk to Dixie Street, turned right and went past the hospital. It was four blocks to the room she and Lucy Diamond shared with Henny, and even though it was cool the night was nice so she walked slowly and whistled some.

Wasn't as good as being whistled at. People were coming and going at the hospital. She still owed them for Lucy Diamond. Fifty-five dollars. Paid forty off in six months, which wasn't bad considering what she made. Seventy, sometimes eighty, a week, when Charlie left her alone. But he liked the young stuff. One week it was every day. He smelled sweaty and his thing was real little and sometimes it got so funny she laughed while he was in the saddle, and he slapped her some, which was good cause being mean got him through faster and she could wash him out like Henny showed her and get back to Singering those suits.

The doc at the hospital was older than Charlie. He touched her all over but it wasn't the same. Even slid his finger up her behind and when she jumped, instead of laughing like some did, he said Hmmm-mmmm. She thought Dr. Spaulding was real nice even though he did cuss. Like when she said she was not married, and never had been. "Goddamn," he said, "and you want this child?" There was another woman in the labor room at the same time. She was older, maybe even twenty-five, and she cried a lot. Her poor husband was there and he had to hold her down. She had her baby and it was all deformed. That was funny cause that woman had everything money could buy and she had nothing, but in the end Lucy Diamond was a real beauty—all the nurses and even Doc Spaulding said so—but the other woman's was a mess. And then she almost died. Not even a private room could stop her from bleeding.

Those niggers in the ward were all right, too. Never troubled her, and the bucks who visited them paid her no mind. Course, they talk strange but they understand each other, so what difference does it make? She took Spanish once in high school. The only year she went

52

and didn't pass, but she liked hearing foreign sounds. *Co-mo est-ta oose-ted?* It was nice knowing you didn't forget everything, even when all sorts of terrible things came in between and tried their best to drive you crazy.

She drew her lightweight coat closer and hurried her steps. There was one thing she could not forget and wished—even prayed—she could. Being buried alive's no fun. It was a holy miracle she was here today. There were two of them and they started out real friendly. At the roller rink on the Bremen Road cross from the root beer place. She didn't know Henny then, or anybody. Had just come to Oughton from Ranburne, over in Alabama. Was going to Atlanta, but on the Trailways met this very nice nigger girl named Clusta and she said Oughton's a very nice town and there's work, and since it's not but fifty miles from Atlanta why not give it a chance?

So she did. It was noon when she got off the bus and by two she had herself a job waiting tables at Miss Saxon's Tea Room. Miss Saxon was a very particular woman who wouldn't hire just anybody, but she took her on because she was young and pretty and lots of men working downtown came in for lunch rather than go home. Bought her a pink rayon uniform too. Henny says the old lady hired her cause she was green and would work for the next to nothing she paid.

They said they'd pay but they didn't. Not that she did it for pay. She touched her firm, flat stomach. It was fun. Always was and would always be, and it was part and parcel of being a woman in a world run by men. When their things got hard it was up to a woman to make them soft. Man couldn't do much with a hard-on. She laughed as she envisioned a minister shouting hellfire with his pants bulging, and it would surely get in the way of a policeman making an arrest. Now she frowned. Wasn't always fun. With Charlie it was just another lousy thing to put up with at the mill. That Jim Bird back at the motel— probably still peeing—was different. Like part of a plan. After what happened with them and she was knocked up with Lucy Diamond she came to see it different, so now she didn't turn them down, unless they were nasty or mean or drunk or diseased. He wouldn't miss the ten dollars. Drove a new car and wore good suits. She knew suits, made them herself. H,S,&M does all right. Put the cash away in a secret place with the rest till Christmas. Good time of the year. Even when she was a kid and it was tough, Christmas was good. Mama always

53

had something for them. Nobody knew where she got the money. She smiled. Poor Mama!

She stopped, looked both ways, and hurried across the railroad tracks. Mama's pet brother Uncle Hines got killed by a train. Car stalled and he wouldn't jump out. Everybody thought him crazy, but Mama knew why. Had a load of whiskey worth plenty in Anniston where they sold it to the boys at Fort Mac. Uncle Hines had a houseful of kids and they needed the cash.

"Them two wouldn't give me none." She was trying to stand up on those roller skates when they came in. She had on a short skirt and a tight top which showed off her boobs real good. And everytime she fell, which was every time she let go the rail, her legs shot up in the air and they saw her panties, which were very thin and yellow like the skirt. The big one—his name was Reg—helped her up and said he'd show her how. His arms were strong and covered with black hair tough as steel wool. On skates he was real smooth; said he could've been a pro only hanging round rinks all day and night wasn't really fun, since lots of crazy people did the same. He danced her round that floor and every time her feet went the wrong way his arm held her up. Course, his big hard hand was cupped under her tit.

The other one—Julius—he watched. Even when Reg took off her yellow panties and gave her a solid bang. He touched her there while Reg was going for all he was worth, which was plenty. They were on the back seat of his car, which they pulled out and set up in the woods. And when Reg finished she thought Julius would hop into his place. Not that she was happy for that, but they were nice. Bought her hamburgers and root beer and taught her how to skate, and it wasn't like she was losing anything by giving them a little. It was natural. But that Julius was different. Wanted her to do something else. She had done it before and it was all right. But she didn't like this Julius' weasel looks so she said no, but with a smile, and offered what she gave Reg.

She turned right on Lewis Street and left the walk for the pavement to avoid the pitlike shadows. That's when they got mean. Reg was big and he grinned a lot but he was just as bad as Julius. He told her she better, if she knew what was good for her, and she said she knew and it wasn't that. When she wouldn't they made her. Held her down and twisted her arm and pinched her nose till she had to open her mouth

54

to breathe and then Julius did it. But she got even. Bit him till he bled red blood.

She tried to run away. But Reg caught up and beat her so bad she knew her teeth would drop out. They hit her with their big hard fists and kicked her with their heavy boots till they thought they'd killed her. But she saw them and heard what they said, only it hurt so bad she couldn't move. They put her in a big sack they had in the trunk of the car and they dug a hole and buried her alive.

She hurried now through the night, the shadows clutching at her dress. She felt like she was in a hole whose opening was the sky and it was so black it looked tied with a rope.

"I would've died and nobody would've known or cared!" Only it was a miracle, just like in the Bible maybe where that fellow got puked by a whale. Only out of it all came Lucy Diamond. Yes, something, someone, dug her up and untied the sack. She did not know who he was, but he told her he saved her life and it was true. She could breathe. She could see the moon! It was dawn when she crawled from the grave. What a mess! Her new skirt and blouse were filthy with blood and clay and her panties were gone. Her pretty yellow hair was matted with dirt and leaves and she smelled musty like earth. But she was alive! She wandered through the woods, found a highway, waited for a ride. A deputy sheriff picked her up and she thought she was real lucky cause now she'd show those two.

The blue name plate on his tan shirt said Wills and she told him who they were and what they did. He was a young fellow for a deputy and he wasn't quick to believe cause, he said, "In this work you jump to conclusions and somebody'll jump you." Since he had to be sure, she let him look and touch and the next thing she knew that blue and gold official car was parked on a dirt road and he was going just as strong as Reg. But he did give her a ride to town. And some advice: "Don't fool with them two. They're plenty mean and what good is it if you turn them in and they kill you later? A pretty girl like you deserves better."

And for a while he gave her just that, till his wife found out and took a shot at him with his .38. Wills was his name and she still saw him, but he didn't even say hello. He had nice blue eyes. So does Lucy Diamond. But she has red hair too.

On the birth certificate Doc Spaulding put down her name—Lola

Sue Banning—as mother and another name she'd heard in school—Winston Churchill Banning—for father. The nigger girl who changed sheets told her Doc Spaulding liked her, cause when he disliked a single mother he'd put down a name like Adolf Hitler or George Wallace for the daddy. She went into the hospital with nothing but a bulge and came out with sweet Lucy Diamond and a husband who was king of London, or something.

Not that it meant anything. Didn't pay no bills. Welfare did some. Doc Spaulding made sure she got it. She was b-r-o-k-e broke. Had to quit Miss Saxon's soon as it showed. Met Henny then. Doc was treating her for sore gums. She told her about the mill, but Charlie wouldn't hire her in that condition, so she had to get something else, which wasn't possible. You learn something every day, though. Only reason they hire a girl like me is I look pretty and work cheap and do it. Lose your shape and it's like a bitch mutt. Nobody gives a damn. Soon as you're ready to do it again come back! Yes. If the doc hadn't helped where'd she be now?

Dead.

Inside a zillion worms. You could feel them in the damp earth, wiggling, trying to get in through the sack.

She shuddered and turned across the street and hurried up a leaf-covered walk. The front door was open and people were talking in the downstairs rooms where the landlady Mrs. Holliday kept Lucy Diamond while she worked. Charged fifteen dollars a week not including the baby food, milk, and diapers. Rent was twenty and food for herself another fifteen. There were hospital bills and medicine and Lucy's clothes, not to mention taxes and the social security. The two five-dollar bills in her shoes hurt good.

She unlocked the door and went in. The lights were out and when she flipped the switch she saw Henny was already in bed, only she wasn't alone. Some fellow naked as nature was atop her, his white, hairy behind splattered with heat bumps. Over his bony shoulder Henny said, "Lola, I told him not here but he wouldn't leave. Said he'd make a mess if I didn't."

Lucy Diamond was in her crib with the Mother Goose decals in the alcove between the closet and the counter where they cooked on a hot plate. Her little eyes were shut tight and she was sleeping. The fellow slapped Henny's pale face and told her to shut up and do it or he would take the baby next.

"That's my baby, jack!" cried Lola. "You get!"

Without getting off Henny he looked back at Lola. "You talk mighty big for such a little bitch. I think I'll give you a screw when I finish this bag."

"I told you get!"

The fellow laughed. "All I'm gonna get is some of your tail, girl, and if it ain't sweet enough I'll have me some fun with that baby!"

Being in the same room with him was like being buried alive only maybe worse. He just kept on going in an out with Henny and cussing and telling her to squeeze him just so. I can't stand it, she thought. People got to know it can't be everywhere like this all the time. She looked at Lucy Diamond. Pretty little thing! Getting raped and buried alive was worth it for her and so was doing it here and there for a little extra money. But.

"You gonna get or do I make you?" she said.

He rose up, bending Henny's thick legs back till her knees touched her chin, and said, "Quit running your mouth while a man's fucking!"

No good talking with him. "Grab him with your legs, Henny," she said. And as Henny put a tight scissors hold around his skinny waist, Lola broke the pretty vase she won at the West Georgia Fair over his greasy head. Just like in the movies, she thought. Only a piece clipped Henny on the forehead and her blood mixed with his on the pillow.

"I'm hurt!" she cried. "Why'd you go and do that?"

"Be quiet, you'll wake Lucy Diamond."

Henny unlocked her legs. They rolled the unconscious man to the floor and dressed him. They had to get rid of him somehow. But if they tried to lug him downstairs Mrs. Holliday would hear and what would she think?

"We'll drop him out the window," said Lola.

"The window?" said Henny. "It's twenty feet to the ground!"

"More like fifteen. Why, he something special to you?"

"He's right nice."

"He's right bad! You heard him!"

Henny shrugged. Her large breasts trembled. "He's just talking. Nobody'd do that."

It was like she was suffocating. "There's bushes down below and the ground's soft. Won't kill him. If he comes to here he'll kill us."

Henny sighed. "Guess we got no choice?"

57

"None," said Lola. "You grab his feet and I'll take out the screen."

It was hard work but they dragged him across the faded rug and slid him feet-first through the window. He hit with a thump, then rolled down the hill behind the boardinghouse into the woods.

While Henny went down the hall to the bathroom to clean herself, Lola bent over the crib and whispered to her daughter. "Nobody's gonna hurt my darling, not ever, and when you grow up you'll be the prettiest girl in seven states."

Lola couldn't resist picking her up. She was so soft, so warm, and when she held her breath and listened she could hear her little heart working. She hummed a happy, wordless tune, and smiling, danced her all around the furnished room. Later she hid the five-dollar bills in the crib mattress, and when Henny came back she took a sponge bath, brushed her teeth and said her prayers, and went right to sleep.

Chapter Six

transferred

S inging "I saw Wimpy kissin' Santa Claus underneath the X-mas tree las' night," Billy Joe Wimpton finished his nails and considered them from arm's length. For a moment he fancied he saw his smooth, oval face and soulful eyes reflected in their tiny mirrors and he smiled. But as though the fine lips and white teeth devoured the face, the images faded, and once more the nails were only pink wedges jammed at the tips of his fingers.

Wimpy put the buffer in the manicure set and contemplated the future. Roses, he thought, it's coming up roses for me and Joe. Humming the tune, he rose from the bed, folded his purple gown about his hips, and placed the manicure set in the cabinet above the sink. As he closed the cabinet door he saw in the patchy mirror that he needed a shave. It was a daily act that he could not escape no matter how thickly he applied makeup, and he hated it. Once he heard that the North American Indians never had to shave because they plucked their whiskers with oyster-shell tweezers. He was sitting in Manuel's bar when he heard and he got dead drunk and went home and tried. But even the whiskey wasn't enough to stop the hurt, so it was back to the razor again. After the hormone treatment, though, he wouldn't have to worry anymore. He smiled at the thought, and took Joe's mug and brush and lathered up.

When he finished shaving Wimpy moistened a cloth and gently patted his face, at the same time noticing that he should do his head. But he was too nervous. I'm in a state, he thought, I'd surely nick myself. He decided to wait for Joe. When he gets home I'll be all right. I'll do my head and put on my nicest clothes and we'll celebrate before we catch the plane. He winked at himself in the mirror, and wished he hadn't, for then he saw the thick wattle of flesh dangling below his chin. He was going to fat and he hated it as much as he hated shaving. But he could do something immediate about the fat. He jutted his face toward the mirror and patted his chin with the back of his hand the way they taught at beauty school.

After a dozen pats he wasn't satisfied, but his throat was going red so he quit. He wrung out the washcloth and spread it on the window ledge to dry. Beyond the streaked glass, the sun stared like a jaundiced eye, striking yellow all it beheld. Wimpy sighed and looked out at the discolored buildings. Oh Atlanta, you city of sorrow, he thought, Oh pale, bitchy city of flesh, FALL DOWN! But the city stood unmoved, and now the sun seemed to seek him out as a shaft of light passed through the window and fixed his eyes in a yellow haze.

Wimpy pulled the blue curtains and the room darkened. Fuckin sun! he thought, always trying to put a person in the spotlight. Fuckin city! San Francisco would be different. I'll have my operation and everything will be changed. To reassure himself he started singing "Ca-li-forn-ya here I come" at the top of his lungs. After two choruses his breath failed and he sprawled across the bed and watched the door.

At first he thought it was his heart racing in his throat from the singing. Then he heard footsteps and he knew it had to be Joe. He sat up and pulled his robe about him as Joe burst into the room. "Joe-babe!" he cried. "You've been gone *so* long!"

Joe slammed the door and leaned out of breath against it. "Yeah, Wimp, I was how do you say de-tained."

Wimpy placed one bare foot on the floor. "Did you get it, Joe. Did you get the money?"

"Yeah, I got it. And that ain't all I got." He turned around.

A circle of blood blotted through Joe's shirt, staining the blue cloth purple.

"Jesz!" said Wimpy.

60

Joe faced him and sat down on the footstool beside the window. "That's quite a bonus, ain't it?"

Wimpy leaped from the bed and touched Joe's shoulders with quick, light fingers. His voice trembled. "Did—did *she* do this to you?"

"Who else?"

"The bitch! The lousy stinking—"

"Yeah, and it hurts."

"I know, I know," Wimpy cried. "Take off the shirt, Joe-babe. Let Wimp have a look."

Joe peeled the shirt over his head and let it hang from his elbows. Wimpy's hands made quick attacks across Joe's back, his fingertips skimming the white skin.

Joe wiggled and hunched his shoulders. "Hey, Wimp," he said, "Jesz, that ticks!"

The fingers jumped away. There was a wound, a slash in the white skin, and Wimpy bent close to inspect it, his lips pursed, his eyes opened wide so the veins in the corners showed bloody against the white.

"I think she bit you," he said.

"Bit shit! That ain't the half—she chomped!"

"Yeah, she bit you, the slut!"

Joe bent his arm around his back and searched for the wound, but the shirt pulled against his elbow and stopped his hand short.

"Sit still, babe," Wimpy said. "Could get infect. I got ointment in the cab."

"It sure does pain," Joe said. He got up and went to the mirror over the dresser and tried to position himself to see the wound, but it was in the hollow no-man's-land between his shoulder blades.

Wimpy rummaged in the cabinet. He took down a can of lilac powder and a manicure set, but the ointment was not on that shelf so he moved to another. While his fingers carefully fluttered between Joe's shaving lavender and his own jar of dipilitant, he said, "Hey Joe-babe, how'd it hap?"

Joe made one last twist to see his back and gave up and went back to the stool. "I went to see her, Wimp, and she bit me."

"Sure, but straight, babe. Fill in."

"Well," Joe stuck his fist under his dimpled chin and looked out the window at the sun. "Well, Wimp, it was like we figured, you know? I caught the bus at 14th and changed at Buckhead." He laughed. "There was a spade faggot on. Cute! One o' them apple-hipped cherries in green stretch-pants. Didn't ball me, though. Had an engagement ring on his pinky. I about crapped when I saw that ring. So I tried 'im out, you know, to see if he was true and all that shit. Shot 'im a big wink. Stopped 'im cold. Man, he smiles down at me and blinks them mascaraed eyes. For a sec I thought he was about to flip, but I guess his fiancé must've warned him about honkies, 'cause he shook his pinky at me and said, 'Naughty man.'" Joe slapped his knee and laughed.

Wimpy dropped his Max Factor eyebrow pencil in the sink below the cabinet. He picked it up and discovered it was broken at the point. He found the sharpener in the cabinet, inserted the tip, and ground out a new one. He replaced the pencil on the shelf and shut the door. Then he crossed the room to the dresser and began searching the top drawer.

"Hey, Wimp," said Joe, "You find it yet?"

"Not yet. What about you and her? What happened?"

"Well, I got to her place. Gee, Wimp, I hate to tell you, but at first I couldn't go in. Guess I was chick or something. Anyhow, I went in the tavern down the street and had a couple of beers and watched the ball game on TV. Well, my money gives out with the beer so I know if I don't want to walk home I better see her."

"How did you get the money?"

"Give me time, Wimp, I'm comin' to that."

Wimpy looked under the diploma he had earned at the *Tres Chic* Academy of Hair Styling and Beauty, then covered it with Joe's neatly rolled socks and closed the drawer. "I hope you got it, cause it means the world to me," he said, opening the next drawer. "You know we've got to make it to San Francisco and get a clean start, together."

"Sure, Wimp," Joe said, "I know what it means to you. It means the same to me, Wimp. Just give me a chance to get on, ok?"

"Okay, babe."

Joe traced the thick black hair on his chest and said, "Well, I goes up to her place. The same card was on the box—Mr. and Mrs. Joseph Me, it read. It was kind of funny seeing that, Wimp. I mean it was like comin' home, you know, only it wasn't. Know what I mean, Wimp?"

"Sure, babe, I know."

"It wasn't that I felt like *homesick* or anything like that, Wimp. I just felt—Jesus, I don't know how I felt. It was like me calling on myself, like I was a stranger in town who just happened by and saw my name on the door, and at the same time I knew how it would be behind the door. Jesz! It was nuts!"

"Have you seen the ointment?" Wimpy asked. He slammed the bottom drawer and stood in front of the dresser, his hands braced on his wide hips, the sash of his purple housecoat falling in a loose tassel below his knee.

Joe shook his head.

"Well, I know it's here somewhere." He went back to the cabinet above the sink and began searching again.

"Yeah," Joe said, "It was strange, Wimp, nuts with a capital T. Anyhow, I read the card a couple of times—Mr. and Mrs. Joe—, you know, and finally I pushed the buzzer. It was the same buzzer. You know, Wimp, you remember how it goes *Buzz-buzz-buzz* and then peters out? I was always gonna rewire that damn buzzer but one thing and another I never got around to it. Remember how I said I was gonna rewire, Wimpy?"

"Yeah, babe, you told me last time I was there."

"Last and *only* time you was there, Wimp. Remember what happened? Jesus, what a scene! Remember how Jeannie bounced that vase off your skull cause you called her—"

"I called her what she is," said Wimpy. "And I thought you promised to never mention *her* name in my presence!"

"Jesz, Wimp, I forgot. I'm sorry, 'kay?"

For the second time Wimpy was searching the shelf on which Joe's shaving lotion stood. He took down the bottle and sniffed the stopper. "I've got feelings, too, Joe. Just like everybody else."

"I won't do it no more, Wimp. Promise."

"When she said I should look up Barnum and Bailey I went blank."

"I promise, Wimp."

Wimpy placed the bottle gently on the shelf. "Okay, you're forgiven. What did she say?"

"She called you a *queer*, don't you remember?"

"Not *that* time, *this* time. And don't use *that* word in my presence either!"

"I'm sorry, Wimp. Slip of the ol' tongue and all that."

"You're forgiven, babe."

"Thanks Wimp. You're swell like that. I wouldn't hurt you none, for the world I wouldn't. I mean, hell, I know how it is and all."

Wimpy opened the leather case in which his manicure equipment was bedded down on a slab of red velvet. The ointment wasn't there.

"Well," Joe continued, "I pushed the buzzer and this voice said, 'Who's that?' and I said—Jesz Wimp, I don't know why I said it. I mean it was just the first thing that popped. You know, I just couldn't say, 'It's Joe, baby,' cause she never would've opened up, I said—guess it was cause there was this truck parked out front of the bar and I thought it was funny it should be in front of a bar of all places. I mean it's not because some guys who go in bars couldn't use them, but— jesus, I laughed when I saw that truck!"

"What truck are you talking about?"

"The diaper truck. See, there was this pink and blue diaper truck parked in front of the place where I had the beers. And when I came out and saw it I laughed like hell. Then, when she said, 'Who's that?' for no good reason I said, 'Diaper man!'"

Wimpy frowned. "Did she open the door?"

"Yeah, but first she says, 'Diaper man?' like she's thinkin' what-the-hell? She opened the door a crack and when she saw me she tried to slam it shut. But I jammed the ol' foot in. She gives me that go-to-hell-Joe look and says, 'What do *you* want?' and it was just like the old days, Wimp, like when I was comin' home reg and she'd say that and I'd say, 'Whatcha got, baby?'

"Well, I said that and pushed the door open some, only she was tryin' to stay hid behind it. Know why, Wimp? She was in the middle of takin' a bath, that's why. I could tell cause you know how that mirror is located opposite the door? Well, I could see her in the mirror and she was all shiny from the water. She had one of those little towels held up in front of her, but it was worse than nothin'. I mean, well, it just called attention to the fact—I should say *facts*, cause as you know she's—"

"Look, sweetheart," Wimpy said, "Here I am killing myself trying

64

to find medicine for *you*, and you are making me positively *furious*. I don't know why I bother. Please, *please* spare me the lurid details. Did you get the money?"

"Sure, Wimp, I got the money. Ain't that what I went for?"

"Yes, but what else did you—? No, don't tell me!"

Joe smiled. "Gee, Wimp, it's a crazy thing. I gotta tell you."

"Very well," Wimpy said. He turned back to the cabinet. In the excitement he had forgotten which shelf he was currently searching, so he began again from the top.

"So I'm in," said Joe. "She's hiding the towel like we wasn't married and I was some guy who just busted in. Well, I wanted to keep her happy—in view of the money and all—so I suggests she continue her bath and I will sit on the john by the tub and we will talk.

"'Are you nuts?' she said. 'Get outta here before I call the cops!'

"I wasn't lookin' for no trouble, Wimp, so I tried to quiet her down.

"'Jeannie-baby,' I said, 'I honest don't wanta bother you none but I absolutely gotta. Now if you will please sit down we will talk nice the way we used to and then I will leave you to your bathing.'

"She justs looks at me for a sec like she is thinkin' I-know-what-you-want-and-you-are-nuts-if-you-think-you-can-get-it. So I said, 'Like old times, honey, when you and me used to live here.'

"'Okay,' she says, 'but no trouble.'

"I tell her that there will be no trouble, that all I want to do is talk. Course, Wimp, I didn't tell her then what I wanted to talk about, you know, the money. I didn't say money cause I didn't want her to come after me like she did you.

"Anyhow, I sat down on the sofa, which I paid over six bills for the year before. The yellow sofa that converts, you know. Six bills for that damn sofa. When I sat down I thought about that and I thought, Christ! six bills, couldn't I use six bills now, instead of a yellow convertible sofa which I will never convert again!

"I sat down and she went in the bedroom and slipped on a robe, only she was still wet, so when she came out again it was like with the towel, only worse. I mean that robe was thin to begin with and with her being wet—it was like she was in a cellophane bag, you know, Wimp, you could see through it like a bag of peppermint candy."

Wimpy slammed the cabinet door so hard that the bottles inside rattled. He stalked across the room, his purple robe swelling behind like the trailing edges of a butterfly's vaporous wings. He yanked open the top drawer of the dresser and dug into the neatly folded socks above his diploma.

Joe smiled and went on. "I took it slow, Wimp. I asked her how she was doin' and she said 'okay,' but it wasn't like she meant *okay*. It was just *ok*. Then I asked her about her mother, and she said the old lady was doing all right, except that she wondered where I was. The old lady's always liked me, Wimp. She was all the time comin' over to the apartment and doin' things for me. I mean it wasn't because she felt she oughta. Hell, most guys' mother-in-laws do it just so they can be on the scene and get some snoopin' in. But not the old lady; hell no. She did it for me cause she liked me. Know what, Wimp? This'll kill you, but I liked her too. She was okay.

"So we talked like that for a while and Jeannie began to—Jesz, I don't know, Wimp, I'm not good with words like you. She began to—I guess *you'd* say *melt*. She got quiet and serious and she was lookin' at me the way she used to when we'd talk like that. Pretty soon she moves a little closer and a little closer, and then she puts her hand on my knee and the top of that robe is pressin' soft against my arm and she looks up at me with those big brown eyes and says, 'It's good to see you, Joe. It's good.'

"'It's good to see you, too, Jeannie,' I said. And to be true, Wimp, it was good. I mean, well after all, when a guy's been with a woman that long and everything between them's okay—you know, Wimp, I been married to her for—Jesz!—it'll be six years come July 12th!—when a guy's been with one that long and then he goes off for a while like me, I don't care who the guy is, Wimp, he feels pretty good when he sees her again. That's the way I felt when Jeannie said that. Know what I mean?"

"Yeah," Wimp said, "yeah, I know." He was still looking in the top drawer, only now he was not so much looking at the socks piled there as at what was not there. "I know, babe. How do you think I feel when you go away from me like you did today? It's terrible when you go to work, Joe-babe. Imagine how it was today when I knew you were going to see *her*."

Yeah, Wimp, I'll bet it was real bad. But hell, it's not exactly the same. I mean I was only gone a couple of hours from you. But me and

Jeannie we been away from each other for about—*damn*—we been apart for six weeks now. No wonder she—"

"Have you seen the ointment? It's in a red and white metal tube."

"No, Wimp, I ain't. Say, there's some boxes in the top o' the closet. Might be in them."

Wimpy shut the dresser and opened the closet door. The boxes were stacked neatly on the shelf above. He took them down, put them on the bed and began searching.

Joe watched him open a large, flat box. "What's in that one, Wimp?"

"Wrapping paper, babe. Whenever I get a gift I always save the paper. It's so pretty I just can't throw it away."

"You too?" Joe said. "Gee, Jeannie does the same thing. Crazy!"

Wimpy slammed the lid on the box and knotted the ribbon that held it shut. "I asked you once, Joe-babe," he cried, "*please* don't mention her name!"

"Did I do that again, Wimp? Gee, I'm sorry. It positively won't happen again. I guess it's cause I just saw her. You know, it kinda sticks in my mind? Yeah, that's more than likely it.

"Well, we're sitting' on my six-hundred-dollar yellow sofa and she tells me how good it is to see me again and I says the same to her. And then, really husky, she whispers, 'What do you really want, Joe?' I started to say 'Money, honey,' but I figured it was too soon for that. So I said, 'Gee, honey'—see, Wimp, I'm bein' careful not to mention her name—I said, 'Gee, honey, I want what you want, same as always.' And she runs her fingers down my arm and over my chest and says, 'Do you really, Joe? Is that really what you want?'

"'Yeah,' I said, 'What you want is what I want. Name it, baby.' She smiles real sweet and her hand is now at my neck and she's usin' my neck to pull herself against me and she gives me a kiss and when it's done she smiles and stands up close and undoes the robe and lets it slide off. I guess the robe soaked up all the water, cause now her skin is dry—only it's not. You know what I mean, Wimp? It's slick and shiny lookin', but it's not *wet* wet.

"Well, then, one thing leads to another—if you know what I mean—and finally that's that. Then, it's now sometime later, she is fixin' my collar and she is soft and quiet and in a way she is happy, I guess, cause then, out of like nowhere, she says, 'Do you need money, Joe?'

"'As a matter of fact I do,' I says. 'That's just what I need.' She gives me another kiss and walks over to the desk, takes out the business checkbook and asks how much.

"I thought about it, Wimp, and I figured since we were goin' out to the coast and I'd have to look for work, maybe six hundred would be okay, so I said, 'Make it six big bills, baby.'"

Wimpy plopped on the bed. "Six hundred? You got six hundred?"

Joe smiled. "Yeah, six bills. I mean, Jesz, Wimp, I don't know why. I guess it was like the diaper truck, know I had been thinkin' about that sofa costing six bills and that was the first number that popped. Well, she wrote out the chec—"

"You got *only* six hundred dollars? Only six?"

"Yeah, I—"

"In a check?"

"That's right. She wrote—"

Wimpy sprang from the bed. The box of wrapping paper spilled red, yellow, and blue to the floor. "She gave you a check for six hundred dollars after submitting you to *that?*"

"*That?* That what, Wimp?"

Wimpy paced the room, his hands jammed elbow deep in the wide pockets of his robe. "She has her nerve!" He stopped. "And you! Why didn't you ask for more?"

"Gee, Wimp, I don't know. Six seemed right. I mean, hell, I don't know."

"No, you don't!" said Wimpy.

"Yeah, but that's nothin'. Let me tell you what else she did."

Wimpy strode behind him now, looking down at his broad back and at the wound that stared at him like a raw, grotesque eye.

"She gave me the check, Wimp, handed it over real sweet—and even gave me change for bus fare—and up till then she hadn't said a word about where I'd been, about you. Then—I'm at the door—she gives me a kiss and I turn to go. She grabs me around the neck from behind. For a sec I think she's just being playful the ways girls are, you know? Then WHAM! She sinks those teeth in me and they are capital S sharp! *Ch-rist*! It was like she hit me twix the blades with a white-hot slab o' steel! Man, I spun around tryin' to get her off, but she held on and chewed harder. Jesus! I whammed her against the wall and I could hear the air whoosh out of her, but she still hung on. I thought—Know what I thought then, Wimp?—I thought, Christ, the sun don't go down till six and here it is only four!"

Now Wimpy stood behind Joe. The wound was dry now, and the blood had caked in twin converging purple ridges circumscribing the bright red oval where her teeth had cut away the skin.

"That's what I thought," said Joe. "But then she lets go and I spin around and then I'm mad enough to jerk a knot. But she's *smiling*! She says, 'Don't take that personal, Joe, that's just my present for little Miss Wimpy.' And then I'm in the hall and the door shuts."

Wimpy stared into the wound. Nestled as it was in the hollow between Joe's white shoulders, it seemed to smile at him, to laugh. Then Joe straightened up and the wound withdrew into the deep furrow that cleaved his shoulders. A shadow fell in the space and now, as Wimpy looked down in horror, it was not Jeannie's mouth that mocked him.

"And that's the way it was, Wimp," said Joe.

Wimpy looked away from the gash that was no longer a wound.

"And here's the check. I done endorsed it already."

Wimpy unconsciously took the check. "Yeah, Joe," he said. "Listen, babe, do Wimp a big favor?"

"Sure, Wimp, sure. Name it."

"Listen, Babe, slip into a fresh shirt—there's one in the closet—and run over to the drugstore at Five Points. I can't find the ointment and we've got to do something for your poor back. Mind?"

Joe stood and stripped his shirt from his arms. "No, Wimp, you know I don't. But Five Points is a long way to go. I mean, well, comin' and goin' it'll take at least an hour. I could go to the Rexall. It's closer."

"The ointment's special and they don't carry it. Tell the pharmacist I sent you. He knows what I want. Charge it."

Joe changed his shirt and left. Wimpy watched him from the window. When Joe turned the corner, he took two suitcases from beneath the bed and packed. Then he slipped off the robe and pulled on a girdle and hose. He took a chic green wool suit from the closet, where it hung beside Joe's blue sport coat, and dressed quickly, but with care. Finally, he painted on eyebrows and tenderly took the blonde bouffant

69

wig from the improvised rack in the top of the closet. Slowly he drew the wig over his head. A few dark bristles showed at the nape of his neck and he felt them, but there was not time. He looked into the mirror and carefully drew a mouth with a tube of purple-tinted lipstick. After he blotted his lips on a fresh tissue, he held the lipstick firmly in his left hand and wrote on the mirror as many vulgar words as he could squeeze into the space, and at the bottom of the mirror he printed boldly, GOOD-BYE JOE, GOOD-BYE.

He picked up the suitcases and went down two flights of stairs to the street. Halfway up the block he stopped and looked at himself in a shop window. A man and a woman were inside the shop talking to a clerk behind the counter. The woman tried on a hat. As she turned to admire herself in a small round mirror down the counter, the man saw Wimpy. He smiled, shot a checking glance at his wife, and then winked so hard that his canine tooth showed yellow-white against his red gums.

Wimpy was tempted to teach him a lesson he'd never forget, to drop the suitcases and lift his skirt and show the bastard what life was all about.

But what would that get him? Sixty days in jail.

He spun on his heel and walked away, heading downtown to the bus terminal and the 8:37 Trailways that would take him fifty miles through rolling, pine-covered hills to the little town in which he was born and raised.

The thought of Oughton was almost enough to make him puke. But Atlanta had lost its glitter; it was a city afflicted with terminal jock-itch.

He'd go back to the Blue Note Cafe his mama ran by the railroad tracks. Yes. He'd boil grits and make red-eye gravy and fix those baloney sandwiches with gobs of mayonnaise that he used to spit on to teach the railroad bullies a lesson.

Wimpy smiled. Sure, he'd save his pay, and if Joe's check cleared, it wouldn't be too long before he could strike out again for that city by the bay where everyone lost her heart.

70

Chapter Seven

After eating a light lunch and washing the dishes, Velma and Louise went out on Velma's shady back porch to cool down. They were sisters and sisters-in-law both, having married the brothers Reg and Julius in a double ceremony at the Free Will Chapel three years ago. Reg and Julius had gone fishing for the day and so the sisters were visiting.

Velma stirred the still summer air with a palm-leaf fan and speculated on what the brothers would catch. "I'd like a mess of catfish myself," she said.

"Me, too, sister," said Louise. "We could fix some hush puppies and if you got a cabbage some coleslaw, too."

"And have ice tea to drink."

"Law, you're making me hungry talking about it!"

Velma fanned herself more vigorously. Louise used her cupped hand to move the warm air across her sweaty face. Velma allowed her to sit in her rocker. She wasn't about to give her the only fan as well. Since they were sisters and were married to brothers, Louise understood. But it didn't make her any cooler.

"You know what I'd like right now if I could have it?" she asked.

Velma giggled. "A good-looking man with a carload of money!"

Louise smiled. "Besides that."

"Two men and two carloads of money?"

"Sister, you are too much," Louise squealed. "What if Reg heard you? He'd give you something to remember."

"You started it," Velma replied. "And what about your Julius? He's not the most even-tempered man I know."

Louise's smile faded. She stared down from the porch past Velma's well-kept garden to the pasture and the distant woods. Summer heat hung over the green grass like mist. Storm clouds were building beyond the trees. After a moment she nodded. "None of our husbands is kind men."

"That's not the half of it," said Velma.

Louise looked sideways at her sister. She felt a responsibility for Velma since she was older by two years, and besides it was her dating Julius that brought Reg into Velma's life.

She asked, "Has Reg been after you again?"

Velma pulled up her sleeve to expose her meaty upper arm. A set of fingerprints blackened the milk-white skin. "He grabbed me there last night. Shook me till I thought my eyes would pop."

Louise tenderly touched the marks. "He's got a meanness, that's for certain."

Velma dropped her sleeve and commenced fanning again. "How about you and Julius?"

"Don't ask me," said Louise. "Please don't ask."

"Why, he been up to his old tricks?"

"Law, the things I could tell you!"

Velma watched Louise rocking furiously in her own best chair. She waited till she got up a head of steam, then said, "It's none of my business. But we're sisters. And I told you."

"If you insist," said Louise, who needed little prompting to discuss her husband's cruelty. "Julius is worse than ever. I swear he's as mean as a snake on a hot road." She slowed her rocking and watched her sister from the corner of her eye. "Some days I wish I never laid eyes on him."

Velma exclaimed, "Why sister, I'm surprised at you!"

But Louise saw by her expression she really wasn't. She commenced rocking again. "You aren't no more surprised than that billy goat down there in the pasture or that thunder cloud swelling beyond the trees."

She paused and slyly considered Velma again. "In fact, you feel the same about Reg."

"Sister!"

"You do and don't you deny it."

Velma frowned and made the fan fly so fast the hair at her temples fluttered. "Reg is as mean as he can be. Somedays he gets so bad I wish—"

"What? Don't stop now, sister."

"It's awful what I wish."

"Don't matter. Get it out in the open."

Velma turned and placed her moist hand in Louise's. She closed her eyes and whispered, "*I wish he was dead*!"

Louise squeezed her fingers. "Sister," she said, "I been wishing the same for Julius."

"Oh!" cried Velma. She took back her hand. "Louise, we are bad!"

Now the rhythm of Louise's rocking changed. It was more regular, more determined, like a carpenter driving sixteen penny nails.

"No we're not," she said. "We're sisters. No wonder we got the same feelings."

Velma shuddered. "But it ain't right thinking those thoughts. They'll come back upon us a hundredfold!"

"We're God-fearing girls," Louise went on, as though she hadn't heard her sister. "Our mama and daddy raised us in the fear of the Lord. Reg and Julius ain't got no background at all, unless you call a daddy on the county roads something. We got to face facts, sister. We was dead wrong to marry them."

Velma fanned herself furiously, as though she was being singed by flames. "What are we going to do? What can we do?"

Louise rocked and thought. "We can't divorce them. They'd kill us. Yes sir, they'd pull out their knives and cut us into cat meat."

Velma shuddered and touched the bruises on her arm.

Louise said, "We can't run away. We got no place to go."

"I was raised here," said Velma. "This is my home. I don't want to go."

The thunderheads beyond the pasture were rising in a gray wall against the sky. Shafts of sunlight fell like searchlight rays across the fields, then abruptly went out as the wind shifted and the rents in the

73

clouds closed tight. A pale finger of lightning sputtered against the horizon.

Velma looked at Louise and said, "Well, sister, ain't there nothing we can do?"

Louise stopped rocking. "You recall what mama always told us to do when we had problems so big we couldn't handle them ourselves?"

"Well—," said Velma, thinking back to those happy days when she was a chubby little girl in a short pink dress.

But Louise didn't wait for her answer. "She said take them to the Lord."

"In prayer!" chirped Velma.

"Yes, in prayer. And He would show us the way. Sister," Louise looked Velma straight in the eye, "are you willing to pray about Reg and Julius?"

"Yes, oh yes, I am!"

"Then let's," said Louise, rising from the rocker and dropping with a heavy sigh on her knees.

The thunderclouds stood before the house like a gray mountain range. Invisible lightning generated volleys of thunder which trembled the steady earth like so much jelly. The animals in the pasture loped for the safety of the red barn. Martins zipped across the dark sky and dove after swarms of bugs stirred by the coming rain. Now forks of lightning speared the earth and the sisters quivered as the nearing thunder rattled the washpans hanging on the porch wall.

"Oh Lord!" Louise bellowed, "deliver us from evil our husbands put us to. Please, dear God, talk to them, to Reg and Julius. Show them how bad they is." She paused. "Velma?"

"Oh yes, Lord," Velma began, "help us like sister says. We're good girls, Lord. Always have been." She rubbed her arm. "Please do something so Reg and Julius will set us free."

Now the rain came, a great wash of water sweeping in from the pasture and cascading across the porch. The sisters scrambled into the house. Behind them the washpans floated across the yard and Velma's rocker tipped back and forth crazily, then flung itself down the steps.

"Law, what a torrent!" cried Louise, flinging water from her fingertips.

Velma hurried about the small house unplugging the TV, stove,

74

refrigerator, and an electric clock-radio. She also took the phone off the hook.

A darkness fell over the house. The rain and wind lashed at the windows. Puddles appeared beneath the front and back doors. While Velma stopped the leaking with old newspapers, Louise squinted through the front window at the hardtop road.

"Can't even see the center stripe," she announced. She pulled the curtains tight, then adjusted them top and bottom to keep out the fearsome sight of the storm. "I'd surely hate to be out in that."

"So would I," Velma said. She was sliding a pot in the fireplace to catch the steady drip-drip coming down the chimney.

Louise went to the kitchen window and looked down at the empty pasture. "Animals must've got to the barn," she said.

Velma finished with the pot and stepped back. "Yes, well, I guess everything's safe and sound now. Oh—!" She threw her hands to her mouth.

But Louise knew what she thought. Wordlessly, the sisters looked at each other, each seeing in the other's face the reflection of her own fear. Their husbands. Reg and Julius. They were out in the storm.

"Oh—oh—oh—!" Velma moaned.

Louise fell into a ladder-backed chair by the fireplace. What had they done? She heard thunder, felt the house shake. Julius, *her* Julius, and Velma's Reg were out on the lake in their rowboat in the midst of this tempest.

"Sister!" cried Velma. "Reg can't swim no more than a rock!"

"Oh law," moaned Louise. "Julius can't neither."

The dreadful image of the brothers dragged down into the green depths of the lake appeared like a common vision to both of them. Julius, once long and lanky, with freckled face and fiery hair, lay convulsed and tangled in the weeds like a rusty, half-opened jack-knife. And Reg, short, thick, black-haired, was embedded in the slimy mud like a discarded beer bottle.

Weeping and trembling, the sisters fell into each other's heavy arms and called out for God to forgive them. Lightning fell about the house in terrible, crackling bursts. Thunder shook dishes in the glass-front cabinet. Silverware rattled in the drawers.

"Oh, it's the end of the world!" sobbed Velma.

But in the steady roar of thunder Louise could not hear her. She concentrated her attention upon that dismal spectacle at the bottom of the lake. Catfish were lazily inspecting Julius' gleaming head. His mouth was open, the thick dark lips curled in a silly smile revealing the missing teeth he lost in countless honkytonk battles. The bristly hair in his red ears trapped bits of flotsam from the lake water like sea plants she studied in school books long ago.

The apparition was too much for Louise. She flung Velma aside like a feather pillow, rose tottering to her feet, and reaching her hands into empty space, bellowed, "Oh Julius, Julius, why was you so mean?"

A boom of thunder replied. She fell back on the sofa in a dead faint.

Velma almost fainted herself at the sight. And it was so frightening to be alone in such a storm! But try as she would, she could not swoon. So she did the next best thing, her duty, and ministered to her stricken sister.

As she patted Louise's clammy wrists and called her name, the thought crossed her mind that since she had to face this ordeal it wasn't fair her sister should shirk her responsibility. So Velma did all in her power to bring Louise back to consciousness. She sprinkled ammonia on a washcloth and clamped it over her sister's nose. The blistering fumes got results. Sputtering, Louise sat straight up and wildly swung her meaty hands in all directions.

"Where—where—am I?" She demanded. "What—happened?"

Velma jabbed the ammonia at her again, and as Louise made a terrible face, said, "You're right here in my house, where else, sister, and you fainted. But I didn't."

"Fain—Julius!" Louise cried out. She sprang to her feet and ran around the room, ending up at the front door.

The rain had slacked to a steady drizzle. A car stopped on the hardtop and turned into the muddy yard.

"Someone's coming!" Louise said.

Velma pressed her face beside her sister's at the window. Through the beaded glass they saw the blurred shapes of two men climbing from the car. They wore yellow slickers and wide-brimmed hats.

"It's not Reg and Julius," Velma said.

Now the men were on the steps. Louise saw them plainly. "Sheriff Lee and a deputy!" she moaned.

There was a knock. Velma opened the door. The two lawmen stood out of the rain on the porch. Water ran off their slickers and formed black puddles about their boots.

Louise pushed past Velma and said, "It's about Julius and Reg, ain't it?"

"Yes'm," the sheriff said.

"Well, they ain't here!" Velma declared. "They went fishing."

Louise elbowed her. "What—what is it about Julius and Reg?"

At her sister's touch Velma lost her courage. "Oh-oh," she moaned. "They're dead!"

Louise slipped her arm around her and became all business. "Did you find the bodies?" she asked.

"Bodies?" said the deputy, who looked quickly about the room as though expecting to see the stiff feet of a corpse poking out from beneath the sofa.

Now Velma blubbered like a baby. She gnashed her teeth and called Reg's name.

"Yes, the bodies," said Louise. "We want to give them a Christian burial. Even though they was mean, they still was God's children."

The sheriff shook his head so suddenly water sprayed into her eyes. "There ain't no bodies," he said. Then he said it again, louder, adding, "Reg and Julius didn't go fishin'. They got themselves good and drunk and tried to hold up the bank."

The deputy smiled. "Would've got away, but they rammed a utility pole."

"Wouldn't got away neither," the sheriff growled. "There's half a dozen eyewitnesses."

Velma had stopped crying at the mention of a bank. Now she said, "They told us they was going fishing. Where are they? They all right?"

"Right as two fellows can be who're in the hospital," the deputy said.

"Hospital?" both sisters exclaimed.

They got pretty broke up in the wreck," the sheriff explained. "But the doctors say they'll live to go to jail."

"For a long time," the deputy added. "They shot the guard. He ain't dead. But they shot him just the same."

Bank robbery. Shooting. Wreck. Hospital. Jail. The sisters clasped each other and swayed at the words like pines in a windstorm. Louise felt Velma's quick breathing. Velma was aware of Louise's racing heart. Each gathered strength from the other's encircling arms.

"I tried to get you on the phone," the sheriff said. "But the lightnin' must've knocked it out."

The storm! The prayers! Was this the answer? Louise fiercely hugged Velma and said to the lawmen, "Are you sure it's *our* Reg and Julius?"

"They went fishing at the lake!" said Velma.

"Julius is tall and Reg is short," Louise said. "They're—"

"Ma'm, I've known them two all my life," said the sheriff. "There's no mistake."

The deputy grinned. "Everybody knows Reg and Julius."

Now the sheriff removed his hat and shook away the few remaining drops of rainwater. "I figures you ladies would want to go to the hospital. We'll drive you."

"Sister, we can't go," said Velma. "They'll be coming with all them catfish. And if we're not here—"

"No, Velma," said Louise. "It's them all right." She squeezed her hand. "We got to visit them at the hospital. Let's freshen up."

All the way to town the sisters sat quietly in the back seat of the sheriff's car. At first the deputy tried to make conversation. "Ten years at the very least," he said. "That's the minimum." But when the sheriff only grunted and neither sister responded, he lit a cigarette and looked out the window at the passing telephone poles.

Velma and Louise held hands. The same thoughts passed through their minds and each knew how the other felt. Now they were alone. Reg and Julius had been taken away. They hadn't been drowned in the lake, sucked down in those muddy depths to rise again gas-bloated after three days. Ten years, at least, the deputy said.

They would go back to the way they lived before Reg and Julius. Velma felt her bruises vanishing. Louise tried to decide would it be best for her to move in with Velma, or for Velma to come live with her? They had a lot to forget. Reg and Julius were strong, hard, violent men and they were only girls. But time heals all wounds, and ten years was quite some time. Maybe they'd change. It was possible. All things were. After all, they weren't dead. There was a great consolation in that fact. It made Louise sit a little straighter and smile almost sweetly. At the same moment, though, a little, nagging voice located close by the region of her conscience posed a silly little question which she knew was foolish, but which she could not for the life of her either answer or ignore.

"Why, why, why on earth," asked the voice, "did Reg and Julius get drunk?"

In desperation, Louise looked at her sister. But Velma only shook her head. "I don't know neither," she whispered. "I just don't know."

Chapter Eight

Perhaps there wouldn't have been a problem if Miss Cora hadn't spent two weeks at Panacea, Florida, during August of 1899. She was twenty-four years old then, had been reasonably educated at the academy in Oughton, and was generally accepted as the sort of grammar school teacher who'll handle the job for fifty years, since she wasn't exactly a pretty girl, but more of what ladies call handsome. She was tall and well put together; her dark hair was always combed back straight; and her gray eyes were sort of frosty. Miss Cora went to the Baptist Church, where she taught Sunday School, because her people had always worshipped their Creator there. Needless to say, she had no recognizable vices, and was the sort of young woman to be counted on in a time of need.

Which is why she was down at Panacea walking barefoot on the beach in August of '99. The Middletons, of which Cora was one, had relatives in Thomasville. A cousin there, Mrs. Betsy M. Fuller, chose the summer of 1899 to have a baby. Since school was out and there was nothing much to do except sit on the porch and damn the heat, Miss Cora decided to head south and offer comfort. She went the fifty miles east to Atlanta in a buggy, then caught the Southern Railroad south. All told the trip took three days. Shortly after she arrived the baby boy did also, but as long as she was there in Thomasville she allowed the

Fullers to convince her to tarry so as to take part in the event of the year—the annual migration by Thomasville's finest families to Panacea, Florida, where they maintained cottages, and where the chief entertainment was catching and devouring fresh mullet.

So soon as the baby Fuller—now called Reginald M.—was of sufficient poundage, and his mother had recaptured some of her healthy glow, they set out down the clay highway on a trip of some sixty miles, more or less, leading through Tallahassee and down past Wakulla Springs, where clear, cold water gushed out of rock and it was fresh and delightful no matter how hot the day.

Well, Miss Cora did what everybody else did at Panacea. She oohhed and ahhed the Gulf of Mexico, ate mullet fried, boiled, baked, with grits and without, slapped gnats and sandflies, and protected her bare face and hands from the sun with applications of glycerin and rose water.

She also met a young man by the name of Kermit Westmoreland, whose journey to Panacea began in Cuba where for several years he had managed a plantation for a Spanish family who themselves had never ventured further west than Lisbon. The changes brought about by Teddy Roosevelt and his boys caused Kermit's departure and because he had known a relative of the Fullers, he wound up on the same strip of beach with Miss Cora. As he consumed the requisite number of fresh mullet and slapped at the gnats and flies pestering him, Westmoreland also noticed Miss Cora's person and found it—as well as her—to be most interesting.

As they say, one thing led to another, and at the end of the Panacea vacation Westmoreland discovered he had pressing business in Atlanta and even—wonder of wonders—must take the same northbound train as Cora. Chaperoned by the wife of the Fullers' minister, they passed the hours traveling together profitably. By the time the conductor announced Atlanta, they were in love. As soon as Kermit concluded his affairs in the city, he came westward to Oughton, met Cora's extensive family, was judged by them to be suitable, asked for and received the promise of Cora's rose-scented hand. He also secured a position with Cora's daddy, William, as manager of one of his cotton mills. The only stumbling block in their hasty romance was religion. He was, as his name indicated, Presbyterian; she was Baptist. It was agreed they would be married in her church and then both become

Methodists, with the stipulation their children might pick and choose for themselves—among those three denominations, of course. Which explains why their eldest son, Oliver, became a Baptist, and his son, Walter, an Episcopalian. The other children, who don't figure in the problem, ran true to breeding and remained in the Methodist fold.

So much for that aspect of background. I'm getting all of this down because my task promises to be formidable, if not impossible. There were eyewitnesses to the shooting, and it was common knowledge in Oughton that Walter Westmoreland and Richard Leeds were not on the best of terms. In fact, they despised each other.

But before the law mutual hatred is no justification for attempted murder, the charge which the district attorney, Ben Lewis—a man quick to make use of any political advantage—spoke of bringing.

"Had they met in some private place, like the back nine of the golf course, and opened fire, it would've been one thing," he said. "But on the city square, on a Saturday afternoon! Why, women and children might well have been injured!"

He went on to add, for the benefit of the Atlanta reporter who had driven over in the interest of preserving quaint Americana, that he believed the only way to settle political differences was through the ballot.

That comment moved the story from the C-section to page 2-A. It also gave Ben Lewis a bit of political exposure from which he had never been known to run, and which might now come in very handy since both candidates for the Sixth District congressional seat were cooling their heels in adjoining cells at the county jail. After their shootout on the square, anyone who came out for ballots over bullets would look pretty good, even if his name was Lewis.

But the problem didn't relate to politics. No, it was just a whim of chance that dictated Westmoreland and Leeds would be engaged in campaigning when that little so-called "fact" Granpa Westmoreland uncovered years before should accidentally come to light and cause triggers to be squeezed.

Which brings me back to Miss Cora and the connection to be made between her Panacea mullet-eating vacation and the problem.

Kermit Westmoreland's compelling interest, after making money, of which he made a great deal, was "family connections and/or history." He was an amateur genealogist who knew every leaf and twig of his Westmoreland family tree and set out to solve the curious mysteries of the bloodlines of many important Oughton families, defining, along the way, "important" in terms of those who had progressed in 1903 to indoor plumbing and thereby narrowing his sights to five households. Since most of the females of these families held membership in the UDC, it was not too difficult to chart timelines reaching back into the eighteenth century.

Of course, not all were willing to have the real truth of their backgrounds examined too closely. The Georgia Colony was, in fact, a noble experiment whose end result was the cleaning out of several large British prisons. And while it is true historically that felons were transported to Australia and debtors to America, somehow it seemed less grand to have ancestors who left their motherland due to reasons of impecuniousness rather than out and out criminality. Even today bankrupts are looked down upon, while bank robbers, though incarcerated, are secretly admired.

Kermit Westmoreland's greatest source of pleasure was investigating "the shady side of the family tree," as he called it. The strange freaks that are hidden up there in the branches of everyone's bush gave a quick spring to his step and a roguish twinkle to his eye, especially when he happened to meet the clan's present-day representative at some cultural event.

The genealogical discovery which Kermit considered to be the most splendid feather in his cap had to do with the very heart of the town of Oughton, the square, that little rectangle of earth peculiar to small towns where the main north-south and east-west roads cross. Ranging in size from no more than a few humble yards to several acres, and containing here a single monument, there the county courthouse, ringed with benches and rusty cannon, the square is considered by each citizen to be the focal point of God's benevolent gaze upon the world. Lining the streets running round it, regardless if they be paved or dust, are found the shops catering to the multifarious tastes of the townspeople, stores selling shoes, hats, overalls, needles, flour, nuts, bolts, Bibles, and occasionally culture in the form of lithographs of famous religious themes, not to mention cigars and long underwear.

Now in the year 1904 when Kermit was delving into ancestral affairs, Oughton's square was distinguished by a certain statue which served as a sort of common denominator for all small southern towns.

Done slightly bigger than life in semidurable stone, it portrayed a young Confederate soldier, rifle at the ready. Perhaps the most striking aspect of this often-repeated monument was the certain steady and northward gaze of its eyes, carrying in their resolute expression the clear announcement of "Retreat, hell!" These statues serve another, more pragmatic function, known to all small southern boys. If lost, they will give the direction of true north more faithfully than Polaris and the Big Dipper combined. This orientation of the Oughton statue in particular caused a bit of difficulty when, in 1940, the highway department decided to route a main road through the center of town. The square—at least the park in the center—had to give way to progress. The moving of the statue required a crane, a stout truck, several strong men, and Miss Cora. Armed with a compass, she rode alongside the stone image making sure that, while the truck must on occasion shift directions, the stone eyes overlooking the scene did not, for when the driver signaled for a turn, so did Miss Cora. The workmen shifted the statue about toward north, again and again, so that the one-mile trip from the square to the monument's new home in front of the county hospital took almost two hours. This exodus was marked by a following cloud of pigeons, whose circling flight allowed those not on the line of march to determine the statue's progress by simply looking, like Joshua, to the sky.

Kermit Westmoreland's inflammatory footnote to history was only tangentially concerned with the Confederate statue. It was the event it marked—the War Between the States—that he dealt with, in particular a certain event during that war which occurred on the Oughton square.

A pigeon's-eye view of the square back in those days would've revealed four L-shaped blocks of property caused by the intersection of the north-south and east-west roads. The southeast block was owned by the Leeds family, ancestors of the same Richard Leeds involved in the recent gunplay. The southwest block was held by Cora's people, the Middletons.

What makes these boring land descriptions important is the historical fact that on the afternoon of July 14th, 1864, a company of yankee soldiers under the command of Captain D. Griffin rode into Oughton. When they departed along about seven o'clock in the evening of the same day, they left the buildings on the square in flames—excepting a chosen few, namely those standing on the Leeds block. In a sea of fire it remained an island sanctuary. Oh, a few windows were shot out, and smoke from the nearby infernos blackened the bricks somewhat. But when, two days later, after the ruins had cooled, the proprietors surveyed the extent of their ruin, they discovered the Leeds buildings had ridden out the yankee storm with virtually no damage.

"An act of Providence! A Miracle!" many cried.

The Leedses did nothing to suggest any other explanation. Nor did anyone else. And so the encounter with the enemy on Oughton square fell into the gray area of that grayest of myths—Confederate deeds—where it swelled and grew for forty years and became so ingrained in the people's experience that when they walked into the stores on the southeast corner of the square they felt safe and smiled a little more openly.

Kermit Westmoreland smiled, too. He told Doc Spaulding he realized that where there was a smile there might well be a damn good laugh. And so he looked into the matter by tracking down the family of Captain D. Griffin through letters to the War Department. The captain had passed away in 1892, but his eldest son was quick to answer as many of Kermit's questions as he could, explaining that his father had to his dying day thought the "Civil War" to be the one great experience of his life; "this feeling was due, no doubt," the son added, "to the war's being the one time father was able to get away from mother for any considerable length of time."

Sitting before the fire, his children at his feet, a large glass of whiskey in his hand, the captain had more than once mentioned the episode at Oughton. It seems he hadn't really wanted to burn the square. But war being the hell it was, the knowledge that other units were liberally applying the torch left him no choice. Yes, he did spare the southeast corner, but neither God nor angels had anything to do with it.

"A fellow came out on the walk," the son related, "and told Daddy, in a low voice, that he owned the property and that his entire sympathy was with the northern cause."

"'Very touching, now stand back or be burned up,' my father replied.

"'Sir, I don't believe you understand,' the fellow said. 'I don't intend to have what's mine burned.'

"'Oh? And how do you propose to stop me?'

"'Since my words have not moved you, perhaps my money will. How much will you take for that torch?'

"Well," the son continued in his letter to Kermit, "my father said he laughed pretty good at the fellow's cheek, but when he saw he was dead serious, he dismounted and went into his office to talk business. He handed over a thousand in gold and two fine diamonds, unset, as 'fire insurance.' And that was that. Father called off his troopers and they left Oughton. But the adventure didn't end there. Father gambled away the gold in Atlanta. After the war he made the mistake of allowing my mother to take him to a tent meeting, where he got so fired up he momentarily lost control of himself and dropped the diamonds in the collection plate. The next morning when he realized what he'd done, he went looking for the preacher, but he had taken off for parts unknown."

Having laughed over the truth about the conflagration on the square in the privacy of his study, Kermit shared the revelation with his wife, Miss Cora, saying at the conclusion, "So you see, it was God who saved the Leeds property—God, not in His Providence nor from the Good Book, but God just the same, in fact the one and same who is still worshipped daily on the square—I mean Mammon! It was gold and diamonds, not prayer, that saved those buildings from the flames. Too bad your ancestors were so tight!"

Miss Cora did not argue. She merely swore her husband to eternal silence, not by forcing him to take an oath on the Bible, but rather by the sober threat of making absolutely sure he would father no more of *her* children should he speak.

So Kermit wrote down the account in the large leather-bound volume he had ordered from London for the purpose of recording Oughton lore. He wrote it neatly in thin jet-black script easily readable today. After his death in 1945 and Miss Cora's in 1950, the book, along with his other papers, was deposited in the regional library's local history collection, where it lay untouched and un-thought of until a month ago, when a fourteen-year-old boy from the high school, a sharp lad with a bright future (if he lives so long), opened it as he engaged in research for an original paper for his history class.

Well, his paper was so original, and so entertaining, especially to those who didn't care too much for the Leedses, that the newspaper printed it on the feature page. Some feature. What happened was quite a few of the more noisy readers—and I don't mean the kind who read out loud—made a political issue out of old man Leeds's act of bribery, proclaiming that anyone whose ancestor would do that should by all means be *in* Washington, or Paris, or Bombay, or anywhere else, so long as he was *out* of Oughton and *for* good.

Now, as for the shooting in question.

Let it be understood that Walter Westmoreland did in no way seek to profit politically, or otherwise, from his grandfather Kermit's account of the acts of Richard Leeds's relation. As a matter of fact, he went well out of his way to make sure history should not become an issue. But this action backfired; in contrast to Richard Leeds's rage, Walter's cool courtliness brought voters flocking to his cause.

But the shooting.

As stated earlier, it happened on the square at that busiest of all times, Saturday afternoon. It was also dove season, another institution as gilded with tradition as the square. Some people have even gone so far as to claim Oughton was built where it is because of the location's proximity to the path taken by dove as they make their yearly southward migration to Cuba where they winter.

Maybe so, maybe not, but regardless, most every human being wearing trousers and a few in skirts put their normal lives on hold when the doves are passing. The lanes and fields around Oughton resound with the pop, pop, pop of shotguns till a person doesn't much hear them anymore.

So on the Saturday afternoon of the shooting the two parties, Westmoreland and Leeds, were on the square armed with shotguns. There are two stores on the square where hunters—serious hunters, the kind that like talking about it almost as much as doing it— congregate. One is the Ace Hardware, the other is the Economy Auto. They face each other across the intersection where once the Confederate statue stood gazing northward.

What happened was this:

Walter Westmoreland, gun over his shoulder, was coming out of the Ace Hardware at the same time Richard Leeds, gun over his shoulder, was getting ready to go into the Economy Auto. There was a noise remindful of a gunshot. Both men's reflexes were sharpened by years of hunting. Each saw the other standing there armed glaring at him. And so both fired.

Each man claimed he did not take direct aim at the other, but rather sighted somewhat above the target and fired merely to warn, or to scare, or, in other words, to let the other know that if he meant business, well, by damn, so did he. The shot pellets rained down like the Bible says on the just and the unjust, striking parked cars and pickups like hail, and scaring the bejabbers out of Sergeant Sikes, whose beat for thirty years was the square. Shot at, the policeman figured, he must defend himself as well as the public welfare. So he drew his .32 hammerless and shot himself through the boot. The spent bullet ricocheted upward through the window of Jake's Jewelry, triggering the alarm system. The clanging of the rusty bell so unnerved one farmer, who was more adept at steering his tractor than his truck, that he rammed a fire hydrant, releasing the pressure that was waiting for just such an opportunity out in the tank on Oak Mountain. A geyser spewed higher than the People's Bank Building and some sport in the nearby pool hall cried it was the end of the world, at least.

Well, something had to happen to bring order out of this chaos. And it did. Both of the instigators (to exclude the nameless and unknown so-and-so whose backfire or firecracker or popped brown paper sack, or what-have-you, served as catalyst) tossed their weapons in their cars and tried to calm the multitude. They succeeded in calling an ambulance for Sergeant Sikes, when an event occurred I still shudder to recollect.

It is said by those who ought to know that when a shark smells blood he goes into a frenzy, during which he will sometimes even bite himself. Well, the crowd went into a frenzy, too. Only these usually kind and friendly folks didn't nip themselves, except maybe indirectly by bringing shame on their town. If there's any justification for their madness it would have to be fear. They were most certainly frightened.

Someone spotted Richard Leeds and cried, "That's the polecat trying to kill us! Let's get him!"

A large red-faced man carrying a baby tucked under one beefy arm like a sack of chicken feed, dashed into Ace Hardware and demanded a rope. Before the clerk could think of what to say, the fellow tossed him the baby, who started yowling, and reeled off twenty feet of all-purpose one-inch hemp, cutting it loose from the spool with a swipe of a tobacco-stained Tree-Brand knife. With one quick flip he bent a sturdy noose on the end and started for the mob in the street, who had meanwhile caught up with Richard Leeds and were telling him in twenty-five different voices, all pretty ungrammatical, just what he could expect.

Well, they got the rope up and over a lamppost still bearing red and green traces of the Christmas decorations put up annually by the Jaycees. They were trying to get the noose close to Leeds's neck, when help arrived in the person of the sheriff, John Lee, a local man famous for never toting a gun, except when there was real trouble, and like that saying of some Russian writer, a man determined to hear a gun go off once he'd seen or shown it. This time John Lee was packing a pistol and handling a shotgun, cut off down close to where the slide-holder joins the barrel. He let the 12-gauge do his introduction. The mob froze like it was posing for an old-time photographer, and all the roaring and cussing seemed to ooze from their open lips like cartoon balloons and float away on the breeze.

"I'm gonna close my eyes for a spell," said John Lee in his normal quiet voice, "and when I open them up I expect not to see nobody on this square who don't want to go to jail."

You could almost hear his eyes click shut. For a moment no one knew what to do; the next moment every one knew precisely. When John Lee next surveyed the scene only two persons stood before him, Westmoreland and Leeds.

"You two is under arrest," he said.

"What?" cried Leeds, at last getting the rope off his adam's apple.

"Any more fool questions and I'll cite you for resisting."

"But they were trying to string me up!"

"Yes, and we didn't do anything," said Walter.

"Everybody's did something, one time or another. Get in the car."

So like in Monopoly they went straight to jail, where they still sit, side by side in a sort of poetic justice, which may well be the only kind of justice handed down when the Honorable Judge Green gets back from his hunting trip on a reservation down by Bainbridge. The charges aren't felonious—just discharging firearms within the city limits, inciting a riot, and causing a commotion.

The boys pass the time swapping insults, the best of which being the following:

"Damn it all, Walter," said Leeds. "None of this would've happened and I'd be outside today, winning the race for United States Congress, if only you'd been more picky in choosing a granpa!"

"Oh yeah?" replied Walter. "Well it's just too bad one of your illustrious ancestors isn't around right now, so he could slip John Lee a bribe and spring us both!"

Too bad old Kermit Westmoreland wasn't alive to make a note of that exchange and get it down clearly for the benefit of future historians. Or maybe it's better he isn't. If he was he'd really have a laugh, and there's something about old men's laughter that gets me, something sort of terrible, if you know what I mean, when they drop back their bald heads and their wrinkled necks like roosters getting ready to crow, but the sound spewing over their gums is a clutching, a rasping, which brings to mind the truth that theirs is only the next-to-last laugh, that the final chuckle is on them and, therefore, on all of us.

Chapter Nine

When Flora saw Mr. Billy come down the back steps and walk toward the cabin, she knew something was wrong. The time was right—5:30 in the morning—and Mr. Billy was dressed as usual in a tan short-sleeved shirt and tan trousers and was wearing his Silver-Belly Open-Road hat, his cowboy boots, and his wide leather belt with the silver longhorn buckle. Everything looked right, but instead of stopping off at the blue and white air-conditioned shed where he kept Mr. George, his prize Angus bull, he came directly to the cabin.

"Mr. Billy's comin' this way, Charles," Flora told her husband, "and there's somethin' wrong."

"There is that," Charles said. He sat at the kitchen table holding his chin in his hands. "This jaw tooth is about to kill me. I never had such an ache in all my life."

"You better get yourself up and get out on that porch."

Charles got up. "Don't you know better than to boss a man with a bad tooth?"

"Daddy's tooth still hurt, Mama?" a voice in the other room of the cabin asked.

"Now you got the kids up," Flora said. "I don't get no time to myself."

Charles shrugged his shoulders and, wrapping a red bandanna

around his head and tying it under his chin, went out on the porch just as Mr. Billy closed the gate behind him. Flora's four dominecker hens scurried out of his way, raising faint puffs of dust.

Mr. Billy took off his hat and swiped at the satin lining with his fingertips, then eased the hat on the back of his head so his wispy red hair showed from under the cocked brim. In the sty behind the cabin Charles's sow flopped over in the cool mud.

"It's gonna be a hot one," Mr. Billy said.

"It surely is," Charles said.

"Hot and dry. Be a cloud of dust against the sun by noon."

"Could rain by night. Signs is right."

Mr. Billy slapped his leg. "Not a chance. Weather bureau in Atlanta says no rain today and none in sight." He squinted at Charles. "Bad times, hard times are upon us. Some folks are sayin' it's like the days of Joseph in the Bible. Course, I haven't had no dreams. Have you?"

Charles looked over the flaring brim of the gray hat. Something was up. Something was wrong. Every other day Mr. Billy would first thing go see how Mr. George was feeling. Then he would come down to the cabin and tell him what work was to be done for that day. That was the way it had been all his life and his father's before him. There had always been a Charles Jefferson in the first cabin nearest to the big house, and there had always been a Mr. Billy Green in the big house. Mr. Billy told Charles Jefferson and Charles Jefferson told the people living in the other cabins, and all together they got the two thousand acres of the farm worked.

"Yessir, the days of Joseph," Mr. Billy said again. His blue eyes narrowed. "What the hell's that wrapped around you head? You got the toothache?"

"Yessir, that's it all right. One of my jaw teeth got a big hole in it."

"That's a shame. But it happens to all of us, I guess." He smiled. The gold crowns on his teeth shone. "Old Mr. George had a little tooth trouble himself a while back. Had to have a false tooth. Some folks thought it was silly for me to spend good money on such a thing, but it's a fact that when a prize animal's teeth are bad he gets thrown off his feed and loses weight. Appearance suffers too."

"Yessir," Charles said. "That's a fact."

Behind him Charles heard the children whispering as they gath-

92

ered around the kitchen table for breakfast. He looked up at the pink and gold dawn sky and asked Mr. Billy what he wanted done that day.

"Well," said Billy, "to tell you the truth I don't want nothing done, not today and not—" He pulled off his hat and punched out the crown with a pop, then carefully pinched it in and set the hat back on his head, the brim low now, so a shadow hung over his eyes. "I don't want nothin' done today, and I don't want nothin' done tomorrow. In fact, I don't want nothin' done no more."

"No more?" Charles said. His toothache suddenly ceased. "You mean you done sold the place?"

"No, I haven't sold it."

"Well thank god for that. This farm's been part of your family for a long time."

"Been part of yours, too," Flora said from inside the cabin.

"That's so, Mr. Billy," Charles said. "Course, a woman shouldn't—"

Mr. Billy stepped away from the porch and put his hands on his hips. His face was the color of his hair.

"Now I got to tell you this, Charles, and you got to get it straight and tell the others. I don't like it, but it's the way it's got to be. So that's it. You and your people are gonna have to move off this place."

"Move? Why, if we move then who'll do the work?"

"You are gonna move. I got men with tractors and machines coming in and they can do the work a lot cheaper. That's the way it's gonna be!"

"But we can't move off like that! Where'll we go? What'll we do? I got a wife and family. I ain't got no place to go. You—"

"Now you listen here to me! This is my land. Mine! And everything that's on it is mine and I can do with it what I want. If I want to blow it up with TNT I can. If I want to leave it fallow till doomsday I can. It's my land! That's the law! You understand?"

As his voice grew louder, Flora led the children onto the porch in a line behind Charles. All were barefoot. The two oldest girls, Clusta and Louise, wore faded dresses that Mr. Billy's wife, Miss Eugenia, had given them for tending her children. The oldest boy, Charlie, wore a torn sweatshirt and a pair of patched work pants that had once belonged to Charles.

Mr. Billy's voice seemed to batter the line of bodies. Charles said, "I got to have time. I can't just up and go. I ain't got no place to go."

93

"You got all the time you want," Mr. Billy said. "But you haven't got any more work. I figure you and your people before you earned a right to that cabin—that's damn sure more than the others are givin'—so it's yours as long as you stay in it."

He pulled a white handkerchief from his pocket and wiped his face.

"But let me tell you this," he said, his voice no longer loud. "It's all finished here. It's done with and that's that. You hear? There isn't anything I can do—nothin', absolutely nothin'. Even if I wanted to. But what I want or don't want is beside the point. We are using tractors and machines now and there isn't any place here for you and your people." His voice grew loud again. "That's it as simple as I can put it. You can stay in this cabin as long as it takes you to find a new place. You can have the produce in your garden but you can't plant any more. You can use the well. Your account at the store is closed. No more credit. And you can't work here."

"We'll die!" Flora cried. She opened her arms to her children. "As sure as day we'll starve to death!"

The younger children hid behind her.

"Nobody's gonna starve," Mr. Billy said, "if they'll pay attention and do what I say. You all can move off to a city somewhere, to Atlanta even, and make a lot more than you ever did here."

He went through the gate, hooked it behind him, and walked quickly to the shed where Mr. George was bellowing for his morning feed.

The windows were curtained with blankets. In the circle of lamp light Charles listened to Flora's brother Russell who had come in after dark from the farm next door where he lived and worked. Three men came with him, and they and Charles and his son Charlie watched as Russell supported his speech with loose diagrams sketched with his blunt fingertips on the red oilcloth table cover.

"Heard it all last night," he said. "Mr. James called a meeting of the bosses in the county. They was all there, every one of the rascals."

"Tell them who else was there," said one of the men who had come with Russell. He was tall and heavy and wore a narrow-brimmed black hat.

"I'm coming to all that. There was Mr. Billy and Mr. Barnett and old Mr. Williams and Mr. Rutledge. They was all there laughin' and drinkin' and havin' a good time. The preacher, Mr. Suggs, was there too. And Judge Green, Mr. Billy's brother. Oh, they was quite a group!

"Well, my wife was up in the kitchen when they all come in. She heard what they was up to and sent down for me. It was dark then, so I hid in the bushes outside the library window and watched and listened."

"Tell them what you heard," the man in the black hat said.

"They're out to get us. They're gonna get us for good!"

"I talked with Mr. Billy," Charles said.

From the other room Flora said, "You mean *he* talked to you!"

A child cried out in its sleep. Flora hushed it.

Russell said, "Then you know what's up. The bosses and the judge and the preacher worked it all out. It was Mr. Barnett's idea."

A man wearing a huge silver ring snorted and said, "Leave it to that fella if it's bad!"

"Yeah," Russell said. "Right off he held up his glass of whiskey and said, 'Let's us drink to the United States of America and to our dear wives.' They all liked that. Then he told them the meeting was his doin'. 'Got the answer to all our troubles,' he said. 'Got it right here in my hand.'

"I eased up and saw he was holdin' a book about tractors and farm machines."

"Ain't nothin' new about them," Charlie said.

"This time there is, boy," the man with the silver ring said. The third man who had come in with Russell, and who was wearing an old embroidered sateen warm-up jacket whose faded letters spelled KOREA 1952 above a spitting dragon, nodded his head. "I know machines," he said. "I knowed it was comin'."

"It ain't the machines," the man with the black hat said.

"Hell no!" Russell said. "It's them bastards that owns them!"

For a moment the cabin was quiet, the only movement the flicker of the lamp.

"And what did Mr. Barnett say?" Charles asked.

"He said he didn't know about them, but he was goddamn sick and tired to death of bowin' and scrapin' like some damn nigger before the federal government. They all said 'Yeah sir!' to that. And then he said

95

he wasn't gonna let the communists and the jews and the niggers tell him how to use his land, and he'd be double-dogged damned if he was gonna stand around one more day and let them officials in Washington D.C. steal away all his hard-earned cash money and give it out to lazy good-for-nothin' black and white sons-a-bitches who do nothin' 'cept lie around like wormy dogs in the shade all day and beget bastard children all night!

"That's what he said!" Russell cleared his throat.

"And then he held up that tractor book and told them his plan. 'We're gonna solve our problems, boys, by getting at the root,' he said. 'Them folks in Washington been pickin' on us cause we got every other nigger in the nation livin' amongst us. All right then, I say, if we want to get them off our backs all we got to do is get rid of the goddamn niggers! And we are gonna do just that!'

"But then Mr. Rutledge said, 'Hold on there Barnett. If we get rid of the niggers, who's gonna do the work?'

"Old Barnett just laughed and shook all over at that. He said, 'Machines is gonna. Machines! This is the twentieth century we live in. We forgot that?'

"He gave Mr. Rutledge the book and while he was lookin' at it, he said, 'These machines will do everythin' them niggers has been doing except loaf, get sick, waste food, and try to get in white schools. What's more, they don't show up on welfare rolls. Now I'll grant you they cost a little to begin with. But you all got to remember them niggers did too, back when our ancestors was startin' out. We tend to lose sight of that, but gettin' them slaves from Africa and bringin' them across the ocean was one of the great sacrifices our fathers done to make this land what it is today. So the machines cost somethin', and they cost somethin' to run, too. But look right there—'

"He took the book away from Mr. Rutledge and read them some figures about how one man with this machinery could do the same work in one day as one hundred men without. And then he slapped that book shut and said, 'Every machine you buy is a hundred niggers you can get rid of. All you got to do is look around and find some young bucks without families to drive them. Teach them how and turn them loose!'"

Russell stopped and tugged at his collar. His dark face was slick with sweat and almost white in the lamp light.

The man in the Korea jacket whistled. "One hundred to one. Might be more than that."

"That's plenty enough for us, ain't it?" the man in the black hat said.

Flora stuck her head around the corner. "Well, you all ain't gonna let them do it, is you?"

"That's why we come over, sister," Russell said. "We got our plans too."

"Ain't gonna lie down and be run over by no man no more," the man with the silver ring said.

"No sir, no more!" the others said.

Charles looked into the burning globe of the lamp. After Mr. Billy had gone through the gate that morning he had sat down on the porch and made himself deaf to Flora's words and the children's cries. He had to think about it. It was his job to tell the others what to do and he had to be sure he told them the right thing. But he could not sit on the steps all morning. The people were up and waiting to go into the fields. Then he had gotten up and walked slowly down the clay road that started behind his cabin and curved between the other cabins of the settlement. As he walked he scratched his head and suddenly realized that the red bandanna was still knotted under his chin. He took it off and slipped it into his pocket, deciding as he did that he would not tell them just then, that he would wait for at least a day. Maybe he could talk to Mr. Billy. Maybe he could find out what was wrong and set it right again. So he had told each man he came to that today was a holiday and that Mr. Billy had said take it easy and rest up. They whooped and ran inside to tell their families, and when he came up the road on his way back to his cabin, men, women, and children were sitting on the porches laughing and carrying on.

"And what do you think, brother?" Russell asked.

"I don't know. Just don't see how Mr. Billy could say all them things."

"He's just like all the rest, Daddy," Charlie said. "They's all alike!"

"That's the truth!" Flora said.

"Now you's talking!" said the man in the black hat.

"Well," Russell said, "that's not exactly the way it was. At first Mr. Billy didn't like the plan and said so. Said it wasn't right."

Charles smiled. "I thought I knowed Mr. Billy."

"Now just hold on, brother," Russell said. "He said that *at first*. But he said something else too. When Mr. Rutledge and Mr. Barnett told him it was his duty to stick to his own kind and do what the others done, he changed his tune. Judge Green said, 'I'd sure hate to think what daddy and gran'daddy would say to that.' And preacher Suggs said folks had to be constant on guard against all them godless communist red-devils who goes around stirrin' up the nigger and tryin' to destroy the American way of life."

"I seen them red-devils when I was over there fightin'," the man in the Korea jacket said. "They're more brown than red."

"And what did Mr. Billy do?" Charles asked.

"Do? Why, what could he do? He went along with the rest of them. He's one of them, brother, not one of us. Don't you forget it."

"I ain't forgettin' nothin'. It's just hard to figure. This mornin' Mr. Billy told us we got to leave, but then he said we could stay in this cabin long as we like."

Russell laughed. "Now ain't that white of him! He's gonna let you stay here till you starve. Ain't no work—ain't no credit—ain't no food. Maybe you got a little saved up, maybe you ain't. Don't matter. You sit here in this fine old cabin and don't do nothin' but wait till Mr. Billy changes his mind, and they gonna plow your dead kids under and you ain't gonna mind cause you gonna be starved to death, too!"

"Machines don't eat," the man in the Korea jacket said. "They gonna take young fellas like your boy there and they gonna pay them ten dollars a day to drive them machines. That's five times what they pays now. They gonna get their pick of drivers. Crazy peoples gonna be standin' in line to sell out."

"I ain't gonna do it!" Charlie said. "Don't care what they do, I ain't gonna!"

"You don't somebody else will, boy," Russell said.

"And them that don't pick up and move will be starved out," the man in the black hat said.

"That's right," Russell said. "Ain't gonna be no more welfare. Judge Green seen to that. Told them the law. Said, 'If there's a man in the house fit to work it don't make no difference if there's no work for him. Long as he's able we don't have to give him welfare.' And then the bastard said, 'If they don't move on they'll starve to death. Either way we can't lose.'"

Charles went to the window and eased back the blanket. Through the narrow opening he could see the back of Mr. Billy's house. The lights were out. Mr. Billy and his wife and children were in bed. He closed the blanket and came back to the table and sat down.

"That's the way it is," Russell said. "We come over here to tell you what we gonna do."

"Do?" Charles said. He looked first at Russell, then one by one at the three men who had come with him. "There's only one thing you can do and you know it."

"Well, brother, that depends," Russell said, spreading his fingers flat on the table cover. "That depends on what you think is right and what you think is wrong. See?"

His right hand darted beneath the table and emerged holding a nickel-plated revolver. He pressed the pistol against his cheek in the circle of lamp light. The brilliance of the metal reflected in his eyes like white fire.

Now as Charles watched, the three other men took out pistols and placed them on the table.

"We'll kill them all!" Charlie screamed.

"And we'll burn them out flat to the ground and cut down their trees, and then we'll plow up their graveyards and fling the coffins in the river," the man in the black hat said.

"Oh, yeah!" said the man with the silver ring. "We'll kill every livin' thing that belongs to them, just like they done in the Bible when the children went into the Promised Land."

"And then we'll burn their Bible too!" the man in the Korea jacket said.

"No," Charles said.

"No? What do you mean no?" said Russell. He shook the pistol in Charles's face. "Everything they got they made with our sweat. Nigger sweat! It's all nigger sweat! Every house they got, every piece of land. Hell, even themselves! We done made every crop that fed them!"

Charles pushed away from the table. Flora stood in the doorway behind him holding the restless child.

Russell looked at the pistol and put it in his coat pocket. "Never thought I'd live to see the day when my own sister's husband would go Uncle Tom!"

99

"He ain't no Uncle Tom and you know it!" Flora said.

The baby cried.

Charlie sat between the two men and looked first at one, then the other.

The man in the black hat said, "Maybe he thinks he'll go up to Detroit and get himself a job making them tractors and machines!"

Charles got up. "You fellas ain't lookin' for nothin' but trouble." He pointed his finger at Russell. "Always thought you had good sense. They'd just love for us to start shootin'. That'd be all the excuse they need."

"That's right," Flora said. "And they got bombers and machine guns."

Russell nodded toward the man in the Korea jacket. "We got men who knows how to fight. We ain't scared of nothin' they got. They done it all to us anyhow. There ain't nothin' left. It's the end. We figure we might as well teach them bastards a lesson!"

The man with the silver ring struck the table with his fist. The lamp shook. "I'm a man and I'll be damned if I let my wife and kids starve to death and do nothin' about it! Gettin' shot's better than lyin' down and being run over!"

"And brother they ain't got no right!" Russell said. "Look what all we done for them. Not just me and you. Look at all the folks that come before us. They ain't got no right!"

Charles looked into his brother-in-law's eyes and saw himself as a tiny black dot in the tears of anger that had gathered there. "Well," he said, "it's true they ain't got no right, but it ain't doin' us no good."

"Then tell your people to get ready."

"I don't know about that. I got to think about it. Got to have time."

"All right," Russell said. "You come to see me tomorrow night. We won't do nothin' till then." He got up and went to the door. Charles turned down the lamp wick. One of the men said to Russell, "I ain't never liked no Uncle Tom. You sure you can trust him?"

In the dark shadows Charles could barely see Russell nod his head.

Charles sat half asleep on the porch and watched the sun rising. The summer sky was barred with shafts of red and purple. Birds were fluttering and singing in the trees in Mr. Billy's yard. "Pear trees," thought Charles, "and pecans too." They grew behind the white fence that separated the big house from the barn and the cabins beyond.

Flora came out on the porch. "What are you thinking about?" she asked.

"Nothin'," Charles said. He watched the sun rise beyond the big white house. The light framed it in a red haze as though it was blazing. It was a wooden house, an old wooden house. It would burn almost as fast as his own cabin.

"Nothin' ain't much to be thinkin' about now," Flora said. "You hungry?"

"Naw, I ain't hungry."

"That jaw tooth hurt?"

Charles looked up at his wife. "You know that ain't what hurts now." He looked down at the steps. "Ain't never had nothin' like the hurt I got now."

Flora placed her fingertips on his head. "What we gonna do, Charles? You know what we gonna do?"

"Don't know."

"You 'fraid, Charles? Is you scared? I got to know!"

"Yeah." He stood up. Her hand fell away. "Sure I'm scared. Ain't you? If you ain't you never gonna have reason to be 'fraid again."

"Sometimes I feel just like brother!" she cried out. "Them sons-a-bitches! What right they got? Sometimes I wish I was a man! If I was a man I'd get me a gun and I'd go up there and shoot every last one of them! I'd do it! I would!"

"Hush! You gonna wake the kids."

"Let them wake! It's high time everybody woke! It's past time!"

"All right, all right," Charles said. He put his arm about her shoulders. "Be still now. We're gonna find a way. Come on now. Easy. Yeah. Now you get me a cup 'a coffee. Can you do that? Good. I'll just sit down here and think about what we're gonna do. You get me the coffee and I'll think."

But even with the coffee he could not think it out. The children woke, ate, and were sent to play with the other children in the settlement. Two men came up to the cabin and asked Charles about the work for the day. He told them it was a half-holiday and there'd be no work till noon. "I'll come down there then and let you know," he said. The men were puzzled, but they did not question him, and went away laughing down the road to their cabins.

The sun was up above Mr. Billy's house now. He had come down to the shed to see Mr. George. Charles saw him come out and pitch new hay in through the door. Then he went back up to the house. Charles wondered how they were making out up there. It was a large house, lots of rooms to be cleaned. Who had cooked breakfast? Could Miss Eugenia cook? Maybe Mr. Billy would have to send her off to cook school.

It was hot on the porch. In the exposed beams a family of black and yellow wasps went about building a nest. Sap was rising in clean amber beads on the firewood stacked by the steps and around the blade of an ax embedded in one log. The sun was full in Charles's face. A sheet of light reflected from the metal roof of Mr. George's shed and shimmered in his eyes. His straw hat lay on the floor just beyond the reach of his arm. He wanted the wide brim to shield his face from the intense glare. But it was so warm and still, and the buzzing of the wasps was so insistent, that he closed his eyes and lazily allowed his thoughts to drift on the soft warm air. He yawned and leaned against the porch rail. The light against his closed eyes was a pleasant reddish tinge.

Mr. George was talking to him. The fine black bull opened the gate, came up to the steps, flicked his tail to one side, and sat down on the steps beside him.

"Why can't people do right?" Mr. George asked. The brass ring in his thick black nose bobbed as his gray lips moved.

"Don't know," Charles said.

"Why can't they?" Mr. George said.

"Don't know," Charles said. "Don't know, can't know, won't know. How'm I supposed to know? I done wrong? You got the wrong man, Mr. Bull George!"

"When I was a little bull my mama told me," said Mr. George. "She said, 'George, you're just a little bull right now, but if you do right, someday you'll grow up. Then you'll be a big bull. You know what big bulls do?' I said, 'No Mama, what does they do?' She said, 'They makes little bulls.'

"And that's all I do," Mr. George said. "I stay up there in that shed and I give Mr. Billy every drop of my juice just like his cows give him milk."

"Or his niggers give sweat!" Charles said.

The sun was very hot now and struck him full in the face. Moisture ran into the corners of his clenching eyes.

"I ain't never worshiped no bull!" he cried. "Ain't never listened to no bull! Don't care about you, Mr. George! Got a notion to get me a butcher knife and cut you good! Gonna make you sweat!"

Mr. George got down on his knees. "Do it! Do it! Do it!" he begged. "Put an end to me. Cut off my pizzle and make yourself a stew. I'm sick to death of sending my kind to the slaughterhouse. Every drop comes out of me goes into the bellies of you-know-who!"

Now it was no longer hot. The redness went out of Charles's eyes. Mr. George vanished. Charles yawned and stretched, and as he did, his forearm brushed back the brim of his straw hat.

He sat up straight and felt the hat with both hands and looked up slowly at the sheltering brim. His hat was on his head. He had been dreaming and someone had come along and seen him sweating in the sun and had picked up his hat and placed it on his head to shield his face from the heat.

He jumped up and searched the yard. No one was there. Who would do such a thing for him? He went in the cabin. Empty. Behind the cabin there was no one. He came back to the front steps and cupped his hands above his eyes and squinted toward Mr. Billy's house. All was still, motionless in the late morning sunshine. He fell to his knees and examined the earth near the steps. There were many scuffed markings, some barefoot, some booted, too many to be sure of any one. He sat down again on the steps and looked at his hands. They were coated with red clay dust. From his blue and white air-conditioned shed Mr. George bellowed once and was quiet.

Charles looked up at the sun. It was almost noon. He stood, brushed himself off slowly and carefully, and went up the path through the gate to Mr. George's shed. Mr. Billy was inside. He saw him through the frosted window and came out in a rush of cold air.

"I can't do anything about it," Mr. Billy said. He pulled his hat low over his eyes. "I told you how it's gonna be and that's the way it's gonna be."

"I know," Charles said. "That's why this once I ain't gonna take off my hat."

Mr. Billy looked at Charles's wide-brimmed straw hat. He ran his fingers across his lips and wiped them on his trouser leg. "Suit yourself. Too hot to go without a hat anyhow."

"I didn't come up here to talk about hats," Charles said, jerking off his hat.

"That so? Then what did you come for?"

"Ain't gonna be run over by no man no more!" Charles said. "You look at me and what do you see? You don't see nothin'! But you is wrong, I's a man! You see that?" He held up his fist. "I got me nine kids and a wife. Got me the respect of all them people livin' down there in the cabins. I ain't nothin'. I ain't no tractor, no machine. I is somethin'. I's a man!"

Mr. Billy folded his thick, red-haired arms over his chest and looked Charles straight in the eye.

"You take that back to Mr. Rutledge and Mr. Barnett and all them others!" He spit in the dust at Mr. Billy's feet and wiped his mouth on the back of his hand. "And I'll tell you this, your daddy and grandaddy wouldn't like what you're doing! No sir! They was always good to us. They knowed how it was. Why, many's the day your daddy and my daddy went off fishin' or huntin', and sometimes they even went down in the woods and got drunk!"

Charles pulled his hat on so the wide brim was on a line with his eyes.

"That all?" Mr. Billy said.

"No, that ain't all!" Charles said. "I told you I's a man, and I come to prove it. I owes you money at the store. I ain't leavin' here till I got it paid."

"There's no more work," Mr. Billy said.

"Ain't talkin' about that. Talkin' about work that's been done and done and done. I figure that sow I got is worth somethin'. And them chickens of Flora's. On top of that I got the cabin you say is mine. You take all that and we'll be even just like we never met!"

"I don't want your stock."

"Well you got it!"

"That cabin's yours. I'm not gonna take it in trade. I told you all the accounts are closed. The books are shut. Nobody owes nobody nothin'."

"Well, I ain't gonna take that stock with me! I pays my debts, *all* my debts!" His face was running with sweat. He pulled his red bandanna from his pocket, wiped his face and the back of his neck, and handed the damp rag to Mr. Billy.

He went through the gate and down the road to the settlement and told the people how it was going to be from then on. He would not take no for an answer, and when some, like Russell, vowed they would die first, he shouted them down and said, "For what? If that's the way you think, then brother you is dead right now!"

He told them to get their things together, to load their trucks and cars, and to be ready to leave after supper. "Ain't gonna spend one more night on this land," he said.

Toward sunset the people were ready. Charles stood by his old pickup truck which was loaded down with kids and belongings. Flora and Charlie came around the corner of the cabin. Charlie was leading the grunting sow on a short rope. Flora had packed her hens in a flimsy crate which she carried on her hip.

"Where you all going?" Charles said.

"You know," Flora said. "Gonna pack these on the truck."

"Gimme that!" Charles said. "And you, boy, tie that sow to the porch."

Charles tore open the crate, pulled out the first hen, and wrung its neck. Flora stood open-mouthed and watched. Then he methodically destroyed the other hens and tossed their broken bodies and the splintered crate on the porch.

"All right, boy," he said. "Lead that sow in the cabin."

Charlie pulled and tugged, but the sow smelled blood and backed off.

"All right then, have it your own way," Charles said. "Ain't nobody gonna escape nohow."

He pulled the ax out of the log by the steps, walked slowly to the sow, and struck a terrible blow to the head. The beast squealed, rolled over, and pawed the air, as its thick, hot blood gushed on the dusty red clay. When the sow was still, Charles and his son lugged it into the cabin and placed it in front of the stove.

Then Charles told all the people to load into their trucks and start out for the highway. As they passed his cabin, the last before they went by Mr. Billy's barn and house, Charles sprinkled coal oil over the porch, struck a match, and sat the cabin afire. The ancient pine boards went up in a swoosh. Fierce currents of icy air raced across the dusty yard and swirled through the door and windows. Flames leaped above the roof and chimney. The earth shook from the roar of the fire.

Charles came away from the burning cabin and started the truck. It was so hot that he was sweating as though he had been at work all day in the fields. He eased the old truck in gear and moved off down the rutted road.

"Where we goin'?" Flora said loudly over the crackling flames.

"To tell your brother what we done," Charles said.

"And then where?"

Charles steered the truck around the barn. Mr. Billy and his wife and children were nowhere to be seen. The pens and yards were empty. The red light from the burning cabin bathed the big white house. Its windows reflected the glow as though it was blazing inside.

Charles turned onto the highway and set out in pursuit of his people.

"After that where're we goin'?" Flora repeated.

"Away," Charles said. "We is goin' away, and we ain't never comin' back no more!"

Chapter Ten

The Howard Johnson's opened for breakfast at six. A trucker was having coffee at the counter. In the second booth a man and his wife and two groggy children ate doughnuts. A young man and young woman parked beside the building near the front door. The hostess and a sleepy waitress watched as they got out of the car and came up the walk. The young man opened the door for the young woman and she waited for him to find a booth.

"It's six-thirty," said the young man. He took a sip from the glass of ice water the waitress sloshed in front of him, then picked up the menu.

"Want coffee now?" the waitress asked.

The young man lowered the menu and looked at the young woman. She turned toward the window. "Two coffees," he said.

As the waitress went to the counter, he said, "This number six looks good, Molly. Two eggs, toast, grits or potatoes. With number seven you get the same plus ham or bacon."

"I'm not hungry, Frank."

He put down the menu. "I find that hard to believe. How do you feel?"

"It's not that. You'd like it to be that, wouldn't you?"

"I don't want you to feel bad. I've told you. If you don't feel good maybe I can do something."

She laughed. "You're plenty good at that, aren't you, Frank!"

The waitress brought the coffee. "Want to order now?" she asked.

"No," he said, looking at the young woman, "we haven't made up our mind yet."

The waitress went back to the counter, lit a cigarette, and talked to the trucker.

"You've made up your mind, how you've made it up, Frank!" Molly said. "I wish I could be like you. You're so damn positive."

"I think I'll have the number seven with ham. You?"

"I'm not hungry. I feel like I'm going to be sick."

"All right, I'm not going to ask you again. You can't starve yourself to death. You'll need all the strength you can get."

He motioned to the waitress, and when she came to the table he ordered two number sevens with ham.

"How you like the eggs?" asked the waitress.

He looked at the young woman. "My god," she said, "you don't even know how I like my eggs. My god!"

"I like mine over light," said Frank.

"Sunny side up," the young woman said.

After the waitress gave the order to the cook she went back to the counter and talked to the trucker. "They're eloping," she said.

The trucker turned on his stool and looked at Frank and the young woman. "How do you know?"

"I can tell."

"She probably asked them," the hostess said.

"I was young once," said the waitress. "Besides, car's got Georgia tags. Lots of young couples stop here. They head for Miami and the bright lights. Gives them something to talk about back on the farm."

Frank took another sip of ice water, then excused himself and went to the men's room and scrubbed his face and hands. His eyes were burning from driving since midnight. He came back to the table and drank his coffee. Molly watched him.

"Don't you want to freshen up?" he asked. "The rest room's clean."

"Like the last one?"

"When you travel at night you have to take what's open. I told you that."

Molly laughed. "You told me a lot of things, a hell of a lot. You can really tell when you try!"

"Look," said Frank. "Get it out in the open. I thought we settled it two days ago."

She took a sip of coffee. "*You* settled it. I didn't."

"And you agreed."

"What else could I do?"

"It's not dangerous. We've been over that in detail. It's really very simple."

She slapped her hand on the table. "*Simple*! Is that all you can say?"

"What do you want me to say? I'm sorry? Okay, I'm sorry. You don't know how sorry. I've never been so sorry."

"If you're so goddamn sorry why don't you do the right thing? That's all I want to know. Tell me why and I'll never bother you again. Just tell me. You owe me that much."

"I've told you."

"Tell me again."

"Because I've got two more years of college and then the Air Force, and because I can't be sure."

"Sure? Jesus, I swear it's yours!"

"Not so loud. What about the others?"

"Others? I—I *admit* I went out with other guys." She smiled and touched the top button of her blouse. "I'm not unattractive, am I, Frank? Even your daddy, the all-powerful Judge Green, thinks I'm pretty."

"What he thinks doesn't matter."

"Ha!"

The waitress brought the breakfast. As she arranged it before them, she said, "I hear the weather's nice in Miami."

"Is that so?" said Frank.

"Very nice. Temperate, the radio says."

Frank ate breakfast. As he buttered a piece of toast he looked at Molly and said, "Eat. Going hungry won't help."

She started crying.

"Neither will that. Wipe your face and eat. It's too late for anything except having breakfast and getting back on the road."

Molly slipped from the booth and ran to the rest room. Frank tried the ham and eggs. She came back and sat down. Her young, fresh complexion was bright from being scrubbed with commercial soap and dried on paper towels.

"I think I'll have breakfast," she said.

"Wonderful," said Frank. "The eggs are good and the ham's great. Try the hash browns."

Molly smashed the sunny-side-up eggs with her fork and mixed the runny yellow into the potatoes and took a bite. "It is good," she said.

"It's great," said Frank. He glanced out the window. When they had come in the sky was lavender. Now it was blue. The sun was up and traffic was brisk on the highway.

"Eat fast," he said. "We've got to be in Miami by two this afternoon."

"Anything you say."

"I'm glad you've decided to be sensible."

Molly took another mouthful of eggs and potatoes and chewed rapidly, speaking as she swallowed. "Hell, I don't know what's sensible. I know I'm still young and attractive and I'm going to make it a point to forget this as soon as I can. After all, it's not like it was somebody. I mean it's not murder. I'm going to forget you, too."

"Eat," he said, "we've got a long way to go."

When they finished, Frank paid the check at the counter. As she gave him change, the hostess said, "We hope you enjoyed your breakfast. If you're going south you can eat lunch at Howard Johnson's in Fort Lauderdale."

Frank dropped the change in his pocket. "We might do that," he said.

Then he told Molly to wait in the car. He went back to the men's room. His stomach was churning. He gagged and threw up his breakfast.

He cleaned himself and went out and got into the car. The waitress and the hostess watched through the window as they pulled onto the highway and headed south.

"Nice kids," said the hostess.

"Yeah," the waitress said, "real nice." She walked slowly back to the table and began clearing away the dirty dishes.

Chapter Eleven

Box 53
Oughton, Georgia
June 11, 1884

Mr. Samuel Clemens   *Bones Mark Twain too*
Farmington Avenue
Hartford, Connecticutt

Dear Mr. Clemens,

   I trust that your journey down the Mississippi to New Orleans with
Mr. Osgood was successful, and that soon you will be publishing a
book about your adventures. I have ordered a copy of *The Stolen White
Elephant*, but I suppose that it will be some weeks before I receive it.
Such was the case with *The Prince and the Pauper*, which, though
requested January last, did not arrive till March, and which I read at
one sitting with *great* delight!

   Since you have expressed interest in the various "curiosities" of life
in this small town in Georgia, I am taking the liberty of passing on to
you the following account of still another which I witnessed recently—and which moves me to ask that question again, "What is
Man?"

Friday and Saturday of last week, the 2nd and 3rd of June, 1884, were days long to be remembered in Oughton. Friday was the day designated for the execution of C. R. Reynolds and L. K. Sapp—both of the Mt. Nebo community—the former for murdering Alfred Lewis, May 2, 1884, just outside the incorporate limits of Oughton, and the latter for murdering Ash Dunway, January 4th, three miles west of Oughton, near the farm of J. W. Rutledge.

It being generally known that the execution would be public, and that Friday was the day set apart for it, a great many people from a distance came in on Thursday evening—to the delight of the merchants—that they might be present to witness it. But on Friday morning the main crowd came—from east, west, north, and south—so by eleven o'clock it was conceded that the largest number of people were in the town to be seen at one time, the crowd being estimated at from five to ten thousand. Of course, with so many people gathered together, on such an occasion, there was a good deal of suppressed excitement—and no little bartering of goods and produce—which was augmented by the announcement, early in the morning, that Sapp had attempted suicide the night before, and was in an unconscious condition, and could not possibly live.

Investigations soon proved that the announcement as to his attempted suicide was correct. At about two o'clock Friday morning, Sheriff Roberts, who was sleeping in the corridor of the jail opposite Sapp's cell, heard his difficult breathing. Going into his cell, he found him unconscious and soon discovered that he had taken poison. Dr. Austin was summoned and every effort made to revive him, but, to all appearance, without success, and the doctor thought he would certainly die. This was the condition of affairs at ten o'clock, when the sheriff, as the time for the execution approached, telegraphed a statement of Sapp's condition to the governor in Atlanta, and asked what he should do. The governor ordered him to suspend Sapp's execution and await further instructions, and by the next mail sent a reprieve for twenty-four hours.

At 11:40 A.M. C. R. Reynolds, accompanied by the sheriff and his deputies and his father, was brought down from the jail and put into a hack to be called to the place of execution, a large lot behind the town square where on the first Tuesday of each month townspeople and farmers meet to buy and sell. Reynolds was seated on the front seat of the hack, his father on one side and Sheriff Roberts on the other. On the rear seat were the deputies, Messrs. Parkman, Bowen, Martin, and Bray. Reynolds was cool and collected when brought down from the jail, and also throughout the ride to the place of execution. He held a beautiful bouquet of red and white roses which had been presented to him by Mrs. M. C. Beckwith, president of the Baptist Missionary Society. A guard, under command of Captain B. S. Hinson, armed with breech-loading shotguns, surrounded the prisoner.

At twelve noon the gallows, erected by F. D. Spence and sons, was reached. The condemned man, still accompanied by the sheriff, deputies, and his father, mounted the scaffold with a firm step. By request of Reynolds, Messrs. Benton, Barnwell, Spofford, and Mudd, ministers, were with him upon the scaffold, for the purpose of administering to him the consolation of the gospel, in these last sad moments.

Perhaps it was due to the heat of the June sun or to the dread expectation of what was to come, but the multitude surrounding the gallows was silent, save for the occasional cry of an infant in its mother's arms. The religious services were opened by the Rev. Benton, who said, "Friends and fellow Christians, it is in accordance with law that we are gathered on this solemn occasion. That the condemned is soon to die reminds us of the shortness of our own lives. While our hearts might be sad under the circumstances, we have God's assurance that if we trust in Jesus, all will be well. It gives me great pleasure to say that Reynolds has always received me and the other ministers in all kindness and utmost seriousness."

The Rev. Benton concluded by reading a portion of the 57th Psalm: "Be merciful unto me, O God, be merciful unto me; for my soul trusteth in thee; yea, in the shadow of thy wings will I make my refuge, until these calamities be overpast."

The Rev. Barnwell spoke next, saying, "It is by request of the condemned that I speak. I am glad to say that Mr. Reynolds assured me that he is not afraid to die, that he has put his trust in Jesus who has promised to be with those who pass through the valley and shadow of death."

Turning to Reynolds, who still held the bouquet of roses, Barnwell said, "You, having committed yourself to God, need fear nothing."

Now facing the crowd again, the Rev. Barnwell said, "Mr. Reynolds has given the local ministers a written communication authorizing us to say to all the world that it was through whiskey and bad company that he was brought to this untimely end."

The condemned man was seen by all to nod in agreement. Then the Rev. Spofford rose and said, "Friends, this is a sad occasion that brings us together this lovely summer day. Let us remember that we will all soon be called to meet our Maker. I appeal especially to all young men to take warning from the fate of Reynolds, lest they should come to some such end. This man, it is true, has committed a crime, but the atoning blood of Christ is able to wipe it away. Many say that no murderer shall enter the kingdom of heaven, but this means that no murderer can enter without repenting. The Bible tells us that all sins—yea every one—may be forgiven, except sin against the Holy Ghost. I have talked with Mr. Reynolds; he has faith and he finds peace through the blood of Jesus."

At this moment a flock of crows, gathered in the pecan trees below the lot, rose with a clatter. Several horses shied and a baby squalled.

But in a moment all was deathly still again and the Rev. Mudd, a great favorite of young people in the community, stood beside the condemned, laid a hand on his shoulder, and, smiling, said: "This man is my brother in Christ. I know for a fact that he has always been eager to receive religious instruction and that he has professed Jesus Christ as his saviour. I trust that his death, like that of Samson of old, will be beneficial to all of us."

Now the Rev. Mudd faced the condemned, placed his hands on his shoulders, and said, in a loud voice so all the multitude might hear: "May the Lord Jesus Christ receive your spirit when done with this world."

The Rev. Benton advanced to the edge of the scaffold and, raising his hands to heaven, said, "Let us pray." Every head was bowed, every eye shut, and it was as still as the tomb, though from a great distance the mournful shriek of a train whistle was barely heard.

"Oh Thou great and holy one, who hearest prayer, and who art a present help in time of trouble, we lift our voices to Thee in this time of sorrow, for we have no other to go to, as Thou and Thou alone, have the words of Eternal Life. We pray that the circumstances of this day may resound to the good of this audience, that many souls may even now at this moment turn to God. We pray that our friend, the condemned, may feel that strength and fortitude which comes alone from on high, and that he may feel assured that all is well and put his trust in Thee. Have mercy we pray Thee oh Lord on his wife and children, his parents and brothers and sisters, and sanctify this affliction to the good of Thy people. And may we all, when done with this earth, meet in an unbroken assembly around thy throne, there to praise Thee forever more. Amen."

A gentle "Amen" swelled from the crowd and there was a flutter of bandannas and handkerchiefs to dry many damp eyes and moist cheeks.

Now after the religious services were concluded, the noose was adjusted around Reynolds' neck. He then with a firm tread stepped to the front of the gallows and spoke:

"What has brought me to this place? Whiskey and bad company. Eleven months ago I came into Oughton and bought the whiskey. How I wish that I had not! But I am prepared to go in this way which is fitting and proper according to the law. I did not choose to attempt suicide as did Sapp. While I do not judge him, nor any man, I advised him not to take poison, that one murder upon his soul was sin enough. Yet Sapp said that he did not intend to be an example to Oughton County. But if my execution will be a warning to the rising generation, I am glad that I am here. You must shun whiskey and bad company lest someday you will stand here in my place!

"I am at peace with God. What a friend we have in Jesus! And I have friends here, too. The sheriff and his deputies have treated me with kindness while I was in their keeping. Eleven months ago I was brought to the jail unconscious, and when the next morning I asked a fellow prisoner why I was in the cell, he replied that it was for cutting Alfred Lewis, a man with whom I had no acquaintance and against whom I entertained no malice."

As Reynolds closed his speech he said that he had some of his pictures for sale and hoped that all of his friends and everybody else would buy them as he had nothing else to leave his wife and children.

A great many went forward and bought copies of Reynolds' pictures. He was very much interested in the sale. During this time the express train from Cedartown to La Grange passed through the distant station, and many men in the crowd by force of habit withdrew their pocket watches and noted the time. The great solemnity which had pervaded was somewhat relieved.

But now the fatal hour was at hand and but a few minutes remained between the condemned man and eternity. The time had come for him to bid farewell to his friends and those around him. He called for the sheriff's little boy, Latham, and, having told him good-bye, handed him the bouquet of roses. He bid the sheriff and his deputies and the ministers farewell. Many others went forward and shook his hand. Last of all, his father, a poor but honest farmer, advanced to take a whispered last parting with his son. What passed between them could not be heard.

It remained for the sheriff to perform his duty. Reynolds was placed upon the trap, his arms and legs were pinioned, and the black cap, ominous of death, was pulled over his face. The last moment had come. The sheriff seized an axe to cut the rope, and in a clear and distinct tone said, "In the fear of God and the name of the State I now execute the law."

The axe fell. The rope was cut. The body of the condemned plummeted from sight to be stopped by a terrible snap. A moan passed through the crowd. In five minutes after the fall Reynolds' pulse was 38, and in 10 minutes it had ceased to beat. In 19 minutes the body was cut down and turned over to his father, who with the aid of male relatives, loaded it into a wagon and, head bowed, drove slowly away.

Upon the return of the sheriff from Reynolds' execution Sapp was found to be much better, being conscious, and during the evening he so far rallied as to call for food. He wished to know of Reynolds' fate, and when told he had been executed at the appointed time and his troubles were at an end, he exclaimed: "I wish mine were, too; I wish I were with him!"

During the evening the sheriff telegraphed to the governor the improved condition of Sapp, and received a reply from him to guard Sapp carefully to prevent another attempt at suicide, and to proceed with his execution the next day, sometime between the hours of the day designated by the judge. The reply was not received till late, about six o'clock, after the large crowd had dispersed to their homes.

During Friday night Sheriff Roberts and his deputies remained in the cell with Sapp. He talked freely with them, telling them he had attempted suicide because he did not want the citizens of Oughton County to see him hanged and that he did not want to be buried in the county. He seemed to entertain a great deal of feeling toward the county, as he thought everyone was against him and always had been. He said the poison he had taken was made by putting match heads in a bottle of liniment which had been obtained for him some time ago by Dr. Austin for heart disease. He suffered a good deal during the night from paroxysms of pain, but at times he was easy and would drop off to sleep. He was not told till next morning that he would be hanged, and he then said to the sheriff that he thought he ought not be that day because he was not well enough.

At twelve o'clock Saturday Sapp was brought down from the jail and placed in a hack with the sheriff and his deputies. He looked much better than was expected under the circumstances. He sat upon the seat quite erect and as he was carried to the gallows he looked first one side, then the other, at the crowd, which was considerably smaller than the day before and was estimated to be at no more than 2,500.

He was accompanied to the scaffold by the Rev. Leathers and the Rev. Diamond, the latter of whom said that by request of Mr. Sapp he would say a few words:

"The condemned is sorry that he attempted suicide. He has confessed his sins and he hopes that God has pardoned them. Mr. Sapp does not believe that he killed Ash Dunway; it was an error that he bought the gun to kill him with since he bore Mr. Dunway no malice."

The Rev. Diamond then drew a picture of the hanging yesterday and the lesson to be learned from it, saying how it should sink into the hearts of the young. In closing, he said, "May God sanctify what has occurred not only to the good of this man, but that sinners may be saved."

Mr. Leathers next spoke. He was glad that Mr. Diamond had told of the moral effects of these executions, that we may have a higher regard for not only the laws of the State, but those of God, that we may resist the beginning of crime.

Sapp had nothing to say, claiming that he was too hoarse to speak, no doubt from the effects of the poison he had consumed.

"Jesus Lover of My Soul" was sung by the multitude under the direction of Mr. Leathers, who then offered a prayer closing the religious exercises. Mr. Diamond then stated on behalf of the prisoner that the reports in circulation about his having committed other crimes elsewhere were false, that Sapp made this statement in the presence of death.

The ministers then left the scaffold and the officers prepared the condemned man for his execution. After the noose was adjusted a good many went forward and told the prisoner good-bye. In a croaking voice, Sapp requested that the black cap not be put over his face because he wanted to look into the faces of those who gathered to watch him die. This plea not being in accordance with prescribed custom, it was denied. Sapp was pinioned and at 1:20 P.M. the ax of the sheriff struck for the second time in as many days. The condemned man's neck was broken and he was pronounced dead in 13 minutes by Dr. Austin. There being no relatives of Sapp present, his remains were carried away by the deputies and on the next day were buried in Potter's Field.

Thus ended the last act of a scene which we trust we may not see again in Oughton. The lives of four men gone, in the prime of manhood, and all on account of whiskey. While there was present at Reynolds' execution on Friday the largest crowd ever seen in Oughton, the best of order prevailed, and not a single drunk was observed.

Finally, it was learned the next day—Sunday—that the bouquet carried by Reynolds had been sought by the crowd, and that the sheriff's son Latham had sold it leaf by leaf, petal by petal, stem by stem, and even thorn by thorn, keeping for himself a single rose as a memento of these sad days.

In closing, Mr. Clemens, I trust that my choice of words has rendered a clear picture of these happenings. A public execution is a terrible event, but if it serves to uplift the morality of a community it may indeed be of some useful purpose. Since Saturday last there has not been a single killing reported throughout the county.

My best regards to you and yours, sir. I look forward to reading *The Stolen White Elephant* and all other works that flow from your pen.

Respectfully yours,
A. C. Henderson (Mrs.)

Chapter Twelve

Harry Edwards heard them as he came from Corday's Department Store and stood out of the rain under the awning on the corner across from the Acropolis Newsstand. They were howling. Like wolves. Johnny Demos who ran the Acropolis heard too. He stuck his bald head out the door and looked up and down the street. And when he didn't see anything except Harry, he waved and ducked back inside.

Harry opened the umbrella he'd bought at Corday's and moved into the misting rain that kept Oughton's square all but deserted. Dogs? he wondered. He went across the square toward the sound.

He had grown up in Oughton but he'd never heard dogs howl so. Of course, he'd been away at the university playing ball and earning a degree in education. This fall he would teach history at the high school and coach junior varsity. But dogs? There was a curious quality about the sound, mysterious, that seemed to affect his nose more than his ears. Made him think he smelled wet fur.

He stopped. Sniffed the air. Shook his head. It was the dampness, not dogs. How could anybody smell them when there weren't any? But what was that sound? Was he being followed? He glanced over his shoulder. Nothing. Except rainwater pattering from a rusty spout. No, there positively wasn't a sign of a dog. Except the howling.

He followed the sound another half block to the corner and called himself stupid. No reason for dogs in the neighborhood. No restaurants, no groceries. In the next block was Bird's Funeral Home. Down the street to the left was the old McIntosh Hotel. Across to the right sprawled an empty lot which fronted the county jail and maintenance garage.

The howling seemed to be coming from the jail. Maybe there's been a break, thought Harry. Sheriff's putting bloodhounds on the track. He listened carefully. No alarms. No shouting. He started to turn back. But then a truck engine revved up to a scream and backed down crackling and popping. The howling stopped. Then, in the lazy hum of rain, it began again, softly—like a whispered question.

Well, I've come this far, Harry told himself. He crossed the street, passed the sheriff's office, and turned down an alley between the jail and the garages. Now the howling was louder. The truck engine sputtered and stopped.

At the foot of the alley beyond the cell block a hill marked by a single large oak sloped to an enclosure inside of which stood several low wooden houses. A chain-link fence taller than a man and topped with glistening barbed wire ringed the area. The dogs were inside. He saw them clearly. They lined the fence like spectators and watched two men standing between a new green pickup and a waist-high wooden box painted the same slick yellow used on stop signs.

Harry found a dry spot beside the oak and folded his umbrella. Beyond the tree to his right a young man in white coveralls was hooking the thick hose from an orange and white Gulf delivery truck to the garage storage tank.

Harry leaned against the oak and observed the two men at the foot of the hill. One was tall and young. He wore his sandy hair in a crew cut and had some sort of purple smudge on his right forearm. The other was older. He was short and stout and had a blue baseball cap pulled low over his eyes. Both men wore khaki trousers and short-sleeved shirts streaked from the rain. Their high yellow boots were splattered with mud.

"All right, George," said the older man, "let's get on with it."

He undid the latch to the yellow box and threw open the lid. A cloud of oily black smoke puffed out. The dogs within the enclosure howled and whined. Harry felt the hair on the back of his neck bristle.

As the young man waited for the smoke to clear, he took a pair of black rubber gloves from his hip pocket and carefully pulled them on. Then, drawing a deep breath, he leaned over and reached so far into the box that only the toes of his boots touched the wet ground. He straightened up slowly and struggled to pull something heavy from the bottom. Harry squinted. Was it a—dog? Yes. The limp body of a large brown and white hound. Harry saw its pink tongue dangling like a worm from its gaping black mouth. Now grasping the dead animal by its fore and hind legs, the young man heaved him into the bed of the pickup. He went back to the box and fished out a small taffy-colored dog and tossed him into the truck.

"All right, Mr. Wiley, that's it," he said.

"Good, George," the older man said. "I'll bring you some more customers." He unlatched the gate and went into the enclosed area.

Up on the hill by the oak Harry rubbed his eyes. It was a joke. People just didn't. Sure—was some kind of act, like in the circus. He watched the dogs in the pen. Didn't try to escape. They cowered and crawled on their bellies across the wet concrete floor toward the man who was coming for them. They whined and nuzzled his muddy boots. And when he reached down to grab them, they licked his fingers.

He seized a black dog and a yellow bitch by the scruffs of their necks. They rammed their haunches flat on the concrete and stiffened their forelegs. But he scooted them to the gate, and held one against the wire with his knee while he undid the latch. They slid easily across the muddy ground to the box.

"Better watch that black one, George," he said. "Rascal tried to nip me."

"He's had his last try," said George. Scooping up the dog by his ears and hind legs, he threw him in the box. The older man heaved in the yellow.

Harry felt his hand aching. His fingers gripped the umbrella handle so tightly that his knuckles showed bonewhite. It was no joke. He had to do something, to run down the hill maybe and—well, do *something*. Tell them to stop. Let them know. Anything!

"It's a hell of a show, ain't it?" said a voice from behind the tree. Harry leaned around the trunk and recognized the driver of the gasoline truck.

"It sure is!" said Harry.

"Yeah, but watch what they do. Man, they got it down pat."

George latched the top of the box and checked the joints on a chromed metal tube that snaked across the mud and connected the truck's exhaust pipe to a fitting at the bottom of the box.

Mr. Wiley got in the pickup and pressed the starter.

"If you listen real close," said the Gulf man, "you can hear them fall down inside the box. They just go plunk, like this." He slapped his fist against his palm.

When the engine caught and raced, Harry looked at the cloudy sky and tried not to listen. A frantic scratching came from within the box. The metal tube slithered sideways as Mr. Wiley gunned the engine. The dogs watching from behind the fence whined. One howled.

Harry heard them fall. It was clear, distinct, no mistake. One. Two. Just like when you take off your shoes and drop them on the floor. And that was all there was to it. George opened the lid, let the smoke clear and dumped the twisted bodies into the pickup. Mr. Wiley swung from the cab and went into the enclosure.

"See?" said the truck driver.

Yeah, I see, thought Harry. He bit his lip. Jesus, he couldn't let them get away with it!

Loudly he said, "That's a brave thing to do!"

"It's a hell of a thing," said the truck driver.

"It's rotten!" said Harry. He turned the umbrella about so the handle was away from him like the head of a hammer. He put the umbrella over his shoulder and started down the hill.

George looked up at Harry coming toward him. He pulled off his gloves and stuck them in his pocket. When Harry reached the bottom of the hill, he unlimbered the umbrella as though he were stepping in the batter's box and said, "That's a rotten job you've got!"

George grinned. "Boy, you can say that again."

"All right. It's a goddamn rotten job!"

"I know," said George, eyeing the umbrella. "Some days it gets me in the stomach."

The driver of the gasoline truck had followed Harry down the hill.

Now he said, "I don't see why you do it. I don't see why you have to go and kill dogs. You ought to find homes for them."

"That's a real good idea," said George. "But nobody wants them."

"Then take them way out in the woods and turn them loose."

George shook his head without taking his eyes off Harry. "It's not as easy as that. They'd go wild and there's no telling what they'd do."

The dogs in the enclosure howled and jumped against the wire.

"It's still a goddamn rotten job!" said Harry.

George nodded. "Yeah, but I just got out of the service and this is the best I could do. I'm still looking, though. I check the paper every morning."

Harry pointed his umbrella at the older man inside the enclosure. "Is he still looking, too?"

"Mr. Budge Wiley? He's the official Oughton dog catcher." He glanced up at the sky and shaded his eyes with his right hand. Now Harry plainly saw the smudge on his arm was a scar, a red-brown patch ringing his forearm.

"Boy," said George, lowering his hand, "this rain is picking up. That umbrella work?"

Harry glanced at the futile bundle of silk and flimsy metal, then reversed the point and handle and flicked it open.

"That's a nice one," George said. "Looks good and waterproof. My school teacher had one just like it. Course, I always use a rain-coat myself. Hey, you're a pretty stout fellow. You play football somewhere?"

"I did," said Harry. "And it's still a rotten job."

Mr. Wiley banged on the wire fence. "George, you ready?"

"Sure thing! I'm always ready, always!" He laughed.

"I don't see nothing funny about killing dogs," said the truck driver.

"Me neither," said Harry.

George looked at one, then the other, and grinned. "You don't?"

Then the dog catcher dragged out two more dogs and a spotted puppy, and he and George tossed them in and shut the lid. Just as the older man was climbing into the pickup, a new Buick pulled in by the enclosure. The driver rolled down the window and waved. The dog catcher swung from the truck and plodded across the mud to the car.

It was, Harry decided, an act of providence straight out of Walt

Disney. Somebody had come from somewhere in the nick of time to stop the madness that was taking place in front of him. Everything would be all right now. They would probably resuscitate the stiffening animals in the rear of the pickup and give them to orphans who need furry pals. While the little fellows choked back their tears and said, "Gee, thanks, Mister," the dogs would whine and lick their thin faces.

The truck driver sensed the same thing. "That guy is after his lost dog," he said. "Son of a bitch. Hope he ain't too late!"

But then the driver of the car reached into the back seat and gave a brown paper bag to the dog catcher. A big grocery sack. The sides sagged and wiggled.

As the Buick drove away the dog catcher held the bag carefully with both hands and brought it over to George. "There's a cat in here," he said. "Going to have kittens. If she gets ahold she'll tear you up. So watch out."

"Wait!" said Harry. "You can't put her in there with those dogs!"

George was holding the cat by the nape of the neck. She yowled and twisted back to grab him. But she could not quite reach his arm because of the weight of the kittens in her belly. "Why not?" he said. "Don't make no difference. They'll get along just fine."

He dropped her in and shut the lid.

Harry listened. No sound, except the rain.

The dog catcher gunned the truck engine. Before Harry could count to three the dogs keeled over. The cat took a little longer, but finally he heard her plump body collapse.

"It's a terrible job!" said Harry.

"I know," said George, unlatching the lid. "Sometimes I get so nervous I almost re-up." He let the smoke clear and then hauled out the bodies. When he came to the cat, he swung her limp body under Harry's nose, laughed, and said, "You know, the gooks eat them." Then, "You play for Georgia?"

In the face of such truth Harry could only turn and start up the hill. The rain was a little heavier now and it made a soft patter on the taut black fabric of the umbrella. When he reached the oak, he looked back. They were loading the box again. The driver of the gasoline truck still stood there with his hands in his pockets, talking to George, and watching.

124

Christ! There was nothing he could do. He laughed bitterly. Oh hell yes—write a letter to the editor! Yeah, nothing concrete! Damn! He kicked the ground. A rock came loose under his shoe. He looked down at the man and measured the distance. They would have a hard time running up the wet hill. He could stand there and give them hell and if they came after him, he'd give them more than that.

He picked up the rock. Sharp and heavy, edged with moist clay, it felt good. There was no telling about a rock like that. He held it out before him and drew careful aim.

Down by the open yellow box George glanced up.

Harry dropped the umbrella and braced himself, his left arm extended, his right cocked behind his ear like a catcher setting to nail a thief at second.

George waved both hands.

"You better do more than wave, you bastard!" cried Harry.

"Sure!" yelled George. "That's all right!" He and the truck driver ducked behind the box while the dog catcher crouched inside the enclosure with the howling dogs.

Harry gritted his teeth and threw the rock. It flew over the box by a good ten feet and bounced off one of the kennels. The dogs whined and raced up and down behind the wire.

George poked his head above the box. "Not bad," he said. "But it's hard to throw downhill. Everybody misjudges the distance. You gonna fling another one?"

"No, that's all," he said. He wiped the mud on his trousers, picked up the umbrella, and walked away. As he went through the alley he heard the ping of wrenches striking metal in the garages and the incomprehensible buzz of voices behind the cell block bars. When he reached the street he thought, *because* there were fewer of them, the sound was worse than before.

At the square he went into the Acropolis and took a *Time* from the rack and looked at the pictures. Demos smiled and said, "Hey Harry, what's up?"

"Two guys are killing dogs behind the jail."

"Yeah," said the Greek. "They used to do that at night, but a couple of months ago Budge Wiley demanded overtime, so now they do it days. And speaking of dogs, what about Georgia this season? They gonna win the SEC? Me, I think Bama and the Bear look good.

Auburn ain't bad. But what do I know, huh? I mean it takes a guy like you Harry who's been there to know what's really what, right?"

Harry frowned, more at himself than at the world. He put the *Time* back in the rack and leaned against the counter and shared his wisdom with the Greek.

Chapter Thirteen

B y now the urge was so much a part of him that the phone call was unnecessary. An anonymous voice whispered: "Full moon, Senator Rutledge." The line clicked dead.

They were proud he was a state senator. Face to face at the gathering they said, "We made you what you are and we will make you more, but do not forget us."

As if I could!

He dialed an outside line and called his wife. Abby's pretty face appeared in his mind's eye as he heard her happy voice.

"Davey, that you?"

"No, me," he kidded. "Put on your clothes and listen."

"Why, sen-a-tor, you have your nerve, and I'm glad you do."

When he told her he wouldn't be home till very late she was disappointed. They were married only two months and the honeymoon wasn't over yet.

"Honey, it's business," he explained. "You know there's nothing I'd rather do than—"

"Don't whisper—I can't hear!"

"—you know. But this is important, swear. Don't wait up."

As he put down the phone, Davey Rutledge visualized his beautiful wife alone in their new house in Sunrise Hills. The big colonial home was a perfect setting for her. Yes, it was as if he built it with her in mind, although the place was finished and he moved in before she came into his life. Their relationship was very romantic and, therefore, very strange. Sometimes he could not help wondering.

He leaned back at his desk. Strange. Of course, *they* said she was part of the plan. They told him the same night they said he would marry her. They proclaimed he had *always* known her—the two years before when she was in the Peace Corps in South America, and prior to that when she was at college, earlier still when she was just a little girl. Their belief wasn't strange. They had ways of knowing. But from the first time he saw her in Judge and Mrs. Green's living room he had this feeling, a nagging—*doubt*. Maybe it was love, pure and simple. "I *do* love her," he declared. She was such a beautiful, intelligent, gracious woman, who wouldn't fall in love with her? *That* was the trouble! And contrary to what they said, he had no recollections of her, none whatsoever.

"There is knowledge and there is knowledge," they said at the time of the last gathering. He felt the full moon sucking at his brain like a white tick. But it wasn't a new experience. He was a senior in high school when they met him after football practice one October evening and said, "Davey, we're taking you home."

He recognized them—important people in Oughton. But names were forbidden because they were too powerful. "A man's name is his identity," they said. "It is enough to know. Put names behind you and trust in knowing."

Davey rose from his desk and paced the thick carpet. Everybody had secrets, and he was no different. That was excellent political rhetoric but he knew it wasn't true. Their influence made him special. He felt the moon rising unseen beyond the horizon. They did not take him home to Rutledge Farms where he lived with his mother and father. It was to another place they drove, far into the primeval country southwest of Oughton, where the giant trees grew, fell, decayed, and renewed themselves untouched by man. There were dark, hidden ravines and swift black streams pulsating through the fearsome land like arteries and veins. The winds breathed hot and cold across the rugged hills and the living stones oozed dank, bitter moisture.

The phone rang. It was Abby, giving him one last chance to come home.

"I wish I could," he said, wondering why she was so insistent.

"But, Davey, I miss you. You don't really have to go? I mean, can't it keep? I've been waiting for you all day. I *need* you!"

He could tell her pretty lips were pouting. She had never been so upset. Still, he had not failed to come home for supper before. "Tomorrow night we'll drive into Atlanta and eat and see a show, okay?"

"But tonight?" Her voice was resigned. "All right, then, if you won't. Don't be too late."

The moon was peeking over the rim of the world and his heart skipped a beat. "I'll be home when I can."

From the beginning the property belonged to them. The deed was secret because the recorder of documents at the courthouse was always one of them and he kept their book hidden. They claimed the land before the Indians. Davey at first worried over that bit of lore, had even tried to check in the regional library. The Indians were here ages before the white man—long before Oglethorpe and his debtors, de Soto, Columbus, the Vikings, before even the mythical Welshman Madoc and the legendary Irish priests. They were hunting the land before the Egyptians and Phoenicians sailed into the Unknown Sea. The red men possessed the land, but they did not venture into this tract. There were tales handed down by shamans and betrayed for rotgut whiskey to whites of strange events in these forbidding hills. *Wheg-gap-nee*. "The Place of Shadows," they called it.

Davey slowed and turned off the highway onto a gravel road. Suddenly, a white face shone from the darkness. He recognized the wild eyes and bushy gray hair. It was Bobby-bob the crazy little man who collected cold-drink bottles for a living. He stood on the road shoulder and watched the car pass. Davey didn't stop. In these woods it was every man for himself.

He focused his attention on the road. It was treacherous now, sudden turns, rises, dips—his muffler scraped, and now it seemed the wide automobile would never squeeze between the hovering clay banks. On every side was night so dark it made him dizzy. The gravel played out and now the surface was soft dirt, till it too disappeared and he drove through the forest on no road at all but a wide rutted path cut in the native stone and filled here and there with drifts of pine straw and cones that popped like dry bones beneath the heavy wheels.

The others were ahead of him, but he was not late. The full moon did not yet float above the massive oak whose gray, splintered trunk was ripped to the heart by lightning ages before; the silver eye of night, that saw into all things, was not yet staring into the cave. He parked beside the last car, a Buick whose tag he recognized, and hurried across the rocky ground to a black hole in the hillside that devoured him like a hungry mouth.

The pine torches sputtered against the January cold, hurling huge blunt shadows through the trees beyond the clearing. Inside, the bonfire burned, hissed. Already they were moving back and forth before the throbbing flames. The three leaders sat above the altar beyond the fire. In the shifting light the symbols daubed upon their skin seemed to crawl like red, yellow, and blue creatures met in dreams.

Davey shed his clothing and joined the circle of dancers. The young woman whose warm hand he held had come to Oughton the year before. He played bridge and golf with her and her husband at the country club. Her lovely small breasts were tinted a delicious pink by the firelight, and the taut flesh of her thighs rippled as she moved gracefully across the stone floor. He felt her casting a spell on him. But he was not here just for that, although sometimes it was necessary if knowledge were to come. Once he did it for all of them, high upon the altar, with a lawyer's wife who was his mother's friend. But now he danced and watched the fire and concentrated on the one thing he wished to know above all else.

The moon entered the cave.

The dancers stopped and faced the light. Behind them, the leaders spoke, their voices made wise by veils of smoke and fire and endless time:

"We gather to know. If our hearts are right we shall know. How then shall our hearts be set right?"

"By dedication," the dancers chanted.

"How?"

"By consideration."

"How?"

"By consecration."

"Aye, and truly our hearts shall be set right and we shall know."

The dancers turned to the fire and, holding hands, moved slowly round it, in the same direction as the moon circling the earth. Their eyes fixed upon the five blazing logs set end to end upon the stone hearth like a falling star. Outside the cave a cold wind howled through the skeletal trees. But Davey was warm. The Circle was formed.

As her spell came over him, he freed his right hand and cupped her breast while they moved. Now she touched him and he felt his power rising like sap in a tree. He loosed his other hand and danced with her alone, their bodies becoming an urgent, conscious one. He laid upon her, her flesh softening the hard earth. About them others were dancing and sinking. He knew a joyous burden drained from his body. When they rose and parted the dancing stopped.

The leaders spoke: "Those who would know may know, if their hearts are right. Who among you would know?"

Davey looked about the cave and saw a cross section of Oughton. There were common laborers, slender of waist with heavy, muscular arms. The Baptist Church and all the other denominations, even a rare Catholic and a lonely Jew stood in the Circle. The wire factory was present, and the plating company, as well as the cotton and clothing mills and all of the enterprises on the square. He saw Rotarians and Lions, Jaycees and Optimists, the courts, doctors, teachers, the rich and poor. The oldest was confined to a wheelchair; the youngest was a girl in junior high whose small perky breasts were hard as green fruit.

"Is there one who would know?"

A man whose body was as unkempt and gray as his hair raised his hands to the fire. Davey knew him as the senator who retired in his favor. The old man said, "I would know the day of my death."

"Are you worthy to know?"

"I am."

"Come to the altar."

His age makes him worthy, if nothing else, thought Davey. As the questioner passed close, Davey saw his trembling body. The knowledge he sought was terrible, yet it would free him for he would know what remained. Davey did not want to know. He was thirty-one. There was much time. If there isn't, he told himself, seeing the elderly man struggling to climb the altar, I don't care to know—yet!

The leaders came together and spoke with him who would know. The fire gnawed the roof of the cave. Someone was coughing in the thick smoke. Now the questioner returned to his place in the Circle, a faint smile on his thin lips.

"Is there another who would know?"

Sometimes it was best to remain ignorant. No, that was a delusion. It was better to know, regardless. Davey felt compelled to ask. Abby was a loving wife. And they had chosen her. Still, there was much he did not know about her. She was with the Peace Corps in the back country of Peru. She was not a virgin. She was a good wife, but she said things—nothing specific—but *things* which made him doubt. He was a state senator and they said in time he would be governor and then something much, much more. There was only one office that was much, much more, and he would not name it because names were too powerful and he did not want to break his spell. Many reputable figures said the Peace Corps was questionable. Abby was a loving wife but how would she affect his career?

He had to know, even though his doubt made him unworthy. He raised his hands to the heat of the flame, saying, "I would know but I am not worthy."

"What would you know?"

"The loyalty of my wife."

He felt the dancers of the Circle tense.

"You must be made worthy. Come to the altar."

The flames bit his legs as he mounted the stone steps. The leaders conferred among themselves. It was not easy being made worthy. Davey tried to free his mind of thought and thus bring knowing unto himself. But he was filled with memories of the other time he stood here upon the great black stone. They had summoned him, Davey Rutledge. It was fated he would be a state senator. His election would come to pass after certain obstructions were removed. Soon afterwards his mother and father died in an automobile accident. It *was* an accident—the sheriff and deputy swore to the fact. Their insurance made possible his successful campaign.

132

"This will make you worthy," said one of the leaders.

He held forth a white chicken. The bird struggled, kicked, made a terrible cry that echoed in the cavern like the stirring of spirits. The fire curled and held the altar in its red hands. It was only a chicken. The moon watched from the mouth of the cave.

"Take, eat, and be worthy," said the leaders.

Davey grasped the chicken by the feet and neck. Its crazed eyes loomed larger than the moon as he plunged its head between his jaws. He chewed the flesh and brains and bone and swallowed it with gulps of the hot gushing blood. He ate the scaled feet, then the dry, feathered wings. The breast was tender and sweet, and the heart's blood washed the clinging down away. He swallowed the warm entrails, but the bones were too pliable to crush, so he spit them into the fire.

"Now you are worthy to know."

They told him all with a simple gesture. He looked. Abby! She was here, in this place. Doubt left him forever. She came into the cave on the arm of Bobby-bob. While Davey uttered a silent prayer of relief, her lovely body fell willing prey to clawlike hands, yellow lips. The dancers wove a narrowing circle about her. She touched them all and they touched her. A minister laid her upon the altar at Davey's feet. The leaders anointed her with black blood and wiped it away with bare hands.

"From this day onward," they said, her beautiful eyes bloody with fire.

Leaves and berries were cast upon the white-hot coals. Bright smoke filled the cave, absorbed the darkness. They danced, together and separately, and while one could not see another, wherever they turned they found the sweet reassurance of warm, willing flesh.

As Davey turned from the highway into Sunrise Hills, the moon hid behind the trees and he felt his body start as though awakening from a deep, mindless sleep. It was always that way. Coming back was worse than going out. Yes, because after it happened he could never be sure what happened. The leaders were powerful. There was nothing they couldn't do. But what did they really do?

It was impossible to say, except in his own case. From no political background and connections, he became a state senator. He remembered his mother and father and gripped the wheel tighter. Abby? "She was there; I saw her," he told himself. "She's one of us, now, a helpmate for my future."

Yes, that settled it. She was to be trusted. Only—

He could never be sure she was there because it was forbidden for one member to speak about it to another. "The power lies in being One," the leaders explained. "We must lose ourselves in order to gain our Self. You must never break the Circle of Self formed by unquestioning faith."

He parked in the garage. Abby's red Triumph was already here. Suppose it was a trick? What did they want, really? According to them, it made no difference which political party was in office, and he had seen Republicans and Democrats at the place. Did not matter either if this was still the United States. The Circle was a thousand times older.

But Abby? He got out of his car. Did he really see her? It wasn't good to doubt them, especially since they gave him knowledge. "But she's my wife and I have a right!" he argued with himself.

And he would exercise his right. He crossed the garage and placed his hand upon the hood of her car. Stone cold!

But he knew he saw her! Someone must've picked her up. After all, how could she know the way?

"Davey, are you in the garage?"

He turned toward her welcome voice. She stood in the kitchen door, the light outlining her lovely figure through her yellow gown.

"I thought it was you. I waited up. Don't be mad."

"Haven't—," he began, starting to ask if she'd been out. But if she were one of them it would break the Circle.

"Haven't I what?"

"Been to bed?"

She smiled and opened the door for him. "You know I can't sleep without you. Besides, I have a great idea for redecorating. Come on, I'll show you."

As Davey trailed her up the stairs, his mind wandered. Where were the bedrooms in the White House? The moon winked at him through the landing window.

134

Chapter Fourteen

J
udge Green cleared his throat and said: "It is the opinion of the court that there is no sufficient reason to bring charges against the accused, George Demos. This hearing is closed."

Deputy George Demos looked at the judge and listened, hearing the words and the hum of the fan turning slowly on the ceiling. Beside him at the table in front of the court sat the sheriff. Demos knew that he was listening. It was very important to the sheriff, a matter of political life and death. The sheriff was a steady man, a just man, even, who greeted the mysteries of life with a half-smile. He was a man to be trusted, thought Demos, recalling how, when it happened, the sheriff told him, "Don't worry; it'll come out all right."

The judge raised his gavel and ended the hearing with a bang. The people in the courtroom stirred, rose, whispered first, then spoke aloud. Demos heard someone chuckle, another laugh.

Now the sheriff squeezed his hand and through the half-smile said, "That was a close one, Demos, but it came out the way it should."

The sheriff told him take the week off. Demos nodded, thinking, Is that all I get? It's not much for killing a man.

"I'll tell Rayfield and Wills," said the sheriff. "Guess they'll like to know how it came out."

"Yes," Demos agreed. They'd like to know. Rayfield with a bullet through his lungs. And Wills, he might never know anything again except that last instant when the rifle leveled on him. "Yes, you tell them," said Demos.

"And you do like I say. Take the week off. You need a rest."

"I'll do that; might even go fishing."

The sheriff patted his shoulder. Then he started around the table. Demos looked up and saw the boy leaving the courtroom. "Wait!" said Demos. "What about him?"

The sheriff's smile faded but only slightly. "Well, what about him? We've been through that. It's done, for now."

"But you know—" It was no use. It was of no importance to the sheriff, to anyone, for that matter, except him, that the boy had caused the whole thing. He caused me, thought Demos, as surely as if he held and aimed the gun, to kill an innocent man!

"Don't think about it," said the sheriff. "See you next week." His shape merged with the other shapes moving from the room.

Demos followed them out, acknowledging with nods the congratulations of the crowd on the courthouse steps. He wanted to stop and tell them again what really happened, how he and the other deputies had been suckered to do a boy's killing, but they did not want to hear that story. They were satisfied that justice had been done, that the reputation of Oughton was not soiled, that it would be business again—as usual.

Demos crossed the parking lot and slid into his car. It wasn't business as usual for Old Red. He started the engine. Old Red was ninety-one when he died, and even though he wounded Rayfield and Wills, he was innocent of any crime.

Demos turned down a shady side street edged with neat little homes in which lived the citizens he was sworn to protect, with his very life, if need be.

He passed the street on which he lived and turned onto the highway leading to Atlanta. He'd go fishing tomorrow. Right now he had to see it again. He had to get the facts straight once and for all.

Left at the store and down the clay road through the pines. The store, the coke sign, BAIT SOLD HERE, and flour and bacon and tobacco— how many times had Old Red come down this road to the store, Demos wondered. An old man with a sack slung over his shoulder trudging along, hearing the mockingbirds and jays, smelling the pines, feeling the sun.

The car lurched in the ruts. Demos wrenched the wheel to the left and pulled into the clearing before the old man's house.

Still sitting behind the wheel, he told himself, It's just a house, no more. Yet, looking at the house, seeing it outlined by the afternoon sun, the first thing you notice is that it's neat, not run-down like some farmhouses. Small, not much larger than a child's playhouse. The old man had painted it recently, had colored it a light blue. Around the door and the single shuttered window he traced a broad white trim— made it somehow remindful of a ship. The shotgun blasts showed black against the trim. The yard was swept clean, but now some weeds were sprouting. A lawn broom still stood against the house, and next to it was a patch of flowers. They were alive with color when Demos came before. Now they were brown.

Demos got out of the car and saw the shed set back from the left side of the house. He smelled the dead mule before he saw the bloated carcass underneath the shed. Buzzards were clawing at its swollen belly. Demos threw a clump of clay at them. They looked at him, then went back to eating. He picked up another clump, then dropped it. "Take it! Pick it clean to the bones!" he said.

He went past the car to the other side of the house. The plowed field opened beyond a clothesline strung between two dogwood trees. A yellowed sheet and faded blue shirt still hung on the line, but now they were tattered from the wind. In the field the corn was half as tall as a man. It was planted right, spaced, but now the weeds were trailing up the stalks.

Demos went back to the woods in front of the car and found the tree, an oak, bigger around than a man's outstretched arms. Up in the thick branches were squirrels and birds. He sat behind the tree, took off his hat, and edged around the trunk till he saw the house.

This is the way it was, he thought, just like this, only it was noon and the sun was flashing off the tin roof and it was hot and still.

Demos went over it again. "Proceed," the radio said, "support Rayfield and Wills. Shooting, man gone crazy, proceed!"

Demos squinted around the tree. He knew the old man was in the house but he couldn't see him, saw only the neat little blue house with white trim. Rayfield was back in the car with a bullet through his chest. The boy was with him. Wills was on the other side of the house.

Ka-boom, ka-boom! Wills fired into the house. He's shooting blind, thought Demos, no windows on that side. He's trying to catch him through the wall.

The impact of double-ought shook the house. The shutter swung slowly open. Demos pressed the shotgun to his cheek and fired. The shutter jumped shut.

"Hit him?" Wills yelled.

"Don't think so." Then the rifle appeared in the window and a bullet dug into the tree. "No, he's still shooting!"

"I'll fix him!"

Ka-boom, ka-boom!

Demos glanced at the small shed to the left of the house. A gray mule watched him disinterestedly. He was chewing a mouthful of hay with slow, deliberate motions.

"How's Rayfield?" Wills called out.

"Don't know!"

"The old goat! I'll fix him!" Wills fired twice, reloaded and fired again.

If I can get across the yard to the window I can take him, Demos thought.

He eased around the tree and stepped forward, crouching, flexing his legs to run. The shutter snapped open. For an instant he saw the rifle bore, black, round, and empty like the mouth of a cannon, then the flame and a bullet creased his cheek. He hit the ground and slithered back to the tree.

"You okay, Demos?"

Demos felt his face. The bullet cut a furrow on line with his ear. Blood ran quick like water into the corner of his mouth.

"I'm okay! Just nicked me!"

"Who the hell does he think he is?" Wills screamed. He fired twice into the walls.

"How about tear gas?"

"How the hell you gonna get it in?"

The house was tight, no openings save the door and window. The door was shut, probably wedged with a dresser or bed. In the center of the door the buckshot had torn a jagged *0* at the place a man's belt buckle would be if he were standing in the opening. It would be hard to lob a gas shell through the door. But the shutter at the window kept swinging open as though the shot poured into the house had rocked it off its foundations.

"Well?" said Wills.

"I don't know, maybe!" He spit out a mouthful of blood and leaned around the tree.

"Get the gas! I'll keep him busy!"

Demos backed away, careful to keep the thick trunk between him and the window. The car was back on the road. All four doors were open. Rayfield was—

Was how? Demos leaned against the tree. Bloody. He was sprawled across the back seat like a side of beef, moaning.

I got the gun and gas shells, Demos remembered. The ambulance Wills called was on the way. I got the gun, then Rayfield started talking. I told him no, but he wouldn't stop. All the time the boy was sitting in the front seat, cool as could be.

Rayfield warned him, told him it was all wrong. "Haven't got a warrant, George," he said. "It's not legal." Then he told him what happened. The boy was a stranger, said he came from the next county, said his dead mama was Old Red's granddaughter. He told Rayfield the old man owed him money and wouldn't pay, said when he went to get it the old man beat him with a stick, said he was so old he was crazy.

They had gone to the house, the three deputies and the boy. Wills knocked once and when the old man didn't answer, the boy said he was deaf. Wills started in. The old man was waiting. Never said a word. Aimed the rifle and fired. He was trying for the boy but he missed. They ran. He fired again and hit Rayfield just before he got to the woods.

"Let him alone, George," Rayfield said. "Let him cool off. Stop shooting before somebody gets killed."

Then Rayfield passed out and Demos asked the boy, "What about this, is this what happened?"

"He crazy," the boy said. "He so damn old he crazy." Then Demos noticed the boy's eyes were cold and lean and hard. And the mouth below the eyes was like a pair of shears hacking the words out of the hot air. "All that his, every damn foot," the boy said, indicating the land with a sweep of his black arm. "One whole section, 640 acres of the best land in this county. Think he know what to do with it? Hell no! Plant ten acres in corn, leave the rest to the damn birds and squirrels. That sound right to you?"

"But the money? He does owe you money?"

Then the boy laughed. "Money? You call twenty dollars money? Hell, I would'a paid it back in a week!"

But we couldn't go off and leave him, not the way he was, thought Demos. Somebody might have come along and the old man would have killed him, thinking he was one of us.

"I tried to tell him," said Demos aloud. "I called to him and told him it was all a mistake."

But the old man said nothing—he never said a single word, not even at the end.

Demos leaned against the tree. Before him the house was still. The shutter, torn ragged with buckshot, was half open. I stepped out and fired the gas shell through the window, he recalled. I saw it go through, heard it pop. Then the house began to smoke like it was on fire.

But the old man did not come out.

Demos waited, crouching behind the tree, shotgun in hand. The gas boiled inside the little house. He heard the shell spinning and twisting on the wooden floor.

"Get it in?" Wills called.

"It's in. Now sit back and give him a chance to come out!"

Wills laughed. "After what he did to Rayfield? Hell no!" He fired into the wall, waited, and fired again.

"Come around to the front!" said Demos. "Let me explain!"

The other deputy worked his way through the bushes. He stopped behind a tree on line with the door of the house. "Okay, what's up?"

Demos told him what Rayfield said.

"That don't make no difference, not now!"

"Give him a chance, he's an old man. He's scared."

"Well, all right. Holler in there and tell him throw the rifle out."

Demos told the old man to give up and he wouldn't be hurt. Then it was quiet, not a sound except for the breeze across the dirt yard and the old man's washing flapping on the line. The mule stood frozen under the shed, his mouth half full of hay.

The door creaked open and the old man stepped into the yard. Demos saw just a man, old, slim, dressed in faded work clothes. His hair was steel-gray, parted cleanly down the middle, and he wore a pair of gold-rimmed glasses.

It happened.

Wills raised his shotgun a fraction and the old man swung the rifle to his hip and fired.

The slug took Wills through the throat and flung him back into the woods. Now, in a single motion, the old man levered a fresh shell, swept the muzzle across the yard toward Demos, past Demos, and shot the mule dead-center through the eye. And in the one blurred motion, Demos pointed and fired the load of buckshot into the slim black figure and saw him bolt back into the house as though he was snatched by a steel spring.

"And that's all there is to it!" Demos said, bitterly. I shot him because he shot Wills, but Wills might have been trying to shoot him. He shook his head. I shot because he was trying to shoot me. But he could've shot me because he went past me and killed the mule. Maybe the tear gas affected his vision. He shook his head again. No, no, it wasn't that. He could've killed me if he wanted, but he wanted to kill that mule more. Now he nodded his head. And I shot him because the gun was there in my hands and he was shooting. Law and justice had nothing to do with it. I shot him without thinking.

He nodded his head again. And all because of a lying boy and twenty damn dollars!

Demos left the tree and moved toward the car. The boy was there, leaning against the fender, a rifle in his hands.

"You trespassing, jack," the boy said, "less you got a warrant." He smiled, his lips cutting back tightly, his eyes changing to slits. "Well, you got a warrant?"

Demos stepped forward.

The boy aimed the rifle at his chest, his finger going gray on the trigger. He laughed. "Why don'cha try it, big man? Wish you would. I'd like to shoot you. One thing I don't like is a trespasser. Guess I got that from my great-grandpa."

"A good licking's all he ever gave you," Demos said, his hands unclenching.

Now the smile broke, the tongue behind it flicked once. "That too. But he give me all this land to boot. That's right, left it to me. Seems I's the only blood he had."

"He had mighty thin blood."

The boy stepped away and brought the rifle to his shoulder. "You sure beg for it, don't you? Guess that goes with being a deputy. Brave man! Hah! Maybe you be brave but you ain't too smart, no sir!"

A bluejay sang. Demos said nothing.

"You ain't talking?" The boy laughed. "Look like I got the drop on you more ways than one." He wet his lips. "I got the law and justice on my side. All legal as a twenty-dollar bill. Got the land, the house, and everything in it. How you like that?"

The breeze reminded Demos. "You got the mule too, didn't you?"

The boy's face went blank. "That was a damn good mule! He done that to spite me. He was a spiteful old bastard!"

Demos got into the car, started the engine and drove away. The mule was still a damn good mule, yes sir. By the time he came to the end of the red clay road and turned up the highway, he felt better— not good, but at least not so bad. What happened was terrible, no doubt about it, but now he felt pretty sure he hadn't seen the last of that boy.

Chapter Fifteen

D riving home he could not stop looking at his reflection in the mirror. He studied it so intensely he lost control and scraped the curb, shooting a screaming shower of sparks into the cold night. Ordinarily such a mishap would unnerve him. Now he gripped the wheel tighter, aimed for the center-stripe, and looked into the mirror again.

That's me, he thought, *me. I've been that all my life, I'll be it till I die.*

Time had made certain changes. In high school his hair was jet black. It started changing in college. Now at thirty-one he was gray. Came from mother's side of family. She was snow white before thirty. There were compensations though. Gray was an asset when you were a VP at Community Bank. Lent maturity, dignity. Inspired confidence. Was worth at least six thou extra per year and all he had do to get it was be born.

The car swerved and he discovered himself careening through the parking lot at Dex Robert's grocery. He wrenched the wheel, hit the brakes, and managed to angle past the windows marked SPECIAL.

In that moment he forgot. But his square chin, blue eyes, and gray hair again appeared in the mirror. He realized with a frown there was more than himself. It was a time machine, the bits and pieces of himself going back, back to the caves and beyond. He glanced away from his reflection. The sky was burning with stars. The moon floated yellow-gray in the west. The dark trees on both sides of the road were losing their leaves. Next Saturday was the Georgia-Auburn game, after that Thanksgiving.

Louise would be home by then. Maybe they'd go to the game, if she was up to it. Football weekend would be good for her. He laughed. "Anything'd be good now!" Yes, get up a party. Ask the Rojacks and some other couple.

Party. He signaled and turned left on to his street. It was the correct prescription. "Maybe we should have a real party, engraved invitations, caterer from Atlanta, the works, and announce the blessed event publicly."

Hearing his own banker's voice speak those words caused another laugh. The thing couldn't be kept secret, not in Oughton—not in any town.

Even now someone at the hospital was telling it. The age of electronic miracles, instant communication. Some good in everything. Taught you science doesn't know it all, not by a long shot.

"Hell of a consolation!"

He parked the car in the driveway, didn't bother to lock it, and went into the empty house. A quart of Cutty was lurking in the cabinet above the refrigerator.

"Have a drink, ol' buddy. Celebrate," he said in a deep voice.

"Thanks, don't mind if I do. After all it's not every day," he replied in a higher pitch.

He downed a swallow. "Slugging from the bottle's not sociable," he said, "or too sociable?"

He took another drink to decide. It was childish, infantile. There was that word! Drank again. Ah, nice, smoother. He pulled out a chair and sat at the kitchen table.

"Bottles are curious objects," he mused, taking another swallow. Could put most anything in one. Even a bottle in a bottle. A bottle in a bottle in a third bottle? An infinite number of bottles. There were Chinese boxes, why not Chinese bottles?

"Ah so," he hissed, "I give you humble Chink bot."

He drank to this toast and added a second. "Also gents, I give—gave—you something to put in it. Hoo-ray!"

144

He was dizzy. Nothing to eat since lunch. Rushed Louise to the hospital before supper. Hours in labor room. Head was spinning. But not from hunger. Was the kitchen. Sonabitch had a curious way of merry-go-rounding when he took a few pulls on the bottle. Yes, right now the stove was eyeing him. And the frig was taking down every word. Dishwasher lurked beneath the counter like always.

Everything would be used against him. He took another drink. The room whirled. He put the bottle on the table and looking the stove straight in the oven said, "I'm a reasonable man so I'll give you a warning—stop!"

He might as well have been talking to a stove. All right, they had their chance. He lurched to the broom closet and flipped the switches, killing them dead. Ah, it was good to have a private drinkie again, so he had three, which was so funny he sobbed.

Poor Louise, was she crying too? "She's just a girl," he informed the lovely sailing ship on the label. "Just a young thing and cannot leave her mo-ther."

Poor damn Louise. He saw her now, in that bed; her face as white as the pillowcase.

Poor goddamned Louise! She was still out. After it happened—came to pass—Doc Spaulding took one look and gave her something. He took a drink. Wouldn't give him anything but a hard look and harder advice.

"You're a man, act like one!" he said. "These things happen. Don't get tough with me, dammit! I delivered you and I'm not too old to give you another slap on the ass! Go home. We'll see what develops."

Develops, like photography. What a negative! Had he not with his own two eyes seen, he could not believe! The nurses wore masks. But their brows spoke volumes.

He took another drink, wiped his mouth on the back of his hand. He wiggled his fingers, glanced at his arm. "I'll never trust my body again, never!" he whispered. It was guilty of treason. He always took such good care of it and now—

There were phone calls to make. Long distance to Louise's parents. Friends. Everybody would want to know.

Poor Louise. At least she didn't know, not yet. Still out. *Out?* Out where? "Am I *in?*" *Out* would be a fitting name for a kid.

What would they call him? Steven Eldridge Floyd, the Third. Number three. His father expected him to do his duty. Three on a match?

"If only I hated my father."

He took another drink. No sweat then. Just say, "Keeping the family line moving, pop. See the resemblance? He's got your—"

A voice called from the back door. "Steve? Anybody home?"

It was Molly Rojack from across the street. Her auburn hair was up on metal curlers and she wore a shapeless quilted robe fastened to the chin.

"Saw the light," she said. "Boy or girl? How's Louise? It's cold, ask me in."

Steve made a clumsy flourish. "Abandon hope all ye who enter here. Have a snort?"

"You're drinking," she said, brushing past him, "but it's part of being a father, I guess. Ken got smashed when I had Kenny." She sat at the table. "You didn't answer me. How's Louise?"

"Beautiful. You want scotch?"

"It's five in the morning. Did she have any trouble?"

Steve found a glass in the cabinet, poured a sloppy drink and slammed it on the table. "Never too early for a snort, only too late." He sat across from her. "She didn't have trouble, not yet."

Molly pushed away the glass. "What's wrong? You aren't very happy for a new father."

Steve laughed. "*Father*, that what you call it?"

Molly's green eyes narrowed. "Something *is* wrong. Louise? What happened?"

"Nothing. Every damn thing!"

She started to rise. "If you won't tell me I'll call the hospital."

"Ah, drink your scotch. I said she's okay."

Molly's fingers circled the glass. "Is it the baby? It's not—?"

Steve took another swallow from the bottle. "Moll, how long we known each other?"

"A long time, all our lives. But so? Why won't you answer me?"

"Drink up. You'll need it. You know, Moll, I could've married you instead of Louise. Don't say anything till I'm finished."

He examined her confused expression. No mask on her face. And confession was good for the soul, or something.

146

"I could've cause we grew up together. Remember we dated some in high school? What all this means is I know you pretty good and vice versa. So I want you to tell me straight. Promise no matter what you'll be honest, okay?"

"Oh, can I speak now? All right, cross my heart."

"In time, as the B-i-b-l-e tells us, all things shall come to pass."

"Good grief."

He pushed the glass at her and smiled as she downed the scotch in one cool swallow. Refilling the glass, he said, "You always could put it away, Moll. That was your tragic flaw. Every guy in high school admired your action, But after that summer day at Jekyll Island when you drank those SAEs under the table they lost heart."

Molly giggled. "All this nostalgia is interesting, but so what?"

"*What* is the clincher," Steve replied. He went to the counter. A bone-handled carving knife was snoozing in the second drawer. It didn't like being rudely wakened, he could tell. Now he opened the frig and, wondering why the light was out, rousted a large frisky carrot from the freshener. Facing Molly, he held the carrot waist-high and said, "This is to test the knife," and slashed it in two.

"You're drunk," said Molly. "Put it down."

He tossed the knife on the table, then unzipped his trousers and exposed himself. As Molly turned away, he found the knife and pressed its glinting blade to his pale flesh.

"Thumbs up, thumbs down?" he asked her. "To be or not?"

"Steve, stop! Just the idea makes me sick!"

"But look at it, take a good look! Tell me what you see!"

He caught her neck and forced her face forward. She struggled but she looked. "What do you see?"

"Dammit, you know!"

Steve released her but he did not cover himself. For a moment he thought Molly would cry. Let her. He might too. But no, she swore softly.

"I'm going to chop it off," he announced.

"Good!"

"I mean it, Moll. It's a fire sale—everything goes."

Now she looked at his face, then at the pale spectacle. "You're crazy, Steve, you really are."

He laid the edge to his flesh. An involuntary shudder shook his

147

head. Body will look out for itself, he thought, but *only* for itself.

Molly touched his arm. "Don't be a fool. What would Louise do?"

"Don't you understand anything?"

"Yes. You said we've been friends a long time, so I'll tell you the truth. If I were Louise I'd want it here when I got home."

"If you were her you'd chop it off yourself!"

Molly frowned.

He laid it on the table. It lumped there like a bloated grub. "It must've been made in Japan, 'cause it doesn't work right. Molly, the kid's a monster!"

"A what?"

"He doesn't have a face. A slit of a nose and another for a mouth. Doesn't really need a mouth, though, cause he doesn't have a rectum."

"But Louise—?"

"She doesn't know, not yet. Did I tell you he has six fingers on one hand? Be a hell of a pianist!"

"Stop, Steve! Listen, doctors can perform miracles. Plastic surgery. Put that ridiculous knife away."

"I'm gonna chop it off and put it in a bottle. Then when anyone laughs and says, 'Why?' I'll say, 'Ask it, not me!'"

"Steve, quit. These things happen. Nobody knows why for sure. There's no deformity in your family, is there? And Louise—?"

"See! You're thinking it! I don't know. If monsters perched in your family tree would you talk?" He felt the thing on the table stir, as though he'd called it by name and it was answering.

"It happens, all the time," said Molly. "I don't know why."

It tightened, stretched, swelled. He watched. Let it go—wouldn't be easy to miss in that shape.

Molly saw it now. "Steve, control yourself!"

"Can't, Moll. Like the joke goes, it's got a head of its own."

It raised up from the table like a reptile testing the air for hostile vibrations. Steve planned his attack. First slash would be downward. Then anything went. Testicles wouldn't escape. Toss 'em on the floor and use a heel.

"Well, Moll, ready for first aid?"

She reached out and took the wavering thing in her hand. "Steve, don't. How can you be sure it's your fault? Abnormalities occur—one

148

in a thousand, ten thousand, I can't be sure. But it happens and nobody knows why. Maybe Louise took a drug, like thalidomide?"

"Doc Spaulding knows about that."

"Okay. Suppose you have a bad gene. That's no reason to mutilate yourself. Get a vasectomy. Lots of guys in our crowd have, like Bill Middleton."

"Screw Bill Middleton! What does he know? He's got four kids and no monsters!"

"He knows how to say when."

"Shit!" He felt the urgent pressure of Molly's fingers. "That's not enough. Somebody's got to pay. You didn't see him."

"Did Louise?"

"Not yet."

"Maybe she won't. Maybe he'll die and she'll never know."

"*I'll* know!"

She looked at the thing in her hand. "It'll know, too, won't it?"

Steve shook his head. "I can never do it again, never."

Molly's green eyes were all seriousness. "Is that what this means to you?"

"It means everything! Don't you understand—I'm the father of a monster! There was a sliver of tongue. It crawled around in his mouth like a red worm!"

"Keep talking, I hear," said Molly. With her free hand she unzipped the front of her robe and pulled it back on her shoulders. In the harsh neon light her small breasts were pale, the nipples bluish. The room was spinning again. Steve found the scotch, took another swallow, heard Molly say, simply, "Well?" heard himself answer, "I can't" and felt his fingers touch her cool flesh.

"I can," she said, standing. The robe settled about her ankles. She wore black bikini panties. There were delicate traces of veins in the whiteness of her thighs. "Come with me," she said, leading him.

"It's not possible!"

"Wait."

They went into the guest room. As she removed the spread he said, "Are you crazy, do you want a monster of your own?"

"I'm on the pill."

"But Ken?"

"I thought you said you couldn't?"

It was not the same with her as with Louise, but it was very good. In twenty minutes she was gone. He stayed in the guest room. Poor Louise. On top of everything he'd committed adultery. But he and Molly had been friends all their lives. That was no excuse. There wasn't one, not even the monster. But he felt different now. The son would die. Under an angel tombstone in the family plot who would know the difference? There were many angels in the Oughton cemetery. But did he have a soul? And what if only his little body were deformed?

Steve left the rumpled bed and examined his body. He was not a Mister America. But he'd played ball in high school and he jogged daily and watched his diet. The hair on his head was gray but everywhere else it was jet black. Moll was amused by that. So were the young wives who hung around the club pool in the summer. Not that they said anything. But he knew.

Still naked, he went into the kitchen, sat at the table and took another drink. Moll was all right. Maybe she knew what she was up to. He grinned. Ship wasn't drawing much scotch now. When he was a kid he dreamed about running away to sea. All kids shared that dream. "Suppose he lives?" he asked himself aloud. "What can I do with him?"

The fair came every August. He'd have a future with the freaks. Nature had a way of compensating. Gave with one shaggy paw, took back with the other. Maybe he was a genius.

As he pondered these mysteries the phone rang. Rojack with murder in his middle-class heart? No. Doc Spaulding.

"Is something wrong? Complications?" asked Steve.

"No, but your dad called."

"You—told him?"

"Dammit, I told him he had a grandson and his daughter-in-law was doing fine. Your dad's on his way over to your place. See you in the morning. We've got to make plans."

"But wait—the baby's—all right?"

Doc Spaulding sighed. "Right enough to live."

He hung up.

Steve dropped the phone on the hook. It was still alive. They all were still alive. Nothing had changed, yet everything had changed, and—the knife. Under the table. The blade making its bright grin at him. He gripped its bone handle and spread his legs. Poor damn Louise. The laughing blade rose over his head and screamed down and stopped.

He tried again.

It was no use. He could not do it.

He stood with knife in hand until the sound of a car door closing stirred him and he saw he was naked. He could not let his father see him like this. As he slipped into his wrinkled clothes, he tried to understand, but reasoning failed him, and when his father called his name, he went out to look into his face with the same dread that sickened him as he peered expectantly into that bundle held by a nurse and discovered his son.

Chapter Sixteen

The doorbell rang as Tom and Ada left the dinner table and came into the living room still cluttered with crates left by the movers.

"The neighbors don't waste time," Tom said.

Ada glanced out the front window. "I don't think it's them. Who do we know drives a black sedan?"

Tom shook his head. "I don't know anyone in Oughton except Ken Rojack and he drives a station wagon."

The bell rang again as Tom opened the door. A young man faced him across the threshold. He wore a conservative dark suit and his blond hair was cut short. In one hand he held a gray snap-brim hat, in the other a small gift-wrapped package.

"Good evening, Mr. Walters," he said. "I have something for you."

"No, my name is Smith," said Tom.

"This is 550 Cedar Street."

"Yes, but my name is Smith."

"Who is it, Tom?" Ada asked.

"Wrong address," he said over his shoulder.

"It's the right address," said a second man who had been standing against the wall out of Tom's line of sight. Now he stepped into view.

A giant of a man, he wore a neatly tailored dark suit which, except for size, was the mate of his partner's.

Tom glanced at his square, solid face, then said, "It may be the right address, but we're new here. Just moved in this morning. Our name isn't Walters. It's Smith, plain Smith. Sorry."

He tried to close the door but the big man put his foot in the opening. "Now, see here—" Tom protested.

"No, *you* see here," the big man said.

"The address is right," said the young man, "so this belongs to you." He placed the package in Tom's hand. "Our employer wants you to know he has his eyes on you, no matter where you go. Open it."

"But I'm not—"

"Do what he says."

"You have your nerve!" cried Ada. "I've got a good notion to call—"

"No, Ada, wait," said Tom. The two men seemed to mean business. Besides, what if it were some kind of practical joke cooked up by the fellows at the new job? He turned to his wife. "Shouldn't you put the dishes in the washer?"

"I'm not afraid of them! This is America!"

Tom balanced the package in the palm of his hand. "Yes, of course. But see about the dishes, okay?"

As Ada retreated to the dining room Tom loosened the gay ribbons binding the package. There was a lacy silver bow, and the red and green paper was of a slick metallic finish. He peeled away the covering as carefully and steadily as he could. He did not want to drop it. For a reason he could not quite understand, it seemed important that, like Ada, he not let them know he was frightened.

Beneath the paper he found an ordinary small white box, the type jewelers use for bracelets and necklaces. Tom examined it and hesitated. It had to be a joke. Sure, when he opened it, an elastic snake would zoom out and the two ominous callers would yell, "Surprise!"

"Open it," the young man said, a smile on his lips.

Tom sliced the tape on each side with his thumbnail and, bracing himself for a shock, slowly lifted the lid. A layer of cotton greeted his eyes.

"Go on," the big man said.

153

"All right." Tom drew a deep breath, lifted the cotton and blinked at the two shell-like pink objects resting on a second layer of cotton. Ears! A pair of human ears, crusted with dried blood along the edge!

The shock of such a terrible sight drained the blood from his head. This was no joke. Whose ears were they? Each lobe bore a small dark dot. Pierced. They had to be a woman's ears, or a girl's.

The young man laughed. "Now do you know who you are, Walters?"

"I—I'm—what does this mean?"

"Mean?" said the big man. "Tell him what it means."

"It means our employer wants you to be a very, very good boy. It means you should keep your big mouth shut. It means if you play ball with us you'll see your kid again. That's what it means."

"My kid?" said Tom. He strained to look past the two men on his porch. Yes, there were his son and daughter playing across the street with the neighborhood children—and his Sue's ears weren't pierced.

"Now you know what we mean," the young man said. His cool blue eyes narrowed. "Stop playing dumb, Walters. You're wasting our time." He pointed to the ears. "Keep quiet till the investigation dies and you'll get the girl back."

"Ears can be fixed," said the big man. "Death can't. Understand?"

Tom nodded slowly. Who wouldn't understand that? The small box cupped in his fingers weighed a ton. He had to put it down, to get rid of these monsters, but he couldn't forget he wasn't the man they were after. Replacing the lid on the box he said, as calmly as he could, "Suppose you're wrong, suppose I'm not Walters?"

The young man frowned. "In that case we've made a mistake, which is very bad for us. But we never make mistakes. You *are* Walters."

"Yes," Tom lied, his mouth as dry as Death Valley. "Yes, yes."

"Sure you are," said the big man.

"Yeah, okay, we'll see you around," the young man said. "No hard feelings, Walters. We're just doing our job." He extended his hand and, as in a trance, Tom shook it, feeling the cool dampness of his flesh.

Tom stood in the open door, the box in his hand, and watched them go to their car. The children across the way ran in crazy patterns over the green lawn, squealing incoherently, as a third man came around

154

the garage and slid into the back seat. The big man started the engine and backed down the drive. Good grief, they weren't going to—but yes, they were. At the street the car stopped momentarily and all three gave him a cheery wave.

Not until the car passed out of sight around the corner did he move. Then it was at the hurried insistence of Ada, who brushed past him to shut and lock the door and exclaim, "Quick, call the police! I got their license number!"

"But the children—" he said.

Ada dropped the envelope on which she had jotted the identifying numbers and slapped her hands to her mouth. "I forgot them!" she bawled. She shoved Tom aside, undid the door, and ran down the walk, frantically calling, "Sue! Tommy!" The children stopped playing and stood dumbfounded as she swooped down upon her two and convoyed them home.

By then, Tom regained his presence of mind enough to turn his son and daughter back from the door and take his wife into the kitchen. He searched through the cabinets, found a half a bottle of bourbon and two glasses, and poured a pair of neat drinks. He placed the small box on the table between them.

Ada said, "This is a hell of a time to drink! They're getting away!"

"I don't think we want them caught," Tom replied. He nudged the box toward her. "Do you know what's inside?"

She had forgotten the box. Now she took it in both hands and wrenched off the lid. The contents spilled across the table. For a moment she was speechless. Then, choking, she sobbed, "Ears! Human ears!"

"Yes, ears," Tom said, and then he told her the young man's message.

As he spoke, Ada stared at the ears. When he finished she said, without looking up, "They've made a terrible mistake. What can we do?"

"I don't know. Calling the police would be insane."

"We'll move away! Right now, this minute!"

"No, that would be worse than calling the police. Don't you see, if we leave town this *employer*, whoever he is, will believe we really are the Walters. We've got to stand fast as though nothing happened."

"Nothing? But something *has* happened. What about those?"

Tom picked up an ear in each hand, gingerly with thumbs and forefingers, as he'd grasp a pair of kittens.

"You touched them!" Ada cried.

"Do you want me to leave them on the table? They do belong to someone, you know—they said to a little girl."

"I don't care. Drop them into the garbage disposal."

Tom studied each ear, then packed them in the box between the two layers of cotton. "We can't throw them away."

"What do you mean, we can't?" Ada said. "I can't live in this house with them! You've got to do something."

Tom took a generous sip of bourbon. "What if I do and those men realize they've made a mistake and come back? They'd be overjoyed to hear I threw them away."

"There must be some other way," said Ada. "Maybe we'd better do the right thing and get it out in the open. I'll call the police if you won't."

"I told you we can't. Listen honey, did you see the third one? He was watching the back yard."

"While I was in the kitchen?"

"Yes, he was out there keeping an eye on you and the back door."

Ada looked over her shoulder at the unlocked door. "I don't believe you. You're trying to scare me into keeping those—those *things* and doing nothing."

Tom opened the back door and went down the steps into the yard. A set of deep footprints marred the flowerbed beneath the kitchen window. "Those are fresh tracks, see?" he said.

Ada saw. "There *was* another one." She glanced along the wall and into the hedges. "Are there more?" she whispered.

"I don't know," said Tom. "But I wouldn't be surprised."

As they went back into the kitchen Ada tried to speak. With desperation in her eyes, she said, "What—what are we going to do?"

Tom picked up the box and went to the counter. The only thing we can. Nothing."

"But the ears, what about the ears?"

"We'll keep them," he said, rummaging through the counter drawers.

"But how, where? Not in the house! Tom, I couldn't stand it. Go to the bank in the morning and get a safe-deposit box."

156

"Won't work. After a while the smell—ah, here's what I want."

He withdrew a package of plastic bags, shook one open, dropped in the box, and twisted the plastic closed.

Ada collapsed in a chair at the table. "You're not going to put those ears in the—"

"Yes, the freezer," Tom said. He opened the refrigerator, and as a cloud of icy air settled about his head he reached deep into the snowy box at the top and deposited the package between containers marked "turnip greens" and "liver." Then he closed the door and turned to face his wife.

"Let that be a warning," he said.

"A warning?" she moaned. "A warning of what?"

He leaned his dead-tired weight against the refrigerator and thought about it. After some moments he replied simply but honestly, "I don't know, of everything, I guess."

While his wife cried softly, he took her hand and they went out and sat on the porch of their new home and watched their children play.

Chapter Seventeen

There was a forbidding air to the mountains, an ominous cast which McBride sensed was caused by something more than intelligence reports of enemy in isolated pockets.

He pulled the jeep to the shoulder of the sinuous road and looked back beyond the steaming jungle to the clearing far below. The wire protecting the HQ resupply compound glinted in the sunlight. Plumes of dust marked the planes as they landed with ammo and fresh troops, then wheeled about, loaded, and took off with the wounded and dead.

He watched one plane climb and draw away until it vanished in the Asian sky; then he turned to the peaks at his back. It would be good to go home, to leave this jungle, this war, and have a small church somewhere, and deal with civilian sins again. It wouldn't be as exciting, but—even chaplains got killed. The enemy made no exceptions.

McBride shifted into low gear and steered off the shoulder. Two hours later he was in among the peaks. The jeep strained over ruts which passed for a road but were really watercourses down which muddy torrents poured in monsoon season. As he drove upward, he kept his carbine within easy reach. "Not that I'd kill anyone," he told himself, "but I'll bluff if I have to."

The shadows grew and gathered as the jeep groaned on. McBride felt he was being stared at, that things were moving there in the dark rain forest where no light came even at noon when the sun stood still as Joshua's in the blue sky. Once as the jeep lurched into a hole he felt a barely perceptible sliding, and when he looked back a huge snake was thrashing in the throes of death. There were creatures in the jungle, eyes nonhuman as well as human watching the road. Now he was glad he brought the carbine. He heard himself say, "I still won't kill anyone, but I might shoot at them."

As he came around the next sharp turn he had to brake suddenly to avoid crashing into a tree that had fallen across the road. Ambush! He shut his eyes, bent down in the seat, and prayed for his enemies, at the same time feeling for the carbine. But the quick stop had thrown the weapon to the floorboard and his fingers found only his Bible. McBride clutched the book. Asking God for strength, he thrust it above his head and shouted, "I come in peace!"

"Peace yourself," a voice replied.

McBride opened his eyes. From the murky shadows at the exposed roots of the tree stepped a soldier. He carried a M-16 over his shoulder, his finger on the trigger, the gray muzzle aimed at the heavens. An inch of yellowish cigarette dangled from his cracked lips. "You lost, buddy?" he asked.

"I'm a chaplain," said McBride, pointing to the cross on his helmet. "HQ says you men in the mountains haven't had church services for months."

"Today Sunday, sir?"

McBride swung out of the jeep. "No, but it makes no difference. In this man's war you have to take church when you can get it."

The soldier laughed. "Just like everything else, sir."

McBride almost smiled at the ironic tone of the man's voice. But there was something about him he didn't like. His torn uniform was streaked with sweaty dirt. McBride smelled a foul mustiness. His rifle was clean, though, and so was the long bush knife stuck in his web-belt.

"Where's your command post?" McBride asked.

The soldier spit the cigarette from his lips and pointed behind him to the slope. "We got us a nice place up there."

159

As they started up the hill, McBride said, "Who's in command? HQ said there's a Captain Garcia and two lieutenants."

"*Was*," said the soldier. "Ragusa's boss now."

The clearing at the top of the mountain was less than two hundred feet in diameter. In the jungle around the edge the men had dug bunkers and built hutches. In the center of the clearing stood a pile of stones higher than a man could reach. Around the stones on four sides, like cardinal points of a compass, were shallow fire-pits.

As McBride and the soldier stepped from the jungle, a tall man with a short red beard trotted from a nearby hutch. He snapped off a salute and said, "Master-sergeant Ragusa, sir. Acting company commander, sir!"

McBride returned the salute and looked the man over. He wore fatigues chopped off above the knees. The milky skin of his chest, arms, legs, and even his feet was decorated with scores of intricate tattoos—hearts, girls, daggers, strange animals, stranger inscriptions. His eyes were blue as tropical sky; his smile was even and very white.

"At ease, sergeant," McBride said. He told him who he was, why he had come to this outpost. Ragusa saluted again, did a smart about-face and barked commands across the clearing.

As if by magic men appeared in the jungle, the hutches, the bunkers, and moved quickly into the clearing. Near the rock pile they formed four ranks and came to attention. Ragusa reported to McBride that the unit was ready to hear him.

"Have them fall out, then, Sergeant," he said. "Let them relax, sit, have a smoke. God's word comes as a comfort and a strength, not as an exercise from the drill manual."

"As you wish, sir," said Ragusa, grinning.

The men settled in a semicircle facing the rocks. McBride climbed upon a large stone at the base so they might see him clearly and so he could look into every face. Before he spoke, he glanced past them to the jungle and beyond to the empty sky, the far peaks. The sun was lower now, and shadows were closing in like hungry mouths over the bright spots in the valleys. Soon it would be night. The enemy was out there, too.

160

McBride opened his Bible to Psalms and read slowly in a tone calculated to drive back the dread that crept into all men's hearts. "Yea, though I walk through the valley of the shadow of death I will fear no evil, for Thou art with me. Thy . . ."

The men listened, quietly, patiently. They heard the scripture through and allowed him to explain the verses in terms of their own lives.

"Never doubt that God is with you," said McBride. "He is with you always, just as He was with His people in the time of David. Yes, even here in this outpost so far from home, so close to the enemy, He is, too."

When he finished his sermon, McBride invited any who wished to establish or to reaffirm their faith to come forward while all sang the first verse of "Onward Christian Soldiers." Sergeant Ragusa joined him on the rock pile and led the singing in a loud, pleasing voice which seemed to reach across the jungle slopes and echo from the distant hills. To McBride's surprise and delight, fourteen said they wished to unite with God. After he spoke to them, Ragusa led them all in singing the doxology.

McBride jotted down the fourteen names for the Chaplains' Record, then raised his Bible above his head and blessed them all with a benediction:

"In the name of the Father and of the Son and of the Holy Spirit, may peace abide in your hearts now and forevermore, amen."

A breeze stirred the darkening trees and raised small dust devils near the pile of stones.

As the men dispersed, Ragusa said, "A good service, sir."

"Their response is heartwarming."

"Yes sir. Will you be leaving now, sir? Night comes fast in these mountains, and then it's Charlie's turn."

McBride squinted at the sun. Perhaps two hours of light remained, probably less. Going down would be quicker than coming up. And he hadn't planned to spend the night.

"We'd ask you to take chow with us, sir," Ragusa said. "But if you don't go now you'll have to wait till morning."

Several men in the clearing looked at McBride. He sensed the way they felt. He could come and go. They had no choice. A power over which they had no control held them captive atop this peak. Some would never come down alive.

Going down the slope to the road, McBride asked the sergeant if he had any messages for headquarters. "None, sir," he said. "Just tell 'em we got a handle on things up here. Old Charlie's hanging tough, but so are we."

As they neared the jeep, McBride heard movements in the jungle. Ragusa threw his automatic rifle to his shoulders and gestured for silence. McBride crouched by the front wheel, his Bible over his heart.

A soldier came out of the trees and walked up the road. Ragusa lowered his weapon. "Hey, sarge!" the soldier yelled. "We got just what you ordered!"

Now a half-dozen troopers came from the shadows. McBride stood up. The first soldier saw him and froze. McBride read the name tag on his filthy shirt: Garcia. The captain's tracks on his collar blinked like narrow yellow eyes.

"Come on in," said Ragusa. "This is the chaplain. He doesn't bite. Give him a salute."

The soldier wiped his hand on his pants leg and made a halfhearted salute. McBride nodded.

Ragusa said, "All right, you guys, hump it to the clearing. The chaplain was just leaving."

Four of the six men carried poles over their shoulders from which something heavy was slung. In the gathering darkness McBride couldn't make out what kind of animals they'd killed. Pigs and deer lived in the jungle. When the men passed the jeep he saw, but he didn't believe his eyes. Two natives, blindfolded and gagged, were suspended hand and foot on the poles. One looked like a boy. There was no mistaking the other—a girl. Her shirt was ripped open.

"Prisoners, sir," Ragusa said.

"What will you do with them?"

"Questions and answers, sir. You might let S-2 know we picked them up."

"I'll do just that. And what about Captain Garcia? One of your men told me—"

162

"That Garcia's dead? He is, sir. That was no spook you saw. Smith's shirt rotted off his back, so we gave him the captain's, since he didn't need it anymore."

"You should strip the insignias."

"Yes, sir." He smiled. "But this way the natives think we still got leadership."

McBride got in the jeep and started the engine. "I'll tell HQ to send you an officer."

Ragusa snapped to attention and saluted. "Yes sir. If you make it to the valley before dark you'll be okay. On behalf of the men, I want to thank you for coming, sir. What you said up there in the clearing means a lot."

Now the shadows were closing in and the narrow road was a tunnel leading him deeper and deeper into the dark heart of the earth. Through scattered rents in the treetops he saw the blackening sky, and he thought how good it would be to drive into the HQ compound again, and shower and change clothes and have a hot meal. From a distance these mountains were beautiful. But when you reach them, thought McBride, they're strange. Some sort of low, furry creatures darted into the road. He swerved the wheel to avoid them.

Ragusa's face flashed before his eyes. What were those troops doing on the peak anyhow? Where were the enemy?

McBride's foot touched the brake. And the boy and woman, what about them? Ragusa said questions and answers. The jeep slowed. Those tattoos. Questions? Ragusa looked like a man who knew how to ask questions that would be answered, eventually. A woodcut in the musty volume at the seminary library came into his mind. Hooded figures. Whips weighted with lead. Tongs. The Inquisition.

McBride pulled onto the shoulder of the road and shifted into neutral. It was all but dark now. Another thirty minutes and he'd be safe in the valley. He glanced back at the way he'd come. A hot breeze fanned the jungle with a hum like beating wings, or breathing. And now, softly, he heard a second sound. A cry? Moan? The flesh on the back of his neck tingled. It was an animal calling to another animal, that was all. Or was it?

"It can't be them," McBride told himself. "Sound carries in the mountains, but not this far."

Yes—but what if it were them, the boy and the woman? They had been trussed like beasts from poles. Suppose Ragusa were putting questions to them for which there were no answers? McBride saw the carbine on the floorboard, the Bible on the seat. He was an officer, even if he was a chaplain. Someone had to be responsible.

McBride turned the jeep around. Now almost all light was gone from the sky. The trees on either side stood like overhanging layers of rock that would bury him without a trace. He switched on the headlights from time to time. It would be better not to march straight into camp. Best to scout them first. Then if nothing was wrong—No one liked to be suspected. If Ragusa was torturing the prisoners in violation of the Geneva rules— McBride drove with one hand and felt for the carbine on the floor.

He parked the jeep by the fallen tree and backtracked the road a good hundred yards before striking into the jungle. Wet branches and sticky vines grasped at his body as he felt his way uphill through a darkness that blotted everything, even his hand held before his face. As best he could, he kept to a route paralleling the one he had taken to the clearing.

The way was growing steeper when McBride heard noises. He paused, choked down his labored breathing, strained to hear. A steady thump-thump like the beating of a drum—no, more like pounding on a tree trunk. And now he heard a second sound, mournful, not animal. Human chanting.

McBride clutched the slick vines and pulled himself closer to the top. Now the sky above lightened and he saw sparks rising through a veil of smoke. For a moment he felt silly. What if Ragusa and his men were doing nothing more than cooking chow and singing native songs? He would have to spend the night on the mountain or try to drive the jeep down in the darkness. The enemy would be waiting in the jungle. McBride cursed his stupidity. A chaplain was supposed to believe in his fellowmen, trust and love them. I could barge into the clearing and say I got lost, he thought. Sure, they'd like that. Such idiocy would confirm the enlisted men's opinion that officers were fools.

McBride continued up the slope. When he reached the top he

164

crawled across the level area toward the light. Through the undergrowth he saw the dark shadows of the hutches. The fires blazed beyond. The men were gathered in the clearing.

He moved closer, careful now to prevent the slightest noise that would give him away. The soldiers sat in a semicircle before the rock pile, chanting words McBride could not understand. He reached a hutch, then darted forward into a bunker within the flickering circle of light cast by the fires. Ragusa's voice rose above the chanting. He stood atop the rock pile, naked except for some kind of animal skin draped like a cowl over his head and shoulders. The grotesque markings upon his body seemed to come alive in the wild firelight. Holding his hands to the heavens, he exhorted the men to louder and more frenzied chanting, crying:

"Yea, though I walk through the valley of the shadow of death, I will fear no evil, for Thou art with me!"

From his hiding place McBride watched. Out of a hutch across the clearing came four soldiers carrying the captive natives slung on poles. What was Ragusa planning? McBride felt his hands instinctively raise the carbine. He forced it down. No, Ragusa was no ordinary man, that much he had seen by the way his men obeyed him. This is just a clever trick he cooked up to get information from prisoners, McBride reasoned. Sure, they were uneducated, were highly superstitious. Ragusa was simply playing upon their fears.

But now from the other side of the clearing came five soldiers dressed in skins like the sergeant. Four carried among them two logs. The fifth dragged a rope on which were tied a number of round objects. As they came nearer the fire, McBride's hands trembled. Skulls! Strung together on the rope. The soldier placed one skull in front of each fire and handed the fifth to Ragusa. The other soldiers put a log in a hole by the rock pile and raised it high above the clearing. Now they lashed the second log across the first. McBride recognized the form they built. A cross. But it was inverted. The horizontal piece was barely three feet above the earth.

Ragusa kissed the skull, held it above his head, and sang: "Praise Him from whom all blessings flow, praise Him all creatures here below, praise Him above ye heavenly host, praise Father, Son, and Holy Ghost."

Now the soldiers cut loose the boy, untied his blindfold and gag, and brought him before Ragusa.

When the boy saw the terrible shape above him, he cried out and tried to flee. But the soldiers caught him in an iron grip and Ragusa made over him the sign of the cross and chanted: "*Hoc est corpus*!"

Now McBride knew. Witchcraft. Black magic! Ragusa had no intention of questioning the prisoners. He would use them in a bloody heathen rite.

Unless he, McBride, stopped them. He checked the carbine, released the safety. No time now for reasoning. Some ideas defied reason. If he could get the jump on them and deal with Ragusa, maybe the others—

McBride leaped from the bunker, aimed the carbine at Ragusa, and shouted, "That's enough, Sergeant! Let him go!"

"Ah, you've come back," Ragusa said. He nodded once, and McBride cried out in pain as the point of a knife jabbed between his shoulder blades. A soft voice said in his ear, "Drop the weapon, sir. Don't make no trouble." McBride let the carbine slide through his fingers and tried to bluff it. "You're in trouble, soldier, big trouble!"

"Yes sir. Now head for Ragusa."

The sergeant came down from the rock pile and faced him. "Took you long enough to get back," he said. "We thought you wouldn't leave in the first place."

"Take off that costume and get back in uniform, sergeant! Call off the show." McBride tried to laugh, but the dryness in his mouth choked him. "Black magic went out with the Middle Ages."

Now Ragusa grinned. "And your white magic, is it still in force?"

"Religion is not magic."

"That's right," said Ragusa. He held the skull before him. "This is our religion."

"*Our?*" McBride searched the circle of faces. "Does Ragusa speak for you, men? Have you forgotten the God of your fathers?"

"He don't listen to grunts, sir," one soldier said.

"Nor to fools!" McBride said. He went from face to face, trying to convince the men. "Don't let this maniac destroy you!" His eye caught the soldier wearing the captain's shirt. "I'm not blaming you, men. You're without leadership. But you must do what's right. Take Ragusa into custody. Free your prisoners."

166

The soldier with Garcia's shirt stepped forward. "Don't let anybody fool you. We've got officers. *I'm* Captain Garcia."

"What?" said McBride. "But you said—Ragusa— You're a disgrace. Pull yourself together, man, before it's too late."

"And getting later," said Ragusa, as the fire sprang to life anew. "Garcia, take three men and tie up the chaplain. A man of God shouldn't hurt himself. Put him by my bunker so he won't miss anything."

"Want me to gag him?"

"No, let him scream his holy guts out." The sergeant looked up at the night sky. "*He'll* like that."

McBride made a futile effort to break away, but they had him before he moved two steps. As they tied his hands and feet he said, "God is with you! He will save you!" But they ignored him.

When he was bound securely, Ragusa knelt at his side. "Man of god, we need you for this ceremony just as we need those men who affirmed their faith today. In order to know the Power, one must renounce the other power. We have the Power. Two nights ago we almost summoned Him. Tonight He will appear."

"It won't work!" McBride said. "It can't!"

"It can, and it will. Don't you believe in Satan? If you believe in god you must believe also in Him." He raised his arms and drew them about his chest as though seeking to cloak himself with the immensity of the night.

"He is here. He was at Bull Run, at the Little Bighorn. He was present at Verdun, at Normandy, at Hiroshima. He was in Korea. He is out there, in the darkness, waiting for our prayer. I can feel Him near. Tonight He will come!"

From where he was placed in front of Ragusa's bunker, McBride could not avoid the ghastly spectacle. As the drummers cast an hypnotic spell, the soldiers moved like sleepwalkers in a weaving pattern among the four fires and the pile of stones. Ragusa sang a monotonous chant. The men answered with howls, then fell silent.

"The time has come," said Ragusa.

In the stillness broken only by the crackling of the fires, they put the boy upon the inverted cross, feet up, head down, and spiked his limbs to the logs with bayonets. The boy screamed, but no one, no

167

thing, came to his aid. McBride roared at the men. They did not, would not, listen to him.

Now as the boy twisted upon the blades, five soldiers dragged the woman out of the shadows into the circle of light which twitched in the darkness like a ravenous mouth. They stripped her, spread her upon the rocky earth, and raped her, silently, methodically, one after the other.

McBride answered her screams with his own, mixed with curses and prayers, until his voice died to a croaking hoarseness. But he could not stop his ears, and as long as he heard, he could not shut his eyes to the fear, the suffering, the evil.

Now Ragusa approached the cross. Chanting the name of Satan, he took a glistening knife from a soldier's hand, kissed the blade, drew its razor sharpness once across the boy's throat, then once from his severed head upward to his crotch. A fountain of steaming blood gushed over Ragusa. He accepted it with eager lips, caught it in cupped hands, sprinkled it upon those near him. And now, crying like a beast, he tore open the boy's chest, plunged in his fingers, and wrenched free the heart still hot with life.

Bearing the dripping heart uplifted before him like a brimming chalice, Ragusa scaled the pile of rocks, moving upward until he stood upon the pinnacle outlined against the leaping flames. His immense flickering shadow eclipsed the clearing and rushed out for the distant peaks.

"Oh Holy Father Satan!" he cried. "One only true God! Our Creator and Preserver! Appear to us, Your children!"

McBride strained to shout down this sacrilege. But only a whispered "no" passed his dry lips. He fought the ropes binding him. It was no use. The abused woman at the foot of the cross pulled herself to her knees and screamed. At a nod from Ragusa, the soldiers hacked her body into four pieces. They laid these quarters of human flesh like offerings upon the campfires. As the meat spat in the flames they wiped their bloody hands upon their faces, and cried again and again, "Satan! Satan!"

McBride shut his eyes and implored God to strike them down. But no angelic trumpets resounded in his ears. There was movement behind him in the jungle. A heavy coldness slipped across his legs.

Then another. Snakes! They were coming out of the shadows into the light. By the hundreds, their slant eyes burning with green fire.

Now other creatures followed the snakes. Four-footed, furry things. Rats! They swept over McBride like a wave of foul water. And now other forms swarmed and scuttled. Horrible shapes with hard, bristly bodies and thousands of churning legs. Spiders, centipedes, all manner of crawling things.

The creatures of darkness converged upon the center of the clearing and flung themselves upon the pile of rocks. Up, up, they slithered, crawled, scurried. Ragusa greeted them with open hands and guided them about his naked, sweating body. A mist rose hissing from the earth about the stones, shattering the firelight into jagged rainbows of green, purple, yellow.

Ragusa tilted his face to the yawing pit of darkness above and cried out: "Our Father, who art in Hell, hallowed be Thy Name! Come unto us, Father Satan, come!"

At the sound of his voice, a pair of red lights kindled in the heavens overhead. A humming stirred the night. The lights grew larger and larger, brighter and brighter, and blinked like gigantic eyes awaking from eons of sleep.

The men fell upon their knees and howled with Ragusa: "Satan, we are Yours!"

Now the red lights opened into a yellow, feline brilliance illuminating the clearing, the jungle. Another light, dazzling white, appeared below the pair and flickered like the tongue of a reptile testing for flesh before striking its fangs.

Extending the bleeding heart above his head, Ragusa cried out, "He, He comes! Satan, Father of Darkness, set Your children fr—"

The pulsing white light exploded downward in a shaft of fire. For an instant McBride saw Ragusa, the crucified boy, the kneeling soldiers, the snakes, and rats transfixed upon a million needle points of light. They vanished. McBride felt himself being overturned and swept down, down, down into the earth.

The patrol found McBride half buried in a bunker. The ropes that held him were torn away. When the medic brought him to a semiconscious state, McBride saw the clearing was empty. A light rain was falling. The soldiers were gone. The cross, the pile of stones had disappeared.

McBride pulled himself to one elbow and called Ragusa's name.

"Easy, padre," said the officer leading the patrol.

"Ragusa, Sergeant Ragusa," McBride whispered.

The officer shook his head. "There's no one here but you. They're gone. Without a trace."

"He was blond—had tattoos—a beard—"

"Sure, padre, sure. Now tell us what happened. Who was here? Did you see the rockets before they impacted?"

"Rockets?"

"Yeah. We figure the enemy zapped this place with four or five of their specials."

"No—rockets—it was—" McBride whispered. He tried to wrestle free, to make them understand. But the officer held him down and the medic gave him an injection of morphine.

The needle burned his flesh. And now he was slipping again. Into darkness. Mountains. Spearing the stars. Night. In the distance lights winking, smiling. Things. Slithering, crawling. On the peak stood—no! He tried to stop, to turn back. But the power had him in its grasp. Ragusa was there, and above him, vaster than the sky, loomed—McBride clawed the earth and screamed so that every man in the patrol heard—"He!"

Chapter Eighteen

It was a secret, so he kept it to himself and never even hinted at it when he spoke to his wife or drank from the circulating bottle with his friends on Saturday nights. Often, though, he dreamed of it—images from long ago that swept by his dozing guard and invaded his consciousness. It was the way it had been, then, he twenty years younger and trimmer. There were five more teeth in his mouth. In his dream he saw them when he smiled. He smiled a lot in the dream, smiled and laughed, and when he wasn't afraid he had fun. It was like he had died and gone to heaven; but instead of being lifted up in a sweet chariot drawn by angels, he thundered through the broken gates in a medium tank and saw the smoking celestial city hazed and dark in the bright prism of the gun sight cushioned to his eye. In the black cross hairs stood the buildings. The mill gradients climbed one by one like the rungs of a fire ladder up the broken windows. His hand clutched on the rumpled sheets and closed about the firing mechanism. A 90mm round lay ready in the breech.

But it was not that. There was no roar and heaving up and rocking down as the shell whined on its way. No metallic clang or mechanic whir as the red-hot casing popped on the armor-plated floor and the turret traversed, searching a new target.

He had recalled those things so often that they had become as much a part of him as his hair and his eyes. Those thoughts were integrated, and so they came and went into his consciousness as they would—when they came he lived them again and whistled a little tune he had learned in Paris from a huge dark woman who cooked at a cafe. But he could not remember the words. He would go about his business and sweep the floor and whistle. They were not dangerous thoughts, so they were not kept secret. If anyone had come up to him—why, even Mr. Frank—and said, "Sam, what in the hell are you so damn happy about?" he would have told them that he was just going through the war, that was all, and probably—if it was Mr. Frank he would have because he had been there too, only in Italy—probably they would have talked about it together right there in the hall.

But even though he wore his OD jacket until it got so ragged he couldn't patch it anymore, no one asked him. He had taken off the insignias, but any veteran who saw the dark peaks on the faded material would've known his rank. And then they could have said, "Corporal, eh? What outfit?" He would have told them how he got the medals—he had three and he wore them on special days down on Alabama Street when the Legion post had celebrations. Then the little boys would cluster around and ask about the "metals" and he would tell them. The Purple Heart he got for being cut by a tiny piece of shrapnel, which was jagged chunks of metal and which, he discovered in a dictionary in the library, was named after a man, a Captain Shrapnel, who invented it. It was curious; nothing else like that was named for a man, as far as he knew. Well, the shrapnel had done it. The Bronze Star he got for not letting the little piece of shrapnel stop him from crawling into his tank and killing two German Tigers, one—two. The Good Conduct he got because he was cut by a little piece of shrapnel and still destroyed two enemy tanks. And because of the little piece of shrapnel, the Purple Heart, the two tanks, the Bronze Star, and the Good Conduct, he got an honorable discharge. It was the honorable discharge that got him the job as janitor at the Oughton high school. He was responsible for the English, History, Math, and Home Ec rooms. His friend, old Edgar Green, did the science rooms and the offices. Willie Pike had the gym and grounds.

When he thought about it—really thought about it—stopped, leaned on the long handle of his push broom and gave the matter his undivided attention—it made him smile. Twenty years before he had raised maybe a quarter-ton of dust, dirt, and debris everytime he caught a target in the hairs and pushed off a round. And now—now he swept dust, he caught and smoothly pushed with his twenty-four-inch broom the soft balls of dust that came as if from nowhere, sifting down through the sunlit air. It made him wonder what was going on up there in space out of sight. And he cleaned windows—having personally broken enough glass to reach from—well, from here to there and back again. And he mopped and polished floors. The ladies in the Home Ec department were very, very particular about their floors, but—and this made him smile too—they couldn't hold a candle to the mess sergeant he had in basic training. Now *that* was a man who loved clean floors. He would make them get down on their hands and knees and scrub, and then dry, and then he'd cook their chow and put it on the floor and make them eat it up. And when they were through he'd study them for a minute with his bright blue eyes, and then make them lick their plate clean and scrub the floor again.

The ladies liked the floors scrubbed and waxed and polished so bright that when they clicked over it on their high heels they could look down and see the fluttering white of their slips. They could have seen as well the small tracks their sharp heels made in the glow, but moving like hens unconscious of their trails, they did not notice the marks until the surface was bleared by all of them coming together as though a squad in hobnailed boots had marched through. Then they were astonished, and called him.

The secretary in the principal's office did the calling. It was very simple—he often wondered about the simplicity and tried to figure out whether it was because they thought he was stupid or because the simple arrangement required little effort on the secretary's part. She would reach to the side of her desk and press a small black button which was connected to a pair of insulated wires which, in turn, ran to a cigar box in which was a pair of dry-cell batteries. One wire went to the batteries, the other paralleled to make the circuit. From the box the wires crawled up to the juncture of wall and ceiling, out the transom, down the hall, across the hall ceiling, and down the stair-well to the small basement room where he stowed his brooms, rags, cleaning powders and fluids, waxes, toilet paper, soap, and sanitary napkins for the machines in the rest rooms. It was his room—they called it his office, and in the beginning—he was young then, broad shouldered and narrow at the waist, the scar from the shrapnel still pink on the black skin of his tight cheek—they had said *office* with straight faces but with a sound like their lips were smiling inside next to their teeth. But now they were used to the term, and his room was his office and that was that, just as he was him, and it was him you called when the floor needed attention. You called him by pressing the button and at long distance ringing a bell in his office. It was like the apparatus he had once seen used in the movies in a fancy mansion when, to interrupt a folksy scene among the help in the kitchen, the master pressed a button and in the kitchen a gong sounded and in the window of a neat box over the stove a number sprang up to show which room the master was in.

But that was not his secret. He did his job and he did it well, and he never pushed himself on anyone. So through twenty years of not asserting himself, of being, simply, an absolute nothing except the "Boy Who Cleaned Up" and hid in a little room in the basement, they came to accept him as a part of things in the same way as they considered the desks and lockers and the stoves on which the girls ruined cuts of meat and cakes and pastries that he couldn't buy on his salary, or the refrigerators, in which they stored—under lock and key—the food before it was ruined and thrown out in the garbage, or the sewing machines or health charts, or movie projectors, or, for that matter, the bathroom fixtures, which he daily cleaned until they shone so white and slick that he laughed first to think maybe he had worn through the porcelain skin and touched the bone, then frowned to wonder if everything was that color after all, except him.

The secret he kept to himself, deeper than his bones. Sometimes it came as he sat in the dim light of the small lamp he had rigged in his office, as he sat in the sweaty sweet smell of his own body in the close room on the chair which, years before, an overweight girl had broken by pouncing on it when she thought she saw a mouse—and which caused panic resulting in a ring to him who came, and amidst lifted dresses, exposed thighs, and screams and tears, discovered that the mouse was no mouse at all, but a woolly gray glove someone had dropped in a dim corner. The screams and tears stopped, and the dresses came down and were curled around the legs and held tight, and he had known the hatred they felt because he had saved them—

174

not from a mouse but from a glove and their own foolishness; a mouse was silly enough, but a glove?—and in front of him, he being what he was? As he went out of the room, the broken chair in one hand, the glove in the other, he heard one of them say—he heard it but he did not let them known he heard—walked straight as though on parade—one said: "Just like a damn nigger!," and shut the door and did not think about it for at least one full step. And when he did, he saw it in the only terms he could, because he was ten years younger then and he could not control the secret as he could now—he had thought as he went down the hall carrying the chair shattered by the trembling bulk of a crazy white girl—the seat of the chair still warm from the heat of her bottom—he thought about the women he had had. Not the women of his own kind. He was tall and trim, a hero with three medals and a scar, his own kind came to him naturally because they knew him for what he was. But these were different.

And it was not the same as whores. They were not whores who came to him. Some of his buddies told the women in England that they were genuine American Indians; others said they were secret weapons of the army—night fighters dyed black to be invisible as they infiltrated the enemy lines. He said nothing. That was before the shrapnel and the German Tigers and the medals, and he was afraid. They saw him and they liked him—they liked him more because he was afraid, not cocky-smart like the others. But if he was afraid of the war, of crossing the channel and going against the Germans, he was terrified of the women.

And carrying the still-warm shattered chair down to the secure place of his room in the dark basement of the building he had thought of what happened between him and the women in terms as splintered as the broken thing he held by one leg. He had taken them. He squeezed the chair and gritted his teeth. He had taken them. And sweet God in heaven they had taken all he had and cried for more! They loved him. Once two of them fought over him; battered each other with their fists, tore their flesh with their bleeding nails, and, wallowing, biting, kicking, wrestled all around the dirty beer-stained floor of a dingy flat, their thighs and hips exposed, their hard breasts torn out of their ripped blouses—they made beasts of themselves for him. And he let them, and watched it, and took the winner.

But he kept it all to himself, even then. You never could tell, not

175

even there, in the war. There were men there—not his own kind—men from the same section of the country, from the same state—there was Captain Rutledge from Oughton, too. You had to be careful. The war took up their time and when they were not fighting the enemy, passes and furloughs in the English and French towns kept them busy. But still, there were things, he knew, that no man would forget. He had never forgotten the mess sergeant who loved clean floors. Captain Rutledge owned land, good farmland; he would not in ten thousand years have forgotten what he did with the women.

Then, they were not so much as women go. Oh, he knew they were attractive. But it was not the same. They were low women because the war had run over them, had killed their men, had left them alone, hungry for—if not love—the things that stood for love. They were low, then, lower even than him. And that was what excited and terrified him. It was not the way it was supposed to be, not at all. Back where he came from—he had told himself every time they came after him—back there they would have cut him up and tarred and feathered him, and finally lynched him for attacking one of their women simply by virtue of being located by hearsay in the vicinity. But in the war it was different, even for the men who would have been sticking the knife, dobbing the tar, and pulling on the rope. The women had fallen and it was every man for himself but don't come up with a clap—that was all. If you got sick you didn't get rank.

So he never told a soul. He worried now about the dreams mainly, because in his conscious memory the pictures from the past were not as sharply focused as they had been. And there had been so many of them. Blondes, brunettes, and one redhead. Sometimes, when he first came to work at the high school, he watched the women and the girls—watched them slyly from the corner of his eye as he swept or cleaned because then they were not used to him and they had not yet blended him into the surroundings in the same way that kudzu vines slowly overtake and conceal trees, or a cabin, if left unchecked. He watched them and played a game in which he tried to pair them off with the women he had known. But then his memory was too good and the pairings made him nervous. Could they read his thoughts? He had given it up—had driven the secret deep under, beyond his throat and vocal cords, and had done his job.

But once, five years earlier, he thought he had come very close to

176

giving himself away. A guest teacher came from England to the high school for a term, and he was sweeping the hall outside a classroom when she spoke. He stopped the broom and listened to her voice, not to the words—he could not understand them—but to the tones and accents. He stood motionlessly propped on his broom listening, until Miss Willton, who taught dressmaking, came late to hear the lecture. She laughed and teased him, saying, "Why, Sam, I didn't know you were interested in nonorganic food!" And he, he started sweeping and replied, "No, ma'am," and moved away as she went into the room with the voice.

So he guessed they never knew. It was good they didn't. He could picture what would happen if they found out. Suppose—just suppose—he once told himself—suppose that someone came to Oughton who knew and saw me and told them what I did. It would be like the mouse, only a thousand times worse. He had laughed at the thought. They would fire him sure, and then they would dredge up every notion of every move he ever made, and make up a few, too, and relate them all to rape. But—and this was what made him laugh not only at the mouth and lips but deep within, even in his heart—for one instant, a single satisfying moment, they would see him for what he really was—for a man. And after that? Well, he knew what word they'd use.

But that was what twenty years before had made all the women in England and France act toward him as they did. Well, it was a secret and it had to be because—well, because for one thing he liked living, and for another he had kids so he needed a job, and in twenty years more, if he kept his nose clean and was a good boy, he could retire.

Maybe he would go back then, pack a bag and take a liner across the ocean, go to the places he had seen. Maybe there were still people who remembered. They would not recall him—he was only one and there had been thousands—but maybe by seeing him they would think they knew him because of the thousands. Or maybe there was something else. He had kept this deeper and more hidden than the other secret. But in his dreams it too came to him, fresher and more alive and real than even the women. Maybe there were children. Why should there not have been, he asked himself each time before he squeezed the thought from his mind—I have children of my own here. I am a man.

That was twenty years in the future and he would hold it secret until then. He would not breathe it; it would be like the scar on his cheek, thick, stronger than the surrounding tissue, but invisible. And so the women would never know. They accepted him now. He was like the building and the fixtures. He took three rolls of pink scented toilet paper from a freshly opened case and went up to the faculty rest room.

He walked in without knocking. It was all right. At Oughton High School they accepted him for what they thought he was.

Chapter Nineteen

They were all seventeen, young men of the new generation, born in Oughton and raised up together by parents born there; they had passed through the elementary school and junior high; in another year they would graduate together from high school and then, if breeding proved true, go off together to the university at Athens, to pledge SAE, drink to the brink of insanity, and—without fail—root those hairy Bulldogs on and on. In time they would complete four years there, and one or two might come home with degrees, while the others traveled for their health or worked for their fathers, and then, a year or so later, finished up their course work at a smaller college or, in extreme circumstances, in schools across the state line in Alabama.

But this August night they were seventeen and the moon was as full and beautiful as an idol's eye. They were floating naked in inner tubes in Steve Floyd's cow pond and drinking beer chilled in a croaker sack secured to a tractor tube. The pines along the north shore moved gently in the warm breeze and from the woods to the south came the occasional cries of night birds and the sweet song of a mockingbird.

Bill Middleton opened his third beer and said, "Well, what about the team this season?"

Frank Green chuckled. "Team hell—what about the cheer-leaders?"

"They're looking good," said Davey Rutledge. "I've been scouting those closed practice sessions in the junior high gym."

"Exactly *how* good?" asked Steve.

"Well—if this was Hudson Bay country, I'd tell all you trappers to gear up for a bumper crop of beaver."

"How's Molly West?" asked Bill.

"How's Molly West—is that all you can say?" said Frank. "I think you've got the hots for sweet Molly. Right Davey?"

"Right and left."

"Aw—"

"Play good ball and she'll cheer for you," said Frank. "Now listen up, men, just what are we going to do tonight?"

"What would Alexander the Great do?" asked Davey.

"What indeed?" replied Steve.

"Speaking as a Greek myself," said George Demos, "I suppose he would wait for a god, or goddess, to move him."

"Just thinking about a goddess moves me, oh yes," said Frank.

Bill said, "What would Jesus do?"

"Jesus?" said Steve. "Jesus, Bill!"

Bill tried to laugh it off. "Well, isn't that what they tell you to ask when you're faced with a problem—preachers, I mean."

"Yes," said Frank, "and I think in this case Jesus would drown you." He started paddling toward Bill, but since he held a beer in one hand he went in circles.

The others laughed, and then Davey said, "Seriously, men, what are we going to do. The moon is climbing above yon trees and we are growing older by the second."

"And wiser, too," said Steve.

"Well," said Frank, "the way I see it, we could get out of this cow pond, dry off—after a little grab-ass, of course, get dressed, have a chaw, and then go down to the square and see if it's still there. We could exchange philosophical views with Bobby-bob, or drop by the Blue Note and wink at Wimpton."

"That queer? Not me!" said Bill. "But listen, we could sneak in Bird's Funeral Home and see—"

"One thing I want to know," said George, "is does old man Bird diddle those stiffs?"

Davey laughed, "Only the females. Mrs. Bird handles the others."

"Handles?" said Steve. "Well, well and my-oh-my."

"What would Shakespeare do?" asked Frank, opening a beer. "I mean—what would the bard do on such a night. Gentlemen, elevate your eyes heavenward and behold the splendor of the stars and moon. Ah yes, there are songs to be sung of such, not to mention tales to be told, and nookie to be got."

"Well said indeed, noble bard," said Davey. "I drink to your stars but especially to your nookie."

"I'll drink to that!" said Bill.

"Hell, you'll drink to anything," said Steve.

They laughed together, even Bill, and drifted silently for a time, each looking up at the clear August sky. Finally George said, "My uncle John tried to teach me the constellations when I was a kid. I can recognize the Big Dipper and Orion, but the rest are like Greek to me."

Frank laughed. "All I see up there is nookie—look at those four stars to the left, then draw a line over to that reddish one. Got it. Okay, now—"

While Frank amused them, Davey Rutledge smiled and enjoyed the pleasant sensation of the warm pond water on his naked skin. It was good being with friends—even with Bill. Yes, and—he frowned. He smelled something. He shifted his gaze from the stars to the shore. There was still the scent of pines but now there was something else. A sweet, thick smell, as of long hair and soft flesh. And now he heard a sound, a rustling near where they had left their clothes. "Shh!" he said.

The others looked at him, then toward the shore. He held a finger to his lips and gestured for Frank to continue speaking while he investigated.

"As I was saying only the other day, there is nookie and then there is nookie—" Frank went on, while Bill and George laughed.

Now Davey slipped from his tube and swam underwater. He had to surface once for breath. He saw something moving in the shadows cast by the moon. He swam until his hands touched the muddy bottom, then lowered his feet and crawled forward and rose up and charged out the shallows like an amphibian beast.

There was a scream and the shadows divided. One fled to the left, the other to the right. Davey flung the pond water from his eyes and ran naked to the right down a path through the pines. One thief wasn't two, but at least he would teach—suddenly he realized that what he had smelled was woman. He ran into a tree, caught his balance, and continued down the path, going faster now, tasting the scent of pine sap on his tongue and the scent of another sap that was both rising in him and running before him through the moonlit woods.

He heard someone stumble and fall and he pounced over a clump of vine to see a form on the ground in front of him. A black girl, or at least in the shadows she seemed black. One of the girls from his father's farm or from Billy Green's. It didn't matter. She'd been going through their clothes. She had to be punished. He snatched a thin branch off a nearby tree and whipped her. The needles stung—he knew how they could sting—but she said nothing. She rolled up in a tight ball and then he saw that she was naked, too. Yes, she had been swimming in the pond—must've, but he hadn't heard or seen or smelled her till the wind shifted.

He looked down at her. She was no child, but she wasn't a woman either. The moon was moving through the pines. Light fell across his waist and down his legs to her body. She relaxed and sat up and looked at him. Her breasts were small, the nipples erect. She was black all over but her eyes were as round and white as his. She smiled, and then he saw how hard he was. He growled and raised the switch over his head. She fell on her back and parted her knees. He tossed the switch into the woods and fell onto her like a meteor drawn by gravity to earth.

Chapter Twenty

W hen news of Mrs. Alice Corday's involvement spread, no one in Oughton was surprised but all were curious.

"She's taken up with a bum who calls himself a faith healer," Tom Davis informed Mrs. Sam Roberts as he cleaned the windshield of her Buick at his service station. Tom had done a lot of hunting and fishing and not a little drinking with Alice's late husband, Pete. In fact, he was with him only an hour before the stroke that left Alice a widow.

"You don't say," Mrs. Roberts replied. She had gotten the same news earlier in more vivid terms from the postman Walter Leeds.

"It's a true fact," said Tom. "They was here yesterday for gas in Pete's caddy." He stopped wiping and put his face in the driver's window. "And do you know what? *He* was driving!"

"Pete's car?"

"Yes sir, he sat right there where Pete used to, big as ike. He's got hair down to his shoulders just like a girl's. And know something else—?" Tom looked both ways and behind him, then whispered, "He don't wear no pants!"

"He don't?" cried Mrs. Roberts, almost dropping her credit card. This hard fact the usually reliable Walter omitted.

"He don't! Got on some kind of robe hiked up so's you can see his knees. And he goes barefoot."

"Lord!" sighed Mrs. Roberts. "What's next?"

"Something's got to be done about this fellow. That'll be nine-seventy for the gas. Yes sir, driving Pete's car, and with no pants. Poor old Pete. You want me to charge it?"

Mrs. Roberts was in such a hurry to relay the news she paid cash. On her way home she detoured down Alice Corday's street. Pete's car was in the drive, but there was no sign of life, except the pack of dogs that chased her car and barked so loud and long that she slouched down on the seat and speeded up in case anyone was watching.

But she could have laid flat on the floorboards and still be recognized. Alice knew Marian's Buick as well as Marian knew Pete's Cadillac. She was in the upstairs bedroom folding clothes when the dogs barked and she saw Marian cruising by.

Well, now it's started, she thought. Pete's picture was on the dresser into which she was stacking her underclothes. "They're going to talk and say nasty things," she told him. "But I don't care. I feel better than I have for a long time."

And the truth was she did feel good. For a long while she had terrible headaches, the kind men laugh at and women dread. She consulted a number of physicians, first Doc Spaulding who brought her, and almost everybody else in the county, into the world, and then a succession of specialists in Atlanta. They sampled her blood, X-rayed her brain, tested her allergies, examined her eyes, ears, nose, and throat, not to mention her private organs, and took out her tonsils. But they found nothing "organically" wrong. She even went to a chiropractor. He spent a lot of time working on the base of her spine and her breasts, but to no avail. As a last resort, and at the insistence of a friendly enemy, Jennifer Myers, she had her palm read by Sister Faye out on state road 5. The gypsy suggested she was a very strong person and predicted she would someday be wealthy and independent. The headaches she never mentioned. Her husband Pete paid all the bills without complaining, even though the outlay sharply curtailed his activities with Tom Davis and the boys. But the pains in her head never slackened. Morning, noon, and night— especially at night, when she lay in the kingsize bed and tried to sleep—her head throbbed like the big bass drum she marched in front of years ago when she was the Oughton High School majorette and featured twirler.

Her head didn't hurt in those days, she recalled. My, how good she looked in her sequined suit. She had a cute figure, everyone said. And a pretty face, too. And if she wasn't a brain she was bright. Graduated with a B average, almost. She wanted to go to college.

But Pete came along. He was thirty then, twelve years older than she. He knew all the tricks for sweeping a young girl off her feet. Everyone said she'd be a fool not to marry him, if he asked, which they doubted, since he was a veteran just back from the war and was a grown man who made lots of money running his father's department store, the biggest in town.

Not that there weren't other boys in her life. She was a popular girl. In comparison to Pete, though, her high school beaus seemed childish. He took her for long rides in his Cadillac convertible. They went dancing till all hours in the neon-lit places up and down the highway and in Atlanta. He declared he loved her, brought her nice presents, and swore he dated no other girls. And she loved him. She'd be a fool not to, her friends said. So the June she graduated they were married in a big ceremony at the Methodist church. They went to the King and Prince Hotel on Saint Simons Island for their honeymoon, and almost everything they did in that bedchamber overlooking the Atlantic was sweet and wonderful to her.

There were a few unpleasantries. She had never seen a real man. From pictures she knew what to expect. But Pete was a very big man. He wasn't circumcised—she knew the abstract term from Bible class, but now here it was in the flesh. He also had a tattoo from his army days which was hidden by his clothes. It wasn't very nice, and he was ashamed of it. To cover up he laughed and said, "Well, I don't suppose I'll take off my underwear in public!" She laughed too, to be polite and understanding. But she prayed that when she awoke it would be gone.

Though faded slightly, the vein-blue lines were still a part of him when, sixteen years later, Mr. Bird the undertaker removed his corpse from the room she now worked in. Five months ago, in the spring. Alice looked at the bed. How strange he should die when just outside the trees were tapping their buds of life on the windowpanes. Of

185

course, he had been in poor health for some time. His liver, Doc Spaulding said. He drank too much. She tried to help him. But he would not, or could not, give her a reason. She even appealed to his friends, especially to Tom Davis, and they had the audacity to say *she* was the cause of Pete's trouble. That was absurd. She was his wife. She loved him. There had never been a moment she wasn't faithful, not even when Tom and Sam Roberts and the others asked her to dance at the country club and held her so close she couldn't draw a breath without pressing hard against them.

Her headaches got worse then. For a time she thought she was losing her mind, and there were many instances when the pain was so intense she could not remember the day. Aspirin was no good. Doc Spaulding gave her a limited number of codeine capsules, to be used as a last measure. At best they helped her sleep a few hours, but the pain greeted her when she awoke, so she quit taking them and gritted her teeth.

Alice smiled at the image of herself marching around with jaws clamped like someone in a rage. Men would find that funny. Her smile faded. It wasn't easy being a woman. Especially when there were men who didn't accord you the respect you deserved. Not that anything happened. She wouldn't let it. But she knew what they thought. She hadn't been a majorette for nothing.

Alice sat on the edge of the bed on which her husband died. She had changed the sheets and spread, but the brown and white shoes he would've put on had not the clot lodged in his brain were just under the bed out of sight. His tan suit was in the closet, and his shirt and tie. She took his wallet, though, and put the little black book with all those phone numbers and intimate comments in a safe place. She also disposed of the condoms. What a funny name for something like that. She looked it up in the dictionary and was surprised to discover they were named after their inventor, a Dr. Condom who lived in the decadent eighteenth century.

She thought it highly presumptuous Pete should use them anyhow. They were married sixteen years and she never once missed a period. She was capable—Doc Spaulding said so—and she never refused her husband, not even those countless times he came home stinking drunk and called her dirty names while they did it. No, it was Pete who was sterile, not her.

186

That didn't make sense, either. He was a fine specimen of manhood when they married. Well over six feet tall, slim and muscular. There was no sport he did not excel in. I was the unformed one then, she thought. Oh, she was eighteen and beautiful. She had a good figure, but here and there were pockets of baby fat. She absently touched her flesh. Her nipples were so tiny then that she was ashamed to let Pete see. But he liked them that way and kissed her there until sometimes it stopped feeling good and actually hurt. When she asked him to please stop, he got mad and wouldn't answer unless she did other things. After three years—she was twenty-one and had lost all her baby fat—he brought home a big mirror and placed it at the foot of their bed. It was strange seeing herself like that, and she felt embarrassed, as though she was watching Pete with some other girl. But she was a good wife. She did what her husband told her. Sometimes she enjoyed it very much.

Pete died here, she thought, leaning back on the pillows. She looked at the ceiling. There were several discolorations in the plaster. It was like watching clouds. She saw all sorts of things traced in their indefinite designs. A tower, a bull. Stilts. A deep hole out of which a tree struggled to rise. She wondered if Pete saw the designs. It was strange lying there where he died and looking up at maybe the last thing he saw on this earth.

Her head ached. She covered her face with her hands and pressed her fingertips into her closed eyes. Reds, greens, and blues exploded like skyrockets. But the pain did not die with the fading patterns of light. She tried to be strong, to do exactly what he told her. But she was weak and the pain was as bad as when Pete was alive.

The phone rang. Forgetting herself, Alice rose and went to the hall extension. It was Jennifer Myers.

"I hear you have a new doctor," she said.

The pain was so bad she couldn't think what to say. Jennifer was the busiest busybody in town. Her husband Charlie Meyers was a supervisor at one of the Middleton Mills. She was a tall woman with huge jutting breasts and a narrow waist. Alice heard rumors she only wore panties on special occasions, like funerals, tornadoes, and floods. Pete declared her problem was she was horny. "What she needs," he said, "is about ten inches of the finest." Jennifer always liked Pete, and she cried like a baby when he died. Alice wondered what they would look

187

like together in the mirror. Her phone number wasn't in Pete's black book, though.

"Honey, are you there?" Jennifer asked.

"Who told you I have a new doctor?"

"Why everyone. It's all over town, didn't you know?"

"What's all over town?"

"Honey, do you feel all right? Maybe you need another dose of medicine." She laughed and Alice pictured her big breasts shaking. "They say he's a faith healer. Does he favor herbs, or is he a root man?"

Alice hung up without replying. Root man indeed! She knew what they were saying, the shits. Just because for years they did it with any and everybody, they assumed she was doing it with him.

"They can think what they want!" she said, going back into the bedroom. "I don't care a damn!"

But that was a lie. She cared very much. It wasn't that she was morally offended by their conclusions. She was a woman who lived with a healthy man for sixteen years. She smiled. There wasn't much she couldn't do if she had a mind to. Pete saw to that. It was the idea that she'd flaunt such behavior openly. Just because they did was no reason she would. Still, five months was a long time to go without it, especially when Pete was so demanding, even up to the end.

He brought home an outfit made of shiny latex two days before he died. It was for her—tight pants that showed off every curve of her nice legs, and a top so tight you could see her nipples like she was naked. He wanted her to wear it to bed. She did and for a while it was fun, but then he showed her the whip and ordered her to beat him. She couldn't do that, not to her husband, no matter what.

Alice sat on the edge of the bed and rubbed her hand across the footboard. Pete had leaned over there, had exposed himself and implored her to whip him. Deep inside she wanted to more than anything. But she could not. It was as though a switch shut off her arm muscles. They would not raise the whip. First he begged, and then he cursed. It ended with him crying and stomping out of the house. Thirty-six hours later he came back, to die.

Heart failure, Doc Spaulding said. Caused by too much drink and a bad liver. "Ulcers I can cure," he said, "and sometimes even lung

188

cancer. But a goddamn rotten liver is something else. You can live on one lung or with two feet of intestine, but not without a liver. What's more, any fool who'd do what Pete does is asking for it plain and simple, like he had laid down on tracks of the Atlanta and West Point Railroad."

Plain and simple, he got it, thought Alice. She rose and smoothed the bedspread. Her headache had vanished. She did not remember having it. Pete was soused when he came back. He wanted her. Even though it was ten in the morning and her hair was in curlers, she placed herself beneath him. But she knew it was no use. When he realized the same he started choking her. He was very heavy and she was light and quick. His meaty hands hurt her throat. But the once tremendous strength was gone from his fingers. She easily released his grip, and when she rolled over he was dying. Thank God he had not removed his pants. His eyes almost popped out and he lost control and flooded the bed with yellow-green urine. When it rained you could still smell it.

She called Dr. Spaulding, then zipped up his fly and put the shoes under the bed. She had time to comb out her hair and tie it with a blue ribbon that matched her dress. It was strange about death, though. After the doctor pronounced Pete dead and the undertaker's men were putting him on their stretcher, the blanket fell away and she saw that dead he had gotten it up like he couldn't alive.

The worms were gnawing it now and the rest of him, too. Dying was bad, like a dirty joke, almost bad as living. No, that was a lie. Life was fun, at times. She was a widow, but she was still young— only thirty-four, her hip size. Her hair wasn't gray and her figure was better than when she was eighteen. She had matured, aged like wine. She stood before the mirror and raised her skirt to her waist. The thighs were very good, firm, with no trace of that marbling of fat which happens to women in their thirties. She had escaped varicose veins. Her calves were also nice. Pete called them her "grippers." That was because when they did it with her on the bottom she laid them over his back and locked her ankles. She turned partway. Her bottom was as tight as when she led the band. She twitched one hip, then the other. Long ago she overheard boys talking about her, and while she forgot their names she remembered what they said: "When Alice walks, her cute little ass winks at you." That was a nice thing to say.

Alice dropped her skirt and smoothed the hem. Poor Pete. Being a widow was all right. She had a great deal of money and controlled the family store. A lot of unattached men were dying to ask her out. But it was only five months since Pete died and, well, no one wanted to risk being turned down. At least that was what she heard. She would probably marry again. Thirty-four wasn't old. Why, she was young enough to bear children. Five months was a long time without a fuck—that was what Pete called doing it, among other expressions. One thing about being married. It was nice to have a man around the house. Something you could always count on. Pete wasn't perfect by any means. Sometimes his not being circumcised repelled her. But he was all man, and he liked it very much.

Alice moved into the hall and shut the door behind her. She didn't let him before they married. But she had an idea what he had. They played in the back seat of his convertible. Fully clothed, of course. It was what all young women and their steadies did. Only now what was she to do? She could not jump over the front seat like an eighteen-year-old. Still, that was a very important part of marriage and she would have to be sure about her husband before the wedding. Maybe she would forget it and buy one of those vibrators Jennifer was always talking about.

She went down the stairs, paused in the hall, then turned through the dining room and entered the kitchen.

She would bring a great deal to her second husband, if she decided to marry again. There was the house which Ben Lewis valued at a hundred and twenty thousand when he probated Pete's will. The hundred-thousand-dollar insurance payment was in the savings and loan. Ben urged her to put it into stocks under his management. But she refused, saying she didn't want to be under any man right now. Ben didn't catch the joke, even though she smiled. He was like that. She had known him for years. His wife Susie was all right, but she was getting fat. How did they do it? She read somewhere that eagles did it in the air. Ben was no eagle. You could never tell, though. Maybe he kept a whip under his pillow and thrashed Susie's heavy bottom. Of course, there was French culture and Greek culture and all the other cultures Pete ranted about when he was drunk. Still, Ben seemed more interested in a buck than a fuck, to say it like Pete would. She

190

smiled, then frowned. Susie Lewis had ugly hair on her thick thighs. Oh well.

Alice looked out the kitchen window. He was in the garage working on his motorcycle. There was a maid's room on the far end of the garage and she let him use it. That was the least she could do in payment for all he did for her. He wouldn't take money, not a red cent. It was a gift, he said, freely given to him and only good when freely given. All she had to do to receive this gift was accept him for what he was.

But that was a big order. He was so strange. Of course, there were days she believed she was living in Syria or some other Godforsaken land of the Middle East, rather than in Oughton, fifty miles from Atlanta. The sights that passed down her street were better than a carnival. If it wasn't the ragtag junkman in his mule-drawn wagon, it was the boys and girls from the high school in their outlandish getups. And there was an endless succession of salesmen with lean and hungry eyes for her breasts and legs as well as her pocketbook. One— a seller of brushes—even fondled her and when she slapped him had the nerve to ask for a glass of water. She gave it to him, but without any ice. It was a hot day and his hand was sweaty. So was her breast. Afterward it hurt where he touched her and she went upstairs and took off her blouse and bra. The nipple was as hard and stiff as a piece of red rubber. But there was no bruise from his heavy hand. She cried at the sight. Pete was dead only a month. Her head ached. Was this the way life was going to be?

Sometimes beggars came to the door. The dogs that lived on the street usually scared them away. Still, one or two braved the barking. They were curious men, and Alice wondered why they left their homes and moved from place to place. Their breath was rotten. And their clothes were dirty. She tried to be kind, though. It was the least one could do as a Christian. And they never got fresh with her. Not even on one occasion when she answered the door in her bathrobe and later discovered it was unbuttoned from the thigh up.

She looked at the half-opened garage doors. He was in there working on his motorcycle so he could go away. Not that he was a bum or a beggar. He used very good English and he never once said anything bad like Pete. Not that she was judging Pete. A husband should be

191

able to say what he wants in front of his wife. What she meant was like the time Tom Davis called her a good-looking bitch to her face. He and Pete had been out drinking and Pete came home for something. After Tom said it he begged her don't tell Pete. Of course, Pete said much more. He used words she never knew existed and got a big kick out of explaining them to her. Men had curious names for the parts of a woman's body. Doc Spaulding called it one thing. Pete called it another. And Pete seemed more correct than the doctor. At least when he grabbed it and used that word it made her really want to. She never felt that way with the doctor. Then, he was an old man. Think of all the cunt he'd seen! Every one in town.

It probably means as much to him as—as—she searched for the word and spotted the garage—that garage. He was in there fixing his bike. That's what he called it when he stopped in her drive. She was watering the flowers. He came down the street pushing it. It was hot and he was sweaty. So was she beneath her pale blue dress, only it never showed on her because she always looked very cool even though perspiration was running in the ridges cut by her elastic straps.

Anyhow, he stopped in the drive and he was very polite. At first she was afraid of him. His appearance was absolutely foreign. Why, his hair was as long as hers, though not as curly. Yes, it was blond and it fell about his broad shoulders and he tried to push it away from his mouth to speak while holding up the motorcycle.

"I won't hurt you," he said, "contrary to what my appearance may lead you to believe."

His voice was very nice. And she liked his eyes. They were green as grass. He was sort of thin, though, and instead of shirt and pants he wore a robe or tunic of some kind. He was barefoot, too.

He said, "What I need is a place to park my bike while I fix it. If I stop out in the open the police will arrest me because of my looks. Do you understand?"

She dumbly nodded, then felt the strangest sensation. It was like she was walking through a stream. And when she looked she saw that in her surprise at him she forgot the hose. She had soaked her feet and legs and muddied the flowerbed.

He smiled at her. She found herself smiling back and then heard her voice saying, "You can put it in the garage. Nobody will bother you there."

But he wouldn't do it for nothing. He paid his way wherever he went, he said. What could he do? Well, he had been many things at many times in many places, a sort of jack-of-all-trades but master of none.

"I have a lot of good luck with machines," he said.

So he fixed Pete's car. It had been missing for some time. She took it to Tom Davis to be fixed, but it never was and Tom had her bring it back almost very week. She knew what he was doing and it made her mad that he thought she was so dumb she didn't. He made her sit in the car and work the gas pedal while he fiddled under the hood, but all the while he was trying to see her legs. She was tempted to write something awful on her panties and give him a good look. It would be his word against hers, and everyone knew that regardless what Jennifer said she was a nice person. Instead, however, she did not go back until two days ago when she and he drove in. The car ran like it did the day Pete bought it. She let him drive because he wanted to feel how the motor ran and also she wanted Tom to see him. It was better than something written on her undies. Tom turned white, then red. But there was nothing he could do.

There's nothing anyone can do, thought Alice. Yes, she was free to do what she pleased. She had youth, money, good looks and she knew what a man wanted. Maybe she would go to Europe. Lots of people in town with less money did.

"But right now I'll go out to the garage," she told herself.

He was cleaning grease from his hands as she entered. He threw back his head to clear the hair from his face, smiled, and said, "It's fixed. Listen." He mounted the bike, kicked the starter, and twisted the accelerator. The engine came to life and purred so quietly and smoothly it was hard to hear. He cut the switch and sat back on the double seat, the tunic pulling up to reveal a portion of his white thigh.

For a moment she thought she would have a headache and maybe even faint right there on the concrete in full view. But she said, "It sounds real good. Are you going to leave?"

He hopped off and secured the kickstand. "I have to."

Alice did not want him to go, not now. Couldn't he stay for a while? No, it was impossible. Did he have someone waiting? No, there was no one. Why then must he go? There was no good reason except he had to.

"It's not the trip," he explained. "It's the stops, you know, the people along the way. You'd be surprised how many nice people there are like you who'll be kind to a funny looking person like me."

Yes, she was kind to him from the moment he stopped in her drive. It was crazy, and lucky for him. She had thought much about it. Probably she was the one person in Oughton who'd do what she did. Marian Roberts would call the police. Jennifer would make him do it or else. No telling what Tom Davis would've done. But she took him in, no questions asked. Was it fate, maybe?

She was still having headaches then, though not really as bad as when Pete was living. Every once in a while when she thought of how it was, they hit her between the eyes like bullets. But he cured her, and not with Jennifer's root medicine either. That Jennifer would do it with a fireplug! They were in the kitchen when it happened. She was serving him some scrambled eggs. She was telling him how much her husband liked his eggs that way when she almost passed out from the pain.

He made her sit down and they talked. "You know, I can heal people," he said. "I've done it lots of times."

"I wish you'd do it to me!" she cried.

"Do you believe I can heal you? You've got to believe, that's the big thing."

At that moment she would've believed black was white and Jennifer was a virgin.

"Then you're healed," he said, smiling and going back to the plate of eggs.

And the strangest thing of all was that she was. The pain disappeared. One minute it was there, the next it was gone. Just like presto! As he ate the eggs, he said, "Any time you feel a headache coming, you think of me, okay? I promise you'll not be troubled again."

Pete promised her many things and even though she believed him for a time they never came to pass. He swore he would leave the waitress named Henny at the Moose Club alone. But he didn't till her boyfriend started talking. He paid them off, though, with no questions asked, and that was a promise kept, wasn't it? Maybe, but she

194

didn't trust him. How could she after what he did, and all the time? It was hard to believe a man, unless he was doing it and all he wanted was you.

He offered her his hand. "Been nice knowing you, and I really appreciate your kindness."

She accepted his hand. It was cool, soft, and the fingers were nice and long. She wondered where it had been, what it had touched. She felt her lips move, heard her voice asking, "Don't you like women?"

The hand squeezed hers, then pulled itself free. "Of course I like women," he replied. "I like them very much. Why?"

"I'm a woman," she said. And she suddenly wished she wasn't. If she were a man and he were her she would grab his breasts and push her knee into his thing and then they would see what happened. Men could do that. Being a woman was like being—she saw the motorcycle—like being something to be ridden, steered. If only she were a man!

"I know you're a woman," he said. "Have faith, believe in me, and you'll be cured forever and forever."

"Cured? Of what?" she asked. She wasn't sick. Why, she had never felt better in her life, and she was thirty-four and been through a lot. "It wasn't easy being married to an older man who liked doing things that hurt," she heard herself say. "Maybe if you were a woman you'd understand. They take you when you're young and soft and they do it till you love it so much you can't live without it and then they die, and what are you supposed to do? I wish you were a woman. I really do. And if I were a man I'd throw you down on this floor and give you what you need!"

His eyes were nervous. "I can't help you, not that way," he said.

She heard herself crying, "Why, why?"

"They do things to you," he said. "It's your spirit that matters. I'm a man of peace. I believe in understanding, in having faith. It's what keeps me safe as I go up and down in this world. Just let me slip into the ways of the flesh and then you can't guess what happens!"

"But I don't care!" Alice heard her voice say. Why can't I stop it? she wondered. But she could not. "You're a man, aren't you? Well, aren't you? You've got one, haven't you? I know what it is. I was married and to a real man for sixteen years and now it's all of five months since. Did you lose it somewhere? In an accident, a ditch?"

"I like it too," he said. "It's the best thing in the whole world and I've been everywhere. But I can't help you now. Have faith, believe me. There's nothing I'd rather do right now than it with you, but I can't because I'm sick and if we did it then you'd have the same terrible disease and I can't wish that on any creature. Do you understand? Try to understand."

The last she saw of him was his back as he turned out of the drive down the street. The dogs chased him. Standing alone there in the garage she heard them barking. After a while it was quiet again. She closed her eyes, and when she opened them she was in the kitchen fixing a cup of coffee.

It wasn't easy being a woman. He had one of those venereal diseases Pete joked about. "Makes your prick swell up and turn green like a dill pickle," he said. She wanted it very very bad. If he was a faith healer why didn't he heal himself? Oral Roberts and those others cured everything from colds to cancers. Of course, she could not recall them ever once curing a case like that, at least not on TV. Jesus chased out devils, though, and cleansed lepers. It was decent of him to tell her. He could have gone ahead and done it with her and then what a mess! She spooned in sugar and stirred the coffee, absently watching the shaft of the spoon move up and down and all around in the dark steaming liquid.

I am not a weak person, she reminded herself. I will not cry. What was the use in that? Even when Pete died she didn't. Maybe that was why Tom Davis blamed her. It wasn't fair. Why did God make people the way He did, if He did? Women were like flowers waiting for bees. Honey. It was very sweet. She was sweet, too. Wait and something would happen, if it didn't take too long and she withered in the process, or developed breast cancer, or had to have a hysterectomy. Yes, she would have to be patient and to believe and to have faith.

"I will, I swear I will!" she told herself. And for a moment she felt consoled. But only a moment, for then she heard the dogs barking and she rose and went to the door.

Chapter Twenty-One

When Fort Sumter was bombarded in April of 1861, William Middleton was almost seventeen and a member of the Oughton Academy Cadet Corps, which was instituted by the principal, G. N. Brightner, a Citadel graduate who believed that military drill developed mental discipline.

Since the rough and ready land of the county was best suited for subsistence farming, there were few slaveowners and, consequently, little interest in the secessionist movement. But after shots were fired and blood was shed, the citizens gave wholehearted support to the southern cause. The militias of each district mobilized, and all of the Oughton cadets volunteered for duty. Some six weeks later, after a public religious ceremony on the town square, they marched off to join Cobb's Legion.

Moses Middleton, William's father, had gone to war in 1812. In the Battle of New Orleans he was bayoneted in the leg, but with the knife he carried in his boot had managed to cut the throat of the redcoat before he could thrust again. Moses was fifteen then, fresh off his father's farm in Tennessee, and his youthful strength enabled him to survive the loss of blood and the cauterization of his wound with a red-hot musket barrel. But from that day on he walked with a pronounced limp, so his father apprenticed him to a cobbler.

Within nine years, Moses had a shop of his own in Nashville, as well as a wife and two sons. He made a comfortable living, but he dreamed of building something more tangible to leave his children than a name over a doorway on a narrow side street. There was cheap land to be had in west Georgia, land taken from the Indians and divided into lots of 200 acres and given by lottery to encourage white settlement. A few who had little but hope moved into the territory. The Indians fought but in time were vanquished and transported beyond the Mississippi.

When his wife died during the flu epidemic of 1837, Moses took stock of his life. His sons were big boys now and capable of helping a man with one good leg work the land. And though he had not farmed since he was a boy himself, he supposed that even people on the frontier required boots. He would buy acreage there, as close to the main town as possible, and when he was not tilling it he would ply his craft.

So in 1838 he sold his shop, bought horses and a wagon, farm implements and provisions, and with his sons and five hundred dollars in coin, made his move.

The lot he bought for a hundred dollars was two miles, more or less, from Oughton, a village of fifteen log buildings and a jail. Most of the wooded land was as wild as when the Indians possessed it. There were wolves and bears and great tan panthers that had no fear of white men nor of the hides of their brothers that were nailed to log walls to warn them away.

Moses and George and John felled trees and built a log house and an outbuilding for the horses. On the cleared land they planted corn which yielded at best twenty-five bushels. Moses rented space in town beside a tavern and set up shop in a lean-to. It was here that he met the woman who would become William's mother.

Elizabeth Jenkins was the youngest daughter of a large, poor family of Macon. She had married a young man of that area and they had come to Oughton to settle. A year later he was killed in the Creek uprising and the child she was carrying was stillborn.

Her hair was the color of autumn leaves and her plain, fair face was freckled. She could read parts of the Bible and write her name, and she knew how to stalk, shoot, and butcher a buck, and which of the wild plants were edible, so while she had no man to help her, she neither starved nor begged.

Moses and Elizabeth met on a frosty November day when she came barefoot to his shop with a deer skin to be made into boots, offering half of the leftover hide for payment. Her teeth were chattering and it seemed to Moses that her face was as blue as her eyes. He made the boots while she waited. That night he fashioned a carry-all bag from his profit. And when next she appeared in town, bringing eggs to barter, he gave it to her. But she refused to take it as a gift, saying, "The living's too hard in this country for giving without getting, especially between strangers." He accepted eight small eggs.

The next week he had a beaded belt to trade, the week following a purse to match. By now he was tired of eggs, so he spoke his mind, telling her who and how old he was, from whence he came and why, and that he had no wife but two half-grown sons who needed a mother. He ended by limping back and forth in front of her and saying, "I'm a cripple."

She looked him over for a long moment before replying, "Everybody's got something broken. I'm thankful it's not your head."

They were married by the Methodist circuit rider who held services once a month, God willing. Her dowry was a darning needle, a feisty rooster and a dozen dusty hens, and 200 acres that lay two lots removed from his. The hilly land was uncleared, but through it ran Indian Creek, a bold stream that flowed deep and clear in the driest season. In time Moses acquired the land between and built a house on it, another log structure but larger, with an adjoining room for his sons. In 1844 William, their only child, was born. By now George and John had taken wives and settled bordering lots.

Life improved for the settlers though it was never easy. By 1849 Moses owned 800 acres, of which one quarter was under cultivation. He possessed three milk cows and other cattle which he used for meat and for hides that he tanned himself, fifteen sheep, a dozen hogs, and eight horses. The land produced corn, tobacco, cotton, and small grains, as well as vegetables for the table. Two years later he was elected Ordinary. He was also numbered among the founders of the academy at which William became acquainted with Latin, geometry, and military tactics.

After his first encounter with the enemy, William was unscathed but puzzled. There was little similarity between Professor Brightner's lectures and what occurred on the battlefield. It was one thing to lay out Napoleon's maneuver at Austerlitz with twigs and pebbles under a shade tree, and quite another to be one of the pebbles. The officers told them what to do, but after the shooting began and the air was thick with blinding smoke, after men fell screaming and horses bolted, their steaming guts trailing the earth, there seemed to be no plan, unless it was chaos.

Cobb's Legion moved north, taking part in the action at Cold Harbor and Malvern Hill. They were in the thick of things at Second Manassas, South Mountain, and Antietam, where a dozen of the academy boys fell and William's left shoulder was grazed by a minnie ball. A piece of shrapnel ripped through his cap at Fredericksburg, gashing his scalp. He treated both wounds himself. Having heard the story of his father's leg since he was knee-high to it, he reckoned it wiser to take his fate into his own hands than to trust it to the bloody ones of a battlefield surgeon.

The legion fought at Chancellorsville and Gettysburg, in the Wilderness Campaign, and at Spottsylvania Courthouse, where William was promoted to sergeant and given command of a dozen boys, the youngest barely thirteen. At Five Forks they faced Grant, and then, in North Carolina, attacked Sherman, who was moving north after his infamous march through Georgia. This was the only battle in which the legion gave no quarter and asked for none. On April 23, 1865, their decimated army surrendered at Goldsborough. The war was over, but of the seventy Oughton cadets, only eleven survived.

William led them home, traveling by shanks' mare through the wasted country, eating what was kindly offered them by mothers and sisters who waited, many in vain, for their menfolk's return. So far as the cadets knew, the Yankees had spared their people, though they had learned from infrequent letters that part of the town square had been burned before the Battle of Atlanta.

They found ruins and sorrow.

A few days after Lee had surrendered, Wilson's cavalry passed through on their way from Alabama to Atlanta. The troopers had been harassed for weeks by rag-tag rebels and were fearful to the point of cruelty. The livestock they could not eat they wantonly mutilated and killed; the goods they could not use, they burned. And at every house they demanded valuables. Those that resisted were abused and beaten. Three men died.

One of the three was Moses Middleton.

After his mother held him close and, trembling, rested her head on his shoulder, she told him.

"There were four of them, Yankees. They came across the bottom field to the house. We heard shooting before we saw them. They killed the cows, all but one that was down by the creek. Shot the horses in the barn. The hogs scattered so they missed them. We were on the porch, your daddy and me." She gestured behind her to the burned house, beside which was a pine bough lean-to in which she slept.

"The sergeant dismounted and said, 'Give us your gold.'

"Your daddy said, 'Gold? You think if we had gold we'd be living like this?'

"That blue-coat came up the steps. He was a short, stout man with mean eyes and a thick, black mustache. He grabbed Moses by the shirt and slapped his face twice and said, 'I'm through talking to Rebs. Get the gold.'

"I was on my feet by then, but before I could tell him the same, he knocked me down. The other Yanks laughed and said, 'Go to it, Brannigan.'

"But the sergeant didn't smile. He told one of them to get a shovel from the barn. He tossed it to Moses and said, 'Dig it up!'

"Your daddy straightened his shirt front and looked him in the eye and said, 'Haven't got any gold.'

"That damn Yankee slapped his face again, bloodied his mouth. Drew his pistol then and stuck it to Moses' head. 'You're going to dig a hole, old man,' he said, 'and you're going to dig till you find gold.'

"Moses had the shovel. He looked at me, and then he said, 'Where do you want me to dig?'

"The Yank said, 'That's up to you, but you better find gold. Step quickly!'

"Your daddy came down the steps. When the soldiers saw how he walked, they laughed, and one said, 'Jack, that Reb ain't about to step quickly.'

"Mama," William said, touching her cheek.

She brushed his hand away like a fly. "They said some mean things to me, too, in front of your daddy. He stopped, and I knew what was on his mind, so I said, 'It's all right. Go on and dig.' Said that because I thought that after he dug awhile and they saw we didn't have any gold, they'd go away.

"So he did, over there by the south side of the barn."

She nodded her head toward a pile of burned timbers.

"He set to digging. Every few minutes he looked at that sergeant and told him there was no gold.

"Third time he did that, the Yankee cuffed him with the pistol barrel and said, 'Gold or silver—something of value, doesn't matter which—but you better find something.'

"Your daddy didn't let on the blow hurt. Said, 'All we got is dirt,' and kept on digging.

"Meanwhile the others plundered the house. Broke the windows, tore up the bedding, soaked it with coal oil, set it afire. Then they watered their horses and filled their canteens. And when they were through, they took turns doing their business in the well for meanness.

"By now your daddy was waist deep in the ground. His face was flushed and he was breathing hard. 'He's a sick man,' I told the sergeant. 'You're going to kill him.'

"'Hell's fire, woman,' a soldier said, 'Jack Brannigan will kill him anyhow. This way you won't have to dig no grave.'"

She stopped then, shut her eyes. William waited. Her lips moved but she said nothing. He put his arms around her, said, "Mama, you rest, and I'll fetch some cool water from the creek."

Her eyes snapped open. "I can't rest, not yet, not till I get it out of my mind."

She clutched his hand, pressed it to her cheek, said, "He was up to his chest in that hole—up to his chest—and he groaned and fell over. That Yankee sergeant reached down and grabbed his hair and pulled him out of the ground like you'd pull a carrot! Kicked him, told him to get up or he'd shoot him!"

"Mama, Mama!"

202

"I ran to Moses, shoved that Yank aside, took your daddy's head in my lap. His eyes were open but he didn't see me." She drew a deep breath. "He was dead—they killed him as surely as they'd shot him through the heart!"

Tears ran down her gaunt cheeks now. "He was a good man and they killed him. But they didn't lick him, oh no!"

From the pocket of her faded shirt she took a small leather bag. She loosened the drawstring and poured the contents into William's hand.

A dozen gold coins.

"For you and your brothers, son," she said. "For rebuilding, he said, for living again after the war was done."

As the father, so the son. William became a dreamer. Not of building an empire for his children, of which as yet he had none, but of revenge, against one man first, later against all the men for which he stood. A dream that would, however, lead him to become in time the wealthiest man in Oughton County.

All are bought for a price, thought William, as he counted the double eagles in the bag his father's hands had made. And sooner or later all must pay that price, some with interest.

In the months that followed he built a small log house and shed, dug a fresh well, planted the seed his father had hidden, and waited for his brothers' return. Messages came instead. Both were dead, George on the battlefield, John at the hands of carpetbaggers who had taunted him and several other southerners as they were coming home and had lynched them when they refused to kowtow to them. So at age twenty-one, William was the Middleton patriarch, responsible not only for his mother but for his widowed sisters-in-law and his nieces and nephews as well.

He worked the farm from can to can't, and after the crops were laid by he taught at the academy. He had learned to make boots by watching his father; he plied that trade at night, using hides he tanned, then tanning hides for others, and finally bought and sold them. At the end of five years the property he controlled was a sight to behold, and men who lacked gumption to start over again worked it for shares.

But he did not forget his father.

He befriended the small detachment of Union soldiers quartered in

203

Oughton to oversee Reconstruction. In time he thought of a way to discover the whereabouts of Brannigan. He took a post office box under the name Thomas Barton and wrote the sergeant a letter in care of the War Department, telling him they had served together under Wilson, though in different regiments. There was money to be made in the south, he said, for men of action.

The first and second letters went unanswered. Six months after mailing the third, William received a reply written in a fine hand but signed with an X followed by "his mark" in the same fine hand. Brannigan was in the army, was garrisoned in St. Joseph, Missouri, with a year to serve on his enlistment. He was very interested in making money, "by any means."

William left his business in the care of his eldest nephew, George's son. He packed a valise, stuck his father's knife in his belt, and rode horseback to Atlanta, where he traveled by train north, then west.

Three weeks later he returned, bringing with him a second, larger valise and the business card of an Englishman named Dunbar he met while homeward bound.

Having greeted his mother and seen to his horse, he took a heavy bundle wrapped in oilcloth from the valise, unrolled it on the ground near his father's grave, and tacked the salt-encrusted thing it contained on the south wall of the barn. Then he ate, drank a jug of whiskey made from corn grown on his own land, and, drunk beyond feeling, slept through the next day and night.

When at last he awoke, he went back to work as though he had never left. And for the rest of his life he told no one except his mother how he had enticed Brannigan with whiskey and the promise of money, how he had driven the sergeant in a wagon to the woods beyond St. Joe, bound him and slit his throat, how, using the skills he had learned from his father, he had skinned him, packed the hide in salt, and brought it home.

A month later he was in touch with Dunbar. Two weeks after that the Englishman arrived and they worked out a plan.

Since the war the government had changed freight rates, making it cheaper for northerners to ship south and more expensive for southerners to ship north. As a result, cotton growers were at the mercy of mill owners. Dunbar represented a company that sold spinning and weaving machinery. Indian Creek would provide the power. All that was needed was capital, which William acquired by marrying Amanda Lewis, a plain but kind girl who was the daughter of a merchant whose family had connections with Atlanta bankers.

William built one mill, then a second and a third. As he prospered, so did the county. In 1882 the railroad came. At the turn of the century he built the finest house in the area, the first to be illuminated by electricity, which was by now generated by Indian Creek, and which he made available to the homes of his employees, which they might choose to rent but which he encouraged them to buy for a fair price. They worked eight-hour days, six-day weeks. No one under age sixteen was hired. Children attended free schools supervised by him and his wife.

He was asked time and again to stand for office, and once a delegation of powerful politicians came to town to offer him the governorship. But he declined. He was content to grow old surrounded by his family and his good friends in the land with which he had come of age. He sold stock in his mills to the workers and handed over their management to his sons and the son-in-law who married his daughter, Cora.

When he died he was buried in a pine box on the farm beside the graves of his mother and father. His simple headstone faced the barn on whose weathered boards were still visible a number of rusted nails, forming, when the light was right, the shape of something that had once hung there.

Chapter Twenty-Two

The facts of the matter were first revealed to Emma Knowles on an August morning. She got up before dawn, as she always did, to feed her companion of ten years, the yellow cat Leander. She awoke as usual without benefit of alarm clock, slipped into her red, white, and blue quilted robe, removed the green ribbon from her gray hair, fluffed it out a bit, and went into the kitchen. She opened a can of tuna fish and served Leander a generous portion. Then, as was her custom, she drained the oil onto a handful of paper napkins and proceeded out the back door to the garbage cans. A full moon shone down from the gray sky.

It was not till she was boiling water for her first cup of coffee that Mrs. Knowles realized. She blinked, then hurried outside again.

It *had* happened!

But how—and why?

She made herself remain calm, fixed the coffee, and drank half a cup "neat," as her late husband Walter called it, without cream and sugar.

Moonglow cast the backyard in pale light. Steeling herself against what she knew awaited, Mrs. Knowles stood on the steps and looked down at the bits of paper scattered from the empty cans to the rose beds and on, around the house.

Someone had taken her garbage.

She went back into the kitchen and locked the door behind her. I

must be dreaming, she decided, as she closed the curtains. Today is—
she checked the calendar above the sink—Monday. The sanitation
department picked up twice a week, Tuesdays and Fridays.

"Yes, Tuesdays and Fridays, without fail, don't they, Leander?"

The yellow cat cleaned its paws.

"Tuesdays and Fridays, yet my cans are empty and this is Monday!"

Had she slept round the clock? She took down the phone and dialed
411.

"Information."

"What day is it?"

"Day?"

"Of the week, please?"

"Today is Monday."

"Are you sure?"

There was a pause. "Is this some kind of joke?"

Mrs. Knowles hung up. Yes, it was Monday and, yes, they had
come for her garbage during the night while she was sleeping. She
knew they had, because for Sunday supper she ate the last of Friday's
roast and wrapped the remains in Sunday's front page—there was a
picture of the president and something about inflation—that bundle
was on top. Underneath was assorted rubbish which had accumulated
for several days in wastebaskets—tissues smeared with cold cream,
bits of hair, junk mail, gum wrappers, not a few dust balls, and at
least three roaches hunted down by Leander.

And now all of this, every last bit and piece, had disappeared.

She wondered. A thought crossed her mind that made her shudder
and go into the bathroom and study her face in the bright mirror.

Perhaps a prankster had dumped the garbage on her front lawn?
Everyone knew she prided herself on its neatness. And the garden
club awarded her a gold plaque for the symmetrical flower beds. Bill
Middleton's boys were capable.

Mrs. Knowles moved through the house and cautiously opened the
front door.

The first lavender rays of dawn slanting across a neat yard jeweled
with dew and a few misty spider webs greeted her.

She went down the stone walk, surveyed the yards on either side.
Nothing—except, yes! Footprints! Now she saw them and scraps of
paper.

Forgetting her flimsy slippers, she darted across the damp grass and picked up a crumbled gum wrapper.

"Whoever did it came this way," she whispered.

On the other side of the low hedge the smudge of footsteps was evident. He—they—had crossed from her yard into that of Mr. and Mrs. Demos.

Clutching the gum wrapper, Mrs. Knowles went back to her living room. She placed this bit of evidence upon the coffee table and then, hugging her arms close to her sides, paced the rug and wondered some more. It wasn't possible, not after all these years.

"What can I do?" she exclaimed.

Her husband Walter's good advice came to her.

During moments of crisis he always said, "Have two tablespoons of bourbon, breathe deep ten times, and put out the cat."

Walter had been a careful man, a most careful man. All right.

Leander didn't like being deposited on the front steps. The bourbon burned her lips and ignited every breath she drew.

But the advice worked. Now she was calm enough to review her situation objectively.

"Persons or person unknown took the contents of my garbage cans during the night." No, not quite objective enough. "During the hours between 10:20 P.M. and 5:30 A.M."

That was better

"Fact two: City garbage collection is on Tuesdays and Fridays."

She looked down at her extended fingers and thoughtlessly examined the blunt nails which she was always careful to keep painted. She added a third: "Never to my knowledge—and I have lived in this house twenty-two years next November—*never* does the sanitation department work at night."

The sanitation department—of course!

She found the number under "municipal." Wasn't seven o'clock yet, but must be a watchman or—

"Hullow, yeah?"

"Sanitation department?"

"That you Wanda?" said the sleepy voice.

"No, this is Mrs.—*Smith*. Have the garbage collection trucks left?"

"Left where? It ain't even seven."

"Yes, I know, but did they make any collections during the night?"

"Inez? You been drinking? Who is this?"

Mrs. Knowles hung up. The facts spoke for themselves. But what did they mean? She might call the police. But—but stealing garbage? They'd become curious about her. They'd ask questions—after all these years of being a good citizen and neighbor.

And they didn't take the cans. The few bits of strewn paper were no more than what the city collectors left.

She checked the gum wrapper on the coffee table. Juicy Fruit. Millions chewed it.

"It's no crime stealing garbage," she told herself.

But—

She threw out nothing that was valuable—not that she *knew* was valuable. The Demoses next door were ordinary people. No one on the block was more than middle-class.

Maybe the thieves had stolen everyone's garbage? Yes, and then that meant it was nothing personally against her. It wouldn't mean they *knew*.

Dawn was past and the morning light was drying the dew. People were stirring. It would be dangerous; still, she must know for sure.

She crept to the low hedge dividing the Demos property from hers. Their can was just beyond her reach. All she had to do was step through the bushes and lift the lid. But she couldn't take the step. It was as though an invisible barrier as solid as steel had risen from the ground.

She retreated to the safety of her kitchen. The phone rang.

Mary Demos said, "Emma, was that you in my backyard?"

She knew that tone of voice, had expected to hear it every day since she and Walter came to Oughton so long ago.

"Emma? Emma?"

At last, she said, "I wasn't in your yard. I wasn't!" And hung up.

She looked down at her dew-dampened house shoes. Her feet were small; Walter called them feet for Cinderella's slipper. She cried out his name, "Walter!"

There was no reply. He was gone and she would not see him again until—

She pressed her fingers into her eyes. What she and Walter had done wasn't wrong. They had made a choice that was theirs to make.

Of course, it meant not having children, since a son or daughter might've shown the world who they really were. And they decided so long ago. Nowadays people like them didn't hide.

She went to the kitchen window. Mary Demos was by the hedge. Leander was in her arms.

Maybe if she told someone the truth. But who? The new priest Mr. McBride seemed like a nice man. He had suffered in Vietnam, had lost an eye. She thought of his pale, blond wife and shook her head.

No. There was no one since Walter died. Now she knew what she had to do, before it was too late, before the people who dropped the gum wrappers told what they'd found out about her.

She got towels from the closet in the hall. They were fluffy and smelled of sunshine. She wet them in the sink and laid one along the bottom of the back door, another by the door into the living room, then pressed a snow white one along the windowsill. She opened the oven door and, having snuffed the pilot light, turned on the gas.

Chapter Twenty-Three

Think of this as a drama, if you like, a little something for now and then in three or five acts, depending on whose wife is putting up the money. Staging may be as you please, though I'm partial to a sleepy front porch with a swing and cane chairs, and a cozy front room with windows overlooking the street. Those windows must reach from floor to ceiling and must have gauzy drapes so the light even at noon is like mockingbird music.

Dreaming, that's what I'm doing, again, but it doesn't matter.

The truth is that the regular Trailways Bus Company service to Oughton was terminated last March, and the Southern Railroad gave up passenger service long before, so those who wish to visit must arrive the best way they can. There are roads in and there are roads out, and the county keeps them in good repair, with convict labor.

I am doing nothing more nor less than dodging the issue, which has to do with Miss Edwina and what Mrs. Dupont Bailey (who shall henceforth remain nameless) said about her, to wit: Miss Edwina is not a lady.

We were sitting on the porch, a shady porch, I might add, except in the winter when the sun is somewhere over Argentina and its rays slant up from the south and make the swing pleasantly warm.

We were sitting there—myself and this nameless person—when

she said, apropos of absolutely nothing, "Daisy is a lady, but Miss Edwina is not."

Now Daisy is a relative of mine who has had certain troubles through the years. Actually, she is strangely afflicted and so for her own good and mine, not to mention Miss Edwina's, she has passed quite a few years in a certain resting place south of Atlanta, where she has made many good friends and has crocheted any number of prize-winning afghans.

"Miss Daisy," this nameless person continued from the cool shade of my porch, "is a lady and will always be. There is no question of her. But," she shook her head and a fly of which she was unaware raised like a helicopter from the hairpiece which she uses (not knowing that everyone knows) to cover a bare spot above her bangs, then settled again as she stopped, and said, "Miss Edwina's is another case altogether."

I am happy to report that I remained silent, both as to the insect and to her line of talk. She wished nothing so much than that I ask "Why?" and then rush to Miss Edwina's aid. However, I had done business, so to speak, with this nameless person before and I knew her modus operandi, as well as the fact that years before when life was harder she had raised for market oodles of ducks. Yes, in her own backyard, which today is decorated with a lovely little summer house and a Chinese fish pond. In those days the ducks cavorted and honked in an old bathtub, except on Saturday nights, said Miss Edwina, when this nameless person would pen them up and use the tub herself, without bothering to change the water.

Well, Miss Daisy was always partial to ducks, or to anything with feathers and a strange way of talking. That's why Miss Edwina was not too surprised when Miss Daisy and she were sitting right here on this same porch and there was a loud thud on the roof, which sounded, said Miss Edwina, just like that time they were down in Florida and one of those coconuts fell and scared them half to death—Miss Edwina was not too surprised when Miss Daisy smiled sweetly and said, "Another one has arrived."

"Another what, Daisy?" asked Miss Edwina.

"I don't know if I should tell you, but then this is your house, too. Still, there are six—or is it seven—in the front room already. Might we put this one in the breakfast nook?"

Miss Edwina said that she frowned at this messsage from the

interior and therefore unexplored regions of Miss Daisy; she requested more information, saying, "Six or seven of what, please?"

"I suppose you will find out sooner or later, Edwina," said Daisy, making her shiest smile, the same expression which Miss Edwina could never abide and which she maintained made Daisy look like a "dirtroad Mona Lisa."

"Damnation, Daisy, I will find out this minute!" cried Edwina, supposing that Miss Daisy had again gathered up all the little birds that had fallen from their nests and placed them here and there, dead, about the house, to be discovered by Aunt Emma, the maid when she noticed caravans of ants and followed them to their destinations.

Miss Daisy replied to Edwina's strong language by saying, "Watch your tongue. Daddy will be coming home soon and you know how he feels about colorful words."

"When Daddy comes home again I'll bite off my tongue and swallow it," declared Edwina, recalling the fact that their father had fallen during the war and that enough of his remains had been piled in a box and shipped home so that there could be no mistake. "Be quick now, Daisy," she said. "What's been falling on the roof that you've been hiding in the front room?"

Again that quaint smile, which caused Miss Edwina to grit her teeth, and then Daisy said, "I will show you if you will promise to be hospitable."

Miss Edwina so promised and Daisy led her into the front room, which was cooler than the porch. The lovely, dark velvet furniture was unchanged by sunlight, and the delightful arrangement of wild dune grass placed in the corner years ago by the sisters' mother looked as crisp and new as the day it was picked on the beach a few miles south of Panacea, Florida.

"This is Miss Edwina," Daisy announced to no one Edwina could see. "She is a bit loud at times, and sometimes forgets and employs strong language, but she has a good heart, so you must not be afraid of her."

Miss Edwina said she had absolute gooseflesh watching Daisy carry on so; she said it was ten times worse than when she took Daddy's shotgun to Budge Wiley's dog—Old Stud Wiley was his name, a yellow dog with short legs and bent ears—because the mutt, she claimed, stared at her till she could no longer stand it.

"Edward, how nice," said Miss Daisy, standing there in the front room that day with Miss Edwina. "I suspected you would be the first to take heart. And Leopold, good! Arthur, Gregory, Joseph, Clarence, Philip—" She was counting on her fingers and nodding and smiling at thin air. "Yes, I think we are all here now, and out in the open. Leopold, I must caution you that in several weeks Daddy will fire the furnace in preparation for winter, so do be careful about the hot-air vent."

Then, said Miss Edwina, Daisy smiled at her and asked if she had any questions.

"Only one," she replied. "What will the town think if they discover we have seven gentlemen living in our house?"

Daisy clapped her hands. "Why, they will be proud!"

"Proud?" said Edwina.

"Of course! It is quite an honor to have seven angels sharing one's domicile!"

In the minutes that followed this revelation, Miss Daisy and her "friends" informed Miss Edwina that there had been some trouble in heaven and that for reasons best left unsaid, due to certain deficiencies in the mental processes of mortals, it was necessary for a number of the heavenly host (which Miss Edwina later referred to as the HH) to make haste elsewhere. Some were at this moment abiding in splendid "glints" on Mars, said Daisy, while others were taking their ease on the Moon and Jupiter, and a few zoomed through space on meteors. These seven had decided to try Earth and had chosen, of all the towns, Oughton, and of all the homes, that of Miss Edwina and Miss Daisy. Only now there were eight, for Miss Daisy interrupted her explanations to welcome the angel that had just thudded on the roof. His name, she informed Edwina, was Gerald, and his robe was trimmed in a green the color of parsley.

So long as Miss Daisy did not make for the gun rack, Edwina went along with her reveries, and so on this occasion she said, "I will inform Aunt Emma to put two leaves in the dining room table and add eight settings for supper."

At this Miss Daisy giggled and said, "Edwina, you know nothing about angels! They don't eat fried chicken and rice like we do."

"Pork chops?" said Miss Edwina—at least in the retelling years later she claims to have said this, but, frankly, it seems too artsy-craftsy. However, Miss Daisy is alleged to have giggled again before saying, "They don't eat, silly, never! They don't eat because they don't have to."

"Thank God for that," Miss Edwina claims to have said. "Eight more mouths would be about eight too many, and we only have the one bathroom."

"Well," said Miss Daisy, "as far as guests go they will be about the most perfect. They don't need beds because they don't sleep, and who ever heard of an angel taking a bath? What's more, being of heavenly disposition, they won't get into Daddy's cigars and bourbon. And you should see them, Edwina! How lovely they are, like living rainbows, and their eyes—they see only the beauty in one!"

After a time, Edwina once said, she began to feel that maybe something *was* living unseen in that front room. At night when the moon was coming up over the woods below the yard the crickets would all of a sudden switch off and the wind would stop and, well, she heard something moving amongst that velvet furniture and her mind's eye conjured up these eight stately gentlemen sitting around Daddy's leather-topped table playing cards. Why cards, she never could understand herself, but she went on to say that the really strange thing was that every angel won each and every hand and not one of them ever lost.

After a while Miss Daisy forgot about them, though, and so did Miss Edwina. Maybe they left without saying good-bye, though you wouldn't expect angels to be rude. Miss Daisy took leave, also, first of her senses, then of the premises, going first to the state facility after a particularly harrowing night when she allowed the Rome-to-Columbus express to roll over her while she was curled up between the rails. Miss Edwina was in Atlanta that day, so Walter Knowles took responsibility for transporting Daisy the hundred miles to the hospital, a slow, hot journey by car which Miss Daisy thoroughly enjoyed, for she confided to Mr. Knowles's wife, Emma, that all of this had happened once before in a dream, and that what awaited her at the end of this dusty Georgia road was a new life, for the train running over her was symbolic of a new birth and a new variety of experiences, one of which having to do with her being the first lady to swim the English Channel, though for what reason she couldn't tell, since there were perfectly fine boats available to take one back and forth at reasonable prices.

There is more to this than meets the eye, and I do not mean Daisy's insanity, a subject which has been used beyond exhaustion by those dealing with their Southern heritage. As Miss Edwina said more than once, "There are fields of Daisies; they do not bloom alone."

But we were on the porch and the one who shall remain nameless was making a serious charge. "Miss Edwina," she said, "has been frequenting that cafe by the tracks run by that Mrs. Wimpton and her freak son, and in that place she has been seen sitting on a stool at the counter eating doughnuts dunked in coffee. And what is more, she lingers there and converses with the other customers—I almost said 'patrons,' forgive me, please, not a few of whom who have been in Judge Green's court and not as spectators. Finally, upon leaving this place Miss Edwina has been observed—" the nameless one looked both ways and leaned toward me, her motion causing the fly to lift off again and go into a holding pattern remindful perhaps of a halo "—she has been observed using a toothpick while walking down a public street!"

With this bit of news delivered, she settled back and looked at me as if to say, "The point is proven: Miss Edwina is not a lady."

But Miss Daisy, who, it seems, is now determined to turn the state of Georgia into Afghanistan via the dreadful power of her crochet needle, is a lady.

And so, thought I, is the nameless one—a dear, dear lady, of the sort that is not being made anymore.

But of course I said nothing of the sort and ended this little drama by giving assurances that I would have a talk with Miss Edwina concerning her various deviations.

It will be an interesting talk, I imagine, should I ever have the courage to undertake it.

Chapter Twenty-Four

She was neutral about death. It did not terrify her. Nor was it a mystery. Her father was killed in the war. His body was never recovered, so in a way it was as though he hadn't really died. As a child she daydreamed of him living as a god on a Pacific isle. As she grew older her dreams found other subjects.

Her mother died in an automobile accident. By that time she had finished the university at Athens and was married and living in Birmingham. The news of course surprised her and she cried and was filled with a sense of loss. At the same time, however, her husband gave her support and took care of the funeral arrangements and the will. She went home to Oughton and dressed in black and developed a polite yet sadly warm way of dealing with those who, out of love or duty, offered sympathy.

Several months after her mother's funeral she discovered she was pregnant. She did not feel guilty, though to be honest she wondered when it had happened. The day her mother was killed perhaps? But what did that matter? The important thing was that new life was within her.

The child was born, a son. They named him after the husband; he was named after his father, also. Traditional. The boy was beautiful and healthy and looked as though he would live forever.

Death went out of her life for a time. Oh, she was aware of another war. She saw the news on TV every night. The bodies, the solemn ceremonies for the dead. There were accidents, too, not to mention murders and natural disasters. But they stayed away from her. She, her husband, and their son were healthy.

A year and a half later she was pregnant again. This time she thought of death, of passing away on the delivery table. It was silly, she knew. After all, this was not her first baby. And she'd had no difficulty with the boy. The doctor told her she was healthy and strong. She had youth on her side. But it was true that some just like her had died. So she worried.

But there was no trouble. The daughter arrived when expected. Another lovely baby, and once again she felt thankful death had passed her by. But she was also sad. Looking down into the sweet face of her little girl she wondered had she done the right thing. Was it fair to bring life into a world which would eventually terminate it? Maybe it was better not to live.

Maybe it was better, but she had no way of knowing. She was stuck with living till she died, just like everyone else. The idea gave her a sense of community, though it didn't lessen the specter of death.

Life went on. Her husband advanced in his profession. They moved to Denver. They built a big house in a good neighborhood. They bought a foreign car and went from the suburbs to the exclusive downtown shops for clothes, even though she knew the old car was still good and she was paying for labels, not added value.

She gained weight, then went on a diet and lost it, then gained it back. Her husband said he liked her that way, whatever *that* meant, and that she was still his sweet Georgia peach. And since she'd lost pounds once, she knew she could do it again, when she wished, if she wished. But she wondered what use it was to starve yourself, not that she liked food that much. It was the principle involved, the doing without for no good reason. It was like her hair. A few strands of gray appeared, seemingly overnight. At first she used a rinse, but after a time she stopped. What was a little gray anyhow? Covering it up only proved you were ashamed, but why be ashamed of a perfectly natural process?

She watched her children grow, marking their progress on the inside of a closet door, blue marks for him, red for her. Once she backed up against the door and using a fingernail file scratched her height above theirs. When she stepped back and took a look she was surprised how short she was, how little there was of her after all. Not much, yet all that had gone into the making of her! She had to sit down. She had to close the closet door and keep it closed. It was as though something were in there, waiting.

Her aunt died. Her mother's sister, a very dear woman who'd never married and who, consequently, treated her as the daughter she never had. The aunt lived in her mother's house in Oughton, the house she'd grown up in. She died there, in a front room, sitting by the same window she'd stared out on rainy days.

Her husand was upset by this death. He was scheduled for an important conference in Hawaii. He had to go, but if he did, who would take care of the funeral?

She told him she could do it.

At first he shook his head and tried to figure some way he could be in both places at once. She told him again, this time being very calm and gentle, explaining there was a woman who would stay with the children in her absence. She would fly to Atlanta and rent a car. She had her credit cards and checkbook. She was a grown person. Why shouldn't she?

He allowed her to convince him. She made reservations, packed two bags, gave the woman instructions, and took a cab to the airport. Her feelings confused her. Rather than being sad or frightened at the prospect of flying away, she discovered that little pain in her stomach signaling excitement. She hadn't known it in years. She found herself crossing and recrossing her legs. Her palms were damp.

The airport fascinated her. She seemed to be moving through a glass tunnel. All sorts of events took place around her, people rushing, lights flashing, voices booming, but at the same time she experienced a delightful detachment, as though it wasn't exactly real, as though it all happened on the inside of her eyes, as on a screen. Her feet moved slowly, dreamily, past security guards. They searched her handbag, smiled, wished her a good trip. She nodded and glided into the plane, allowing the stewardess to seat her.

The flight took almost three hours. They offered her a cocktail. It was morning. She'd not had a drink before nightfall, not ever. At first she said no. But when the girl passed down the aisle with drinks on a tray for other passengers, she changed her mind. She found it rather interesting to look down at the world from thirty-six thousand feet while sipping a vodka collins. It didn't mean anything, of course. How could it? She was going home to bury a loved one. It was a duty, not an adventure. She drained her glass and watched the clouds. A time would come when someone would have to do the same for her. She held her hand up so that the window glass darkened. The face she saw there was hers. She knew she was no longer young. But she was not old either, not yet. Perhaps she would never be. Perhaps in the youth of her middle age it would be all over.

That made her think. What would happen to the children, to her husband? Could they manage without her? Maybe it was the altitude but she felt silly. They'd have to! Of course, he'd probably remarry. Why not? Maybe another peach. She smiled.

She glanced up and down the aisle at the businessmen. At least they looked like men flying somewhere to take care of business. More than likely they were married, had families. What if their wives died? Did they have lovers in those distant towns they visited?

The seat belt light came on. The pilot said they were going to land shortly. And that if they looked out the left side they could see Stone Mountain. She fastened her belt and stared out the window at the nearing earth. Now she could discern houses again, cars, people. Her husband always said landing was the dangerous time, that and taking off. Things went wrong then. She pushed against the back of her seat, gripped the armrests with her hands, and imagined she was strapped in an executioner's chair. The wheels touched and squeaked. She felt the pressure of wing flaps catching air. The plane ran down the strip, turned, and taxied to the ramp.

She got her bags and carried them to a car rental booth and made arrangements for transportation. The young man behind the counter suggested that since it was such a pretty day she might prefer a convertible. Her first reaction was that wouldn't be proper for the business she had to take care of. But the sun was shining, and she could put the top up when she went to the funeral home, and, after all, it was her aunt who had died, not her.

It was a nice little car, light blue with a white top. She was used to an automatic transmission. The rental car had a stick shift on the floor. At first she had reservations. After she drove down the airport concourse and went through the gears once, missing one in the process and making a terrible grinding sound, she discovered it was fun being close to the ground in a light car that responded to her slightest touch. She pulled into a parking space and let the top down. On the interstate highway to Oughton the wind destroyed her hair. But it felt good and she could always fix it. Once she stopped at a red light. A truck pulled alongside. She glanced up and saw the driver looking down at her. Then she noticed her skirt was hiked above her knees. He was admiring her legs! She was first shocked, then pleased. Let him. She jiggled her knee a little, and when the light changed, she looked up at his tan face and smiled. He waved. She drove away so fast her hair streamed out behind like one of those radiator decorations on cars in the thirties. Her uncle had one and he took her riding and let her polish it.

She pulled off the highway into a shopping center and bought a cheap scarf, blue, to match the car, and a pair of sun glasses, the metal frame kind with wrap-around lens. Did she need anything else? Maybe a plastic box of breath-freshener mints.

The mints made her remember death. Not because she thought it was bitter or foul, but rather because she knew there would be hours of dealing with people and she wouldn't have time to brush her teeth and take care of herself. No, when someone died you didn't have time for yourself at all, never. You had to put a portion of your own life into the grave with them. They demanded it, or at least society did, or thought it did.

It would be so much simpler, she decided, if people self-destructed, vanished in a cloud of smoke, leaving nothing behind, not even a spot of ashes. Let the wind blow them away. Didn't the Chinese think something like that? Not the vanishing but the wind? Her mother had a little thing made of slivers of glass hanging on the back porch and when the wind blew through it made a tinkling sound which was supposed to be the voice of the family's ancestors. It sounded so cool, so dreamy. When she was a girl she hoped that was the way she'd be remembered—a cool breeze and music on a hot summer day, hot as only days in Georgia could be, blue-haze hot with the buzz of bees, days hot enough to make a cat sweat, her uncle said.

The scarf held her hair from the wind and gave her a movie star look. The dark glasses and the sporty car, she fancied, made men look closely as she whizzed by. Men? She wondered about that. Maybe she'd rented the convertible not because it was a nice day but for some other reason?

Reasons or not, she was nearing Oughton and she had to be careful. Things had changed. She hadn't driven these streets for two years. There were traffic lights and crosswalks where before there were none. She recognized the shops she'd frequented. There were new ones, though, and some whose names had been changed. Things did change. The old gave way to the new, even in Oughton. That was simplistic but true.

And this was the town in which she was born, in which she went to school. This town was responsible for the sort of person she was. It supplied the teachers, the books, the adults upon whom she based her self-concept. In a way the town was her and she was the town and would always be, because the town affected her when she was young and defenseless and open to suggestion. It was, she realized, in its own way, like a religion. What was that old saying—you can take a man out of the country but you can't take the country out of a man. Or a town either.

She remembered the way home. Even though they'd made a street one-way and she had to go over a block, she had no difficulty. There was the house. It looked smaller than before. It always looked smaller, every time she came back. Smaller and smaller, yet when she was a child it seemed so big. She smiled. Fifty years from now would it shrink down to nothing? Or when she was ancient and withered would it begin growing again?

She had a key. The door opened with no fuss. She knew the house was empty but was it, really? A person had died in the front room. Did that mean her soul or spirit or whatever was lurking about? Maybe she should say something, like "Anybody home?" Any*body* was appropriate. And if auntie was still about, well, she'd know, and since the dead didn't have a habit of speaking to the living, if indeed they could, why bother?

She closed the door, took off her scarf and glasses. Sunlight streamed through the sparkling windows. The house was immaculate. That was the way auntie lived. No dirt, no dust, no smears.

There probably weren't any fingerprints either. No evidence, of either death or life.

She moved through the rooms, coming at last to the small one on the front where the old woman died. She sniffed the air, bent down and examined the figured rug. She expected traces. It was said that when a person dies she loses control of her bowels and bladder. There was an odor. Or was she imagining it?

The doorbell rang. Probably Mrs. Bailey who'd lived next door always. She took her time answering it, steeling herself for the first confrontation with a sympathizer. She knew, with dread, she had innumerable nods and "Thank yous" ahead.

But it wasn't a woman. A man. He looked familiar. Bill Middleton, sure. From high school. He lived one street over. He'd put on weight and his hair was darker and his eyes were more serious. Still, she knew him.

She opened the door and said his name. He smiled and said hers. His hands moved nervously, as though they needed something to steady them. She offered one of hers. He squeezed it and asked how she was and said she looked fine without waiting for her answer. She smiled and said she'd know him anywhere. He released her hand and patted the front of his coat. He'd changed, he said. She said not that much, to be polite, and then wondered what he really thought about her figure. There was a time when he liked it. She'd gone out with him, danced close with him, even parked with him behind the country club and allowed him to kiss her and maybe pet a little, but she didn't pet him back. He never took off her clothes, not even loosened a button. Now she asked herself why he hadn't. Was it because she'd given him no encouragement? She hadn't, that was true, but it was because she was taught not to, not because she didn't want him to.

He said how sorry he was about her aunt. He asked was there anything he could do. She asked how his wife was. He said all right, nothing more. He wanted to know what she planned to do about the house. He asked because that was his business now, real estate. Did she want to rent it or sell it? He knew the time wasn't right to ask, but still, she was here now and these things had to be done, one way or another.

Rather than asking him in, she came out on the porch and they sat on the steps in the sunlight. She fancied that from the street their pose looked like an illustration from the *Saturday Evening Post*, captioned maybe, "She met him on the steps with wonderful news."

She let him know what she knew. The house was hers. Her mother had left it to her with the provision that her aunt be allowed to live in it till she passed away. What did he think she should do?

Did she mean what would be best, in terms of financial? In that case she should rent furnished, unless she wanted to remove sentimental objects. It would bring in at least three hundred a month. People were coming to Oughton, executives who worked for two new companies. Whoever handled it for her would get a twenty-five percent commission. That was standard. So much for insurance and taxes. He smiled. At the very least she'd clear twenty-two hundred a year.

She looked at him. What had happened? Had she changed that much? No, that was silly, stupid even. Bill was trying to do the right thing. Did she expect him to act like a teenager? What was done was done. He probably had sex with his wife on a casual basis, more to keep her happy than him. Money was what he sought now. It was better than sex, more powerful. Maybe all women looked alike in the dark, just like all money, but unlike women, the pleasure money gave lasted on and on.

He wanted to know what she thought. She rose and told him she'd think about it. Actually, she knew she would let him do what he wanted with the house. She didn't care about the house or about the money, not even if it was twenty-two thousand instead of twenty-two hundred. But she wanted him to have to sweat it out. He'd enjoy success that much more.

He said fine. What else could he say? Then he asked if she were staying in the house. She didn't know, hadn't considered it. But she said yes, and he replied he'd be in touch. As she watched him walk to his car she wondered what that remark meant, although she knew exactly what he meant by it. It was herself she wasn't sure of.

He drove away and she went inside. This house had been her home. The furniture, rugs, pictures, the cracks in the ceiling, all was as familiar as the back of her hand. She turned her hand over and saw things she'd never noticed before and laughed at her stupid reliance on foolish expressions.

Things as well as people changed. She didn't have to be a physicist to know that. The furnishings held memories for her, but she desired neither them nor the memories. They were over, past, through, done. The sooner she was rid of this house and all it contained the better she'd be!

Better how? She asked herself, was she experiencing guilt? For what? For moving away from Oughton, from her family? For not feeling deeply the loss of a loved one? Those people living in the Middle East knew how to lose. She saw them on TV wailing and throwing themselves in the dust. Some leaped into open graves. Soldiers had to restrain them. They were lucky. They got it out of their systems quickly and went back to being normal.

But she couldn't help feeling as she did. Dull, bored, sleepy. That tunnel of glass she experienced at the airport surrounded her again. Beyond its walls things weren't real. It was like hearing your voice on a tape for the first time, or seeing a picture of yourself shot from the rear showing a side of you you never saw.

She climbed the stairs and went to the little room she'd called her own so many years before. How small it was! And the bed, how narrow. How soft. Mushy, even. Had her body changed that much? She had to have a firm mattress now or her back killed her in the morning. She slipped off the dark glasses and stared at the ceiling. To think this bed, this little room, was the place of so many dreams. The summer nights she lay here sweating and thinking of—no, hoping—what would happen to her in the years to come. She laughed to herself. And it had all happened!

She got up and looked in the closet. Empty, thank goodness. Years ago her mother had given all her old clothes to some charity. The dresser was empty too, though a faint trace of a perfume she experimented with still lingered. She looked down at the backyard from the small oval window beyond the bed. Lush, green, she fancied she could smell grass though the window was closed.

The doorbell again.

She slipped on the glasses, deciding to wear them even indoors. People would think it was because she didn't want them to see the redness of her eyes. But really they gave her a comforting shield. She could watch them and not be observed. It was a privacy, of a sort, for the time which was not private.

The mourning began. It was old Mrs. Bailey. Her voice filled with tears and spilled over. She'd been to the funeral home. She'd found the body and called the authorities. Heart attack. She was her friend. Something had to be done. She made the arrangements. She hoped she didn't object, but something just had to be done!

She placed her arm about the older woman's shoulder and tried to calm her, saying yes, she'd done everything properly, and, yes, she knew they'd been dear friends, and yes, she was very sad too, and, yes, it would be all right after a time.

After a time it was all right. Mrs. Bailey blew her nose and wiped her eyes and went back to her house next door. Now she felt hungry. The vodka on the plane had carried her this far, but its effect had passed. A drink would keep her going, but she knew there wouldn't be a drop in the house. She had things to do, the sooner the better. She brought in her bags and carried them up to her old room. She freshened a bit and then drove downtown.

She found a small restaurant in a building that hadn't existed the last time she was home. She forgot the quaint custom of Oughton and ordered a vodka martini, but settled for a glass of white wine. She ate a cheese sandwich and a tossed salad. After a cup of coffee, she went back to the car and drove to the office of her family's lawyer, Ben Lewis.

He was busy, said the receptionist, but when he heard her name, he came out to greet her. She had babysat for his daughter who was at college now. It had been a long, long time. She was looking so well. He offered his sympathy. She graciously accepted. The door closed on the receptionist and the world, and they got down to business. Auntie left everything to her. Her insurance policy was enough to cover the funeral and leave perhaps twelve hundred extra. She could dispose of her personal effects as she wanted. She did bequeath a jade ring to the little girl, her daughter, and a gold pocket watch to her son. Heirlooms. Value was chiefly sentimental. He'd probate the will as a matter of course. But there were no problems, legally speaking. She could do as she wished with the property. Did she have plans?

She told him about Bill Middleton and his offer. He thought it fair, but suggested she hold out for three-fifty per month. Or demand a straight three hundred from Middleton, requiring that he make his profit and pay taxes, etc., out of whatever he got over and above that.

She thanked him and asked he send his bill to her Denver address, which she'd leave with the receptionist. He said it was good seeing her again and would tell his daughter Lauree hello for her. Again, his sympathy. They shook hands. His fingers were amazingly thick to her, and very dry.

She drove to Bird's Funeral Home, arriving there before realizing she hadn't raised the convertible top. Oh well, no one saw her. And even if they did, so what? It was her dead aunt not theirs.

As she entered she remembered the pale coolness, accentuated by a sweet odor of gladiolas, from the last time she was there, when her mother died. She was met by a slim young man in a dark suit. She told him who she was and what she wanted. He nodded and spoke in a gentle whisper and conducted her through several rooms—one containing a casket and flowers and two kneeling persons—to a further chamber.

Her aunt lay in the casket, her eyes closed, her pale hands folded upon her ample breast. It was hard to tell she was dead, at first. But the longer she looked down at her the more she recognized the waxen signs of lifelessness. Her eyelashes seemed as brittle as spider legs, and the pink of her cheeks was cool, not warm. She touched her hand. It was a lump.

The young man hovered like a bat at her shoulder and asked if she were pleased. She nodded. And then she asked when the ceremony would take place. In the morning, he replied. At ten. The minister would hold one service here—a brief one, with a hymn, perhaps, to take advantage of the establishment's fine organ—and another at graveside. Did she anticipate many mourners?

She really had no idea. It didn't matter, actually, he said. They had a good supply of folding chairs, and there were sliding doors that could be opened to enlarge the area, should the need arise. She was impressed by this foresight and told him so, not sarcastically, but sincerely. It was reassuring to know that civilization had progressed to the point where death was institutionalized, even here in Oughton. He said that while Mrs. Bailey had made arrangements, there were

227

papers she needed to sign, if she had time. She did, and picked up an ink stain on the forefinger of her right hand. It reminded her of a birthmark.

It was late afternoon. What else to be done? She knew people in town. She had old friends, from childhood, from school. But why bother them? Maybe they expected to see her. Maybe some would come to the funeral. Maybe not. She hoped they wouldn't. Oughton was getting to her, like an illness. Yes, like the last cold she had. She spotted the symptoms, did nothing to hinder them, and watched them progress—a tickle in the throat, a slight pressure along the top of the windpipe, a heaviness in the upper chest, a sore throat, runny nose, a sneeze or two, upset stomach, but in the end no fever, so it passed in two days. Her husband was out of town on business, so what did it matter? She made the children kiss her cheek instead of her lips. They didn't mind, and they laughed when she sneezed.

And—and—and—!

She wanted to escape, to flee.

But she knew she couldn't, not yet, and so she was stuck with time on her hands—no, around her neck—and if she didn't manipulate it, it would twist her this way and that until, maybe, she broke, and while that might be curiously interesting, it wouldn't be pretty.

She drove, past the grade school, the high school, past the church, past the park she played in long ago. Everything seemed smaller, as though thirty years of summer rain had succeeded in shrinking it. She felt the glass tunnel enclose her again and now she guided the cute blue convertible with her fingertips and hummed along with the radio's gaudy music. She pulled in at a beer and wine store and bought two bottles of Cold Duck, then stopped at a shopette and picked up some crackers and cheese.

Mrs. Bailey was sitting on the steps. She had recovered. Her large face showed no signs of tears. She even smiled as she asked had she been to the funeral home. And then she invited her over for supper. Nothing fancy. She knew she should accept. It was as much for the elderly woman as herself. No, more. But she didn't want to. She wanted to go inside and lock the door and have a nice glass of bubbly wine. And then she wanted to strip and soak in a hot tub, then get out and dry and have another glass. She didn't want to call her children. She didn't want to do anything, really.

She told Mrs. Bailey she was very tired. She appreciated her kindness, but she had to relax. She showed her the bags. She had food, enough for her stay.

She could tell the older woman was disappointed. She nodded when she said if there was anything she could do she'd be next door, and so forth.

Yes, and so they parted and she went in and locked the door and had that drink. She picked up the phone to call home, then put it down and thought, then picked it up and dialed information and got Bill Middleton's number and called him instead. She told him what she wanted. He hesitated. She said she knew what rental property was bringing nowadays. Did he want to handle the house or not? Very well. She gave him her home address. The checks would be made out to her, not to her husband. She thanked him for being so helpful and hung up before he could say anything, if he had chosen to.

She soaked in the tub, the same old relic set up on feet with claws she'd basked in so many times, the same water container, she recalled, in which she'd first become aware of the potentials of her own body. The girl two blocks over—what was her name, Cassie something? Had only stayed in town about six months, long enough to explain the mysteries. Girls like that, moving around all the time, they had to have something to offer, some magic to make others accept them, if only for a short time.

She closed her eyes, let the warm water do its thing, thought about doing hers, decided no. She could always do it if she wanted. No one controlled her. No one. She thought of Bill Middleton, then wondered why she'd been so insistent about the checks being in her name. Was she trying to tell him something, or herself?

She got out of the tub and wrapped in a big towel and pulled the plug. The water rumbled and gurgled. Memory, down the drain. Men left traces, women didn't. They used those traces as evidence in rape cases. Not that she knew firsthand, but on TV and in magazines—

What did they know? What were they trying to tell the world? Or, better why, why did they want to tell? No mystery. To make money. So they dealt with those subjects people craved knowledge of but didn't want to discuss openly. And why was she thinking these thoughts?

She put on her robe, took another towel and wrapped it round her head, found the empty glass and went downstairs and poured more wine. She called the children, dialing direct. The boy answered. He was being good. He missed her. The little girl said she did, too. When was she coming home? Home?

Tomorrow, she started to say. But didn't. Never? That was exciting, but dumb. Of course she was going back to Denver, soon as auntie was in the ground. Of course. Her husband would be gone three more days. There was no reason for her to return so quickly. She told the housekeeper she had to stay two more days. Family business. She understood. She told her children, asked them to continue being good, and promised them wonderful gifts. They understood.

She hung up and finished her wine, then poured some more and opened the crackers. As she sliced the cheese she giggled, not from the bubbly, though it might have helped. She found her little adventure very exciting, not to mention shocking.

It was so ridiculous, her taking the opportunity of the death of a loved one to do things she ordinarily wouldn't attempt. And in Oughton, of all places. The cheese was good. So was the drink. She licked her fingers.

Tomorrow she would do what she must. She would go through the ceremony—ceremonies, there were two, she remembered—and she would stand by dear auntie to the end. Of course, she wouldn't remain till they filled in the grave with dirt. People didn't do that anymore, not even in Oughton. No threat of body snatchers. She'd do exactly what she should, depending upon the young man at the funeral home for guidance.

Afterwards she'd speak to Mrs. Bailey. She and auntie were such good friends. All right, Mrs. Bailey could have all of auntie's things, excepting the ring and pocket watch, to do with as she pleased. That would leave the house furnished, but still ready for occupancy, soon as Bill Middleton went to work on tenants. Maybe she'd tell Mrs. Bailey that auntie had left her five hundred dollars in the will. Yes, money makes all things easier because it takes the place of explanations. The deaf can count.

So by noon at the latest she'd be free. To do what? She propped her feet on the chair facing her, leaned back, took a sip, and thought of possibilities. She had a checkbook. She had credit cards. She handled the household accounts, not her husband. She could do whatever she wanted and he'd never be the wiser. Not that she, a Georgia peach, would do anything to upset him.

She laughed at that.

Another stupid thing to say. How could she know what would upset him? Mismatched socks upset him, even when both were navy blue. No, she wouldn't worry about him. He wasn't here. She was. He wasn't she, anyhow. What she wanted to do counted now.

She'd drive to Atlanta, climb back into that glass tunnel, and fly away. Mexico City? That was said to be an exciting place. She'd never been out of the country. But Mexico City, she reflected, was immense. And there were lots of poor people. They'd make her feel guilty. Not that she was. Poor people made her think of death. Death reminded her of Oughton. She was tired of that subject.

What made her think of life?

She closed her eyes and tilted back her head and looked up at the light above the table. A rosy warm hue filtered through her eyelids. The sun, that was life-giving. Go to someplace on the Mexican coast. To Acapulco. Of course, she didn't have a bathing suit. Maybe they swam in the nude? Why not? Underneath that shroud they'd slipped on auntie was bare flesh. When it rained— When the casket—

Why did she think of that? Sometimes it seemed that her mind was against her! But she wouldn't let it win, not this time. She'd go to Acapulco and buy whatever clothes she needed when she arrived. They had fine shops there, beautiful places. She'd stay at the best hotel, the one with individual pools for each suite, and if she wanted to swim nude she would. She'd go down on the beach, too, and lie in the sun, and maybe have drinks in one of those huts with grass roofs, and if there was music and some handsome young man asked her to dance, well, she knew how, she could dance as well as the next woman, maybe better—no, absolutely better!

She saw herself dancing on the sand. She saw herself clearly. She saw she was dancing with a man but she couldn't see beyond his manliness. His face was unclear, but that didn't matter. She was on the beach under the hot sun dancing for herself, not him. She could've danced alone just as well.

Now that her plans were made and she could see beyond the ordeals of tomorrow, she felt better. She had one more glass of wine, then went upstairs. She slept in the soft bed of her youth, and she slept soundly, believing it was the last time she would have to deal with home.

Chapter Twenty-Five

the bottle collector

Everybody said, "Him? Why foot, that's nobody but <u>Bobby-bob</u> and he's nuttier than a fruitcake!" But he knew better. They were nutty. The voices told him so. The voices said they were nutty because they didn't have voices to tell them things. That made him feel sorry for them. That made him not get mad when they laughed at him and tapped their fingers to their heads or flapped their arms like he did sometimes. He felt sorry because he couldn't figure how it would be not to have voices. Except lonely.

He was born hearing them. Right from the start they told him the true from the false. That woman he had to call momma wasn't his momma no more than the Atlanta Highway was. And his pa wasn't his pa neither. No. The voices told him they used those two to give him shape. He was something mighty special, something made somewhere else, a long way off, and sent down to this little town called Oughton.

The voices said, "Don't be afraid. They can't hurt you or help you. But we can, and we will." The voices gave him a body like no one else's in town. They made him short and quick and bent his back so he could get down low to the ground and not waste time when he turned into a squirrel or a fox or a spotted cat. The voices told him what he was from moment to moment. Sometimes he'd be walking around

233

the square looking at himself in store windows and the voice would say, "Right now you're really a bird dog." And sure enough the next window he passed would show him as a brown and white hound with big teeth and a long red tongue.

Living without voices must be terrible. How could they know things? The voice told him all about the Indians who lived on the land long before the whites. The voices told him how to find old paths through the woods and things the Indians had buried. Bones mostly, and sometimes piles of arrowheads. There was a big box, though, and it was filled right up to the top with money. Gold coins as big as quarters and shiny as the sun. Money for looking at and holding, not for spending. The voices put deposit bottles along the road so he could have money. That box was way back in the woods in the place the voices let some of the townspeople know about. When the moon was full they'd come to a cave there and do things. Not all of them had voices all the time. But on those full-moon nights they heard things. Did things, too.

The voices sent him everywhere, it seemed. He thought maybe that was his job, to go and see things for the voices. Maybe when he looked at what was happening, the people who made the voices saw too, wherever they were. So he kept his eyes open. One time he saw those two mean fellows, those brothers, do it to a girl. And when they were finished they dug a hole and pitched her in and covered her up. She didn't die, though. Another fellow was watching too. Man who ran a grocery store. When the two bad brothers left, he dug her up. He watched close but nothing happened. The grocery store man just went away and left her there. The voices told him she was hurting because her clothes were tight. So he took them off. At first she didn't seem to understand but then she did. So when the voices told him to do it to her, he did, and she didn't mind. She just laid back in that hole and looked up at the full moon so it shined like two moons in her eyes. And he did it real good. He did it twice without stopping. He did it every bit as good as when he did it to those girls who heard voices too.

He could always tell who heard voices. They smelled like animals that want to be petted. He never heard their voices though. His voices told him that didn't matter. There were many voices. There were enough to go around for everybody to have one. But some folks didn't want them. That fellow who spit on sandwiches at that eating place by the railroad tracks, one time he smelled like he heard voices, but his own voices told him he heard something else and to leave him alone because he could change into things that weren't animals or people. He could turn into something nobody had ever seen and lived to tell about.

Those girls that heard voices smelled good. Like animals that wanted to be petted. To be touched all over. They said he smelled good too. They did it in the woods. Sometimes it was when they were squirrels. Sometimes they were rabbits. Sometimes birds. Once they did it when they were rattlers. Being a rattler was all right, and he'd be one whenever the voices told him he was. But all that hissing dried his mouth out something awful and made his throat sore.

He was a lot more when he was an animal. But maybe that was because there were more things to look out for. Take being a cat. Had to watch out for dogs then. Could smell them. But some knew how to sneak up downwind. And if you ran quick without looking you might get hit by a truck or a car. Lots of people liked hurting animals. The voices didn't want them to do it though. One time they told him what to do about it. They said, "Hit him with a big stick, tie him up, stuff his hat in his mouth, cover him with leaves, leave him for the ants." So he did. A long time passed and then the voices told him to go and see how the man who liked to hurt animals was. His clothes were there, and his bones. But he was gone. He was ants now, underground. He himself had never been an ant. Maybe it would be fun to sting somebody. But it wasn't good to think about being stepped on.

Those girls that heard voices and smelled like animals wanting to be petted, they always had children when he was through with them. He was very good at making children. The voices told him this was his real gift. "Those children hear voices too," they said, "so that means there are more voices." More voices was good. Even if they didn't look like him, he knew they were his children because of the way they smelled. They smelled like him. Sometimes when he was a squirrel he climbed trees by the houses they lived in and looked at them through the window as they slept. Sometimes they smiled and moved their mouths and he knew that was the voice working inside of them.

The voices told him he was like the old trees, even the ones chosen

235

by lightning. He was like the rocks too and the creeks. They said he was just like them because he would never die. They said it didn't matter what the ones who didn't hear voices did. It didn't matter if they built their roads and their houses and tore up everything doing it. "It doesn't matter, Bobby-bob," they said, "because nothing they do will last very long." The old trees would last longer, and the rocks and streams too. They were as old as the moon. He was that old too. And he would last just as long because he was slowly passing over into those children.

Once the voices showed him what they meant. They slipped him into one of his children. A little, dark-skinned girl with red ribbons in her hair. He had been a lot of different animals but this was the first time he was a child. Things looked pretty much the same through her eyes, though. But he didn't like it when her momma beat him with a strap just because he did something she said he shouldn't in the corner of the kitchen. The voices told him not to worry. They said momma heard voices sometimes only later she didn't remember. That was what made her so mean. So he put down the butcher knife he had gotten when she turned her back.

He wondered how long it would be before the town went away and the highways wore out. He asked the voices when things would be like they once were. They told him it would be sooner than he thought, and so long as he listened to them and did what they said, he'd be all right.

So he did.

And it didn't bother him when the other people, the poor ones without voices, laughed and said he was nutty. Didn't bother him at all. He just waved and laughed right back, even though inside he felt sorry for them.

Chapter Twenty-Six

It was another sweltering day in late July. The sky was a hazy blue and the only breeze along the Oughton bypass was lazy dust-devils caused by passing trucks loaded with gravel, pulpwood, or chickens. The convicts from the county work camp were cutting weeds under the sleepy gaze of guards armed with shotguns.

A prisoner with scraggly red hair chanted, "Ain't gonna go to hell when I die, oh no, oh no!" Another picked up the rhythm: "I'm down in hell right now, oh yeah, oh yeah!"

The dozen men, all wearing sweat-stained white uniforms with black stripes down the baggy legs, sang in time to their flashing sling blades. The sultry air stank of weeds and sweat, of exhaust and of tobacco juice the guards spat on the blistering pavement.

"Got me a place in heaven," the convict chanted, "where there ain't no weeds no more, oh yeah, oh yeah!"

As the men sang this verse, one in the line wiped the sweat from his eyes and looked toward the cool shade of the kudzu-covered pines edging the right-of-way. He hunched his gorilla shoulders and looked, then he dropped his sling and shaded his eyes and stared at the vine-draped trees.

One of the guards shifted his chew to the other side of his jaw, spat, and yelled, "You—Reg Dunway—get your tail in gear, boy!"

Dunway made no move to pick up his blade. Instead, he dropped to his knees in the weeds, raised his calloused hands, and cried out, "Sweet Jesus!"

The chanting ceased. The cutting stopped.

The second guard said, "What the hell is it, Roy?"

"Don't know, Walter. Looks like the heat got'im. Where's the water bucket?"

"Right there, but you be careful. He's a mean one."

"Yeah," said Roy, hefting the bucket of tepid water. "So you keep me covered."

The guard moved through the weeds, the shotgun in one hand, the bucket in the other. He stopped behind the kneeling convict and said, "What's the matter, boy, sun fry your pea-brain?"

"It's Jesus Christ," Dunway whispered.

"Sure," Roy said, laughing, "and I'm Saint Pete, so I'll jus baptize you."

He poured a dipperful of water on the convict's shaggy head. When Dunway didn't move, he poured another, then poked him with the shotgun and said, "Whatcha want, boy, three days in the sweatbox?"

"It's him—it's Jesus, look!" Dunway said.

He pointed toward the kudzu-covered trees at the edge of the right-of-way.

The guard stepped back a pace and looked. "Shee-et!" he exclaimed. "You see what I see, Walter?"

The second guard's voice trembled. "I see somethin', that's for sure."

"It's Jesus Christ Hisself!" said Dunway.

Another convict said, "It *is*, jus like that pitchur'a Him in my mama's Bible!"

For a long moment the prisoners and their guards were as still as figures in a photo, a great colored print showing a line of men in sweaty clothes staring at a huge green figure, a bearded, kneeling man with hands clapsed in prayer, a figure formed of kudzu vines growing in thick tangles over slash pines.

"Jesus!" Walter muttered, the shotgun slipping from his shaking hands.

"Jesus in the garden 'fore Judas suckered him!" a convict said.

"Jesus prayin' for the sinners of the world, red'n yaller, black'n white!"

"Oh sweet, sweet Jesus!"

238

"It's a sign," said Dunway, "sent down from heaven on high."

A convict wailed, "It's the end'a time—the last day! Oh Jesus, I done some meanness but I ain't all bad!"

"I done worse'n him, Lord," another sang out. "But I loved ya all the time—cross my heart!"

"It's Judgment Day and I done lived to see it!"

Dunway sprang to his feet, wheeled and faced the guard. With head bowed he said, "Brother, you done splashed me twice. Now baptize me for real cause I'm born agin."

"The heat's gotcha," said Roy.

"It's Jesus got me by the short hairs with a downhill pull, brother. You're a holiness, ain't you—a God-fearin' man? Wet me down!"

Roy poured another dipperful over Dunway's head. As the water trickled down his scarred face, Reg hugged the guard to his chest and whooped, "I'm set free as a little bird! The Lord Jesus Hisself done touched my heart!"

Roy pulled loose and raised his gun. The other convicts moved toward him. He yelled, "Walter, watch out!"

But Walter was on his knees, tears glistening his sun-burned cheeks. "I feel it, Roy," he groaned. "I feel the power. It *is* Jesus."

"We all feels it," a black convict said, "and mister we ain't fixin' to hurt ya."

"Ain't gonna hurt nobody no more!"

The red-haired prisoner said, "I ain't felt no such power since the night I handled a rat'ler and drunk strychnine both."

"Gotta get to town," Dunway said. "Gotta spread the good news!"

Roy's fingers tingled. He had been to camp meetings, had seen strange things, heard stranger. He took a long, hard look at the green figure. Right where the eyes should be he saw something moving in the leaves, a fluttering, like eyelids, and now the leaves parted like eyes opening, sky-blue eyes.

"Walter!" he screamed. "You see that? It's the wind, ain't it?"

"Ain't no wind, Roy. Nary a whisper."

"Not none *here*—but over *there*?"

"It ain't the wind," a convict quietly said. "It's the Holy Ghost."

A chill shot through Roy's bones and froze his legs. He sank to his knees and stared at the great green head which now seemed to be slowly nodding. "Oh sweet Jesus," he sighed.

"We're set free and we're goin to town to tell 'em all!" Dunway said.

Roy's legs were numbed but his sense of duty was not. "You ain't goin' nowhere 'cept back'ta work," he said. "You're doin' time for the state."

"There's state time and there's God's time," a convict said.

"And what's more," said another, "all guvermints is ruled by God."

"Maybe," said Roy, "but I'm the guvermint here. It's my ass what's on the line."

Dunway knelt beside the guard, laid his weed-stained hand on his shoulder, looked him in the eye, said, "Brother, you're a God-fearin' Christian and you got the feelin' just like us. So you gotta do what's right in the eyes of the Lord Jesus."

"Amen," said the convicts and the other guard.

"And," said Dunway, "you gotta remember that ever'thin' what is got a purpose 'cordin to God's plan. There was a reason for Poncho Pilot, cause if'n he didn't step out'a the pitchur when he done, then Jesus couldn'ta died for our sins, right?"

"Well, I guess," said Roy.

Dunway squeezed his shoulder. "Yeah, and now you're the guvermint like Poncho Pilot, ain'tcha?"

The guard nodded weakly.

"Well, brother, you gotta do what ol' Poncho done. There's water in this here bucket. Go to it. You can use my shirttail to dry off."

Roy plunged his hands in the lukewarm water. As he wiped them on Dunway's sweaty shirt, he looked up into the eyes of the green figure. Something was moving where the mouth should be. The kudzu leaves were fluttering like minnows in a shallow pond. Lips formed, curved into a gentle smile.

Roy blinked his tears and stared at the smiling face. Now the earth shook and at his back was a breathtaking roar like the whirring of a million wings, then a terrible blast—the Trump of Doom.

So astonished was Roy that he didn't realize it was a semi with two flapping recaps saying "Hi there, good buddies" as it high-balled down the bypass.

The guard pitched forward in a dead faint, his hat popping off to reveal a bald, pink dome fringed with a halo of greasy brown hair.

Dunway came to his feet and did a little buck dance, shouting, "Praise the Lord!"

240

"Jesus is Lord!" cried a black convict. "Praise Jesus!"

Arm in arm the men started for town. One said, "We gotta sing somethin'. How 'bout 'Blessed Insurance'?"

"Rollo knows more songs than a preacher," said Dunway.

"Yeah," said the red-haired convict. "I know 'Blessed Insurance' like I know this here tattoo on the back'a my hand. It's real purty. But it ain't right for now. What we need is a marchin' song. Like 'Onward Christian Soldiers,' okay?"

"That's my gran'ma's favorite," said a convict wearing scratched sunglasses. "She even sings it in her sleep, sometimes."

Rollo hummed the key. Singing in unison the men tramped down the median, flagging truckers and telling them to get on their CBs and spread the good news.

Atlanta TV heard of the strange figure on the Oughton bypass two days later. The news director thought it was crazy, but he had been in the business long enough to know that it took all kinds. Since the Jesus was as green as grass, he gave the assignment to his greenest reporter, Ashley Kerr.

"You're from that area, babe," he told her. "It's a down-home natural for you."

Ms. Kerr had been born and raised in a small town twenty miles west of Atlanta, had studied mass communications at Georgia State University, and while she knew from experience not to play barefoot in a chicken yard, she didn't consider herself a country girl.

But Kerr had a pragmatic streak that a dirt farmer would admire, so rather than saying "Why me?" she got her crew and headed west.

They shot some footage of the hundreds of cars and trucks parked on the bypass, then, led by a sweating deputy in a dusty brown patrol car, drove through the multitude of gawkers and set up their equipment a stone's throw from the center of attraction.

Kerr took a long look at the kudzu figure. She had to admit that it bore more than a passing resemblance to Sunday School pictures of Jesus in the garden. The blue sky backdrop, the oppressive heat, the buzzing excitement of the crowd touched her, and she remembered when she was a little girl going to a country church with her grandmother. So when she started interviewing, her voice had a certain tone of sincerity that raised the eyebrows of her sound man, a middle-aged

241

ex-hippie whose only visits to church were to a fast-food joint of that name specializing in fried chicken.

"How do you feel about the kudzu Jesus?" she asked a tall woman wearing a blue sun hat.

"It's Him, Jesus, praise God."

"How do you know?"

"Faith, honey—got it right here in my heart," she replied, laying a pink hand on her flat bosom.

A skinny man in overalls beside her said, "Ain't no bugs neither."

"Bugs?"

"Nary a one, you notice? Go up'n down the road a piece and there's red-eyed flies and dog-pecker gnats thick as fleas. Skeeters, too, big'uns. But there's none close to Jesus."

Come to think of it there *weren't* any insects in the area. Kerr asked him why.

"Anybody goes to Sunday School and fears God knows," he replied, eyes blazing. "All bugs is under the power of Bellsbubb, the devil hisself. This here territory's under the Lord's protecshun."

Kerr thanked the couple and moved to a slender man standing to one side.

"Name's Carleton Brace," he said. "I'm the county agent."

"Oh? Then you must know all about kudzu. Would you inform our viewers?"

"Tell you what I can. Kutzoo was brought into the U.S. from China for the purpose of holdin' down soil erosion, which it does. Only it grows so fast it gets out'a hand, so to speak."

"And what's your opinion of the kudzu Jesus?"

Brace scratched his chin. "Well, it reminds me of somethin' called topiary—that's a tree or shrub that's been trimmed and shaped to grow into a particular figger. Folks in England have done whales and elephants, freight trains, even."

"You think someone made the kudzu Jesus?"

Brace shook his head. "Didn't say that, ma'am. I looked at it up close. It grew that way, natural."

"Isn't that surprising?"

"Well, no. Must be a million acres of kutzoo growin' in all sorts'a shapes."

242

"So you don't believe God had a hand?"

Brace looked at the crowd, a few of which were listening. "I'm a deacon at the Free Will Baptist Church, ma'am," he said. "Only thing I know for sure is God works in mysterious ways."

A little lady on a walking stick tugged Kerr's sleeve and said, "He shore do! Jus ask Reg Dunway, that fella over there with his hair slicked back like Conway Twitty's."

She pointed with her cane to a husky man in a red and green print shirt with the tail hanging out. Standing behind him was a deputy with a shotgun over his shoulder.

Kerr approached him and said, "You're Mr. Dunway?"

"That's me, in the flesh, and call me Reg. I'm the guy what first spotted this here Jesus, and He set me free, praise His name."

Kerr noticed handcuffs around his hairy wrists. "You don't look free right now."

"There's free and then there's free, honey," said Dunway. He raised his hands for the camera. "These bracelets ain't nothin' but man's law. In my heart'a hearts I'm free as a red-tailed hawk driftin' on the breeze, and Jesus done it!"

"Amen," the lady with the cane said. "Tell her how He done changed your life around, Reg."

"He done it, and that's a fact. Why, 'fore I seen Him my soul was darker'n Dick's hatband. I was meaner'n a horny tomcat." He stared at Kerr with the unflinching eyes of a predator sizing up its prey. "I done some bad things, lady. Real bad. And I got jus what I deserve. Only them bad things is all gone now. I feel as clean inside as when I stopped smokin' and chawin' for almost six months. I'm saved, and He done it!"

Dunway faced the Jesus and said, "Thank ya Lord. I'm all yours."

"Praise His name!" someone cried, and the little lady began singing "Amazing Grace." Those close by joined in.

Kerr knew this would be a tough interview to top, so she and the crew went back to their van. Standing in the narrow strip of shade cast by the vehicle were two men in jogging shorts and shoes. One wore a black patch over his left eye, the other a white bandanna around his forehead. Gold crucifixes hung from gold chains around their necks.

A couple of Christian gays, thought Kerr, a different angle. She signaled her crew and said, "Hi, what brings you to the kudzu Jesus?"

The one with the bandanna said, "We're clergymen. I'm Riggins, Catholic. He's McBride, Episcopalian."

Kerr smiled. "So you have a vested interest."

Riggins grinned. "Yes, but without the vestments. We're out for a run."

"So what does the figure mean to you?"

"Well," said Riggins, "it has one heck of a drawing power, doesn't it?"

"And you, Father McBride?"

The priest fingered his cross. "It's very green."

Riggins said, "Mac was a chaplain in Vietnam—he's our resident expert on vines."

Kerr noticed a pale scar on McBride's shoulder, another on his leg. She asked, "Did you see anything like this in Nam?"

He shook his head.

"Of course not," said Riggins. "Over there it would've been a Buddha." He laughed. "Right, Mac?"

"Come on," said the priest, "let's run."

The two men set off down the bypass at a brisk pace. Kerr and the crew loaded the van and returned to Atlanta. The news director cut her film to twenty seconds and played it that night. The next afternoon Kerr received a call from the vice president of the Christian Television Network. He had seen her bit on the kudzu Jesus and was moved by the way in which she dealt with both the subject and the people she interviewed. For some time, he said, CTN had been searching for a person like her, a sincere young woman with whom their viewers could identify. Was she interested in making a commitment to Christian broadcasting, at double her present salary? If she were under contract, their lawyers could work it out. Well?

A week later Ashley Kerr had a suite of offices all her own in CTN's ultramodern facility in Maryland and was the producer/director/announcer of the Christian Weather Report, which was beamed thrice daily into the homes of 2.78 million believers.

United States Senator Davey Rutledge left his car at the end of the long line of vehicles parked on both sides of the bypass and walked up the median, which had been worn bare of grass and weeds by the footsteps of thousands who had come to see the kudzu Jesus.

Davey had heard of the strange figure a week ago in Washington when two colleagues jokingly referred to it as they told him that not even divine intervention could save the budget changes he introduced. But he had not come home until late yesterday, and then at the summons of Judge Green, who called with the sad news that Doc Spaulding had died.

Doc left his body to the Hopkins medical school so there would be no funeral. Nor would there be a memorial service. Doc communicated this in no uncertain terms to the judge while he lay in bed waiting for the stroke that would kill him. "A man's life is his eulogy," he grunted, "or what's a life for?" But he requested that a few friends get together in Gus White's barber shop for a wake. "Of the Irish sort," he said, "with booze and bullshit, on me, of course. And I'll be there," he added, with a sly wink, "in the cheapest damn coffin Buzzy can find," making reference to Charlie Bird, the undertaker, whose affectionate nickname was Buzzard.

"A wake, Doc, are you sure?" Sidney Green had asked.

"As sure as I'm bound for glory. It'll be a fine cultural experience for this booming metropolis. Tell John Lee to provide the best moonshine corruption can buy."

So Davey left Abby and their two children and flew to Atlanta. He rented a car, drove the fifty miles west into the setting sun, and parked behind the barber shop as night was falling. Gus had made preparations by hanging a curtain across the window and waxing the dingy floor. The open pine box was laid out on chairs two and three. A couple of planks on the first chair was a bar on which the clear and sparkling shine was served up in half-pint mason jars.

As Davey entered he was greeted by Gus himself dressed in his baby blue Sunday suit and purple tie. Sidney Green was fooling with a color TV by the first chair. A dozen men and women Davey knew, some better than others, were sitting in a row on the theater seats Gus had salvaged when the Dixie theater was torn down to make way for the new courthouse. Two sat on the shoeshine stand by the cold-drink box, their feet planted on the iron rests. A pair of wooden-bladed fans lazily stirred the warm air.

245

Davey waved and said hello and was greeted by all. He took a swallow of shine before looking into the coffin to pay his respects. Doc appeared pretty much as always, a little thinner perhaps, and grayer, but death hadn't stolen that small smile he bestowed upon Oughton for so many years. His delicate pink hands folded on his chest seemed freshly scrubbed and ready for surgery.

The only thing different was that Doc's mischievous blue eyes were closed. Davey had never seen him when they weren't looking for something interesting to focus upon. With those eyes shut, Doc looked exactly like what he was, a dead man.

A voice at Davey's shoulder said, "I wanted to touch him up—a little color here and there, you know. But Sidney said Doc didn't want anything done. Shame. I could've made him handsome, almost."

It was Bird. Davey shook his smooth, damp hand and listened while he explained that after the wake the body would be taken to Atlanta by the sheriff and shipped by air. No, it wasn't embalmed. Medical schools did their own work. "They claim," Bird said, "they can do it good as the ancient Egyptians. But between me and you, I think they're lyin'. 'Sides, if they're gonna slice 'em into a zillion pieces, why go to the trouble?"

Judge Green clapped Davey on the shoulder and said, "Ol Buzzy's pissed cause he didn't make no big money off 'a Doc. Hell's bells—I might give my carcass to the Bulldog med school. How 'bout that, Buzzy?"

Bird flashed his knowing mortician's smile and said, "You damn better should cause I ain't about to touch that hunk 'a corruption you call a body, not with no ten-foot pole."

The three men laughed. And then from the corner of his eye Davey saw that Doc was laughing, too. Not the Doc in the pine box. The Doc on TV.

The judge noticed Davey's startled expression and said, "Another of his damn-fool requests. Had the tape made by them TV folks on the square after his first heart attack. Handwriting on the wall, and all that. He was one hell of a fellow, wasn't he?"

Davey nodded, thinking, He was that, and more.

As Davey drank the shine, he mingled with those at the wake, talking first about Doc, then about other things, past, present, and future.

246

Richard Leeds was there, and the Westmoreland brothers, one of whom had followed in Doc's footsteps and was taking over his practice. There was an attractive young lady named Lola Banning who was doing very well in the cosmetics business. Alice Corday told Davey she was studying psychology and hoped to become a counselor so she could help people with problems. Tina Jo Sampson, head of nursing at the hospital, swapped dirty jokes with Bill Middleton, who served on the board. Steve and Molly Floyd let Davey know that their marriage was working fine and asked about Abby and the kids. Jennifer Meyers was flirting with young Harry Edwards, who was coaching at the high school after starring at Georgia and playing two years for Detroit. George Demos was in uniform, but he drank a little shine and told those that were interested about the kudzu Jesus and Reg Dunway's miraculous conversion. "First we thought it was a trick," he said, "so he could escape. But damn if Dunway didn't go straight to the sheriff and tell him all about it. Since he's been turned around, John Lee lets him go out there every day under guard." Annie Mae Henderson, the town's unofficial historian, said the sheriff was a fine man to do that, but the whole thing reminded her of her poor sister, Daisy, who was always seeing angels and talking to them, too. Sitting silently in a far corner beneath Gus White's framed arrowhead collection was Bobby-bob, looking like a small, furry animal that had been stuffed and fixed with bright glass eyes.

Davey was half finished with his second jar of shine when a young woman dressed in white breezed in. For a moment he didn't recognize her. But when he heard the laughter in her voice and saw the wicked gleam in her eye, he realized she was Bobbie Sue Butcher, who now lived in Hollywood and made movies under the name of Karla Anitas.

Bobbie Sue Butcher—Davey's heart leaped. She had let her dyed blond hair grow out to its natural color, a shimmering dark brown. It fell to her shoulders and framed her square, honest face that was set with the loveliest brown eyes Davey had ever dreamed into.

He had known her since she was a little girl living in the Mt. Nebo community. He remembered how she met Doc when she was about thirteen, how he took a liking to her and encouraged her interest in nursing. She worked in his office during high school and summers and he sent her to the vocational school for training.

And when Susannah Wheatley, Oughton's ex-movie star who was a great friend of Doc's, was ill, Bobbie Sue was her live-in nurse. Susannah took her under her wing like a long-lost daughter, and after Jack Wheatley died and Susannah moved back to California, Bobbie Sue went along.

As philosophers and press agents say, the rest was history; only it wasn't. In the course of time Bobbie Sue seduced Davey. Not that he wasn't a willing victim. Her uninhibited charm was that of something wild, untameable, that lived spontaneously from moment to moment without thought of tomorrow, like the birds of the air. Or seemed to be. He was willing to leave Abby. "But that would spoil everything!" Bobbie Sue exclaimed as they discussed matters in the Anniston Holiday Inn. "It's not part of the plan."

"Plan?" Davey had asked.

"You know, *the* plan—the same one that made you a prominent politician."

And when he asked her just what this plan had in mind for her, her brown eyes glowed so brightly they would've shone in the dark as she softly said, "Kennedy had his Marilyn; you'll have me."

Bobby Sue had spotted him and disengaged herself from the clutches of Dex Roberts. As she came over, mason jar in hand, she brushed a cool kiss on his cheek and said, "My favorite senator. What's happening?"

Davey slipped his arm around her waist. "One surprise after another."

"Yeah. Well, Doc lived with death. Used to lecture me on the subject. 'Not much difference between the quick and the dead,' he'd say. 'Both are inclined to forget to pay their bills.'"

"How's Hollywood?"

"A fuckathon, as usual. Where's Abby?"

"Home in Washington with the kids."

"Good. It's been too damn long."

They parted company for a while, each talking with other people, as they moved around the narrow barber shop seeing themselves and the group doubled by the large mirrors on both walls. Davey was collared by Ramona Wimpton, who owned a very successful beauty shop. She wore a low-cut green silk dress and squeezed his arm as she told him he simply must support legislation to allow federal aid for trans-sexual operations. She was saying, "Having to handle it on your

248

own is a real bitch, dear—" when suddenly there was an explosion and everyone froze.

Then Sidney Green laughed and pointed at the TV.

Doc faced them with a smoking shotgun. The camera panned to show a hole in the ceiling of his office. Doc grinned and said, "You sorry pack of drunks—thought that'd get your undivided attention. Sidney, the envelopes."

"Got 'em in my coat pocket, Doc," the judge said, as though Doc could hear.

"Pass 'em out and quick," Doc said, "or I'll fire the other barrel. Hell, think I will anyhow."

He blew a second hole in the ceiling, then put the gun on his cluttered desk. "Open 'em now," he said. "Anybody not here, burn his." He yawned. "Sidney will explain. Won't you Sidney?"

"Sure will, Doc."

Doc laughed. "Knew he'd say that—always did talk back to the TV, especially to Mike Wallace." He sat in the battered swivel chair and put his feet on the desk. "I'm gonna snooze for a while and dream about something pleasant, like a flu epidemic. Have fun."

The screen went dark.

Davey opened his envelope. He blinked. Inside were ten crisp thousand-dollar bills, the same as in every one else's.

There were murmurs, giggles, wild laughs. Sidney Green cleared his throat for order and in his hanging-judge tone said, "I didn't know a damn thing about this—just to hand out the envelopes on cue. But Doc told me to say that you're to use what's inside for fun. Got that? Said anybody do somethin' serious he'd haunt 'em."

Richard Leeds said, "This is a hell of a lot of money, Sid."

"Doc had plenty. Inherited a bundle of downtown Atlanta property from his aunt, and he didn't have no relatives."

"He never mentioned it," said Bird.

"Not to me neither," Sidney said, "not till he drew up a will and named me executor. Hard to say how much he was worth." A tear trickled down his cheek. "At least ten million, probably more, dependin' on the real estate market."

A sigh passed like a breeze through the shop.

"Left a million to the school board, provided they fund a crazy program to teach kindergarten kids good table manners and ballroom

249

dancin'. Said that would solve all the social problems he knew of, 'cept the clap."

Everyone laughed, and more than one pressed a handkerchief to his eyes.

"So have a good time now," the judge said, "drinkin' and dreamin' about blowin' your wad on something frivolous tomorrow!"

Davey did just that, and when at last the wake broke up he left with Bobbie Sue and followed her to the lake cottage on the farm she inherited from Susannah. It was a warm night, a long and pleasant night. But when he awoke late the next morning she was gone. A note pinned to her rumpled pillow said, "Oh *yeah!*" and was signed, "Karla."

Davey moved through the crowd on the bypass, shaking hands and being slapped fondly on the back. At the front were six Japanese who had been touring the wire factory. They were snapping pictures with cameras slung around their necks while a gesturing interpreter explained the situation.

On the weedy clay beyond, in the very shadow of the kudzu Jesus, were a dozen people, some in wheelchairs, some on stretchers, others on quilts, the limp and lame in search of healing who had been brought by their loved ones and laid like offerings before the great green figure.

As Davey edged by the interpreter, a stout young man in a wheelchair cried out, "Oh Mama, I can feel somethin' a'stirrin' in my feet. It's in my legs now. It's a powerful thing, more jumpy than 'lectricity! I can feel it, Mama—oh Lord!"

He pressed his hands on the metal arms of the chair and stood up, trembling.

A gray-haired woman behind him screamed like she'd been stuck with a butcher knife. "It's a miracle, praise God! My boy ain't stood on his own two feet for more'n five year!"

The man took a shaky step, another. He lifted his pale arms and shouted, "I'm healed, healed! And you done it, Lord!"

Many in the crowd whispered "Amen" and "Glory to Jesus." But a louder voice shouted them down, saying, "You ain't been healed, brother. You done been duped by the devil!"

The multitude moaned and opened to allow a small, wiry man in a slick brown suit to step up to the wheelchair. He said, "I'm Brother Horsley Leathers, preacher of the Holy Ghost Tabernacle." He kissed the worn Bible he carried, then flipped it open and, pointing a stubby finger at the onlookers, yelled, "The Lord don't work this away. Anybody what believes this ol' mess'a kutzoo is Jesus ain't nothin' but an idolater, ain't no better'n a catlick!"

Someone shouted, "God made all things, brother."

"That He done—made the world'n all that's in it," the preacher replied. "But He done give it over to the Enemy, to Satan." He shook the Bible at them like a landlord showing an eviction notice. "That's what the Good Book says, and that's what all of us what's saved believes!"

"But I'm healed—I can walk!" the stout man said.

Leathers eyed him and said, "You ain't healed. You is duped by the Devil." He wrinkled his nose, sniffed. "Brother, your soul's in danger of the Fire! Why, bet if I touch ya with this here pinky finger, you'll topple over like a rotten tree."

The mother thrust herself in front of Leathers. She shook a sharp fist in his face and yelled, "Mister, if'n ya even blow your hot air on my baby boy, you'll be needin' somebody to raise the dead!"

The Preacher Leathers retreated, but still he shook his Bible at the crowd and called them idolaters.

Now Davey studied the green figure. It did indeed look like pictures of Jesus at prayer. He glanced back at the people and wondered if it too were part of the plan, or if it were just another little joke played by nature, for no other reason than to make life mysterious and therefore interesting.

One of nature's little tricks or not, there were others interested in the kudzu Jesus, people concerned with religion with a capital *R*.

On the third Monday in August the Atlanta office of the American Civil Liberties Union filed suit, claiming that since the figure was situated on state property, namely the right-of-way of the Oughton bypass, its presence was a clear violation of Article One of the Constitution, which provided for the separation of church and state.

In their brief the ACLU lawyers demanded that the Jesus be removed so as to assure the continued religious freedom of all, and urged that the court act "with all deliberate speed" before "irreparable harm" was done.

When the Atlanta attorneys—both of whom looked a little too slick and shady around the jowls to be southern born and bred—made their plea, Judge Sidney Green stared down at them and bit his tongue because he wasn't sure if he would laugh or swear. So far as he was concerned, kudzu was kudzu and Jesus was Jesus. And if for a while folks wanted to ooh and ahh, it was no skin off his ass. Whatever the thing was, it was good for business. At the last Rotary meeting he heard that gas sales and motel receipts were way up, and that many a shade-tree entrepreneur was making a few dollars selling potted kudzu plants, as well as bumper stickers proclaiming, "I love HIM!" the "love" represented by a green heart. Polly his wife had stuck one on her car and had come damn close to pasting another over the red and black booster sticker on his.

The thing was located on the bypass near the country club not far from the judge's house. He and Polly strolled over to see it because she was curious and because Doc Spaulding, who was in the hospital then, wanted an eyewitness report. While it did look like somebody praying, the judge wasn't sure who. It wasn't that he was irreligious; every Sunday he allowed Father McBride to attempt to lead him through the ritual with all its ups and downs while Polly chirped from the choir. It was just that when he tried to visualize a higher power, all he could come up with was the round and squinting face of Coach Butts, under whose tutelage he made all-SEC his senior year.

The kudzu had, moreover, caused only a few problems. Sheriff John Lee said that the influx of pilgrims hadn't raised the crime rate, beyond a few fistfights and one minor cutting—due to doctrinal differences. But it was necessary to reroute truck traffic through the square, so the judge had difficulty getting into and out of his parking space.

As the ACLU lawyers took turns droning on, the judge thought about the proximity of the Jesus to his house. Hundreds of rubberneckers had pitched tents on the right-of-way and held camp meetings every night. More than once he had been raised from a peaceful sleep by screechy singing accompanied by jangling tambourines, cowbells and horns that squawked like gaggles of geese. He had threatened to issue a curfew order, but Polly talked him out of it, saying sweetly, "Who knows, dear? They may be right. Only time will tell."

Maybe. But the law was the law, and Sidney Green believed in it as passionately as he did in the Georgia Bulldogs. So when the ACLU attorneys at long last finished citing precedent and sat down, he glowered at them and said, "You want all deliberate speed, huh? Then get yourselves here at 9:00 in the morning, and be on time or I'll hold you in contempt."

He took the brief home and studied it after supper.

Polly had gotten wind of the case. After plying him with peach cobbler and two healthy bourbons, and after humming the little tune that foreshadowed advice, she said, "Sidney, dear, that old thing isn't hurting anyone. And besides, it's pretty."

The judge grunted and turned to the next page.

"There's too much interference in religion these days," she went on. "Some people say it's a communist plot to weaken the moral fiber of our nation."

He grunted again.

"And if you rule in favor of those radicals, honey, some fool might burn a cross on our lawn. Think what that would do to the grass you worked so hard setting out."

"Grass'll grow back," he said. And that was all he said to her about the case.

The next morning the judge was ten minutes late to court due to still another traffic jam. This one involved a truckload of squealing swine that had tried to turn too sharply and ended up astride the corner in front of Gus White's barber shop. The semi-trailer was leaking like it had been hosed down, and the gutters were running with hog sweat. Gus surveyed the scene from behind his window, an open bottle of lilac vegetal held to his nose.

The ACLU lawyers, in fresh suits and shined shoes, were as fidgety as school boys when Judge Green walked in. His decision, though, was short and sweet to their ears. "Petition granted," he declared. "I've issued an order to be carried out by noon today. Court adjourned!"

The sheriff had been summoned by the bailiff and was waiting in chambers. As he peeled off his black robe, Sidney said, "John, you know that kutzoo Jesus thing out on the bypass?"

"Reckon so," the sheriff quietly said.

"It's gotta go. Here's my order, signed and sealed."

John Lee stuck the folded document in the pocket of his tan shirt below his star and started for the door.

"Hold on now," said Sidney. "How you gonna do it?"

"Fire."

"Fire? That the best way?"

"Kutzoo's too pesky to yank up or cut out."

"You want me to call some state troopers?"

The sheriff frowned. "What for?"

"Might be trouble. There's plenty'a folks who take it serious."

"Won't be none. You're the law inside. I'm the law out there."

Sidney sighed. "Yeah, John, and you're damn good. But a lot'a them people ain't from around here. Hell's bells, I saw an Alaska tag yesterday."

The sheriff squinted as though taking aim. "There's enough knows me. The rest'll meet me fast."

"You're not goin' by yourself?"

"Could, but I'll take one deputy to sprinkle the gas and two more to stand by with fire 'stinguishers in case it tries to spread. I'll send Demos to keep an eye on you."

"On me—why?"

"You give the orders. I jus carry 'em out."

And so it was that toward 10:30 that Tuesday morning in August the sheriff and his three men went about their business. When the crowd saw the five-gallon gas cans there was an angry murmur. And as the deputy started for the kudzu Jesus with one in each hand, voices shouted angrily and more than one of the onlookers bent down in search of rocks.

John Lee turned and faced them then, arms loose at his sides, hat tilted back, his gaze steady as he looked from face to face. His quiet self-assurance was that of a pro fighter with hands so fast he could catch flies as they buzzed.

"Case some'a you don't know," he said, "I'm the law. Got a court order to remove this here thing. Stand back and be still."

A man holding a Bible over his head cried out, "This is the Lord's work! You ain't a gonna do it!"

"I am, and you're under arrest for interferin'," John Lee said. "Sit yourself in the back'a my car." He scanned the watchful faces. "Who's next?"

The crowd grumbled but there were no takers.

After the gas was spread and the deputies were positioned with fire extinguishers at the ready, the sheriff pulled a railroad flare from his hip pocket. As he ignited it, a woman screamed, "The Lord won't let it burn!"

But the flare sputtered and blazed, and so did the gas-soaked kudzu.

The flames crackled and snapped through the weeds around it, then crawled up the twisted vines. The crowns of the supporting trees boomed like thunder as they burst into balls of oily fire. Sparks rained down on several nearby tents and set them to smoking. The owners knocked down the poles and did a stomping dance on the canvas.

As heat waves rippled the blue sky, a six-foot copperhead slithered out. The multitude fell back, parted, and the snaked passed through into the safety of the weeds on the other side of the road.

The fire grew hotter still. The watchers shielded their faces with their hands. A boiling cloud of jet-black smoke rose heavenward for hundreds of feet, where it encountered a current of air that bent it parallel to the earth and pointed it like a blunt finger toward Oughton.

"A fire by night, a cloud by day! Praise the Lord!" the man in the back seat of the sheriff's car shouted.

"Go home," John Lee said. "Whatever it was, it's finished here."